Praise for Kathy George

'It takes great courage, skill and artistry, to broach the mastery of Dickens and lean into his superbly written worlds to create one's own. And yet, award-winning author Kathy George has succeeded with deep sensitivity, respect and care, to offer up a retelling from one of Dickens's often misunderstood and overlooked characters … a compelling tale and one which I enjoyed greatly.'

—*Better Reading* on *Estella*

'A haunting and darkly beautiful retelling of Dickens's *Great Expectations* that gives voice to an oft-vilified character, placing her at the centre of her own deeply felt story.'

—Karen Brooks, bestselling author of *The Good Wife of Bath* on *Estella*

'*Estella* is a beautiful and hauntingly compelling read with a head-strong and enigmatic heroine. I was mesmerised by Estella and really came to like her … I read it in one day.'

—Leanne Dagan, *@leannebookstagram*

'I also truly felt transported into the world of Dickens. The gothic atmosphere, the period language, the Victorian culture and the haunting settings embraced me in such a profound way. … Ms George's command of language captured my imagination so persuasively I could not put the book down … All my senses were engaged.'

—Cindy L Spear, reviewer, on *Estella*

'Kathy George has produced a superb story that has you drawn in from the first few pages. … The writing is descriptive and atmospheric. I found it simply stunning!'

—Julie on *Estella* for *Better Reading*

'So beautifully written, so skilfully plotted, such a masterpiece of tension and atmosphere ...'

—*Australian Book Review* on *Sargasso*

'Dark, unsettling and utterly enthralling, *Sargasso* is a suspenseful page-turner that builds to an incredible and shocking end. It's a marvellous debut from Kathy George, and I'll certainly be keeping my eye out for this author in the future.'

—*Better Reading*

'In the tradition of great gothic novels of the past such as *Rebecca* and *Jane Eyre*, comes the startling new Australian-based gothic tale, *Sargasso.* A harbinger of something that rests between reality and imagination, this soulful novel strikes a strong chord, with its rich air of possibility.'

—*Mrs B's Book Reviews*

'A perfect modern day gothic novel, I would highly recommend this novel for its amazing prose and atmospheric settings.'

—Cathie Sawyer, *@cathiesbooks* on *Sargasso*

Kathy George was born in South Africa, and has since lived in Namibia, New Zealand, and Australia. A hopeless romantic, she fell in love with *Rebecca* by Daphne du Maurier as a teenager, and includes *Wuthering Heights* and *Great Expectations* among her favourite books. She has worked as a legal assistant, but her true enthusiasm has always been for writing, and she holds a Masters of Fine Arts in Australian Gothic literature from the Queensland University of Technology. Kathy lives in Brisbane. She is the author of *Sargasso* and *Estella*.

Also by Kathy George

Sargasso
Estella

The Scent *of* Oranges

KATHY GEORGE

The Scent of Oranges
© 2024 by Kathy George
ISBN 9781038959232

First published on Gadigal Country in Australia in 2024
by HQ Fiction
an imprint of HQBooks (ABN 47 001 180 918), a subsidiary of HarperCollins*Publishers*
Australia Pty Limited (ABN 36 009 913 517).
Gadigal Country
Level 19, 201 Elizabeth St
Sydney NSW 2000
harpercollins.com.au/hq/

This edition published 2025

HarperCollins acknowledges the Traditional Custodians of the lands upon which we live and work, and pays respect to Elders past and present.

HarperCollins*Publishers*
Macken House
39/40 Mayor Street Upper
Dublin 1, D01 C9W8, Ireland

A catalogue record for this book is available from the National Library of Australia
www.librariesaustralia.nla.gov.au

Printed and bound by CPI Group (UK) Ltd, Croydon, CR0 4YY

For Sharyn Pearce

'Women can always put things in fewest words, except when it's blowing up, and then they lengthens it out.'

Charles Dickens, *Oliver Twist*

'No, no,' replied the girl [Nancy]. *'I have not done this for money. Let me have that to think of.'*

Charles Dickens, *Oliver Twist*

CHAPTER ONE

When I first lay me eyes upon Oliver Twist, his face brings to mind the inside of St Paul's. Of chiselled cherubs, of sculpted saints. For the boy's face is angelic, flaxen hair curled against his ruddy cheeks. He has a mouth like—not a rosebud, but a pale pink peony like them flower sellers sell. His skin is dirty, but the clean patches are pale and as fine as onion skin.

I wonder who he is? Why he's with the Dodger in an alley late at night, and wot the Dodger is up to?

The boy looks out of place alongside my friend, for Dodger is snub-nosed and plain-faced, grimy most of the time, and not especially tall. But, to his credit, he has about him all the airs and graces of a man. He wears a man's coat with the gaping cuffs turned halfway back up his arms, and he swaggers along with his hands in its pockets. The coat near reaches his heels, it does, and Dodger thrusts his bony hips forwards and waves one hand airily about him as if he were a poncy gen'leman. He has aspirations. And he makes me laugh, he does, and I love him for it.

The boy, on the other hand …

The boy evokes other feelings in me. I stand in the shadows, clutch the gritty wall as the press of humanity plods past, and stare shamelessly. The boy … The boy is like something out of a book. Not that I can read. I mean them plates in fancy books. He is innocent and pure. He—he … Ha! He's *a vision.* That's wot he is! Where did Dodger find him?

I am out and about. Currently in Saffron Hill. With instructions from Fagin to visit a new client. Usually Bill accompanies me to look the client over and affirm he's half-decent, to ensure I'm paid right, but Bill—Mr Sikes, to you—is nowhere to be found when Fagin gives me instructions. I don' know where Bill is. I don' know where he is half the time, and the other half he's in The Cripples. I been there and Barney, the man behind the counter who talks as if his nose has been sliced clean off and bunged up with glue and sawdust, told me, 'Dobody's here. Dot a shoul,' by which I gathered the establishment was vacant.

'I've met the client,' Fagin told me, 'and I'm happy the man's a decent sort. You'll just have to go alone if you can't find Bill. It's not like you've never been on your own before.'

No, it's not like I've never been on me own before. Think of all the years I *was* on me own, not counting Fagey of course. But I got used to Bill being with me now, ain't I? I got used to feeling safe and secure when I'm working, knowing someone's got me back. There are times when I like me own company, when I grow weary of Bill bossing and bullying me about, but mostly he's good for me. Not *to* me. I didn' say that.

I push meself away from the wall—I must get on—and take one last look at the two boys disappearing into the murk. Dodger is articulating some theory—his voice carries in the fog, and the boy's face is turned towards his new pal. I have a feeling I will see him again. I get feelings about things. I don' know why. Fagin calls them *instincts.* Fagin has some education and is always teaching me new words. The thing you have to understand is that I seem to be blessed with a good ear. You only have to say words once and I don' forget them.

Anyway, I feel I will see the child again. I don' know if it's me imagination playing tricks, but instinct tells me we are connected. I think I could sit and look at the child for a good long while. Wound taut as a reel of spinning cotton in the workhouse I am. Always have been. All it will take is for him to pull at a thread and it'll be the unravelling of me.

The street is narrow and muddy, forlorn with many tumble-down shops, but strangely alive with many children crawling in and out of doors and screaming, whether for the fun of it or because of genuine strife is uncertain. It's threatening rain. I pull me shawl over me head, hitch up me skirts, and skip over a gutter flowing with effluent. The odours of London, eh! Think of the worst smell you ever met. Now imagine wot it is like to have that in your nostrils all day, every day, and all night. Imagine the rest of the world being shut out, a dense layer of smoke and smog hovering above your head. Sights such as a blue sky and fluffy white clouds are notions you only dream of.

A great bear of a man lumbers from out of a dimly lit doorway into me path and grabs at me with his paw—'Where you goin' in such a hurry, love?'—but I sidestep him nimbly (takes practice, it does) and quicken me steps. I cross a courtyard, the cobblestones hard and bumpy under me boots, evade two scampering urchins so filthy they might be little devils looming out of the fog, and slip down yet another lane. It's a cul-de-sac, and quiet and dark. The client is at Number Fifteen, at the end. It would be at the periphery, of course. Still, I ain't scared. I ain't scared when I'm out in the open cos I'm quick. I only take fright when I'm hemmed in. I count tenements and, as I draw closer, light flickers from a feeble candle in the window. The man is expecting me, then. There are steps up to the door, stone ones, which is something, but as I put me foot down upon the first step, a faint sound comes from under the shrubbery.

At first I carnt see anything. But me feelings tell me there's something there. I lift me skirts and go down on me haunches and tilt me head to get a better look.

The fox cub must be moultin' for it's half red and half black as soot. Its snout is the only reason I don' mistake it for a kitten. It growls, showing a dim outline of its fangs, and I draw off me shawl and wrap up me hands and reach down and lift the scrawny, bony body. The fur is wet and cold and the cub quivers violently against my breast. I stroke it and scratch between its ears, and it starts to settle. Its parents must've abandoned it, or been killed. 'Aah, little one,' I murmur.

I swaddle the cub in me shawl so that only its nose peeks out, and place it back down beside the shrubbery. It's a rhododendron, I think. A posh plant to keep a little one company, to be sure. 'Wait here,' I whisper. 'I'll be back quick as I can.'

I climb the stairs and knock quickly and quietly on the door. A bolt is slid back, the wood cracked open, and a sliver of man's face appears above a chain. Not an unattractive face, I have to say. Not young, but not old, either. Curls the colour of cinnamon tumble around his face, and he has deep, dark-brown eyes, freckles across his cheeks, and a dark-red moustache. I am observant, I am, but then in me line of work it pays to be.

'Nancy?' I murmur.

The wood is pushed shut again. The chain rattles back, and the man widens the door and lets me in.

He looks me up and down in the dim light inside. 'Yes,' he murmurs, 'yes, indeed.'

I got no idea wot he means by that.

'Not much more than a child, are you? Even if you're a pretty one.'

He has an upper-class accent, but he ain't dressed posh. He's above average height and his moustache—as I've pointed out—is an unusual colour. The big, brown eyes ain't like pools to drown in, but they're mesmerising all the same. I wonder if he's gentry fallen on hard times. Not that that will make any difference, neither to me, nor to wot we do. In fact, it's often the gentry that's partial to a rougher ride.

'I'm eighteen,' I tell him adamantly, adding an extra year for good measure and keeping me eyes off the grey pillows and the threadbare coverlet on the lumpy bundle that passes for a bed in the background. At least there is a bed!

There's also a rickety wooden table and a single chair, and from where I stand I can see the pot under the bed.

The man says nothing. He seems to have a talent for saying nothing but conveying plenty. He lifts his hand to pat his moustache and I notice a gold ring, not on his marrying finger. So not that hard up that he's had to sell the ring, then. So wot's he doing in a crib like this? He seems to be in two minds, now I'm here. Thinking better of the whole affair, perhaps?

I suspect that if I open the door and step back into the darkness, he will let me go. Which I won' do. If I leave, it'll be along with the coin I need, that Fagin will demand of me, that Bill will punish me for not earning. I suspect I know the man's type. He's the sort that at first has little interest and pretends indifference, the type whose blood is slow to quicken, the type who dilly-dallies getting there. But when he does, watch out! Which can mean I will earn extra. Which can mean once won' be enough. Maybe twice won' cut it, neither.

I flick out me tongue and run it along me lower lip.

'Well? We going to do this or not?' I demand.

CHAPTER TWO

When I emerge in the pale oyster morning, the bundle is still at the bottom of the rhododendron. I been away for much longer than I intended and I don' hold out much hope for the little one. The night has been raw. Believe me, I spent it wrapped up for warmth with me back against me client's chest, his arms entwined around me.

I lift the swaddling to me face. The shawl is cold and damp against me cheek and the body feels light and lifeless in me hands. 'Foxie?' I murmur into the small opening. 'Fox—'

'Get in here,' the man says behind me. I didn' even hear the door opening. He reaches for me collar and hauls me into the place backwards. I almost drop the cub.

'Who said you could depart?'

He turns me round to face him. Worsted trousers have with haste been pulled on to cover his nakedness and one of them braces is twisted over his shoulder.

'Wot?' I say. 'You mean you're not done?'

I am altogether perplexed since we did naught except drift off to the Land of Nod. Lord knows I tried to initiate something, but he asked me not to. He said, 'No, that's not what I want,' and took me hands away and lay on his side and curled me body into his. Seemed he only wanted to hold me and to be held, which were strange. Perhaps the real work is about to start now?

'I want you to make me a cup of tea,' he says, closing the door behind me.

I snort. 'A cup of tea?' I wonder if I'm hearing right.

He nods. 'Yes. Can you do that? Put that down'—he indicates the bundle—'and make me a cup of tea.'

I place the swaddled shawl gently on the table, but the animal doesn' stir and I think to meself that it is probably dead.

'Kettle's there.' He points to the fireplace. 'Tea leaves here.'

The room is sparsely furnished, but he jerks his head at a shelf behind the front door upon which are some rudiments: a tea caddy, a knife, a wooden spoon, a couple of candles in holders, and a single cup. The china is pretty with a floral pattern. And it's no skin off my nose to make him a cuppa, is it? Especially since I were paid only to sleep.

He sits down at the table while I busy meself stirring the embers and getting the kettle over the heat. When I glance back, his legs are stretched out before him and he's picking at the dirt under the nails of his long, thin fingers. A newspaper is opened out on the tabletop and, in between the nail cleaning, he leans forwards to read by the light of the single candle. Now and then he scratches at the reddish bristles on his chin or he pats at his moustache. Or he looks up at me in consideration.

I wonder wot is going through his mind? I wonder wot last night was all about? For, if the truth be known, he treated me like a man would his little sister. He were kind and gentle. He held me against him and kept me close. He never once became aroused, not that I noticed. Is he perhaps otherwise inclined? Is that the explanation? Or is it me? But if it's me, then why engage me services in the first place?

'This'll cost you extra, sir,' I murmur, glancing at him out of the corner of my eye.

'No, it won't,' he says.

He's handsome, he is, seen properly now in better light. He's taller than most, his eyes evenly spaced, his nose and teeth straight. If he has discerning features, it's them cinnamon curls, brown eyes and deep-red moustache. If he has a negative thing about him, it's that he fidgets.

He doesn't look at me as he turns the page. 'You going to charge me for the privilege of drinking a cuppa with a gentleman? I'll share it with you, you know.'

'That'll be a first,' I say.

All the same, the thought pleases me. I hum a ditty and get down the dainty cup and measure out the tea leaves while the fire glows in the grate, and I think to meself that anybody looking in would say it was altogether a cosy domestic scene. Although the place could do with more furniture. Although some new linen would be nice. Although, if I'm a-going to be a wife (or a sister—I don' care either way) I could do with a new dress instead of this old threadbare one.

If things had turned out different, I could have had a life like this. If things had turned out different, I could have had a steady, reliable life, a good-looking fellow. A little family. Instead, I got Bill, unreliable, everything rocky, everything uncertain—

I am pouring in the hot water when the man gives a shout. Swivelling, I find he's up and gesticulating wildly at the tabletop, at the bundle—

Which has taken it into its head to rise from the dead! Which is attempting to crawl from out of the swaddling—

I put the kettle down as the cub's head emerges from me shawl.

The man laughs.

'Where'd you get that?' he wants to know. 'You had it all night in here with us?'

I shake me head. 'I found it outside your door, not ten minutes ago.' I don' admit to finding it last night. Why would I?

'A fox outside my door?'

I nod. 'In the shrubbery.'

He goes to the door, opens it, slips outside in his bare feet, and returns a minute later. 'Give me that shawl,' he says. 'Please.'

Manners, too, would you believe?

He comes in again a minute or two later, shoves the door closed with his foot and the guttering candle goes clean out. He's shivering, his feet are blue with cold, but his arms is all a-wriggle with fur. Black and a deep-red auburn colour, like his hair.

'Oh, Lord,' I say. 'Wot you going to do with all those?'

'Never mind,' he says, offloading them onto the hearth in front of the fire. 'How's that tea coming along?'

'Done,' I say. 'Here.' And I put the pretty cup on the table, with a teaspoon by its side neat-like. 'There ain't no milk,' I say. 'Not so's I could find.'

He glances up. 'If I give you money, will you go and buy milk?'

'I could,' I say. 'I can.' Although the Lord knows I should be getting home. I don' usually stay out all night. And I don' know wot Bill's going to say about it.

'Right,' he says, and ferrets in his pocket for a coin. 'Quick as you can, please.' He hesitates as he holds a shilling out to me. 'What did you say your name was, again?'

'Nancy.'

'Nancy, I can trust you, can't I? You will come back with my milk and the change?'

'Yes, I will.'

'Good lass,' he says. 'Now hurry, these little devils need food.'

I pause. 'Can I have me shawl, please?'

He's down on his knees in front of the fire, two or three cubs milling around in front of him, fair shrieking they are, and a cub in one hand, still half-wrapped in my shawl but trying to escape, and he glances up at me. 'Your shawl?'

'It's cold out.'

'Tell you what.' He rises again and thrusts his free hand into the other pocket, holds out a crown this time. 'Buy a new shawl, won't you?'

'The shop won' be open yet, sir,' I say, not taking the money. 'And … And I'd like me own back, as it happens.'

I don' tell him that I carnt go home with a new shawl, that Bill will be suspicious, that he won' be happy until he's beaten the truth out of me. And then he'll be half-mad with jealousy. I could say I nicked it, but I'd have to invent a reason why I ditched the old one.

The man is distracted by them cubs, and he pushes his curls back with one hand and looks agitated. Not accustomed to little ones, then. He waves at me. 'As you wish,' he says above the racket. 'Just go. Hurry.'

I take one last look at me shawl, and then I hurry out of the door, hugging me arms around meself for warmth. I reach the bottom of the stairs when the door behind me opens again. 'You can't go out like that. You'll catch your death. Here,' he says, and tosses his coat to me.

The coat is the brown of a horse's pelt and has seen better days—the cuffs are fraying—but it's wool and has a silky lining and big pockets for me hands. I think to meself that I *could* do a runner, forget me shawl, and nick off with the coat and the coins from last night that is tucked away, but I ain't like that. That's not to say that I *don'* nick things, only this is different. I've given me word. And them foxes are hungry.

The coffee house is not far. There's a line of people already wanting sustenance and I join the queue and hop up and down to keep warm until the woman behind me says, 'Wot's with you, you got the pox?'

How rude. But it's me. They know wot I am.

I shake me head and try to stand still, and she puts out one hand—perhaps she's sorry she spoke so forthright—and smooths it cautiously down the coat like it's a wild animal.

'Nice, innit?' I say. 'Not mine, of course.'

'Of course,' she says. She gives me a faint smile. I don' know wot she's got to smile about, a woman like her facing an entire day of drudgery in a gloomy factory, straining her eyes, swelling her ankles, breathing in toxics, and earning barely enough to provide a roof over her head and a couple of bread crusts. I may have wot Fagin calls a *wildly fluctuating* position, but at least I don' have to do wot she does.

While I'm waiting, I think about wot it would be like to own such a coat and, turning away from her, I run me hand down the front like she did, only more decisive-like. It feels good, it does. It smells like him, the coat does. Like the man with cinnamon curls.

The milk comes in a metal container with a lid, and I sacrifice one hand to the cold to hold it out before me, and hurry back.

When I push open the door, me teeth are chattering in me head. The man has found a chipped porcelain saucer somewhere and placed it on the flagstones in front of the fire. The cubs mill around it. Some step into it. One sits at his feet and gazes up with its head cocked to one side. Two more are growling and snapping at each other. All are crying. I ain't never seen an orchestra, but it sounds like a clashing of percussion triangles. Them, I've seen at Christmas time.

He takes the milk jug from me and, pushing one cub aside, pours off a quantity into the saucer.

There is silence. Sweet silence. Only the lap-lap-lapping of the little foxes' tongues. He looks across the table at me and smiles. I smile back. He has a nice smile, on his lips *and* in his eyes. It's a small thing, but it's oddly satisfying. The people I know only smile with their mouths, and mostly it's not a smile, but a grimace.

'Wot you going to do with those?' I say, pointing at the cubs.

'Don't point,' he says, covering me hand with his own and pushing it down. 'It's rude. I have an acquaintance,' he says, 'who will take them and rear them. It's just a matter of how I'm going to get them to him. He can't very well come here.'

'I see,' I say. But I don', not really. And you will find that *I see* is wot I say when I don' really see at all.

He remembers the tea then, and reaches across and pours in a tad of milk, and pushes the cup across to me.

'It'll be cold by now,' he says, 'but have some.'

It's lukewarm. I take a few sips and hand the tea to him.

'I must get on,' I say, taking off his coat and hanging it over a chair.

He nods. Half his face is buried in the cup. Above the rim of porcelain, his eyes watch me as I reach for me shawl and draw it round me shoulders.

'Your change,' I tell him, retrieving it from one coat pocket and putting it down on the table. He's still looking at me.

'Nancy?'

The milky tea feathers his moustache.

'Yes?'

'I'd like to see you again. I might have a job for you.'

'Wot, a job like this?' I indicate the cubs. That makes him laugh. He seems to laugh readily.

'No,' he says. 'The other—'

'I don' do no work for third parties,' I tell him.

'You won't, you'll still be working for me—'

'I don' do no weird things, neither.'

'You won't. You won't have to ...' He waves the teacup in the air.

'Have to wot, sir?

'You know what I mean.'

'I see. Wot *will* I have to do?'

'Behave like you're a lady—'

'I carnt be no lady!'

'Yes, you can. As long as you don't open your mouth you'll be fine.'

'How you goin' to stop me doing that?'

'I'll think of something.' He puts down the cup. 'Nice tea,' he murmurs.

'Thankee, sir,' I say.

Then I go out the door and pull it to behind me.

But I think better of that, open it again and stick me head in. 'Wot am I to call you?'

He glances down at his feet, thinking, I suppose, then looks back up at me. 'Rufus,' he says.

'That ain't your name, is it?' I say. 'That name's on account of them foxes.'

'Ooh,' he says in mock horror. 'You're sharp. I'll have to watch out.' And he smiles that smile again that reaches his eyes.

'Maybe that is my name and maybe it isn't,' he says.

He's playing with me, he is.

'Goodbye, Nancy,' he says.

CHAPTER THREE

Mr Sikes is not home when I reach it. Small mercies. It now being beyond the point of any reasonable return on me behalf.

I stir up the embers in the fireplace, add another nugget of coal, and put on the kettle. I push a chair up against the doorknob and then, hoisting me skirts, spread me legs and retrieve the rubber pessary I inserted before I left. I ain't had me courses not at all—Betsy says it's on account of how thin I am—but I don' like taking chances. I'm very lucky to have a pessary, I am. Between you and me, Fagin has devious contacts. Bill says he's a cunning one, all right, on account of him being Jewish. It makes no difference to me wot Fagin is. I don' care if he's a Chinaman. But I digress. Betsy uses a bowl of water and a plunger but, see, you've got to have that at your disposal straight after, and I don' have that liberty seeing as how I don' work from any fixed abode. I get the flannel, pour out some warm water, take off me dress and, shivering and cursing the cold, splash first me face. Then I flannel meself all over, particularly under me arms, and me nether regions. I rinse out the pessary and replace it in the small pocket in my camisole.

Two little pockets are in me cammie. One's bigger and for blunt, the other's for personal paraphernalia. Then I pull all me clobber back on again, fix me hair, grab me shawl and set out to find Bill.

He's not going to be happy I'm late and it's best to get that over with and not dawdle.

Let me tell you about The Three Cripples, situated in the filthiest part of Little Saffron Hill. The establishment is in a mirey and muddy courtyard. It's hemmed in by ramshackle dwellings, and leans precariously to one side. The mullioned windows are opaque with smut, the flagstones on the floor blackened with years of grime and bloodstains. The front parlour is a dark and gloomy den where a flaring gaslight burns all day in the winter, where no ray of sun ever shines in the summer. And here Bill sits, on a wooden bench close to the fire, brooding over a pewter measure and a glass of something. Brandy, probably. The door is ajar and I stand and look at him from the courtyard. I'm looking at him with new eyes after being with the man with the foxes. *Mr Rufus.*

Bill's not pretty, but he ain't altogether ugly neither. A broken nose, a scar that runs down the side of his swarthy face, and eyes the colour of woodsmoke with sparks in them. Brown hair that's thick like rope lies over his shoulders, and he's wearing his velveteen coat, drab shorts, stockings and half-boots. Bullseye lies at his feet licking at wot appears to be a fresh cut on one side of his jaw, which is likely the result of some recent conflict, which was no doubt inflicted by his master, which is not nice, but is altogether better than Bullseye licking his privates.

'Keep quiet, you warmint! Keep quiet,' Bill bursts out.

Bullseye's slobbering appears to get the better of him cos he kicks out and curses the gangly white-haired animal with the shaggy fringe, who yelps and rises to his feet. Fixes his teeth into one of Bill's half-boots, he does, and gives it a hearty shake.

Bill scowls down at him. 'You'd do that, would you?' And seizing the poker from the hearth in one hand, he opens a large clasp-knife that he draws from his pocket with t'other and from then on in, it's pandemonium—

'Come here, you born devil,' he roars at Bullseye. 'Come here! D'ye hear?'

Bullseye growls and lunges at the poker. Bill drops to his knees. He thrusts and parries at the animal with the knife. Bullseye yanks at the poker like a wild beast. Bullseye snaps, growls and barks. Bill snaps, growls and curses. The struggle is reaching a most critical point and I dare not venture in, when Bullseye drops the poker, turns tail and darts out the door, ears pinned to his head, straight past me legs.

'Nancy!' Bill roars, seeing me standing there. He gets to his feet, still clasping the knife and the poker.

There's surprise in his eyes, perhaps even shock.

He's told me before that he's always thinking I'm a-going to leave him, or that I have left him. And that he will kill me if I do. And this is one of those times. One of those times when he's considered I've left him and, by continuing to hold onto the poker and brandish the knife, he might just do so—he might just kill me.

'Put them away, Bill,' I say. 'I haven' left you. I'm not coming in till you do. I mean it,' I add, when he continues to look threateningly at me and does nothing.

He blinks. He has gold-flecked, hazel eyes that would be attractive in a different face, a face without a scar and a broken nose. 'All right,' he grumbles.

He drops the poker back on the hearth, folds up the knife and lowers himself back down upon the bench, and I go in and slide me arse onto the seat alongside him.

'Where you bin?' he asks.

'I been at work, ain't I?'

'I know that.' And tapping the counter, he says, 'Give.'

'That's a warm welcome for someone who's been working, for someone who ain't left you,' I say.

'Give over, woman,' he growls. Under the tabletop he slides one hand down the top of me thigh, squeezing when he reaches the kneecap. That's as much as I can expect by way of gratitude, or affection.

I look around The Cripples to check no-one's watching, but it's not yet ten and it's only me and Bill here, and then I slip me hand down inside me cammie's hidden pocket, and bring out the coins. I nudge them careful-like onto the table. I don' want all and sundry knowing I have some blunt about me, do I?

'That's nice, Nance,' Bill murmurs, eyeing the coins, 'that's real nice. Tha's more than usual. You do something special?'

'I guess you could call it that,' I whisper.

'Wot you do, Nance?' Bill looks askance at me.

'This ain't the place to tell,' I whisper.

'Nancy, my dear,' a voice murmurs over our shoulders.

'Fagin!' Bill says, jerking upright. 'Sneaking in so nobody hears how you come or go. I wish you had been the dog, Fagin, half a minute ago.'

'Why?' Fagin says, forcing a smile, but keeping his eyes on the sovereigns.

'Cos the government, that cares for the lives of such men as you that haven't half the pluck of curs, lets a man kill his dog 'ow he likes,' Bill replies. He raises his not inconsiderable eyebrows. 'That's why.'

Fagin rubs his skinny hands and plonks his bones across from us, and affects to laugh down his long nose at Bill. He's uneasy. He doesn' like it when Bill's having a go at him. Who does?

'Grin away,' Bill says, giving him a look of savage contempt, 'grin away. You'll never have the laugh at me, though, unless it's behind a nightcap. I've got the upper hand over you, Fagin, and damn me, I'll keep it. There. If I go, you go, so take care of me.'

'Well, well, my dear,' Fagin murmurs. 'I know all that. We—we have a mutual interest, Bill, a mutual interest.'

'Hmph!' Bill says. 'Well, wot you got to say to me?'

Fagin stands and reaches over and cups one hand below the edge of the table and I watch as he slides my coins into his palm. Always do feel regretful when I see me earnings disappearing.

'Thank you, Nancy, my dear,' he says. 'Satisfactory, was he?'

'Wot you make her do, Fagey? That's more than usual.'

'It is, isn't it? Well done, my dear,' he says, pocketing the coins. 'Now, let's have a drink,' he says, attempting to change the subject. 'Where's Barney?'

'You didn't answer the question. Wot you make her do?'

Fagin shakes his head. 'I don't know, you'll have to ask her. Barney!' he calls, rising to his feet. 'Where is that confounded man when you want him?'

I stifle a yawn behind one hand. 'If you'll excuse me, gents,' I say, getting to me feet, 'I've got some sleep to catch up on.'

Bill catches hold of me skirt. 'I'll be home soon,' he mutters. 'Then we'll get to the bottom of this, eh, Nance? All right?'

I nod me head and turn to leave. I'm not really listening.

Me mind has drifted away. I see a red-haired man kneeling on a hearth in front of a fire with a fox cub in his hand, fondling its ears and caressing its head. He's tender. And kind. And I think of how he held me against him all night. Strange, it were. But pleasant all the same.

Mr Rufus.

A gentleman like that and a girl like me? It don' make any sense. Wot's his game? Wot's he up to? Where's this going?

*

I don' go straight home.

I take a shortcut and slip down Hosier Lane, then Newgate, then onto Watling. I am whippet thin, I am, and quick on me feet and I can edge meself through the crowds, paying them no heed.

Have you guessed where I am going? Probably not. Perhaps it will come as a surprise. I do hope so. If there is one thing I have found, it's that it is a delight when someone surprises you.

The big doors of the Gothic building are closed when I reach them, but I check around to see nobody's watching and pull at one and steal inside. You're taken aback that I know wot Gothic is, ain't you? Truth is, you pick up all sorts of information hanging around inside churches.

I look up. I carnt help it. The vaulted parchment-coloured ceilings that soar over me head are intricate and designed like fans, and they draw me eye upwards. Nothing moves except the light drifting down. The air is still and cold, like it holds everything in place. There's a faint whiff of matting, of damp stone, of iron, wood, cloth and incense. Of candlewax.

The paintings, of which there are many, are large and ornate. A stained glass window of the Great Fire of London is all flames licking at charry buildings. There's another of the Lord Jesus drooping from the cross, His flesh being torn by them nails, which fills me with horror. And one of Jesus's mother, Mary, holding Him up to the light—His arms are opened wide as if I'm His favourite auntie and He wants to embrace me. It's peaceful-like, but still I carnt hardly look.

The pews are dark wood and homely-looking and I sit for a bit in a dark and quiet corner and think about how many of Bill's crib could fit into this vast space. The danger of falling asleep, however, is never far away. (I'm a bad sleeper, I am, and when I should be sleeping, I'm up half the night, worrying.)

Although religion ain't for me, it doesn't mean I don' believe and I pause to curtsey when I leave. It's respectful. It's acknowledging that I know He knows I been here. That maybe one day when I stand before them pearly gates, Saint Peter will have a ledger with a column that he'll run his finger down, and say, 'Ah, Nancy. Let me see … Have you been a good girl?'

I push open the heavy door. I step outside. It is only fifteen minutes of me time. Fifteen minutes of me day. Fifteen minutes to ensure I done the right thing. Fifteen minutes in which I aspire to greater things. Fifteen minutes in which me soul is filled with peace.

CHAPTER FOUR

I carnt look at Mary Madonna and her baby since …

But I ought to start at the start.

I don' remember much of me early childhood—who does?—but I have incidents that I won' ever forget. One is Fagin finding me.

I subsisted then, on wot I could steal, beg or borrow, but mostly steal. I don' know how I landed up being a street child. I carnt recall hardly anything of me parents or me siblings. I've always believed I must've had brothers and sisters, but that's only because I have a memory of there being others beside me. But who's to say we can trust our memories and believe them to be accurate? The mind is a cunning beast and can play tricks on one. Maybe me mother was a lady brought down low through one or other circumstance? I mean, think on it. That would account for me looks and for me being brighter than average, wouldn' it? Anyway, wot I remember, I think I were five, is that I were an urchin wandering the streets. Loitering outside a bread shop waiting, not like a beggar for a crust, but for the right customer. For the person you need is one that doesn' guess you are up to no good. One that is naïve. And doesn' know the neighbourhood. A stranger to the neck of the woods, if you like.

Anyhow, I wait, looking sharp, for I'm likely to be shouted at and chased away by the broom-wielding owner if I don' watch it. An old gent emerges. He is dressed wot Fagey calls *dapper*, with a cane and top hat and fancy necktie, so straightaway I know coin's no problem for him. I don' immediately accost him, I lurk behind him until he feels comfortable, for his kind *expects* to be pickpocketed. I lurk behind him and shoo away the other street children for there's an unspoken law—he's mine, I found him first. And by and by, me dapper gent relaxes his hold on the basket that he hugs to his chest and lets it swing at his side. And by and by, I come up behind him. And here you ought to remember people are thronging around him every which way. I come up behind him and wait until some hefty types are approaching, and then I brush past, between him and them, jostling against him and his basket and as I do so I lift wotever I can and slip away, run like the devil is after me. My talents are in me running, and the fact that I am small and light and can dart around like a gnat and zigzag like a flea.

However, on this particular occasion, someone approaching from t'other side sticks out a leg and I go flying. The man stops to help me up, encircling me wrist in a steel grip, and pulling me to one side out of the way. The first thing I do is look for the sustenance, the bread that will be the first food I've had since yesterday morning and, not finding it in me hand, gaze all around at the ground. But it's not there, neither. 'I've got it,' the man hisses in me ear. I glance up to see this old goat with a long nose and a puckered mouth and matted red hair glaring at me. 'And you'll get it all in good time. Now come with me, my dear, there's a good lad,' he says, 'or it'll be the worse for you. I'll have to tell Mr Smith there'—cocking his head towards the old gent who is walking away none the wiser—'that I witnessed you stealing from him.'

Fagin told me later he'd been watching me for weeks, could see that I had talent, and that 'we could be of mutual assistance to one another' as he described it. I was so filthy and long-haired and badly dressed, the old goat presumed I was a boy, and it wasn' until he got me back to his crib and set out wiping me face with a wet flannel that he realised I was a girl. I stayed a boy for years—it was easier—until it was obvious I wasn' one, and until a certain type of gen'leman began making enquiries for other things, which I was never going to do. I suppose I began wearing dresses when I were about twelve, which brought about a whole new way of life I could earn money from. Which I didn' at first like, but beggars carnt be choosers.

Wot else do I remember? Let me see ...

This one is difficult to put into words. It feels like a vision more than a memory. Let me describe it … I am walking down the street clutching the hand of a woman. I think she is my mother. The street is crowded, noisy with flower sellers and barrow boys, horses' hooves, carts and hackney-cabs, hammerings and hollerings, clinkings and shuntings, and the air choked with smoke from towering chimney stacks, the ground beneath me feet slippy. The woman with me don' say much, so either she ain't me mother or she is so intent on wot it is she must do, so overwhelmed with grief, she carnt speak. I like to think it's the latter. But it may be that I am fooling meself. Maybe I was a burden. Maybe she didn' want me no more. Maybe she didn' love me in the first place …?

So there I am walking down the street, clutching me mother's hand.

And someone comes between us, and I lose her hand.

Turning in bewilderment, I gaze up—I am only little, remember—but she's not here. She's nowhere to be seen. Gone. All around me people press past, all around me skirts ruffle, trousers twitch, and canes tap tap. All around me are the faces of strangers, threatening to overwhelm me.

I lose her hand.

Or does she deliberately let go of me?

Does she abandon me?

And then there is this: a memory disintegrating at the edges … A long grey passage, the walls looming over me. A grey wooden table with some dilapidated wooden chairs, beyond that an open fireplace in some blackened, smoky and greasy room. I stand in front of the fire, stirring something in a pot, and clutch someone small to me hip. I am a child meself, but I hold another smaller person to me hip, comforting her. Or him.

I *must've* had a brother, or a sister, or siblings.

Which makes the memory of me mother letting me go all the harder to bear.

I were helpful. Surely, I must've been kind, too? Surely I were kind to me brother?

Why, then, did me mother abandon me?

And why carnt I forget this, leave it behind?

I ought to focus on the things that matter—Bill, and the Dodger, and now Oliver, and Mr Rufus.

I ought to remember that me mother made her choices and had to live with them. I should attempt to do the same. But it's easy to say and hard to do. *Hard.*

CHAPTER FIVE

Bill slides into the bed alongside me and wakes me up. 'Wot time is it?' I ask.

'Time to give me your attenshun,' he says, pulling me onto me back. He props his head on one hand and stares down at me and his thick ropey brown hair falls into his eyes. 'So, wot did you do with this … this … Wot was his name?'

'Mr Wright,' I say. It pops into me head. There's no point fighting Bill's questions. I'll only get a fat lip if I do. He don' always want to know every detail, but Bill ain't met this new client and he's naturally curious. And unnaturally jealous. Always has been. I might as well get it over with.

'Go on,' he says, pushing off the quilt cover and slipping one hand into me smock's opening and fondling me breast, the nipple of which has hardened in response to the sudden cold air.

'Oi,' I say, 'give me covers back.'

'No,' he says. 'A bit of cold will sharpen your memory, eh, Nance? Where did you start? The usual, or something different?

'Nance,' he says, when I don' respond, 'wot did you do that made him give you extra? If yer don't tell me I'll make yer.'

'All right,' I tell him. 'Hold onto your hat.' I pause and pretend I'm thinking when in actual fact I'm inventing. How's Bill going to find out?

'We started off usual,' I say. 'Him on me. Then we did it a few ways—he wanted straddling, he wanted sucking off, he wanted to do it from t'other side.' I shrug. 'The money were extra because, well, there were a number of times.'

'You sure?' He's begun to rub himself up against my thigh. His dick has come over all stiff while I been talking and protrudes from his shorts. 'Show me how he did it from behin',' he says, turning me over with a strong arm and hoisting me up onto me hands and knees.

'Bill,' I say, but I might as well be talking to the wall.

'Come on, girl. Gee up.' He lifts me smock, smacks me arse, and prods at me.

Fiddling in me pocket for the pessary with one hand, me weight all on the other, I widen me legs and manage to slip it in just in time.

Sometimes when he's aroused—I call it jealous—he likes to act like he's the client. Lording it over me. This is one of those times. I have to do it every which way. And the bed rocks and bucks until I think the floorboards, which are rotten anyhows, are going to crack apart and we're going to plummet to the floor below. Finally, he's exhausted. And he rolls away and sinks into a deep sleep, his mouth open, his dick lolling to one side like a wrinkled, dirty sock.

I didn' always do wot I do, of course. Started when I began wearing them dresses, didn' I? Earnt more that way, certainly earnt more than being a regular pickpocket.

In many ways Fagin's been like a father to me. All them other lads, Dodger, Charley Bates, and so on, they came arter me. I was the first and because of that I have a certain standing, a certain respect amongst Fagey's boys.

CHAPTER SIX

I want to talk to you about names. Yes, names.

Me name is Nancy, as you know. *Nan-cee.* Two syllables. The first part of me name—Nan—is low-sounding, and the second part—cee—goes up in the air. Say me name and you start off low and end up high, finish bright and cheerful-like. In the clouds. Now take Oliver's name. *Ol-uh-ver.* Three syllables. The beginning is low, practically down on the ground. The middle is higher but not up in the air, and the ending is higher again, but you're still nowhere near the clouds. Oliver's name is three rungs of a small painted wooden staircase, the paint perhaps being a bit chipped and mouldy in places. But it's three steps *up*. Starting low and rising. And this is how I think of the boy: starting small, but having prospects, going places. Becoming someone. Mr Rufus, on the other hand, is two syllables. *Roo-fus.* On a level. Though you could argue it goes up—a peak of excitement, not always obvious—then comes down again. Then stays the same. Smooth and even. Steady and reliable. Like the man. Fascinating, innit?

Don' get me started on *Bill* or *Fagin* …

It's curious, but the boy and the man, Oliver and Mr Rufus, become inextricably linked in me mind.

I meet them for the first time on the same day. I develop special feelings for the both of them, straight off, without any preliminaries. I see them for a second time, on the *same* night, not long after. There is something odd and unusual about them. They are like people in the wrong place at the wrong time. And I cannot but think of one of them without thinking of t'other. They're connected in some way I ain't yet worked out. I'm not explaining this very well. Feelings are such cussed awkward things to explain, ain't they? And you'll find I don' do them no justice.

It's at Fagin's where I see the boy for a second time. By now, I know there's a new boy, know that his name is Oliver Twist, that he comes from the country. Dodger found him half-starving and with nowhere to stay on that night I first saw him.

'He scarpered from wotever he had, wotever he was, and *wherever* he was,' Dodger told me.

'Must've been awful bad for an innocent-looking lad like him to take such a big step into the wide world?' I said.

'Orphan,' Dodger told me. 'Stands to reason. Got no-one. Mother died at birth—in the workhouse, presumably, father unknown.' Dodger's told me all. In me line of work I bump into him all the time. I enjoy him, I do. Got a soft spot for him. He's often returning home to Fagin's when I'm setting out, and we'll always have a few words. Though we don' make it public knowledge. We feign indifference when we're with company. Works better that way, then nobody knows we share information. He told me Fagin's keeping Oliver out of sight, at home, until he's learned the ropes. Which is imminen'ly sensible. That Fagin's got him picking out stitches in pocket-handkerchiefs, and playing the hunting game. And the boy is providing untold amusement to Charley, who forgets that once he was like Oliver, only very likely worse.

The night I see Oliver a second time, I'm with Betsy. We're not working. We been given the night off cos we done well of late and Fagin's invited us to come up to the crib in Field Lane. I mention Field Lane because Fagin has more than one house, and he moves from one to t'other when the occasion demands. He's invited us to give the password *Plummy and Slam* to an anonymous voice and to tread with care up the dark and broken stairs and be his guests. I am used to Fagin's houses, I am, but let me describe this one. First off, your nose is assaulted by the smell of them cooking sausages. Which accounts for the walls and ceiling being black. Run your fingernail down the wall and it'll come away clotted with charcoal. A deal-table is before the fire, with a candle stuck in a ginger-beer bottle, two pewter pots, a loaf and butter, and a single plate upon it.

Several rough beds made of old sacks are huddled side by side upon the floor, and seated at the table are—let me see—five boys tonight, none older than the Dodger, smoking long clay pipes. One of the boys is Oliver. I pick him out before I've hardly come through the door. He ain't smoking, of course. He sits quietly like he's taking everything in. And already I know the boy is deep.

Spirits are produced and we sit around the table with Dodger and Charley and it's all very jolly. Fagin's in fine fettle. He inserts a handkerchief into the pocket of his flannel gown, sticks his long nose into the air, and instructs Oliver to follow him. As Fagin walks about the room the boy must attempt to remove the silky article without him noticing. Holding up the bottom of the pocket with one hand, Oliver draws the handkerchief lightly out of it with the other.

'Is it gone?' Fagin cries, staring into the middle distance. 'Is it gone?'

'Here it is, sir!' Oliver shows it in his hand. He's so keen to please Fagin, he's like a puppy dog. It's almost embarrassin'.

'You're a clever boy, my dear,' the old goat says, patting Oliver on the head with approval, and we all cheer. 'I never saw a sharper lad,' he adds.

'Oi, sir, that's wot you said to me!' Charley says, and practically falls off his chair with laughter.

Oliver turns to survey us. He has blue eyes. Not like me milky blue ones, they're deep blue. He is a serious child. Or maybe it isn't that he's serious, but that he's pensive. *Contemplative*, Fagey would say. He seems older than his years, and it seems to me that his gaze rests on me longer than anyone else. As if there's something in me he recognises. Or something about me he knows that even *I* don' know.

Betsy picks it up, too, for she glances at me and finds me staring straight at the lad.

'Wot?' I say, trying to rattle her.

'Nuffink,' she says. But it ain't *nuffink* and she knows it.

The Dodger, Charley, Betsy and me get up to leave after a suitable interval. I don' look at the boy again. I am scared to in case I carnt drag me eyes away.

Fagin gives us some coin to enjoy ourselves with. We're going out, but we don' have to work. It's only if we come across employment unexpected-like, and even then it's up to us whether we make use of it. It's the old goat's way of making us think we have some freedom and control over our lives.

Freedom and control over our lives? Ha! Hardly likely is it?

*

We find ourselves in Soho, not our usual haunt. A cut above our neighbourhood. Dodger has brought us here. In spite of the frigid night air, the place is awash with humanity. Resounding with shrieks and throbbings. It's a party of sorts, apparently. He winks, and we know he made good use of the event and I guess that's why we're here.

People and professions of all shapes, sizes and kinds are out and about. A regiment of off-duty soldiers is hanging about the tavern where we stop off, and I half regret that I haven' come out tonight prepared to do some work. I don' often do work without the old goat's knowledge, or Bill accompanying me. Let's just say I tried it once and it didn' work in me favour.

We purchase an ale, Betsy and me, and lose Charley and Dodger in the rowdy crowd, which is all right, they can look arter themselves. Then we edge up against the wall where we can keep an eye on things, and it seems we're not the only ones keeping an eye on things for one or two of them soldiers look our way. Betsy says she ain't come out tonight to work, but she don' mind either way and, when a soldier makes his way over and introduces himself to her, I let them get on with it. They move off to find somewhere more discreet, and I'm left high and dry and don' much care for the way them other soldiers is looking at me. I finish me ale and move off. I may as well head home. It ain't much fun all alone-like. And I have a long walk back ahead of me.

I don' know Soho all that well and it isn't unexpected when I take a wrong direction. I turn into a lane and am halfway down it when I realise it's all quiet as a graveyard. The shops are closed and wot houses there are, are in darkness. Even the gas lamp is out. And then I find, not only that, but me route is bricked up one end and I turn and head back, stumbling in the shadows.

But me way is blocked.

Someone looms over me in the darkness. Red coat with gold braiding glimmering at the neck. One of them soldiers looking at me earlier has been following me.

'Hallo, there, my pretty,' he says. Which is not wot they usually say, but it takes all sorts.

'I ain't working tonight, love,' I tell him, thinking of me pessary which is sitting on a shelf in me house behind a pile of crockery. 'Sorry,' I add, so he knows there's no hard feelings.

'I don't care if you're working or not,' he says, one hand fingering the sheathed sword at his side. Over his shoulder, in the adjoining road, there's the racket of the crowd, revellers coming and going, carriages and cabriolets clackety-clacking, but I know from experience that even if I did cry out for help and someone heard me, there'd be no point. There'd be no help for the likes of me. All they'd say is that she had it coming to her.

The soldier removes his hat, drops it to the ground, advances upon me. I reverse. There's little point in attempting to slip past him. He will just catch me and the excitement of that will heighten his blood and I don' need his blood heightened. I step back. He moves forwards. It's like chess, it is.

Until the bricks are up against me spine. Which is wot he wants, innit? Silly Nancy, *stupid* girl. I said I only take fright when I'm hemmed in and oh, Lord! Am I hemmed in now.

I stand and watch as he lifts his jacket and fumbles with his flies, all without taking his eyes off me.

I want to cry out, to fight him, but I know that it will be the worse for me if I do. If I make a fuss. It is easier to submit and let him get on with it. I do make a noise of objection though. It's involuntary.

'No, please. I don' want to do this. Sir?' I say, in case there's any misunderstanding on his part that I am a willing participant.

I do struggle, in spite of everything. It's not that I am against doing it, it's doing it without me safeguard.

I try to push the hand that gropes under me skirt away, but he is strong. And tall. He leans into me, pushes his weight against me, and I get a whiff of his breath smelling of spirits. Then he plants his mouth on mine, forces me lips open and—so help me God—but I bite him.

'Ow!' He pulls away. 'You little—' he says. A word best not repeated. He smacks me across the face. 'So that's how you want it? You want it rough, do you?'

He hoists me up. Pins me to the bricks, his upper body crushing me bosoms, small as they are. One thigh presses between me legs forcing them apart—

'Get off her!'

The voice comes out of the darkness.

The soldier flicks his head. Someone shoves him violently away and I drop from the wall and land on me feet like a cat.

The soldier is sprawled on the ground, his sword clanking against the stones. And I'm vaguely aware of another man standing over him, but it's too dark to see wot's happening.

'Nancy?'

I gaze up.

Mr Rufus. Wot a coincidence.

Mr Rufus straightening his cravat and reaching for his cane.

'Here,' he says, picking up me shawl and handing it to me. He takes me hand. 'We'd best get you out of here. What are doing here, anyway? This isn't your neighbourhood.'

CHAPTER SEVEN

He doesn't mess about, Mr Rufus doesn'.

We return the way I came and he hails a hackney-cab in the main thoroughfare, and gives the address of the crib where I visited him before.

We travel there in silence, the horse wending its way through the crowds, its hooves tapping on the cobbles. It has started to snow and I watch the sooty flakes falling to the earth. Mr Rufus sits alongside me in the cab but stares out, as if lost in thought. He may be far away in mind, but he still fidgets—one hand twisting his coat buttons. He is quite the man about town tonight: deep-brown velvet waistcoat, patterned cravat, frilly cuffs edging his jacket sleeves. Bamboo cane. No shabby coat. I feel awkward. For one thing, I don' know if he has understood I'm not working tonight—and not working means not working. For another, I feel I owe him. For a third, his posh appearance makes me uncomfortable.

When we reach the tenement at the end of the street, we alight, and I wait with me shawl wrapped around me and hugging meself, while he pays the driver.

'I ain't coming in,' I tell him as he joins me on the stairs, making him look up at me. 'I do thankee for your help, sir, but I ain't coming in. See, I'm not working tonight.'

'Who said anything about work?' he says.

He takes me arm, propels me firmly towards the door, and instinct tells me there's another side to him, a devilish, reckless edge that I don' know.

I wait while he unlocks the door, and then I step inside. I carnt help but shiver. The little house is an ice chest. No-one has been here for days.

The first thing Mr Rufus does after he puts down his cane and pulls off his jacket and lights a candle, is to stack some kindling in the grate and light it. He blows hard on the flames until the fire comes to life.

'Sit down,' he says, when he turns and sees I remain standing by the table.

'I don' want to stay, sir,' I say. 'I don' want to take up your time.'

He opens a cupboard under the shelf where the pretty cup and saucer stand, and brings out a bottle. He opens it, reaches for the cup, splashes some liquid in and pushes it towards me. 'You won't grow good, standing,' he says.

I pull out the chair and sit, although I've a good mind to tell him I won' grow good sitting, neither.

He lifts the bottle to his mouth. 'Cheers,' he says.

'Wot are we drinking to, sir?'

'The Queen,' he says.

'To the Queen,' I say, raising me cup. Why not? I have heard good things about her. The liquid is fiery, not watered down, and it makes me eyes smart. But it does the trick, it warms me up.

'Do you remember I said I might have a job for you?' he says, putting his back against the wall alongside the fireplace and leaning on it.

I nod. 'How come,' I say, 'you haven' been in touch with Fagin?'

'Because I don't want to do this through *Fagin*.'

'You don' like the man?'

'It's not that I dislike him, but that much is true, I do dislike him—it's that I don't want to involve the man. He doesn't need to know …' He trails off and pats his moustache delicately as if he wants to assure himself it's still there. 'This is between you and me.'

'To be honest, sir, I don' like doing things without Fagin, or without … without …' I dither for I don' want to say Bill's name. 'He gives me protection, see, if anything goes wrong.'

'I understand that, Nancy.' He smooths down the ends of the moustache and fixes his deep-brown eyes upon me. 'But you have my word that nothing will go wrong.'

'Still—' I say.

'Nancy,' he interrupts. 'If I had wanted to, I could have had my way with you tonight and invited half the regiment to join in, but I didn't, did I? What did I do, hmm?'

'You saved me,' I mumble.

'I saved you,' he murmurs. 'So you might show me some respect, hmm?'

I fiddle with the handle of me cup. Wot am I getting meself into? And why is he so abrupt tonight? I carnt rightly make the man out. Why did he save me, and wot does it mean? Is he trying to deceive me into thinking he is chivalrous when all the time he has other designs, or is it possible he is a man with principles? Or is it neither of those? He unsettles me, he does. With Bill and Fagey, things are straight. I know where I stand. But this one …

'Wot is it you want me to do? You said you want me to be a lady but I carnt be no lady. Just look at me, sir—'

'I'm looking,' he says.

I don' know where to put me eyes. His gaze is so direct, his eyes, so ... so …

For he looks at me like he's actually *seeing* me.

And here it is. Come over me all of a sudden-like. Making me shiver. A feeling I have never felt before and have no words for. A feeling that is hot and intense. A feeling I cannot name. A feeling that bewilders me even further.

'Drink up,' he says, putting down the bottle abruptly and startling me out of me reverie. 'We ought to get you home. Or do you wish to stay here for the night?'

'No, sir,' I tell him, 'but thankee. I ought to get home. There's people that await me safe return.'

'People?'

I look away.

'When am I to do this *work*?'

'Soon,' he says. 'Soon. Which reminds me, how are we to communicate? Is there someone I can leave a message with?'

I think about this and don' have an easy answer.

'The Three Cripples in Saffron Hill,' I say at last. 'There's a man there called Barney. You could leave a message with him. But make it simple, in case it ain't safe.' I sniff. 'Just put a day and a time.'

I don' want to tell him the reason for not making it complex is I carnt read well, do I?

'All right,' he says. 'I will.'

Mr Rufus extinguishes the fire and locks up, and together we walk back to the main thoroughfare. He hails a hackney coach, but I tell him I can jus' as easily walk.

'Don't be silly, Nancy,' he says, holding out his hand to help me up into the coach. 'I'm offering to pay for it.'

'Sir,' I say, being bold. I may as well spit it out. 'Why are you so—so—'

'Irritated? Rude? Forgive me. I'm angry with myself.' He sighs and tugs on the brim of his hat. 'Are you familiar with wanting something you shouldn't have?'

'That I am, sir.'

'Well, Nancy,' he says. His nostrils flare ever so slightly like he's having trouble controlling himself. And Lord, help me, but I come over all goosebumpy again.

'Well, wot?' I mumble cos cat's got me tongue.

'You want me to spell it out?'

'Yes, please, sir.'

'You,' he says, 'are something I want. But'—he glances away—'you're something I shouldn't have.'

'Nobody's forcing you to have me,' I say.

'That's just the point.'

He knocks sharply on the door then, and the carriage jerks away. But I wonder if that's all it were about, whether there ain't something more that's upset him tonight.

I ride in style back to Bill's. But I make sure the coach stops well before the crib, in case anyone should see me, and then I half-walk, half-run the remainder.

The snow has stopped falling, but them streets are icy and it's as cold as a witch's bum.

*

Strange, but I find meself hovering about The Cripples over the next few days. But there ain't no message from Mr Rufus. Eventually, I put it behind me and get on. But that feeling that I spoke of keeps surfacing, tugging at me. And when it does, I hang onto it like a drowning rat does a straw, for it makes me feel good. It makes me feel warm inside. It makes me feel hopeful.

I keep seeing Mr Rufus's face in me mind, too, the way he looked at me when he said … Actually, I carnt rightly remember wot he said. It's the way he looked at me that's stuck in me mind. And I keep seeing this look, feeling the intensity of it, until I can no longer accurately remember wot he looks like.

CHAPTER EIGHT

I pay a visit to Fagey. For one thing, I need to find out where and when me next job is. For another, it's me attempt to find out more about Mr Rufus in a roundabout way. For me curiosity is piqued.

But the old goat ain't there. Instead, I find Oliver keeping house.

It's a dull and dirty afternoon, the sky blotted out by fog and stinky smoke, and the boy is kneeling down attending to the fire when I push open the door. He doesn' hear me. He seems to have been engaged in picking the marks out of them pocket-handkerchiefs for there is a pile of them, and a needle, upon the table.

He starts when he comes upright, looks around and finds me there. His mouth opens, but no words come.

'It's only me, Nancy,' I say, taking off me bonnet and hanging it over the back of a chair. 'We met the other night, remember?'

'I do remember.' He gives me a long stare, knitting his fair eyebrows together in concern.

I pause. 'Wot is it?' I whisper.

He shakes his head. Wotever it is, he's not saying. 'Won't you sit down, miss?' He indicates the chair.

So I sit at the table, and he takes up his work again, and I say, 'Fagey out and about?'

'Yes, miss. And the boys, too. I did so want to go with them—out to work—but they wouldn't let me.'

'I am sure they will … Soon,' I say. 'Have you played all them games? Do you feel sure you know wot it is you must do when you are working?'

'Oh, yes, miss. Only …' He breaks off and looks earnestly at me over the top of his work.

'It's all right,' I murmur. 'You can tell me. Only wot?'

He sighs. Tremulously-like. 'Only the other night they came home empty-handed and Fagin shouted at them and wouldn't give them supper, not that there was much to begin with, and said they were idle and lazy, and he even … he even …'

'He even wot, Oliver?'

'He kicked one of them downstairs. Charley Bates. I heard him fall. It was awful, miss. But he didn't cry, not once.'

'Charley is a hard nut,' I murmur.

'I feel sure …' Oliver begins. And stops again.

I cock me head to one side and look expectant-like at him. I am puzzled by how well the boy speaks. *Eloquent*, Fagey would say. And I wonder how he learnt to speak well, and why he persists in it?

'I feel sure that if I were with them, they'd do better,' he declares.

I carnt help smiling. 'Do you now?' I say.

In the quiet, a log of wood in the fireplace spitters, and the wind taps upon the window, making a shiver go down me spine. I draw me shawl closer round me. It's hellish out and comfortable here and I may as well keep the boy company.

'Wot did you do before, Oliver?' I ask. 'Before you came here?'

'I was working for an undertaker, miss. In the country. For a man by name of Sowerberry. It was my job to go with Mr Sowerberry to see the people, the people who'd lost their loved ones, their children, and to not say anything, and to look what Mr Sowerberry called *angelic*.'

'I see. And why did you run away?'

'They put me with the coffins, miss. Sleeping in amongst the empty wooden boxes. It gave me the creeps, it did. And Mrs Sowerberry didn't like me. *Mr* Sowerberry did, but he wouldn't stand up for me against her. And there was also a girl called Charlotte, working in the kitchen, who didn't like me, either. I don't know why they didn't like me. I tried to be nice. But that was nothing, really. The worst of it was a big boy employed there called Mr Noah Claypole, a charity-boy, not a workhouse orphan like me, who bullied me and bossed me, and kicked me like a dog when he felt like it. See, charity-boys think they're better than workhouse orphans. And Mr Noah Claypole, I think he was jealous because it was me who went with Mr Sowerberry to see the clients, and not him. And he said bad things about my mother. Which I didn't like. Which upset me.'

'I am sorry to hear that.'

The child takes a needle to one of them handkerchiefs, but his fingers are all a-quiver.

'And then wot happened?' I say gently.

'Oh, miss.' Oliver lays down his needle and handkerchief, and the tears start to his eyes. 'I hit him. I couldn't help myself. I hit him so hard he fell to the ground. And then they all piled into me and beat me till I was black and blue, and locked me away. But I wasn't sorry. I won't have them say bad things about my mother.'

'Wot did they say, Oliver?'

'He—Mr Claypole—he said she was a "regular right-down bad 'un" and that it were better that she died when she did, or else she'd have been hard labouring in Bridewell, or transported. Or hung. And he said that last was more likely than either of the others. And that was when I rose up—although he was a great deal bigger than me, miss—and took him by the throat and shook him until his teeth chattered in his head.' The boy pauses to get his breath. 'Oh, miss, did I do wrong?'

'I don' think so, Oliver,' I murmur. I put out a hand and lay it over the top of his to stop it trembling.

'They gave me another lashing, then, and sent me to sleep amongst the coffins, and called for Mr Bumble, the beadle, who was in charge of the workhouse, to take me back. That was when I ran away, when it was just light, and before Mr Bumble came. I didn't ever want to go back to the workhouse. We were that hungry in the workhouse, miss, that we took a vote to pick one of us to ask for more food, and that was me. And after I asked for more gruel, Mr Bumble caned me, miss, and put me in cell all alone. He was cruel, not a nice man at all.'

Oliver pauses to get his breath, then goes on. 'But something else happened, when I left, that I can't forget. I stopped outside the workhouse, miss, and saw Dick, who was my friend, weeding the gardens behind the railings, and I called out to him to say goodbye … And … And …' The boy rises from the table in his agitation.

'And he said "God bless you!" Nobody'd ever said that to me before, miss. It fair made me cry. I felt like it was the end of the world. And what was I to do? Where was I to go?'

'God bless you, Oliver,' I murmur. 'There, I've said it, too.' I open me arms and say, 'Now come here,' and pull him close and pick him up and hold his small body upon my lap until he stops quivering. And when I pull away his head lolls back and he is lifeless in me arms. Like fainted asleep. Like sometimes happens to women, mostly for good reason. The lad has hysteria. It's all too much.

I lay him down on one of them beds then, and cover him with a quilt and, picking up me bonnet, I leave the room as quietly as I entered it.

*

When I get outside, the rain is pelting sideways. Smoke, fog and steam are billowing every which way, and I hold on to me skirt and me shawl and fight through the wind threatening to tear me clothing from my body, and hop, skip and near slip to The Cripples.

When I ease inside, shivering and shaking off the rain, Barney comes to the counter.

'Bere you bin?' he asks, looking round to make sure no-one else is within earshot and talking through his nose as is usual. 'This bin baiting since bay before besterbay.'

He holds out a note. On which is printed: *Thursday: 5 o'clock.*

Printed. And neat. Mr Rufus already suspects I ain't got no reading skills, then.

'Wot day is it today, Barney?' I murmur.

'Bursday,' he says. And together we glance up at the clock on the wall. 'Bursday, and hob-bast bour,' he announces. 'You'd beb-ber get cracking, girl.'

CHAPTER NINE

I don' have time to go home and wash or do wotever else I might want to do to make meself presentable. I must go now or I will be late. And I don' want to be late.

As I dash out the door, Bill lumbers in from t'other side.

'Oi, where you goin'?' he growls, grabbing hold of me arm. He's wet, dripping with rain, and he's filthy. Filthy with rage. His swarthy face dark with anger.

'Ow,' I say, 'you're hurting me—'

'Where you goin'!' he insists.

'I—I—' I carnt think wot to say.

'I'm a-going to help the boy,' I blurt out. 'I'm going to help Oliver. Fagin asked me.'

'Fagin? I jus' seen him and he ain't said nothing to me—'

'Well, I carnt help that. I carnt help it if he has more important things on his mind than me and Oliver.'

Bill growls, 'Don' be long, then.' He releases me arm. 'I ain't in the mood for me own company.'

I don' say yes and I don' say no. I don' own up to anything. I simply pull me shawl tighter round me and scarper.

By the time I reach Mr Rufus's place, dodging the weather and God knows wot else, I am wet through. But I ain't late. St Paul's has just rung the hour, fair muffled by the rain them chimes are, but I hear all five of them. I rap upon the door.

'Good God,' he says, letting me in. 'You look like a drowned fairy.'

'Thankee,' I say, shivering. I don' know whether to be pleased or affronted. A drowned *fairy*?

The fire is not lit. The little house is cold. It has no heart. Mr Rufus still has his coat on as if he has come here express-like to meet me.

'Well, I guess you can't get much wetter,' he says. He runs one hand through his hair. 'Right,' he says. 'I have a carriage waiting. Let's go.'

'Where we goin', sir?'

'You'll see.'

He propels me out the door and holds one hand over his face shielding it from the elements, while he locks up with the other. 'Quick, let's not dawdle,' he says. 'Down there'—he points. 'All right?' He squints at me through the rain with them deep-brown eyes.

'Here,' he says, 'give me your hand.' And off we go, hop, skipping and a jumping over the puddles.

I am not at all apprehensive, only excited!

And true to his word, there, at the junction of the lane and the main thoroughfare is a waiting carriage, the driver sitting out the wet under a greatcoat, the drops dripping off his large hat.

Inside, it is sumptuous, soft and soothing. Mr Rufus takes off his coat and lays it down on the seat so me wet clothes don' spoil the furnishings.

It's not the same coat he lent me previous. It's altogether nicer, warmer and a newer one. I notice—I try not to stare—Mr Rufus is dressed nicely. Not as posh as he were the night he rescued me, but he looks handsome. I've said before that he has looks. I ain't changed me mind.

I don' know where we are going and it's so murky out that it's hard to *see* where we're headed. I jus' hope that when we get there, there's a warm fire and maybe crumpets with butter dripping off them and bowls of hot soup. And clean, dry clothes. Ha! Wouldn't that be nice?

Calm yourself, Nancy. Don' get carried away.

Mr Rufus starts to talk. He tells me that where we are going, he has dismissed all the servants for the evening, that I will have a bath and change into *finery*, that he will help me dress. That we will be leaving the house and going elsewhere. Where I must not open me mouth. Where I must remember that I am mute.

'Mute?'

'You know what that means—?'

'That I carnt speak?'

'Precisely. So, if there is anything you want to say, you should say it now because you won't get another opportunity.'

'Carnt you tell me why I'm a-doing all this?'

He shakes his head. 'It's better that you don't know. Not yet, at least.'

'All right, but I'm warning you if there's any funny business like you promised wouldn' happen, I won' stay quiet.'

'There won't be any funny business, as you call it. Oh, and you're to have a name, did I say?' He pauses, and fingers his moustache. 'You'll be Miss Tweedles—'

'*Tweedles*?' I blurt out. 'Carnt I have a name that's half-decent?'

'What's wrong with Tweedles?'

'I don' know, it sounds betwixt and between. Wot about Miss … Miss …'

'Richardson, then. Miss Titania Richardson.'

'Titania?'

'Yes, and don't repeat everything I say, Nancy. And stop whining.' He pauses. 'Have you heard of Shakespeare?'

I frown. 'I might of. Ain't he some famous poet?'

'Quite right. You surprise me. How do you know that?'

'Never you mind,' I say, smiling. If Mr Rufus can have his secrets, why carnt I?

'Well,' he says, clearing his throat, 'Titania is a character from one of Shakespeare's plays. The Queen of the fairies, she is.'

I raise me eyebrows. Well, fancy that! 'And?'

'And what?'

'Wot happens to her?'

'Oh.' He waves one hand in the air. 'She falls in love with an ass—'

'An ass?'

'Yes, you know, a donkey—'

'Why would she do that?'

'Well, Puck puts a spell on her so that she thinks—'

'Puck? Who's he?'

'A sort of goblin. Mischievous. And the donkey, who's actually a man, is a weaver, a man called Nick Bottom—'

'Bottom? How rude!'

'It *is* Shakespeare.'

'And is she beautiful, this Titania?'

'Yes, very.'

'And does she have children? Fairy children?'

'Yes. But, more importantly, she is besotted with a changeling.'

'Wot's a changeling?'

'A changeling's like a fairy, too, only people believed they were put in place of babies who were stolen away by fairies.'

'I see,' I murmur, and knot me fingers together. I stay silent. I don' know that I want to know anything more about this Titania and her changeling. You understand why, don' you? I mean, wot if something happens to the changeling? In the play, I mean. Or do I mean in the play?

The carriage soon pulls up outside a many-storeyed house with grey shingles upon the roof, long windows and white walls, and Mr Rufus puts his finger to his lips. I think we're in Mayfair, but I don' really know.

He rises and, from under the seat, pulls out a black cape and instructs me to put it on. Then he opens the door and we step outside. The street is in darkness, apart from the glow of the gas lamps, and we move quickly through the front gate and up the stairs, and I wait while he unlocks the door.

'There,' he says, ushering me inside and shutting the door behind us. The hallway is tiled with fancy patterned squares. There are paintings on the walls, of hayricks and wagons and woodcutters' cottages, and of solemn men's and women's faces who, in spite of their grand attire, don' look too happy. A dark and shiny wooden table with fancy curved legs and feet like dog's paws stands against the wall, and there is a bowl of pink roses and a gaslight upon its surface. The hallway smells of burning candles and furniture polish and old books. And money. Lots of money. And I wonder wot a man like this is doing, going betwixt this palatial dwelling and the other crib. It don' make any sense.

'This way.' He takes me elbow and leads me down the passage and into the heart of the house and I don' have much time to look around on account of we are moving too fast. We go up a marble staircase and along a landing. He opens a door and we enter and he closes it behind us.

It's a man's bedroom. The furnishings are dark and sombre. There's a fire burning in the grate. A pile of dark leather books on the bedside table. A man's set of silver-backed hairbrushes on the dresser. More countrified scenery upon the walls.

Mr Rufus pushes opens another door that I ain't noticed because it's part of the walls-like, and standing inside is a copper tub for washing.

'Get undressed,' he tells me. 'I'll go down and get hot water.'

'I'm to have a bath?'

'Remember you can't speak?' He puts his finger to his lips and raises his deep-red eyebrows. 'You're to have a bath, not because you're dirty, but because I thought you might like to before you dress.'

I nod. That makes sense.

He disappears from the room and I want to look around, open drawers and books and peek into cupboards, but I dare not.

I go into the little room with the copper tub, and it's all tiled in white with a big gilt-edged mirror on one wall and a high, narrow window with opaque glass. A pile of towels is upon a stool. There's also soap and a long-handled brush and some liquid in a cut-glass decanter on a shelf. I open the lid and it smells like something you might use on your hair.

Taking off me shawl, I lay it upon a second stool. There's some water in the copper, but it's cold and not sufficient to wash with, and I guess the idea is that I must get into the tub. So I remove me dress and lay that down, too, and then I step in, careful-like. I am standing there shivering in just me cammie and drawers with me arms wrapped around meself, when Mr Rufus returns lugging a pail of hot water.

He looks at me, puts it down. 'Get out,' he says. 'And take those off.' He means me underclothing.

And as I step out of me underwear, I think that it is just as well that I am accustomed to being naked in front of gentlemen.

'Now,' he says, after he has poured in the hot water, 'you may get back in. Wash yourself, Miss Titania, and don't forget your hair. I'll be back soon to help you dress.'

He picks up me clothing from the chair. Since I carnt talk, I grab him by the arm and look pointedly at me things.

'Don't fret yourself,' he tells me. 'I'm merely putting them away. All right?'

I nod. I step into the warm water, which is delicious, and sink down. I close me eyes and lean back, submerging me head, and when I open me eyes again he has gone.

I want to lie in the bath all night, but I'm here for a reason so I get to washing and cleaning meself. Carefully, I pour some of the liquid from the glass decanter into me hand and rub it into me hair. I shut me eyes tight. Betsy—she knows a thing or two—has told me it stings and I don' want to find out if she's right. I don' know wot the point of the hair concoction is. It doesn't seem any better or nicer than honest to goodness soap. Then I lie back down in the tub, rinse it out and start on the rest of meself.

Mr Rufus returns, carrying a jug of water. 'Washed your hair?'

I nod.

'Right, sit up straight,' he says.

I do, and he pours warm water over me head, leaving me blinking and spluttering for air. I wonder how come he knows so much about washing hair? I carnt ask, can I?

He puts out his hand to help me out, and wraps me up in a big fluffy towel and rubs me arms up and down like I'm a child and I carnt help but observe that he seems to be enjoying this whole rigamarole. I carnt help but observe that now and again he pauses and looks at me with puzzled eyes. Eyes that seem to be making some kind of calculations.

In the bedroom, he sits me down in front of the fire and towels me hair, and then he brushes it out and, again, instinct tells me he has done this before. For someone that he perhaps loved? Did he have a younger sister that he lost? Because he is careful with the knots. Because he is gentle, pulling me hair back and untangling it.

I feel weird, I do, this pampering ain't never happened to me and I don' know how to take it. At every step I want to object but I ain't allowed to, as you know.

He tells me to brush me hair in front of the fire to dry it, and then to dress, and shows me fancy clothes that have been laid out on the bed. There's drawers and a camisole, stockings and garters, stays, a petticoat, and a powder-blue silken dress so lovely it takes me breath away. Although I do pause to wonder where he got them clothes? Then he goes away again. Which is just as well as I am so taken with me finery that me fingers are all thumbs.

I have pulled on me new drawers and cammie, stockings and garters, when Mr Rufus returns. He carries a tray laden with a bowl of wot looks like soup—just like I imagined!—and two slices of crusty bread, which he puts down on the dresser. 'Eat this while I do your hair,' he says, 'and then I'll help you with your stays.'

So I sit in front of the mirror with the soup bowl in one hand, and the spoon in t'other, slurping it in, and, honest to goodness, I coulda died and gone to Heaven. Thick, creamy soup with morsels of meat and vegetables in it. I ain't never tasted anything so delectable.

Mr Rufus, meanwhile, is fiddling with me hair. He picks me fair tresses up in one hand, pulls them above me head and looks at me in the looking glass. 'Yes,' he says. 'I think so,' he says. 'Don't slurp, Nancy.' But he may as well be talking to himself.

Next time I raise me head I don' recognise meself. Me hair is all fastened on top, with a few wisps hanging down around me face, framing it like. And I have to say, I don't look half bad.

I put the empty bowl and spoon on the tray and make a gesture of thanks with me hands, and turn to him. He is standing very still, watching me. It's like it's not me he's seeing, but someone else. And I agree, I don' resemble Nancy from Bethnal Green at all.

We put on the stays, followed by the beautiful satiny dress, and he produces some pale leather boots from his closet, which are on the small, pinching side, but I ain't going to complain.

'Go out the door and come back in again,' he says. 'I want to see you perambulating.'

I frown. *Peram? Perambulating*? This is a word I ain't never heard from Fagey before.

'Walk,' he says, waving his hand at me.

I do as I am told. I *perambulate*, wobbling to begin with—I ain't accustomed to heels—and go out the door.

I walk down the passage a bit, and when I look over me shoulder he's watching me from the doorway. He seems pleased—his gaze is gentle and approving—so I turn around and come back again.

CHAPTER TEN

It is enough to know that I soon find meself in the carriage with Mr Rufus once more, heading somewhere. I don' know where. I don' know where I am in the first place. Outside, the foul weather continues, the wind and the rain lashing the carriage. Them poor horses, I think.

Mr Rufus talks along the way. Not a lot, mostly he looks out of the window. He says things like, 'Foul day to be out and about, isn't it, Miss Titania?', but I know the questions are to test I don' reply. He fidgets, too, of course. Straightens his cuffs, taps his cane upon the floor, smooths his moustache. But I am becoming used to his not being able to keep still. He don' look at me much, either, and I wonder why that is?

We reach a destination, another fashionable part o' London town that is not familiar, and Mr Rufus helps me to alight from the carriage. The house is not as grand as the one we were in before, but it is still quite something. It is one of several all joined together along a curve and them glowing lights behind them windows make the dwellings look like golden trinkets strung upon a necklace.

We go up a darkened pathway and mount stairs to a well-lit front door, and Mr Rufus steps up to the door, knocks, and steps back again.

Wot am I doing here? I think to meself. Is this *really* me, here in this opulent part of town? Is this really me in this beautiful dress? With this man? Who is altogether charming, and kind? Not at all the kind of man I am accustomed to.

Where will this end?

Time seems to stand still, while all around me the world rushes past like a violent wind.

A butler opens the door. 'Good evening, Mr Rufus,' he says, dipping his head. Me eyes widen for that means Mr Rufus's name really *is* Rufus.

Mr Rufus murmurs a greeting in return and we pass inside, and in one last warning to me he puts his finger to his lips and winks. To make me feel better, I believe. For he's been holding me hand, and now he lets it go, and I am all a-quiver with nerves.

We are ushered into a sitting room, the likes of which I ain't never seen before. I don' know where to look first. Rich brocaded drapes cover the windows. Heavy Persian rugs lie upon the floor. Precious ornaments are lined up upon the mantlepiece, artworks upon the wall. The Dodger would be in heaven. A fire burns in the grate and it is stiflingly hot, the gas lamps unusually bright. All these things flash through me head—the opulence, the grandeur—as me eyes dart around the room. Dart around and miss the elderly woman sitting in an armchair before the fire. She sits so erect and so still she is easy to overlook. She does not rise, but takes up one of them seeing things—a lorgnette?—and puts it to her eyes and peers at us. Peers at me.

'Aunt Maud,' Mr Rufus says. 'How are you?'

'Who is this?' Aunt Maud demands, still gawking at me.

I glance shyly at her and, 'Oh, Lord,' she says faintly, as if she is seeing a ghost.

Behind the thick lenses of the lorgnette, her eyes are frog-like—large, green and bulbous—but she is dignified, sitting like a queen upon a throne, her silver hair plaited and wound up behind her head. She wears a forest-green dress with a grey shawl pulled over her shoulders, and on her arthritic fingers float many loose rings of gold and green that tinkle as she moves her hand.

'This is Miss Titania Richardson,' Mr Rufus announces.

I feel like a princess at a ball, and bend low to take Aunt Maud's hand. I do not, of course, speak.

'How do you do?' she says.

I nod me head slowly and gracefully in return.

'Speak up, child!' she demands, clinging to me hand. Her fingers are freezing.

'What's wrong with her?' she says to Mr Rufus. 'Why doesn't she talk?'

Mr Rufus clears his throat discreetly. 'She is mute, dear Aunt. Mute, but perfectly capable of hearing and understanding.'

Aunt Maud releases me hand and puts down her lorgnette, but continues to stare. It is most unnerving, I can tell you. 'How did she get like that?'

'I believe it is something that happened from birth,' Mr Rufus says, glancing at me, and it crosses me mind that he is an accomplished liar, for the words roll off his tongue.

'Hmph,' Aunt Maud says.

She looks at Mr Rufus. 'It's uncanny,' she murmurs.

'I know,' he returns. 'It is indeed uncanny.'

I am in the dark here, honest to God I have no idea wot they're talking about. Wot's uncanny?

She glances past me to the butler waiting in the doorway. 'Foxley, the refreshments, please?'

Foxley.

How strange. A name mimicking them foxes. But the world is full of coincidences.

'Yes, m'lady,' he replies.

'Tell your companion to sit down, Rufus,' Aunt Maud instructs, staring at me again. 'What did you say her name was?'

'Miss Titania, Aunt. And you may tell her. She is, as I mentioned, quite capable of comprehension.'

'Well, sit down,' she says to me, but not unkindly.

It seems to me that for the moment she is taken in, that she does not see through the fancy dress, the hair that's perched on top of me head, and the cheap necklace Mr Rufus fastened around me neck, to wot I really am.

I sit. Mr Rufus perches on the sofa alongside on me left.

Aunt Maud leans forwards. 'Unseasonal weather we've been having, don't you think?' she says to me.

I nod vigorously, clasp me arms around meself, as if to indicate I am chilled to the bone. (I am not, of course.) This pantomime seems to please her for she looks satisfied. Perhaps she understands now that although I don' speak, there's nothing wrong with me eyes, ears and brain.

She leans forwards again. 'Are you warm enough, child?'

I nod again and smile tentatively.

Raising the lorgnette, she peers at me once more.

'You are a pretty little thing, aren't you?' she murmurs. 'But then so was …' she trails off.

I told you I ain't accustomed to attention, and the Lord help me but I blush. Fortunately, Foxley arrives with a silver tray of refreshments and attention is diverted from me onto him, to me relief. He presents the tray to me and I pick up a dainty glass filled with brown liquid. Sherry? Or port, perhaps?

I have me eyes on Aunt Maud, waiting for her cue to sip me drink, and it comes as a surprise when Mr Rufus raises his glass and says, 'To Miss Titania Richardson.'

Aunt Maud and Mr Rufus murmur, 'Miss Titania,' and look at me, fixate on me over the tops of their glasses, and I almost blurt out, 'Thankee, much obliged.'

Foxley appears before me again with a plate of dainty pastries. I put me glass down on the small coffee table alongside and slide one of them delicacies onto a plate. And again I wait for Aunt Maud to give me the cue when to eat, but she does not partake, and saliva fills me mouth. I must watch Mr Rufus, then. But Aunt Maud is bending towards him and murmuring something. I only catch the word 'date', to which he replies 'soon'.

Then she says, much louder, as if she's forgotten I'm not deaf, only mute. 'And what of her parents? Are they well-to-do? Richardson, did you say their name was? I have to confess I have not heard of the family.'

'Sadly, her parents are dead, Aunt Maud—'

'Dead?' She seems aghast.

'Yes.'

'That is most unfortunate. With whom does she live, then?'

'She lives alone, Aunt.'

'How unusual. Most unbecoming, I would think—'

'Oh, she does have a companion, Aunt. Miss Tweedles could not be here this evening. She had a prior engagement.'

Mr Rufus is nothing if not inventive!

'Tweedles? Hmph,' Aunt Maud says again. Then, 'Companions,' she mutters. 'I tried one once, do you remember, my boy? Empty-headed, she was.'

The way she says *empty-headed* makes me think there's some story there. She raises the lorgnette to peer at me again. 'I hope your companion is not empty-headed, child?'

I shake me head and give wot I hope is a pretty smile, and think about Bill and how he would appreciate being called empty-headed!

This *soirée* (as Fagey would call it) goes on for some time. While they discuss bits and bobs, I finish me sherry, restrict meself to two pastries, though I would like to consume the entire plate, and sit still.

There is an art to this. I let me eyes wander around the room. Listen for other sounds. I can only explain it by saying I put meself and wot's immediately going on into a box of sorts, and let me mind wander around outside it.

Horses' hooves clip-clop as a carriage goes by in the street outside. There's the swish of rain. A log of wood in the fireplace breaks and crumbles into embers, and the sparks fly. A tap drips. In the scullery, perhaps? Which carnt be too far away if I can hear it. No sounds of other staff from the rest of the house. There only seems the presence of the butler, Foxley. Unusual. Where are the maids? Perhaps Aunt Maud has something against maids as well as companions?

Two enormous, precious-looking vases stand like sentinels in the entrance hall beyond the doorway, and upon the coffee table nearest me is a gold-rimmed dish containing knick-knacks. One of these is a miniature baby made out of two fat, gold beads, a bigger one for the torso and a smaller one for the head. Its arms and legs are fashioned out of gold and can *perambulate*, and its face is drawn on. *And* it has a bit of feathery fluff for hair. It is exquisite. Surely it is very valuable?

Then, particularly *striking*—ha! do you see wot I did there?—is a little clock on the mantelpiece. Encased in a rectangular gold box, it has a *little* tick-tock. I can jus' hear it above the murmur of voices. It looks and sounds ever so dear. If there is one thing in this room I would like, it is that clock. Or maybe the baby? I am undecided.

Wouldn't the old goat like to get his paws on this loot? Not to mention Bill and the Dodger.

I don' learn much from the conversation flowing around and about me. Aunt Maud is sceptical of the new Queen and calls her *a child*. There is talk of Mr Rufus's parents, who I gather are deceased like mine. Aunt Maud is disparaging of them, and says they ought to have been more prudent or Mr Rufus wouldn't be in the situation in which he finds himself, and I wonder wot that situation is? She asks him if everything in the house is in order? Any maintenance needing attention? That sort o' thing. She makes it sound as if the house belongs to her rather than to him. Does it? I wonder. Naturally, I am assuming she means the posh house from which we departed, not the ramshackle crib. It seems unlikely she would know about the latter. I carnt begin to imagine how she would react to news of that accommodation.

The little gold clock strikes nine o'clock ever so sweetly and Mr Rufus rises from the sofa. He says we must not take up any more of Aunt Maud's time. (I couldn't agree more, me backside is stiff.)

The aunt does not get up and I begin to think it's possible she carnt walk, although there's no evidence of a nearby stick or a chair with wheels.

Mr Rufus moves in front of me and takes her hand and kisses it, and there's the tinkle of her rings again. Meanwhile, I rise discreet-like from the settee and position meself with me hands and the coffee table behind me back. Foxley is safely in the kitchen.

When Mr Rufus steps away, I am ready with me curtsey. Aunt Maud says she hopes she will see me again, and I nod in acknowledgement.

Finally, we are free to go!

CHAPTER ELEVEN

We hurry down the steps to the carriage, shielding our heads from the rain. It's been worrying me that I got some explaining to do to Bill when I get home. But I think I will be all right now. I have something to distract him.

After we set off in the carriage, it is all so much easier. Me tongue is allowed to be loose in me head again! Though, to be honest, I am not a girl that talks like a running brook. *Babble babble babble.* That's something you should know about me. Sometimes, I am quiet and still like ink in a well in a rarely used study, and you might wonder why I don' say such-and-such or *feel* this and that? I believe it is better not to state the bleeding obvious. For we ain't fools, are we?

'Well, Nancy,' Mr Rufus says thoughtfully as we set off again, 'what did you think of Aunt Maud?'

'Are you wanting me honest opinion, sir, or some words that will satisfy you?'

He grins. 'Your honest opinion, naturally.'

'She were all right,' I say.

'Really, Nancy? Just *all right*?'

'Actually she was pretty forthright,' I say, remembering the way she stared so openly at me.

'Yes, she is in the habit of calling a spade a spade. That comes, I think, of too many years of living on her own and no-one having the courage to reprimand her.'

Mr Rufus looks at me in the darkness of the carriage. (I think he has horse's eyes, I do.) 'But did you understand what is at play here, Nancy?'

'I think so, sir.' I pause. 'You and me are betrothed-like? So that she—Aunt Maud—will give you something? Will give you money? Is it money, Mr Rufus?'

The whites of his teeth flash as he smiles. 'There will be money, but there'll be something else, too. Something substantial—'

'The house!'

'Yes.'

The carriage goes over a bump, jolting us out of our seats. The driver shouts, 'Whoa!' and we come to a halt.

We both move across to the window to peer out, but the rain is pouring, drenching anyone who is out and about, lashing the side of the carriage, and making it impossible to see why we have stopped.

'*If* I marry,' Mr Rufus says quietly in me ear. 'Did you understand that bit, Nancy?'

'And if you don'?' I glance up at him.

'If I don't, nothing changes. She continues to give me an allowance, but it is hardly enough to subsist upon. She has stipulated that I will get nothing further unless I marry.' He pauses. 'She drives a hard bargain, but I also see her point. She wants to see me happily settled before she dies.'

I catch a whiff of the musky pomade he wears, which is altogether pleasing. I am so close I could reach up and kiss the pale, thin lips nestled under his moustache. It's a temptation, for he ain't kissed me yet and I wonder wot kissing him will be like. If I leant forwards and kissed him, I wonder wot he would say? Would he be taken aback, shocked, or be pleasantly startled? Would he respond?

The driver urges the horses forwards, the carriage begins to move off again and the moment is gone. We ease back into our seats, facing one another.

'There's one thing I'm not understanding, sir. Two things, actually. How come you don' have some fancy lady you can marry?'

He laughs, but it is a laugh filled with bitterness. 'Because actually, Nancy,' he says, 'I'm dirt poor and no lady in her right mind would have me.'

I think to meself then, that I understand the reason for t'other crib. That it's much cheaper to live there than in the fancy house.

He looks sideways at me. 'What's the other thing?' he asks. 'Let me guess, you want to know why Aunt Maud said it was uncanny. You want to know why I haven't had relations with you, why I haven't—' He stops. 'In short, you want to know what's wrong with me, don't you?'

'Well, yes, that, too,' I murmur. I wonder if he also guesses I've begun to suspect there might be something wrong with *me*!

He leans forwards, his arms on his thighs, but he doesn' engage with me, he looks out of the window into the darkened street. As we pass the gas lamps, his features, his tumbling, curly, cinnamon hair, his tawny-red moustache, are lit up, then fall into darkness again.

'My mother—' He breaks off, pauses. Clearly, the subject is painful to him.

'I was very close to my mother,' he begins again, 'and I lost her.' He glances at me. 'You are remarkably like her. Only in looks, of course. In personality and nature, you are quite different.'

'I see,' I say, frowning. 'But how is it that you—?'

'If you must know, I saw you one day out and about and I followed you. I found out all I could about you—'

'You followed me? When? When was this?' I carnt believe someone has followed me and I've not known.

'When you were living in Whitechapel.'

'And?'

'I did nothing. Believe me. For a long time, I did nothing. I told myself your resemblance to my mother was neither here nor there.' He pauses, taps the brim of his hat as if he's thinking. 'But, to my concern, I found myself looking out for you every day. And if I didn't see you, I was distressed, unsettled, as if the day were not complete. Then I lost you when you moved near to Saffron Hill and … And I was forced to negotiate with the man you call Fagin. I wanted to know more—more about you. I thought that if perhaps I knew more about you, I could more easily separate you from my mother in my mind.'

'And this is why you behaved like you did—because I am like your mother?'

He nods like it pains him to admit to it. 'Nancy,' he murmurs, looking at me now.

'No, wait, sir, please. I want to know … I want to know wot I was doing when you followed me?'

He frowns. 'What you were doing? What does that matter?'

'It's—it's not every day that someone follows you, watches you, is it, sir?'

'No, it isn't.'

'Well, to be fair, I am flattered by the attention. Flattered. And … and'—I find meself glowing pink—'is it wrong for me to want more information, sir? To want to know wot your impressions were?'

'I see that you are vain like any other woman,' he says, but I can tell from his tone that he's teasing me.

'Carnt I be, sir? Jus' this once?'

'Well, let me see ...'

He leans forwards and peers out of the window into the dark night. 'There was a girl—'

'Wot? Some other girl?'

'May I finish?' He tilts his head to one side. 'You do want to know, don't you?'

'I don' want no story about some other chit.'

'Shh.' He puts his finger across me mouth.

'As I attempted to say,' he begins, 'there was a girl. In addition, there was a respectable gentleman. Elderly, you understand, dressed in a bottle-green coat, wearing gold spectacles, and with a bamboo cane under his arm. The old gent was standing outside a book stall, reading. He had taken up a book and was reading as if his life depended upon it. It was clearly a good book. And all the time the girl, who carried a basket over her arm, leant against a nearby lamp post as if she were casually waiting for someone, but she didn't take her eyes off the old gent. By and by, she makes a small motion with one hand. And by and by, two boys appear. They saunter up to the old gent and stand close behind him, and such is his concentration on his book that he does not comprehend them. One of the boys then proceeds to carefully, oh, so carefully, withdraw the old gent's handkerchief from his pocket. The pages of the book, however, are old and dusty and out of the blue the elderly gentleman sneezes and sneezes viciously. Reaches for his handkerchief. And finds it half-way out of his pocket. He turns. His jaw drops, his eyes pop, and he grips the handkerchief all the harder in fury. The impudence! The nerve! The gall! The two boys scarper. Their pickpocketing ploy has failed and they move like quicksilver. Slip away. Gone. Never to be seen again. But the excitement, the indignation, is too much for the elderly gentleman. He clutches at his chest, totters on his feet, and the book falls from his hand.

'The girl with the basket pushes herself off from the lamp post. She's got no business continuing to remain there. Whatever she was waiting and watching for has happened, has occurred, and she must move on. She *should* move on. But instead she goes over to our elderly gentleman, who's about to pitch forwards onto the cobblestones, and takes his arm. Props him up. "There, there, sir," she says. "You'll be all right. Take deep breaths," she instructs. She leads him tenderly to a low wall. She settles him down, returns to pick the book up off the cobbles, and dusts it off. Stares hard at the words on its cover. "It were only a handkerchief," she reassures the elderly gent. "It's not the end of the world, is it?" She sits alongside him, takes his hand, pats it reassuringly. And he looks at her, our elderly confused gent does, as he takes deep breaths and his chest rises and falls, because she's fair and innocent-looking. He looks into her pretty blue eyes, and the pain and anxiety drain from his face. His eyes glaze over, a kindly expression settles upon him. They sit for a while, then she takes his arm and he lets himself be led back to the stall, where she leaves him with the book in his hand and a few comforting words. And later, when I bump into him and question him about the incident, all he remembers is the girl and how charming and how pretty she was. How kind-hearted. He would, he tells me, endure another half dozen incidents with near-stolen handkerchiefs and crippling chest pain, to have only a moment of her company again.'

Mr Rufus's eyes come to rest on mine. He doesn' need to say anything, to tell me who this girl was.

I glance away and lower me head. I am at a loss for words. I don' know wot to say.

'Nancy,' Mr Rufus reaches across and takes me hands. 'Will you … Will you stay the night with me like you did before—?'

'Oh, sir. I carnt. Bill'—the name is out before I can stop it—'will kill me. As it is—'

'Who is Bill?'

I shake me head. 'Don' worry about him, sir. He's me problem. But I carnt. Although I'd like to,' I add softly.

'Come here, then,' he says.

He pulls me to him, and steadies me between his thighs, gazing up at me in the half-light. I put me hands on his bony shoulders and he draws me face down to his, and kisses me. It's light and gentle, but it's on me mouth. *Me mouth.* Whether by accident or on purpose, I don' know.

And I see his dilemma. I believe one half of him thinks I am his mother, and the other half wants to know me in the biblical sense.

And I don' know wot comes over me for I am filled with such longings and yearnings. I want him to kiss me again, and to go on kissing me.

But he pushes me gently away. 'You have to get home,' he says firmly. But his eyes are filled with regret, and sadness. That, too.

*

Within the half hour, I am back in the carriage. Within the half hour, I am back in the carriage, back in me own gear, all traces of Miss Titania Richardson gone, and with the driver having instructions to drop me off near The Cripples.

And now I know you're thinking about that one word, that one word that was mentioned earlier, that word which made your skin and mine all goosebumpy, which I have put away for now—because of Bill.

That word was *marry*. That is wot Mr Rufus said: *marry*.

But I know it ain't for real. It's only to pull the wool over Aunt Maud's eyes. Still, I can pretend, carnt I?

CHAPTER TWELVE

I try, I really do. I hunch me shoulders and make meself small and try to be as quiet as a little mouse, a sneaky little mouse, but when I get home to Bill, he's waiting up for me. He has placed a chair against the door and is asleep in it. I push on the wood and it bumps against the chair and he stirs. I would go back, fly down the stairs, but I ain't got nowhere else to go—see, I ain't been living with Bill long. I would slip away until he's in a better mood but he rears up.

'And where the devil have you been, woman?' he roars at me, pulling the chair away.

'Shh,' I whisper, putting me finger to me lips and coming in the door. 'You'll wake the whole street.' As it is, Bullseye has risen from his place before the fire and come to see wot's upset his master.

'Street can go to the dogs!'

Bill lunges for me shoulder to rattle me bones, but he's only half-awake and misses. His foot gets caught up in the chair legs and next thing, the chair is overturned, Bullseye scattered to the winds with his ears pinned back, and his master sprawled at me feet.

'Bill?' I say, reaching for him. 'Bill, are you all right?'

He grabs for me hair, yanks me down next to him. 'No, I'm not bleedin' all right!'

Pinning me down by a hank of me hair, he scrabbles with the other hand behind him on the floor for something. I carnt see it, but I know wot it is.

'Bill,' I say weakly. 'Don't.'

'You deserve it. Fancy leaving me half the night arter I asked you not to!'

His fingers find wot they're searching for, and he sits up and winds the leather belt around his hand and whips it through the air. I carnt help but flinch.

'Bill,' I say urgently, talking into the dirty floorboard cos that's the angle he's got me face at, 'wait! I got something for you. I didn' come away empty-handed.'

'Wot?' he demands. 'Speak up!'

'I got something! I carnt show you like this now, can I?'

'I checked with Fagey and he knew nothing about you doing something with the boy, so this better be good, girl,' he growls, pushing his ropey locks out of his eyes.

He releases me and I sit up. I tuck me knees under me to spring up and run if need be—although that's never made a difference—and ferret in me cammie pocket. Bill sits across from me, breathing heavily. The belt is still wound around his fist and I need to be careful.

I bring out me handkerchief. I unwrap it, watching his face, holding me breath.

But it's all right. His eyes light up at the sight of the knick-knack. I can breathe again.

'Cor!' he exclaims. 'Where'd you get that, Nance?'

He picks it up in his big clumsy fingers and holds the little gold baby up to the firelight. 'That's a right beauty. That's a right beauty, all right.'

He brings the baby back, replaces it in the handkerchief and folds it up.

'But,' he says, leaning forwards on his haunches and jutting his jaw against mine and half-spitting into me face when he speaks, 'I don' know that it's something I can *do* anything with. And I don' know that it's something that explains away where you bin, *Nancy*. And 'ow late it is. Is it now, *Nancy*?'

'No, Bill, it isn't,' I say, and lower me head. For if he hits me face, I carnt do no work. It puts me clients clean off, it does.

'I am sorry, Bill,' I say. 'I am sorry.'

'Aww, stop your whining, girl,' he says, and he gets to his feet and steps away.

And I think that it's all over, that I am safe, that he's not going to hurt me. Not tonight.

I rise and turn to hang up me shawl and the belt catches me viciously across the back of me legs, and down I go.

I stay down. I don' say nothing. I have learnt that not saying anything, not fighting back, is wot I must do if I don' want more of the same.

*

There's things about Bill you should know. But I'm not about to give you his whole life history since, to be fair, there's a lot of detail I don' know, neither.

Wot I do know is that when he were little, he saw his father kill his mother, knock her clean across the room and break her face. They took his father away and Bill watched all four of his brothers and sisters slowly dying, one by one. He was five, and the eldest. He didn' have no Fagin. He grew up on the street. He did all that grovelling, all that begging, that sleeping rough in doorways and parks, and that having strange men accost him and force him to his knees to do favours, he did all that for years. All on his own.

He's not right in the head. He wakes at night, sometimes screaming, sometimes lashing out with his fists and kicking. Other times he wakes up crying. Sobbing. Those are the times I have to hold him close. I have to reassure him I'm here. For he cries like a baby. He cries like a baby and begs me to hold him close. And I have to say that I'll never leave him.

And I won't. I won't ever leave him.

I could, of course. I could always go back to Fagin.

But how could I? For it ain't right wot happened to Bill, how he were abandoned, wot he endured. It ain't right. Someone has to make up for it, to bestow some kindness upon him, help him see the world is not all evil. And it has to be me since there ain't no-one else a-going to do it.

*

I find another church. It's one where I ain't been before. From the outside, it is an imposing structure, and ever so ornate. There are a number of arched windows, a great big arched door, and rounded towers and turrets, and at the top of the highest tower is a low scalloped wall with four steeples. A sign says 606 AD—*Anno Domini*—and I fancy that indicates when it were first built. (I ain't completely illiterate. I can read numbers and understand them, and I know words like days of the week and months of the year.)

I slip inside and wait alongside a towering column. Let me eyes adapt to the gloominess. No matter how many times I visit a church, I always feel overawed. Humbled. Insignificant. No matter how many times I visit a church, I always think that maybe today will be the day the Lord gives me a sign. Shows me a path to a better life. *Helps* me find the right way to live. For I carnt do this on me own. I have no way of getting above it all. I need assistance. I don' aspire to greatness, or to riches. All I aspire to is to be treated with decency and kindness, and to have food on me plate. And I live in hope that the Lord will help me out here, I do. I live in hope.

Light drifts high against the ceiling, but down here, on the floor made of wooden squares, parky-something, it's dark. The place smells of sawdust and polish. I curtsey, but then I hear someone coming and must take flight—for I am standing in the middle of the aisle. I been caught here before and it ain't pleasant. It's funny how they assume you are here to steal something—as if you would steal from the Lord! I mean, would you?

I murmur, 'Please forgive me, please forgive me,' on the way out—for stealing the gold baby from Aunt Maud, and almost trip over a black cat lurking in the shadows. It hisses at me. But then I think I given it as bigger fright as it's given me and I should be kind and gentle. I hold the door open to let it out and it follows me outside and winds its warm and furry body around me legs, rubs its chin against me calf.

'Move along now,' a voice says as I bend low to scratch its head, and I gaze up to see the face of a priest in the doorway. He's talking to me, of course, not the cat.

'Why should I?' I say, coming upright. 'Jesus said suffer the little children to come unto me.'

'Yes, but you're not a child.' He taps the side of his nose. 'I know what you are. *Know*,' he repeats, stressing the word.

'Sebastian, come here,' he says to the cat. 'And you shoo,' he says to me.

Shoo, as if I were a cat meself. The cheek of the man. I'd like to scratch his eyes out, I would.

CHAPTER THIRTEEN

'The very thing,' Fagin says when he claps eyes on Betsy and me stepping into the room.

'The very thing for wot?' I ask.

Fagin ignores me. He smacks his hand upon the table. 'Betsy will go, won't you, my dear?' he says.

Fagin and Sikes, Dodger and Charley, all sit morosely around the table. Bullseye is settled in a corner, his tail wound round his body, the feathery tip ending in front of his nose. He opens one eye to check us over and closes it again. I gaze casual-like around, but the boy ain't here. And I wonder if the question Fagin put to us, the *very thing*, is about Oliver and where he is?

'Where's you want me to go?' Betsy swirls her colourful skirts, pulls out a stool, and perches her ample behind upon it.

'Only up to the office, my dear.'

Betsy snorts in an unbecoming manner. 'I'll be jiggered if I do,' she declares.

She knows wot the connotations of *the office* are.

She reaches for the open bottle of spirits standing upon the worn wood. Only one glass is on the table, the one in front of Bill. Fagin is not drinking, then, which adds to the mystery. When Fagin does not partake it is because he needs all his wits about him.

Betsy pats the seat beside her encouragingly with her other hand. 'Nancy, sit. A glass, please, boys? If it's not too much trouble.'

Dodger magics a tumbler from behind a curtained shelf on a narrow bookcase against the wall, and pushes it over. Betsy pours out the colourless liquid, then holds the bottle temptingly above Bill's empty glass.

'Don't mind if I do,' he tells her.

Fagin, I'm noticing, has lowered his face and is playing with the cord of the dressing gown that's hung loosely about him, as if it were his pet snake. He looks up at me. 'Nancy, my dear. What do *you* say?'

'That it won't do, so it's no use trying it on.'

Fagin's shoulders slump. He throws the cord to one side in exasperation.

'Shift up,' I murmur to Betsy, and put me feet up at last. I nudge her in the ribs. 'Drink up.'

She seems to still be lost in the connotations of *the office*, remembering bad times. We, none of us, like to so much as to reflect upon the place, let alone go there. Betsy needs no second prompting. She knocks back the drink and refills the glass for me.

I sip at the liquor. I like to make it last for the taste of fire it brings to me mouth and the warmth it carries to me gullet, which is both of them all too brief.

'Where's the new boy?' I ask, stating the obvious.

'Where is he, indeed?' Fagin says with a whiff of sarcasm.

I shake me head. 'Oh no,' I say. 'Oh no.' And I look into me lap, not wanting the others to see me face, not wanting them to know me concern. Oliver in *the office*?

'Wot do you mean?' Bill says. He's referring to wot do I mean by saying that *it won't do, that it's no use trying it on.*

Here's a curious thing about me and Mr Sikes. You wouldn't think we were a couple, would you? More like business partners. He tells me when to jump, and I ask at what time? But, see, we know one another. We're intimate. Like I told you already. We know when to step back, and when to step up with each other—only if I'm honest it's Bill always stepping up. I'm the one got to step back. Even though there's no pleasantries exchanged between us when we meet up, even though he never calls me *Sweetheart* or *Darling*, unless he's being sarcastic, I know him. I hold him in my arms when he cries like a baby. I pick him up out of the gutter. I take his bruised and bloody body home after he's had too many and been in a fight and his face looks like he's copped a mouse. And only I know he can be tender and gentle, me Bill. Only I see that side of him.

I wonder if Oliver's absence has put him in a mood? Then again, why should the boy's presence or absence matter to Bill?

I can guess wot's happened. Brainless of the old man to let the boy out onto the streets so early. *Brainless.* And why? Is the old goat getting careless?

'Wot I say, Bill,' I announce with a certain amount of coolness, 'is I ain't going.'

'But you'd be just the girl for it,' Bill says. 'Nobody 'bout here knows anything of you. Seeing as how you only moved from Whitechapel jus' the other day.'

'And as I don' want them to, neither,' I say, 'it's rather more *no* than *yes* with me.'

Bill reaches for his glass and downs the drink in one swallow. 'She'll go, Fagin.'

'No, she won't,' I declare.

'Yes, she will.' Bill touches his index finger to the side of his nose. 'Remember?' he says to me.

Fagin knits his eyebrows together like a heavy quilt. 'Remember what?'

Bill and me, we say nothing, but we each know wot the other means. He's meaning how late I was out t'other night, how he suspects Fagin's not a part of wotever I were doing. I stare into me glass.

'We ain't got all day,' Bill murmurs.

I sniff resignedly. As if it's something I *really* don't want no involvement in.

'Wot is it I have to do?' I ask.

Between you and me, I was always going, I jus' didn' want it to look like I was eager. I have to tread careful. I carnt have Bill knowing there's something I particularly like or love. Because he'll take it away from me. Sure as the fog keeps rolling in. Sure as women will always be fightin' for their share of the quilt.

Fagin tells me wot I already suspect. The boy has been nabbed. Careless. Thoughtless. *Brainless*, I think again. Wot were they on about?

Now, however, is not the time to point this out.

Fagin loans me a clean white apron, which I tie over me red gown, and a straw bonnet, and I bundle me hair up underneath the bonnet so that some strands curl around me face. I have looks and I'm not above using them.

'Wait, my dear,' Fagin says, and he produces a dainty covered basket. 'Carry this in one hand. It looks more respectable.'

'Give her a door key to carry in her other one, Fagin,' Bill suggests. 'It will look real and genuine-like.'

'Yes, yes, so it does,' Fagin says, after hanging a large street-door key on me right-hand forefinger and standing back to survey me. He's almost excited.

'There. Very good, my dear. Very good, indeed.' He rubs his dry hands together and looks delighted with his handiwork.

Which is half me own doing. But I don't like to spoil his moment. See, you can take a potato and dress it up all afternoonified, but at the end of the day, it's still a potato.

'Now,' he says. 'Give us a run through, Nancy.'

I step back. Wait for silence. I been asked to perform before and I enjoy it. I enjoy pretending to be someone else. I enjoy forgetting me own sordid and sorry history.

'Oh, my brother! My poor, dear, sweet, innocent little brother,' I exclaim.

In the corner Bullseye raises one eyebrow. Whether from appreciation or curiosity, I am unsure. I burst into tears and wring both the basket handle and the key in me hands as if I am in an agony of distress. To me knowledge, I do not have a brother, as I've said. But, as I've also said, who is to say that is the case? The years before I came to Fagin are dark and dim and fraught with horror and I remember little. (That's not true, I remember at least some, I jus' don' like recalling any of it.) I think of Oliver, of his innocent face and his angelic and virtuous nature. I think of the boy in despair, being left alone in a dark and dank cell, the seat wooden and hard under his small behind, and it's not hard to become emotional.

'Wot has become of him?' I go on, my voice rising with anguish. 'Where have they taken him? Oh, do have pity and tell me wot's been done with the poor dear boy, gentlemen? Oh, please do? Please?'

I stop. I smile. I wink to my audience. I do a mock bow. 'All right?'

'Oh, my eye!' Charley gasps. He's in stitches. It takes little to amuse him. Everyone else, even Bill, smiles. Betsy even applauds.

Bill says, 'You're an honour to your sex, my girl,' and fills his glass again. 'But don' let it go to your head.'

'No chance of that,' I say.

I turn for the door. I move down the gloomy passage. I overhear Fagin say, 'Ah, she's a clever girl, my dears,' and feel a glow of pleasure. Strange, that after all these years, I still need his approval.

*

I enter the police office by the back way. It smells of mould, of rotten books, and of sweet apples wanting air.

There's enough light coming from the gas lamps out front for me to make out the cell doors, and I tap softly with the key on one of them. There's no sound within. I cough politely and listen again.

'Oliver?' I murmur. 'Oliver, dear?'

Still nothing.

I pass onto the next cell door, and tap again.

'Wot?' cries a faint and feeble voice.

'Is there a little boy here?' I ask with a sob and a catch in my throat.

'No,' replies the voice. 'God forbid!'

I move on. Two more cells, two more bursts of sobbing, and two more prisoners who are not small boys. Or small. Or even boys. One is cocky. 'And wot if there is?' he wants to know when I ask if there's a little boy there. 'And wot if I have eaten 'im, and he wouldn't stay down …?' the prisoner goes on—he thinks he's funny, he does—but I take no notice.

I sniff in readiness, square me shoulders, and go down the passage, making directly for the officer at the front desk. He wears a striped waistcoat and has his boots up on the table and is engrossed in the newspaper, twirling one end of his handlebar moustache as he does so. It *is* a magnificent moustache.

'My brother,' I cry. 'My brother. The poor, dear, little soul,' I wail, making the candle flicker, which gets his attention.

The officer removes his legs, puts down his paper, and taps his fingers on it. 'Now, miss,' he says. 'I haven't got him.'

'You haven' got him? Oh, me. Oh, my,' I say, gulping. 'Where is he, pray?'

'The gentleman's got him.'

'Wot gentleman? Oh, goodness gracious! Gracious heavens! Wot gentleman?'

'Well,' the officer says, pushing the paper away, 'where shall I start, miss?' He takes a breath. 'Seeing as how the young lad fell ill and seeing as how he was discharged, in consequence of a witness having proved the robbery to have been committed by another boy not in custody, and seeing that the gentleman who brought the charges in the first place, you understand, and seeing *that* gentleman carried the boy away in an insensible, *insensible*, mark you, condition, not being any fault of ours, carried him away to his own residence, of and concerning which to be somewhere in Pentonville, myself having heard that word mentioned in the directions to the coachman, and seeing that—' He breaks off. 'Well, in short, miss, he ain't here, is he?'

'Not here?' I repeat. 'Not here?' I say sombrely, thinking, so the boy's been carted away by a gen'leman, taken somewhere in Pentonville, then. Well, ain't he the lucky one!

'Not here,' he confirms.

'Oh, thankee,' I murmur.

Then, snivelling and crying crocodile tears and reiterating *not here, not here*, I make a hasty exit, back down the passage, the way I have come.

At the rear entrance, I stand for a moment in the dark, looking up and down the lane, and when I am satisfied no-one is in sight, I move swiftly to the main road. Where I do not linger, but return by the most devious and circuitous route I can dream up, in case anyone should be following me, to the domicile of Fagin.

Betsy has departed, I see when I enter the room, but Charley and the Dodger, Bill and Fagin, remain seated around the table. Charley, snoring gently, has his head buried in his arms.

'Well, my dear?' Fagin says, turning to me.

Bill stays long enough to hear me account of the *expedition*— Fagin's word— then calls up Bullseye and, jamming his hat on his head, disappears. Without a word to me. Without a word to anyone, for that matter. Which is nothing unusual. But all the same, I wonder at him. Where is he off to tonight? Me Bill is nothing if not secretive. (While I, of course, am not permitted to be.) But I have learnt there is no point in asking. Asking only gets me trouble. Asking only gets me bruises.

'We must know where he is, my dears. He must be found,' Fagin says with agitation, now pacing the room. It seems to me he is unduly worried. Them boys all been in *the office* plenty of times before. Why's this time different? What's different about Oliver? Is it the fact he has been carted off by a gen'leman, and that he may talk?

'Charley, wake up!'

'Why?' Charley says sleepily, stretching his arms across the table.

'Because you have a job,' Fagin says. 'Charley, do nothing but skulk about till you bring home news of the boy. Nancy, my dear,' he says, turning to me, 'I must have him found. I trust to you, to you and the Dodger, for everything. Now go.'

We're about to leave when he changes his mind—he's like that sometimes, in a right dither—adds, 'Stay, stay,' and, unlocking a drawer with a shaking hand, says, 'Here's money.'

'Why didn' you say so in the first place?' I ask, but he's going off. Like a Catherine Wheel. When he goes off, you can forget about putting Fagin and reason in one sentence.

'I shall shut up this shop tonight—you'll know where to find me. Don't stop here a minute, not an instant, my dears!'

He pushes us from the room, half-stumbling with alarm, and the three of us go down the passage and the stairs as Fagin double-locks and bars the door behind us. Locking himself in.

To do wot? I thought we were all departing. I thought there was a reason why we *all* had to leave.

'Dodger,' I say, stopping outside the crumbling entranceway in the dim light. 'Be a dear lad and go back up and ask the old goat where we're to bring the boy when we got him. Surely it isn't here?'

'I wouldn' think so,' he confirms, looking thoughtful. 'Right,' he says. 'Won' be a tick.'

Charley and I hover about, rubbing our hands up and down our sleeves to keep warm, shifting our weight from one foot to t'other. I don' know wot the time is, but it must be after eleven. I have no intention of going out now to look for the boy and if Charley's got any sense, he won', neither. But Charley don' have any sense.

'You're not going to go out *now* to look for Oliver, are you, Charley?'

He glances at me in astonishment. 'Why not, miss?'

'Well,' I say, 'it's dark, for one. And for two, anybody with an ounce of self-respect is in a warm bed asleep. Wouldn' you be in bed asleep if you were Oliver?'

'Too right,' he agrees.

We skip around again, the frost crackling under our boots. 'Hurry up, Dodge,' I murmur, 'I'm a-freezing half to death here.'

In response, an almighty crash comes from inside the house.

'Oh, Lord!' I say to Charley, and push on the door. A dog begins to bark somewhere. Someone tells it to shut its gob, and then all is quiet again.

Dodger staggers out, his cap askew, looking dazed and confused.

'Wot happened?' I whisper.

'I fell, didn' I?'

He starts to laugh. He doubles over and snorts and stamps his foot and clutches his sides, which starts Charley off. All Charley needs is to see someone else in the throes of mirth and he's gone.

I start to giggle meself, and Dodger flicks his head, indicating we should move off. We sneak around the corner, pause under a lean-to and huddle together.

Dodger pushes up his overlong sleeves, sticks out his hips and thrusts his hands into his pockets, assuming an air of importance. It don' last.

'See, I rapped on the door, smartly-like,' he begins, but has to stop for he is convulsed with laughter. He wipes his eyes and begins a second time. 'I rapped on the door and the old goat says, "Who's there?" all alarmed. Me, I say. "What now?" he says sharply. Is he to be kidnapped to the other ken? I ask. Nancy wants to know. But he's not listening proper and has to come closer to the door. "What?" he says. Which is when I know wot he's doing, why he was so anxious to shoo us out the door.' Dodger stops to survey us.

'Go on,' I whisper.

'See, he's put all them jew-ell-ery'—he strings out the word—'all them valu-ables, watches and stuff, in and on and under and beneath his coat, and the whole business tinkles. Tinkles,' Dodger repeats as if he likes the word (and of course it makes me think of Aunt Maud).

'I ask him the question again, and he says, "Yes. Yes. The other house. Wherever she lays hands upon him. Find him, find him out. That is all. I shall know what to do next, never fear."

'I turn away then and cos it's so awful dark—I ain't got a light, remember—I slip on the stairs'—here Dodger begins to laugh again. Charley is in ecstasies, practically rolling on the ground. 'And the old man, the goat, says, "What? Who? Who's there?" in alarm. He's that distracted, he's already forgotten it's me.'

Dodger stops, and I put me hand on his arm. 'I hope you didn' hurt yourself?'

'Just me arse,' he whispers.

CHAPTER FOURTEEN

I've told you how I was the first of Fagey's boys. The Dodger was the second. He's the best friend I got and I don' believe I've said how he came to be one of us.

I was already quite grown, around nine, from memory, when Dodge turned up. I was returning to the crib from being out on the morning streets—that were a good time for me when gen'lemen were out and about, taking the morning air, and were dozy, not quite awake yet or, in some cases, hadn' even gone to bed yet.

Anyways, so's I come in the door and there's a lad sitting on the sofa in front of the fire. Fagey's turning sausages in the pan. If he's home, Fagey's turning sausages. He told me once there's something about turning sausages that makes him right contented. I guess we all have our little quirks, our little eccentricities, that make us happy, don' we? For me, you could say it's dreaming about oranges. I've always been attracted to them fruit. I'll tell you why soon enough. Only had an orange once before in me life. *Once.*

The frying pan, although it's on the fire, is secured to the mantelshelf by a string since Fagey doesn' trust himself not to throw it at me. And standing over the pan with a toasting fork in his hand is the man himself, wot I sometimes like to call *the old goat*. Fagin ain't anything to look at. He's wrinkly and old. His eyes are set too close together, and his face pinched and narrow and mostly obscured by overhanging, matted, red hair.

Fagey's dressed in a greasy flannel gown, and he's dividing his attention between the frying pan and the clothes horse, over which a number of silk handkerchiefs are hanging—cos this is one of me jobs, see. Unpicking monograms and such in the handkerchiefs so Fagey can resell them.

The lad on the sofa turns his head to look at me. He's as dark as I'm fair. He has a head full of hair like one of them bushy reeds you find alongside the river, only it's black, and his face is sooty, the whites of his eyes sticking out like a little chimneysweeper.

'Who's this?' I say to Fagey.

'Oh, this?' Fagey lifts the fork from the pan. 'This here,' he says pompously—he likes to make an occasion of a new boy—'is Mr Dawkins. Mr Jack Dawkins. Only, Nancy, dear, we're not going to call him Mr Dawkins, we're going to call him the Artful Dodger.'

'Why?' I say, frowning, and emptying me pockets of loot onto the table. I got several silk handkerchiefs, plus I picked up a newspaper that someone discarded. Usually that's because they only wanted it for them race results in the first place, but I know Fagey's fond of reading the paper, so I try to nab one if I can.

'Good girl,' Fagin says, looking over at me findings.

'Girl?' The Artful Dodger says from the sofa. 'He ain't no girl!'

I strut over to the fire, hook me thumbs into me suspenders. Swagger a bit.

'Well, actually, I am,' I say. 'Take me word for it.' I tap me finger to the side of me nose. 'But for all *in tents and porpoises*, as far as you are concerned I am a boy. Now,' I say, turning to Fagey and acting pompous-like meself since I don' want no upstart thinking they can lord it over me, 'why the Dodger?'

'The *Artful* Dodger?' Fagey says, waving his fork in the air. 'Stands to reason, my dear. He's artful.'

'I see,' I say, but I don' really.

'Nancy,' Fagey says, 'be a dear and clean him up, would you?'

'Nancy!' the Dodger laughs. 'Why, the boy has a girl's name!'

'Wotch it,' I tell him, narrowing me eyes.

I get a cloth, then, and a dish of water warm from the fire, and kneel down in front of the boy and begin to dab at his face. And while I'm a-doing that, Fagey brings over a sausage, pronged on the long fork, and blowing on it. All he needs is a couple of horns on his head and together with the red hair he'd be a right devil.

'It's hot,' he says to the lad, 'be care—' And he's only halfway advising caution when the boy seizes the sausage and bites it clean in two and swallows the first half whole and puts his mouth around the remainder and quaffs *that* whole, too. '—ful,' Fagey finishes.

I sit back on me heels in astonishment.

'He's hungry,' Fagey remarks. Like the boy's some wild animal that carnt talk. And returns to the saucepan for another.

I go back to me task. And by and by, I uncover some white skin, and it turns out the boy has some freckles, too. And it turns out the second sausage is consumed in a more genteel fashion. And, later still, it turns out the boy's hair is not black, neither, only filthy.

And while I am dabbing at his face—which he surprisingly submits to without fuss—he reaches behind him for the newspaper and says to Fagey, 'Shall I read to you, sir?'

I almost snort with laughter at the idea of this … this *urchin* reading, but I contain meself.

'Don't call him *sir*,' I mutter instead. 'He'll get ideas above himself. He's Fagin. Or Fagey. Or'—and here I lower me voice even further—'the old goat.'

The boy glances at me, and inclines his head. Like he has absorbed everything I said and don' need to comment further. That's when I know he's cleverer than most.

Then he starts to read. And I'm not even listening to wot he's a-saying because I carnt believe he can read! The Dodger can read.

Naturally, it takes me years to admit to him that I carnt.

Later that night, when Fagey has gone abroad and left us—I am quite accustomed to him leaving me, and coming and going at all hours of the night and it don' worry me—I am awoken by something nudging me.

It's the boy. The Artful Dodger. Only right now he's not artful. It ain't completely dark for the flickering flames of the fire, and I open one eye and his head is blocking out the light.

'Wot?' I say, sleepily.

But he don' reply. And I go back to some half-forgotten dream, only jus' aware of another body lodging in next to mine.

In the morning, when I wake, the Dodger is up before me and feeding the fire. His bedding has been removed and shunted to a corner of the crib. But I have a memory, and I don' believe I dreamt it, of a small body up against mine for comfort in the night. A small body wanting to be held. But I ain't a-going to say anything, am I?

I never learn anything more about Dodger. I try asking Fagin sometimes, but he only shrugs and says he found him on the street. Like he did me. Like he has no idea of his history.

The Dodger don' talk about his past, neither. And I don' ever press him for details for I know wot it's like. Recalling the past hurts. It's painful. You don' want to admit most of it. You don' want to admit there were those who didn' want you, who cast you off like you were nothing more than a nuisance and a hindrance and an annoyance. You don' want to admit that your mother abandoned you.

Everybody wants to be wanted, don' they? It's human nature, innit?

Betsy's not in the gang, by the way. Jus' a recent acquaintance, a recent addition for Fagin, doing wot I do. And is much happier working for Fagey, I can tell you.

Why?

Well, if you must know, let's jus' say she was initiated into the business by a family member. I know, it beggars belief, don' it? And, naturally, she weren't paid for her pains. At least now, Betsy has some coin, prefers the gen'lemen Fagin finds for her, and her life is a little easier.

Wot's that you say, you want to hear how I got into it, too?

Perhaps you've forgotten I told you it started when I began wearing dresses when I were only twelve. But I'm not saying any more. It ain't pretty, see. It ain't for your ears. And recalling it don' help me, or you. Recalling it will jus' make you want to clamp your knees together, grit your teeth and suck in air.

CHAPTER FIFTEEN

The next few days is eaten up with searching for Oliver's whereabouts and I hardly have time to give Mr Rufus, or that magic word *marry,* a thought.

I start with the coachmen who wait outside *the office* for fares, and interrogate each one, and on the third day I find the one who gave the old gen'leman and Oliver a ride to Pentonville.

'Who wants to know?' the driver says when I ask if he remembers ferrying a small, fair-haired, handsome boy, accompanied by an elderly gent, from the police station. The driver's sitting up on his box, looking down at me, putting me at a disadvantage. He's a cruel-looking man, not an amiable, chatty sort. His big, black hat is jammed upon his head, his forehead knitted with worry lines, and two flinty, black eyes scowl out at me from under the brim. Hard eyes, they are.

'I want to know,' I say. 'There's something in it for you, if you remember.'

'Wot?' he says.

I lift my skirt, show me knees to the breeze and raise me eyebrows.

'Hmph,' he says, pursing his lips. The idea appeals to him, then. He lets go of the reins and jumps down from the box. Waits until his face is in mine. His breath smells of onions and old meat. 'Tonight,' he mutters, looking round to see who's listening. 'Here. Nine o'clock.'

'And the address where you took the boy?'

'Do you think I'm slow?' he asks, sneering.

I don' respond.

'Afterwards,' he says, tilting his head at me, dismissing me.

Ugh! The bother I get meself into!

*

I make a decision to leave off looking for Oliver and take it quietly for the rest of the day. I have a feeling that by tonight's end I will have Oliver's current whereabouts. I am, I admit it, nervous about the coachman, but I carnt call Bill in for protection, for I don' wish him to be a party to any knowledge I come by. It will only complicate things. Bill will want to go round there immediate-like and bang on the door. Resort to violence, if necessary. If there is some way for me to save Oliver from Bill and the old goat, I must proceed like a kitten, with caution, and on soft paws.

And so I get out of me neighbourhood and make tracks for Mr Rufus's crib. I need distracting, and I am curious.

It's a cold and raw afternoon and the cul-de-sac looks very different in the daylight. Smoke is twisting up from chimneys, and dark lumpy matter tricklin' down gutters. Ever present is that stench that never goes away, and the added smell of days-old vegetables cooking is here. Cabbage. There are people about. A woman is beating a rug, the dust rising. Six or seven children are playing hopscotch outside the tenements. One of about fourteen—although it's hard to tell—has a sunken face and dead eyes, and a baby bouncing on her hip. Most likely it's her baby and the future looks pretty bleak. I perch on a low brick wall at the bottom end of the lane to watch who's coming and going. The little 'uns give me a glance, but nobody seems to mind me. After a while, when Mr Rufus's place is all quiet, I slip off the wall, and I'm about to head towards the crib when the door opens and a man comes out. Moving quickly towards the children I join in their game uninvited, springing from square to square, muttering the numbers of the squares, keeping me face averted. And Mr Rufus passes us by without a flicker of recognition, without so much as a glance in our direction.

Anyways, I decide to follow him, don' I? For he seems too good to be true, don' he?

I leave the children, who ain't too fussed whether I stay or go, and keep a discreet distance between me and Mr Rufus. He don' walk fast. Fagey would say he *ambles.* He is dressed dapper: a soft, flat cap, a red waistcoat, and a rich, russet overcoat. He clearly knows a thing or two about colour. In a world of his own he is, for he almost gets squashed between two carriages passing one another as he crosses the street. 'Oi, watch where you're going, mister!' the driver calls.

Stuck on the other side, waiting for the same two carriages to pass, I lose sight of him, and when I have lifted me skirts and dashed across, he's nowhere to be seen. The Horse & Groom, however, is staring me in the face. He must've ducked in. Which makes it tricky. A person like me has no business being inside such an establishment.

I pull me shawl closer and raise it around me face, and loiter around the entrance, and next time someone goes in I have a good hard look inside.

And see nothing more than the back of Mr Rufus sitting at the counter. A meal and a glass of ale is set out in front of him, and a bunch of papers are at his side. He has a pen in his hand and he appears to be making some notations on the papers. It's all deadly dull and nothing out of the ordinary.

*

Just before nine o'clock, I am back on the streets. Me carriage driver is waiting for me. He flicks his head at me and I make to get in at the door, but he says, 'No, up here,' indicating the seat beside him. It's as cold as an empty bed on New Year's Eve up there, the wind blowing clean through me as we set off and, although I don' want to, I snuggle up beside him for warmth. Before long he's driving one-handed and the other hand is, well, you can guess where it is, carnt you?

I know our destination is Pentonville, and once we reach its outskirts, I try to memorise landmarks and street names, so I can find me way here again, but it ain't easy to concentrate when a man's got a calloused finger up your *whatsit.*

The name that's in me head, when we stop outside a nice house, is Claremont Court. And it ain't far from some gardens. The carriage driver points to a house on the right, and then he takes me arm and marches me to the park, where it's ill-lit and little frequented and I am surprised he can walk at all with that ship's mast protruding from between his legs. Anyway, the business is attended to, and done with. You don' need to know the ugly details. For ugly they are, enough to make me eyes water.

After the carriage driver departs, I station meself beside a tree and study the house. *Try* to study the house for me whatsit's throbbing. Number Seven. The court is quiet and them houses all look solemn and studious, like lawyers on the bench. The dwelling where Oliver is, if I am to believe the driver, is lit at the entrance, and light glows from behind the upstairs and the downstairs windows. Then the upstairs light goes out—possibly the occupant has gone to sleep.

I had hoped to catch sight of the boy, but it's not to be and, thinking of sleep, I realise me feet are numb and me teeth are chattering in me head. I carnt wait here all night, not if I am to survive until morning. Not if I am sensible. So back I go to Bethnal Green and the crib, walking this time, and the walking helps to warm me up and get me bearings. Praying, along the way, that Mr Sikes is not in residence when I arrive home.

I may be cold and tired, but I have something no-one else has, and that on its own makes me heart lighter. I may yet be able to do something for the child!

*

In the morning when I wake, the other half of the bed is empty and them sheets cold. Where is Bill and wot's he up to, I wonder. But I am also grateful he weren' here when I got in after midnight.

Me second thought is of Oliver and his whereabouts, and how long I can pretend to go on looking for him. And me third thought is of Mr Rufus.

It's not yet ten, but I get up. I want to be gone when Bill does come home. I don' want him asking no questions. I also have a long walk ahead of me to Pentonville. As I hurriedly get dressed, it strikes me that I might well kill two birds with one stone and take a stroll to Mr Rufus's Mayfair crib after I check on Oliver. If I can find it again.

I stop in at The Cripples, in case there's a message for me, which there ain't, and then I set off for Pentonville. But I ain't got much further than a block or two when instinct tells me someone is on me tail. I become conscious of the same shape appearing behind me in the glass of shop windows. Even arter I cross the road. I duck into a doorway, but obviously so does me stalker cos when I glance around there ain't nobody in close proximity that appears to be following me. So I do something unexpected. I backtrack. I backtrack and peer into the next along doorway and—lo and behold—who do I find hovering there but Mr Rufus! Me heart does a funny little hop, skip and jump.

'Nancy.' He dips his hat. He has the grace to appear embarrassed.

I step up into the doorway beside him. The shop is unattended, and we are unlikely to be disturbed.

'Wot you doing following me?'

'I did not want to confront you at The Cripples,' he tells me. 'Someone might've seen us.'

'Fair enough,' I say, and cross me arms over me chest. 'Was there something you were wanting?'

'You could say that. Several things, perhaps.'

He glances at me, and I try not to think of the likelihood of us both wanting the same thing.

'But the most pressing of which is the return of the little *bambino*.'

I frown.

'Don't pretend you don't know what a *bambino* is, Nancy.'

'Oh, I do, sir. I know. But I'm frowning for I don' know wot *bambino* you are referring to.'

'At Aunt Maud's the other evening. In a glass dish. A dainty baby, fat and gold. Gone,' he says. 'Do you have it? Did you accidentally take it? Dear Aunt Maud would very much like it to be returned. She is, in Foxley's words, *apoplectic*. She has no idea where it has gone. Foxley alerted me to its absence. If you have it, would you kindly hand it over, Nancy?'

He sighs as if this is tedious. And it is tedious. For one thing, it is keeping me from me primary task which is to keep an eye on Oliver.

'I don' know wot you're referring to, Mr Rufus,' I say, glancing up at him with raised eyebrows. He is fidgeting with his white cuffs, frilled they are, peeking out from his jacket sleeves. He won' look at me. A sign he is uncomfortable, unsure of his accusation. 'Why would I steal from the goose that is a-going to lay a golden egg?'

'Why indeed?'

He looks at me.

I look at him.

I stare into his eyes, deep-brown they are. And that hot and intense feeling comes over me and I feel me cheeks growing pink. I wait for him to blink. He doesn'—

'Ah hah,' he says, 'you blinked.'

'I blinked because there's something I want to suggest.' I pause.

'I'm waiting,' he says.

'Is it not possible,' I say, sounding pompous and a bit like Fagey, 'that one of the servants may have taken it?'

'Not possible.' He taps his cane in agitation on the stonework of the doorway. 'It's a lengthy story and one day I will explain it to you.' He clears his throat politely.

'Where are you off to now, Nancy? You seemed quite determined on your path.' He glances at me, and I sense something more than curiosity here. 'You are not going to see a client, are you?'

Grateful that he has dropped the subject of the knick-knack, I say, 'No, I'm not going to see a client. I'm running an errand for Fagin.' Which is not overly stretching the truth.

'I see,' he says. 'Can I be of any assistance?'

'Assistance?' I shake me head. 'No. Not really, sir.'

He looks dejected. Fair miserable. Taps at the stonework some more. It seems as if the thought of spending the rest of the day with only himself for company will be the undoing of him.

'It's merely a matter of attending at a certain address,' I say. There's no harm in him knowing this.

'Can I take you there?' he asks, hopeful-like.

I bite my lip. He could, I guess. Wot is the danger in that?

'All right,' I say.

There is a lull while I wait on the shop doorstep until he has secured a coach. A coach for privacy or, rather, a coach in which Mr Rufus will have privacy. I am wot I am and he has his reputation to think of.

When I step up into the coach doorway, the driver calls, 'Where to?' and I answer, 'Hyde Park.' This is not correct, but it will do.

Hallo, I think, when I enter, for the curtains have been drawn.

The interior is dim and dusky, but cosy. Mr Rufus sits to one side with a look on his face that speaks of emptiness, and of sadness, and without a word he pulls me gently onto his lap. Like I am a child. He cradles me head against his shoulder. Folds me up into the warmth of his body. Keeps me close. 'Nancy,' he murmurs, as if reminding himself of me name.

The coach moves off with a jerk. The wheels rumble under the floorboards, judder through our bones.

Outside, the clip-clop of horses' hooves, the trundle of carts, and the calls of barrowmen, of newspaper boys, of girls hawking watercress, of women selling flowers—*Two bunches a penny.* Outside, the frigid air, the spittle of rain, the clamour and the cloying dust, the smoky stench of stacked factory chimneys. The river never far away, the dirty Thames treacly with colliers's mire oiling its way through London.

Now all far away, distant. Now nothing more than faint, discordant sounds. The two of us cocooned like babes in a blanketed basket. In our own world. Me body cushioned by the solidness of him, me hip nestled snug into his. Me heart banging, for that giddy feeling is upon me again.

Glancing up then, and finding his deep-brown eyes upon me. Glancing up and lifting me head and touching me mouth tenderly to his, and the prickle of his tawny-red moustache on me skin as his lips open and respond and his thick hair falls across his forehead. And the touch, and caress, the wetness of mouths, and of tongues tipping, of hands moving slowly, discovering, exploring, and the pulsing sensation of heat and the urge to possess, to own, and the wanting, the wanting, and the ache beginning deep inside and growing, and growing—

'Hyde Park!' The coach halts and we lurch against one another.

Mr Rufus blinks. He stares at me blankly. Like he has been in another world. 'Nancy,' he murmurs. 'Nancy!' he says, anxiously, like he would detain me.

I pay him no heed. Quietly, I reach for me shawl that has fallen from me shoulders, open the door, step down into reality and disappear.

It takes courage, it does. And a strong will. But, see, the truth is I need to leave him at this point. You may find this hard to believe, but I ain't never had the agony of bliss with a man. I had plenty on me own, make no mistake there, for pleasuring meself is a known cure for falling asleep and staying asleep. But not with a man, not even with Mr Sikes. They're always in too much of a hurry, too keen to spray you with their pearly showers. And too rough, and mostly it's all over when I am only jus' beginning to feel the faint stirrings of pleasure.

I carnt help observing, then, as I walk to Pentonville, that this time with Mr Rufus is therefore the first I have come anywhere close to achieving that elusive bliss with a man. It is something worth noting. And not only that, but for once in me life I am looking forwards to—would you believe?—you know wot.

It's peculiar how women will discuss fornicating, copulating, riding the rantipole, and the beast with two backs, but as soon as it refers to us—in a personal way—we get all coy and pretend we don' know the words for it. Or we want to use the word *love* …

CHAPTER SIXTEEN

Number Seven Claremont Court, Pentonville, is pleasantly busy. A dog escapes from a neighbour's gate and runs frantically down the road, barking, and the face of an elderly woman appears at an upstairs window, presumably to see wot all the fuss is about. A boy on foot delivers a brown-paper package tied up with string that looks a lot like books. The postman drops off the mail. A couple, arm-in-arm, step out from another house to take a stroll and I am forced to retreat behind me tree trunk. A stout old gen'leman, rather lame in one leg and using a stick, comes to call. He is dressed in finery: a blue coat, a broad-brimmed, white hat, and a shirt frill sticking out from his waistcoat. He is shown inside by a maid. The door closes behind him, and he does not come out again. I do not see Oliver, either at any of the windows or emerging at the front door.

I grow bored. And hungry.

*

I am consuming a plate of boiled beef behind the bar at The Cripples, when Barney comes through. It would be wrong to say I am *enjoying* the beef—it's that unappetising it sticks in my throat, it does, and is a chore to get it down—but food is sustenance and I take it where and when I can get it.

'You're bonted up fron',' Barney tells me.

I have known the man long enough to be able to interpret his words, and I can tell by his attitude who it is wants me up front, and I say, 'In a minute. I ain't going to leave this, am I?'

I finish the meal, soaking up the watery gravy with a crust of bread, and push the plate away. Rising, I draw me shawl back on and make me way to the parlour of the public house. The front is low and there's little light coming through the mullioned windows, but I find Fagin and Bill, the latter looking expectantly at me.

'You are on the scent, are you, Nancy?' inquires Bill, meaning am I still searching for Oliver, and proffering a thimble of liquor to me. Which is unexpected, but I take it all the same, seeing as how it will warm up me innards for a while. Seeing as how it isn't often that Bill gives me something that I can enjoy.

'Yes, I am, Bill,' I say, disposing of its contents in one gulp for it ain't much, 'and tired enough of it I am, too. We know the young brat's been ill and I ain't seen him yet. I understand he's confined to the crib—'

'Ah, Nancy, dear,' Fagin says, looking up, as if he has only now noticed me presence.

I gaze back at him, cocking me head to one side, for he regales me with half-closed reptilian eyes. I haven' lived with him for nigh on twelve years *not* to understand this look or know its meaning, its meaning being not to allow me tongue to run away with me. Fagin does not want Bill to know the boy's whereabouts. Stands to reason. Bill, given half a chance, would be round there hauling the boy out by the shirt collar.

'I'd best be off,' I say, 'the day isn't going to wait for me.'

'Not so fast, Nance,' Bill says, making me suspect he understands Fagin's look only too well, although he is sitting *beside* the man and not head on. He blots his mouth with his neckerchief. 'I'm a-going in the same direction meself. Let me walk with you.'

He rises and takes my arm. He whistles up Bullseye, who has been lying with his big head on his paws in a corner, and we bid Fagin adieu and step out of the establishment together. And I have to say, Bill is in a good frame of mind, and I wonder wot's brought that on?

It's late afternoon outside. The sky glitters like fish scales. The wintry light drains away like dishwater down a gutter. On the corner the newspaper boy stands under the gas lamp, waving the paper and shouting out the news, and lingering in the west is the sun wot resembles a bloody and rusted gibbet cage, and all of a sudden I don' feel good. Like something bad is coming.

The cobblestones are cold, me boots well-worn. I blow out me breath so it smokes in the frigid air and snuggle up to Bill to distract meself and say, 'This is nice,' the opposite of wot I am feeling.

I'd been moved out from Fagin's for some time when I met Bill. It wasn' working out at Fagey's. Them boys brought out me mothering instincts, but the old goat didn' like me pampering them. Them boys didn' like it, neither, I don' believe. They were too big to be molly-coddled. Not like Oliver.

But, see, I couldn' help meself. Wanted to give out me love, I did. Always wanting to give out me love, I am.

Where is it that love comes from? How is it that it keeps getting replenished?

Anyways, I left. Moved out further afield to Whitechapel. There ain't nothing white about it, of course. Dirty grey would be more fitting.

I still came into town, Fagey continuing to provide me with work. I'd look around and see wot's wot, but at the end of the night I'd return to me own crib, and know I'd be left in peace. Me crib wasn' much more than a dingy box the size of a broom cupboard, with a mouldy pane of glass for a window, a pile of rags for a bed, but it were mine and mine alone. *And* it had a lock in which I could turn the key and shut out the world. Me neighbours, the six people crammed into t'other front room alongside, had no idea wot I did for a crust, how I passed me time, and that pleased me although, yes, it's true they could have guessed from the hours I kept. But mostly they left me to me own.

Until one day work followed me home. *Work* being a client who wanted more, who wasn' happy with me services. See, there're some things I won' do. Which I won' mention seeing as how they're delicate, but you have an imagination, don' you?

Back then I didn' have someone looking out for me. But mostly the clients Fagey sent me to were known to him, and to me, and we trusted them, and they never gave me any trouble. This one were different.

He was new, for a start, but the old goat said he had it on good authority that he was all right. Well, Fagey got it wrong.

When I left the man, he was bleating that he was owed more, that I hadn' done wot I'd been engaged to do. He were hanging onto me arm, telling me I had to finish wot I'd started, but I jerked out of his clutches and took flight. I wasn' going to do wot he wanted me to in a pink fit, jus' the thought of it makes me come over all goosebumpy. Jus' the idea brings a sour taste to me mouth.

It weren' until I were almost home that I discovered he was on me tail.

I were tired and shivering from the cold. Maybe that's a reason why I wasn' paying attention. The cold makes you more alert it's true, but it also makes you forgetful—cos you carnt think past how your limbs are all a-tremble, how the feeling's gone from your fingers, and how the skin on your lips is flaking and bleeding. Your toes will sting from pins and needles when you finally get them warm, you know it.

So it's arter midnight and I'm tired and shivering. I take out me key, unlock me door and turn to close it behind me, only I find a boot wedged in me way. Only afore I can say *Dollymop* the rest of the foot follows.

'Oi,' I cry, glancing up in surprise and glimpsing the face of the boot's owner. I understand wot his boot's doing in me doorway, then. Wot he's intending. And although I push as hard as I can against the door, I carnt prevent him forcing his way in and closing the door behind him.

Inside, we're in the dark. It's like floating in a bottle of ink. Something he didn' count on. Naturally, I know me way around and quick as I can I move stealthily backwards, out of reach. Then the door opens again. Shows me the man's figure. He's opened it so's he can see, hasn' he?

Which is a blessing. Because I cry out and someone from the street hears me, and rushes in. Rushes in like he's been awaiting outside. Rushes in like he's followed me home, too.

Three of us in me room now.

None of us saying anything.

Two stumbling around in the gloom. One trying to get a grip on me, the second attempting to grab hold of the first. It would be funny if it weren' serious. Then one says, 'Nancy, get out. Leave!' Which is sound advice. I have a much better chance of getting away outside, and so I take flight, all the time wondering how does he—this stranger come to me rescue—know wot me name is?

But I'm out, and not too far away, cos it's me room and at some point I'd like to lay me head on me own pillow and catch some shut-eye, and I hear the sound of fists flying. *Biff. Boff.* Next thing the man who wanted unmentionables blunders out. Lurches into the lamppost and clutches on for support. Gazes groggily around, seemingly getting his bearings, then reels up the street as fast as his shaky legs can pump him.

I step out of the shadows. T'other man is standing in me doorway, filling it. His bulk don' leave much room either side.

'Thankee,' I call from a distance, cautious-like.

'Nancy?' he says. 'You are Nancy?'

'I am,' I say, drawing nearer. 'Who be you?'

'Bill,' he says.

'And?' I say, whispering loudly. 'Explain yourself!'

'Fagin sent me.'

The man called Bill dusts off his coat, straightens his collar that is all awry. He has dark-brown hair that's wild, and a strong angular face. 'He had a queer feeling about that one'—he tips his head—'wanted me to check you reached home safely.'

'I see.'

I cross me arms. I ain't convinced. 'Stand in the light,' I demand, 'where I can see you.'

'Feisty, aren' you?' he says. But he does what I ask. He walks under the gas lamp and turns to look at me. The light catches his scar and broken nose, and the flints in his smoky eyes. He's downright handsome in a dangerous way.

'And how is it you know Fagey?'

He glances away. 'We have history.'

'So why's I never met you before?'

He sniffs. 'How much longer we goin' to stand out here passing the time o' night, Miss Nancy?'

A cat miaows and someone yells all polite-like, 'Oh, do be quiet!' I carnt decide whether they're addressing us or the cat.

'Tell you wot,' Bill murmurs, thrusting his big hands into his breeches' pockets. 'I'd suggest you don' sleep here tonight. I'd suggest you come home with me.'

'Do you now?' I say, and laugh.

'I do.' He's serious.

'And why's that?'

He jerks his head towards the street. 'He knows where you live now. He'll come back. He's that sort.'

'And you'd know?'

'I would. Go an' get yer paraphernalia,' he instructs.

Paraphernalia!

Bill's partial to trotting out some of Fagey's expressions, too, only sometimes he don' use them the right way.

That first night we don' sleep together. We don' sleep together the next, neither.

Mr Sikes is a right gen'leman, he kips on the sofa. Also, he don' drink. Not then.

He has me fooled, but not for long. But by then it's too late, I am used to him and his ways, used to his company, to the sound of his tread upon the stair, to his looking out for me, to seeing his familiar bulk awaiting me when I leave a client's. He occupies the space where loneliness lived. He fills up something in me I didn' realise were empty.

And I know I do the same for him. Although you'd never know it from the way he talks about me and *at* me. But see, it's only me knows there are things hidden away inside him he never talks about. Only me knows about the childhood spent sleeping under park benches, about the men he were forced to kneel before. Only me knows he has nightmares and wakes himself crying. Sobbing. Or yelling. Fighting off demons. Or wakes and simply wants me to hold him. As gentle as a lamb then, he is.

*

'I 'aven't seen you for days, Nance,' Bill complains now as we walk down the street, and I've half-forgotten me feelings of dread. 'You ain't been on the job, have you? Not *that* job.'

'I haven't had time, Bill, have I?'

He grunts in response. 'I could do with you in me bed tonight,' he says. ''Ow long's this caper going to take you? You know,' he goes on, 'I carnt see the point in hanging about hoping the kid's going to appear after dark. I mean, it's not like he's going to be out and about, is it?'

I say nothing. Bill's right. If I were wealthy and had a kid, I would hardly let him out at night by himself. Still, instructions are instructions and there's a good hour before it's filthy black, a good hour for checking on things, and I must be seen as making the most of it.

For a while we walk companionably. Bill is a big man and the crowds part before him when they see us coming. It's easy walking.

We turn a corner, Bullseye following at our heels, and make our way down a street. This one is filled with quaint little shops, narrow like the spines of books, one after another, and it makes me think of the nursery rhyme: *Rub-a-dub-dub. Three men in a tub. The butcher, the baker, the candlestick maker*—only there is no butcher but a bookshop—

'Bill?'

I stop mid-stride and clutch at Bill's arm. Across the street and outside the bookshop is a boy, a boy who holds some books under one arm, a boy who looks remarkably like Oliver.

I've been a right fool in alerting Bill, I realise, only the word's come out afore I could stop it.

If only Bill wasn't with me. *If only.*

'Oi, Oliver!' I call.

The boy turns his face towards me and I don' lose any time.

'Oh, my dear brother!' I scream, not believing me luck. And scampering across the street, I throw me arms tightly around his neck.

'Don't,' Oliver cries, struggling. 'Let go of me. Who is it? What are you stopping me for?'

'Oh, my gracious!' I say. 'I've found him. Oh, Oliver, Oliver! You naughty boy, to make me suffer such distress on your account. Come home, dear boy, come. Oh, I've found him. Thank gracious goodness heavens, I've found him.' For good measure I burst into a fit of crying.

'Whatever's the matter?' asks one of two women, who happen to come by and stop at the commotion.

'Oh, ma'am,' I reply, 'he ran away near a month ago from his parents, who are hard-working and respectable people, and joined a set of thieves and bad characters'—this bit is at least true—'and almost broke his mother's heart.'

'Young wretch!' the woman says.

'Go home, you little brute,' the other adds.

'I'm not a brute,' Oliver says, looking alarmed.

To be honest, he in no way resembles a brute. He seems paler than usual and, naturally, is very clean and turned out in a fine suit. Not the sort of finery a brute would wear.

'I don't know her,' he protests, grappling with me. 'I haven't got any sister, or father and mother, either. I'm an orphan. I live at Pentonville.'

'Oh, hear him, how he braves it out!' I cry.

In the struggle to hold onto him, me shawl falls back from me head, and Oliver starts in astonishment. 'Why, it's Nancy,' he exclaims.

'You see he knows me,' I say, appealing to the bystanders, for a small crowd has gathered. 'He carnt help himself. Make him come home, there's good people, or he'll kill his dear mother and father, and break me heart.'

'What the devil's this?' Bill says, his voice booming over my shoulder. Finally, he's getting involved, and talking all politely and gentrified. 'Young Oliver, come home to your poor mother, you young dog. Come home directly!'

At the mention of the word *dog* Bullseye bounces at Oliver's feet, snapping at the boy's trousers.

'I don't belong to them. I don't know them. Help! Help!' Oliver cries, struggling now with Bill.

'Help?' Bill repeats. 'I'll help you, you young rascal! What books are these? You been stealing them, have you? Give them here!'

Bill tears the volumes from his grasp, and I wince as he strikes the boy violently on the head. I want to protest, but wot good will that do? And, anyway, an on-looker from a garret window cries, 'That's the only way of bringing him to his senses.'

'To be sure,' cries someone from the crowd.

'It'll do him good,' says yet another.

'And he shall have it, too,' Bill says. He administers another blow, which makes me flinch again, and seizes Oliver by the collar. 'Come on now, you young villain! Here, Bullseye, mind him, boy! Mind him.'

A bit of scuffling follows, but Oliver is a puppet in Bill's hands, and Bill drags him away.

I follow with the dog at my heels, and Mr Sikes leads us into a labyrinth of dark alleyways. They are damp and smelly, but Bill knows where he's going and forges ahead. It is an effort to keep up. I practically have to run. I can tell Oliver has to do the same. He seems to be weary. I can tell from his slight figure and pale face that he is not yet well, and I wonder how long we can keep going at this pace.

The dark alleyways terminate in a large open space scattered about with pens for beasts. There are other indications of a cattle market, in addition to the rich fruity odours of animals, and I realise we are in Smithfield. I know the area. It is, after all, where I spent a great deal of me childhood.

Bill slackens his pace. Realises, perhaps, that Oliver and me can no longer continue at this rapid rate.

'Take hold of Nancy's hand,' he instructs, turning to Oliver. 'Do you hear?' he growls as Oliver hesitates and glances around.

We have stopped in a dark corner, out of the way of passers-by, and it is perhaps clear to the boy that resistance would be useless for he holds out his hand and I take it.

'Now give me the other,' Bill says, seizing Oliver's empty hand. 'Here, Bullseye!'

The dog looks up at his master. 'See here, boy!' says Bill, putting his free hand to Oliver's throat, but speaking to Bullseye. 'If he speaks ever so soft a word, hold him! Understood?'

Bullseye cocks his head to one side. He lets his long, pink tongue loll from his jaw and eyes the boy from under his shaggy fringe, as if he and Oliver's windpipe are predestined to meet, and he drools in anticipation.

'He's as willing as a Christian,' Bill declares of the dog, not having any appreciation for religious types, 'strike me blind if he isn't,' and he regards the animal with a grim and ferocious approval. It is this admiration for one another that binds them. Each one sees that the other has some quality, some trait, that they covet.

'Now you know wot to expect, boy, call away much as you like, and Bullseye here will soon stop that game. Get on, young 'un,' he says, and the dog wags his tail. He knows when he's being praised, he does, and he leads the way forwards.

The night is dark and foggy, and it begins to rain. The shop lights wink and waver through the heavy air, which thickens and shrouds the streets and houses in gloom. I am grateful I know where I am, but this dismal place with its smells will be lowering the spirits of the boy still further. I gently squeeze his hand, remind him that although he is a prisoner, he is not alone. And of course I regret me actions—I wish I coulda left the boy where I saw him—but instructions are instructions. And if I'd been found out, discovered I deliberately ignored the boy, there would be hell to pay. And until I know wot their plans are for him, I am beholden to follow instructions.

We have hurried on a few paces when a church-bell strikes the hour. With its first deep stroke, Bill and me turn our heads in the direction of the sound.

'Eight o'clock, Bill,' I say, pausing, when the bell ceases. Pausing, for I'm thinking this might be a chance to let the boy get his breath.

'Wot's the good of telling me that, Nance. I can hear, carnt I?'

'Ah, but I wonder whether they can hear it?'

'Course they can,' Bill says. 'It was late summer when I was shopped and there warn't a penny trumpet in the fair as I couldn't hear the squeaking of. Arter I was locked up for the night, the row and din outside made the thundering old jail so silent that I could almost have beat my brains out against the iron plates of the door.'

Bill is not given much to talking. For him to say all this is something. And it strikes me that he don' often talk about his time in Newgate.

'Poor fellows,' I say. I still have me face turned towards the quarter from where the bells came, but I'm thinking about Bill, not them fellows. He was imprisoned in Newgate before I met him. I did not know him back then. And it is just as well for I don' know how I would have borne his being locked up. I would have gone half mad, I reckon, getting through the hours, the days, the ticking of the time passing and not knowing the future—the uncertainty of it.

'That's all you women think of,' says Bill. 'Poor fellows, indeed! Well, they're as good as dead, so it don' much matter.' He jerks at Oliver's hand. 'Step on it,' he mutters to the both of us.

'Wait a minute,' I say, holding back, calculating on giving Oliver more time to recover. 'I wouldn' hurry. If it was you that was coming out to be hung the next time eight o'clock strikes, I'd walk round and round the place till I dropped, if the snow was on the ground, and I hadn' a shawl to cover me. Think on that.'

'And wot good would that do?' Bill asks. 'Unless you could pitch over a file and twenty yards of good stout rope, you might as well be walking fifty mile off, or not walking at all, for all the good it would do me. Come on, will you, and stop standing there preaching!'

I burst into a laugh. Although nothing is funny. I do this sometimes to yank meself out of dark thoughts. Drawing me shawl more closely round me shoulders, I follow the other two, but the thought of prison makes me hand tremble in Oliver's. He glances back at me. I meet his gaze. We pass under a gas lamp and I wonder if me face is as deathly pale as his.

We walk on for a full half hour, meeting few strangers. It rains heavily now and I have to watch meself. Twice, I stumble and almost lose me footing. It's slippery-slidey underfoot, with oozing substances and such-like best not dwelt on, and the only thing pressing me on is the knowledge that the boy must be as exhausted as me, if not more so. And that we are nearly there.

At length we turn into a street full of seedy old-clothes shops. Bullseye runs ahead as if he knows there's no further occasion for his keeping guard, and stops before a closed door. The house is in a ruinous condition, and appears to be untenanted. Upon the door a board is nailed, looking like it was to let at some stage, but also seeming to have hung there for many a year.

'All right,' Bill says, stopping and looking cautiously about.

I stoop below the shutters to get out of the rain, pulling Oliver in with me. A bell tinkles somewhere. Then, all three of us, still holding onto one another, we cross to the opposite side of the street and stand for a few moments under a lamp. There is a noise like a sash-window being gently raised, and soon afterward the door opens softly. Bill seizes Oliver by the collar again and, without ceremony, frogmarches him across the wet and into the house, and I follow.

CHAPTER SEVENTEEN

The passage is dark. I wait with one hand on Oliver's soggy shoulder. Rainwater runs off me clothing and pools at me feet while whoever let us in chains and bars the door behind us.

'Anybody here?' Bill asks.

'No,' replies the voice, which I recognise as being Dodger's.

'Isn' the old man here?' Bill asks.

'Yes, he's here, and precious down in the mouth he has been. Won' he be glad to see you!'

'Let's have a light,' says Bill, 'or we shall go breaking our necks or treading on the dog. Look after your legs, people, if you do, that's all.'

'Stand still a moment, and I'll get you one,' Dodger replies.

His footsteps fade away and, in a moment, he reappears, bearing a tallow candle jammed at the end of cleft stick. He grins cheekily at Oliver, raises his eyebrows at me over the boy's head, then turns away to beckon us down a flight of stairs. We cross an empty kitchen and Dodger opens the door of an earthy-smelling room. I have been here before, though not for some time, and know that it leads into a small built-in backyard.

A shout of laughter at our arrival, and the voice of Charley Bates, 'Oh, my wig, my wig!' he cries. 'Here he is! Oh, Fagin, do look at him! I carnt bear it. It is such a jolly game. Hold me, somebody, while I laugh it out.' Collapsing flat on the floor, Charley kicks his heels in ecstasy.

Oliver's clammy hand goes rigid in mine.

I would like to throttle Charley, but I know me place and know better than to interfere. Neither Bill nor I have remarked upon his fancy clothing. It stands to reason. You don' go abide with some posh people and continue to wear the sordid and sorry gear you arrived in, do you?

Charley jumps to his feet. He snatches the candle from Dodger and views Oliver, round and round, even though the boy's fine clothes are sodden and dripping with rainwater. I understand why Charley is so tickled. The thought that he, or any one of the boys, would ever get to wear such finery is cause for hilarity.

Fagin, having taken off his nightcap and clutched it in one hand, makes a number of humble bows to the boy, while Oliver appears bewildered. I do feel sorry for him. The Dodger, meanwhile, is going through the boy's pockets in an officious manner. Dodger seldom gives way to merriment when it interferes with business. He has a moody nature, but I trus' him over and above Charley. He's smart, too. He's always two steps ahead of Charley. And I like to think the Dodger's got me back. That our history together afore the others came along counts for something. That there's nothing I wouldn' do for him, and he for me.

'Look at his togs, Fagin!' says Charley, putting the flame so close to Oliver's new jacket as to make it steam and nearly set him on fire. 'Look at his togs—superfine cloth, and heavy-swell cut! Oh, my eye, wot a game. And look, he has books in his pockets!'

Charley draws one out and waves it about. 'Nothin' but a gentleman, Fagin,' he says, with a hint of envy in his voice.

'Delighted to see you looking so well, my dear,' Fagin says, again bowing with mock humility. 'Dodger shall give you another suit, my dear, for fear you should spoil this Sunday one. Why didn't you write, my dear, and say you were coming? We'd have got something warm for supper.'

At this Charley roars again, and even Dodger smiles.

I let go of Oliver's hand, move to one side and sigh under me breath. I wish they would get on with it. I wish they would leave the poor boy be. I wish for me own quiet fireplace and a tumbler of something warm. I shake off me wet shawl and, as I do, I see that Dodger has discovered a five-pound note in Oliver's pocket, much to his pleasure.

'Hallo! Wot's that?' Bill says, stepping forwards as Fagin seizes the note from the Dodger.

'That's mine, Fagin,' Bill mutters.

'No, no, my dear,' Fagin says. 'Mine, Bill, mine. You shall have the books.'

'If that ain't mine,' Bill declares, jamming his hat back on with a determined air, 'mine and Nancy's, that is'—he glances across and meets me eyes, and it is times like these that me decision to stay with him in spite of everything seems so right—'I'll take the boy back again. Strike me dead, if I don'!'

Fagin starts. Oliver starts, too, though from a very different cause. How his hopes are so easily raised.

'Come, hand it over, will you?' Bill says.

'This is hardly fair, Bill. Hardly fair, is it, Nancy?' Fagin asks, turning to me.

But I don' have a say in this and guard me tongue.

'Fair or not fair,' Bill retorts, 'hand it over, I tell you. Do you think me and Nancy has got nothing else to do with our precious time but spend it scouting arter and kidnapping every young boy as gets grabbed through you? Give it here, you avaricious old skeleton. Give it here!'

Without further ado, Bill plucks the note from between Fagin's finger and thumb and, looking the old man coolly in the face, folds it up small and ties it in his neckerchief. That's me Bill.

'That's for our share of the trouble,' he says, 'and not half enough, neither. You may keep them books, if you're fond of reading, and if not, you can sell them.'

'They're very pretty,' Charley remarks. With sundry grimaces, he has been affecting to read one of the books in question. 'Beautiful writing, ain't it, Oliver?' He gazes across at Oliver and, at the sight of the dismayed look upon his face, Charley falls into another paroxysm more boisterous than the first. He is indeed blessed with a lively sense of the ridiculous. I wish I could find life half as funny.

'Oh, please,' Oliver says, his voice a-tremble, 'they belong to the old gentleman, to the good, kind, old gentleman who took me into his house, and had me nursed when I was near dying of fever. Oh, please be careful with them! Keep me here all my life long but, pray, send them back. Send back the books and the money. He'll think I stole them … The old lady, all of them that were so kind to me, will think I stole them. Oh, do have mercy upon me, and send them back.'

Falling upon his knees at Fagin's feet, Oliver beats his hands together in perfect desperation.

I cannot watch. I turn away. The boy has entered me being and taken hold of me heart and is twisting it this way and that, and back and forth. Please, Oliver, pull yourself together!

'The boy's right.' Fagin looks round at all of us and knits his woolly eyebrows into a lumpy quilt above his eyes. 'You're right, Oliver, you're right. They will think you have stolen them. Ha ha!'

He chuckles and rubs his hands together and flakes of dry skin drift down to the floor. 'It couldn't have happened better if we had chosen our time,' he says.

I am puzzled. Wot couldn't have happened better? Wot's he on about? And I wonder wot plan he has for the boy, and how will I find out?

'Of course it couldn't,' Bill agrees. 'I know'd that directly I see him coming through Clerkenwell with them books under his arm.' Which is a lie, of course, since it was I who saw the boy.

Oliver, still on his knees on the floor, looks with bewilderment from one of us to t'other, his glance finally falling on me. And wot a look he gives me—supplicating, earnest, pleading. *Oh, Nancy. Oh, Nancy,* his eyes are saying. My knees feel weak.

'It's all right enough. They're soft-hearted psalm singers,' Bill says, referring to Oliver's carers, 'or they wouldn' have took him in at all, and they'll ask no questions arter him, afear they should be obliged to prosecute, and so get him lagged. He's safe enough.'

Oliver cannot follow the conversation, that much is clear. But, at the mention of the word *lagged*, he jumps to his feet. It may be that is a word he knows, for his face wears a look of horror, and he tears from the room shrieking for help, his cries echoing to the roofbeams.

Fagin and the two boys dart out and up the staircase in pursuit, but I spring in front of the door before Bill, who has not been as quick thinking as the others.

'Keep back the dog!' I cry. 'Keep back the dog or he'll tear the boy to pieces.'

'Serve him right,' cries Sikes, as he grapples with me hands. 'Stand off from me woman or I'll split your skull against the wall!'

'I don' care, Bill. I don' care,' I scream. Spittle flies from me mouth while Bullseye jumps up upon us both. 'The child shan' be torn down by a dog—not unless you kill me first.'

'Shan' he?' Sikes grinds his teeth together. 'Oh, Nancy, I'll soon do that if you don' keep off.'

He flings me from him to the far side of the wall, just as Fagin and the two boys return downstairs, dragging Oliver between them.

'What's the matter here?' Fagin looks around.

'The girl's gone mad,' Sikes mutters.

'No, I ain't,' I say, panting with exertion and pushing meself away from the wall. 'No, I ain't. Don' think it, Fagin.'

'Then keep quiet, would you?' the old man says with a threatening look me way.

'I won' do that, neither,' I declare hotly, standing with me legs apart, me hands on me hips, me chest heaving. 'Come, wot do you think of that?'

Fagin ignores me. Damn the man! Damn the man to hell!

I breathe deeply and try to bring meself under control. I suspect he is sufficiently well acquainted with me moods and customs as to feel it unsafe to prolong any conversation with me at present. He has, after all, known me since I were five.

Instead, he turns to Oliver, 'So you wanted to get away, my dear, did you?' he says, and he takes up a jagged and knotted club that lies in a corner of the fireplace.

The boy does not answer. Watching Fagin, he breathes quickly. His face is as white as the mist that rises from the river on a chilly day, and his deep blue eyes just as unfathomable.

'Wanted to get assistance, to call for the police, did you?' Fagin goes on, sneering. 'Well, we'll cure you of that, my dear.'

He catches the boy by the arm—Oliver's expression one of alarm—and smacks him smartly between the shoulder blades.

And the boy cringes. Stoops. And Fagin raises the club for a second blow and Oliver cowers. He cups his hands over his head and waits. His face is a picture of anguish, his face—

Rushing forwards, I wrest the club from Fagin and fling it into the fire with such force that glowing embers are brought out whirling into the room.

'I won' stand by and see you do this, Fagin,' I cry. 'You got the boy. Wot more would you have? Let him be, let him be, or I shall put that mark on some of you that will bring me to the gallows before me time!'

I have said too much. But I cannot stop. Something black and vile has got a hold of me and I am all a-quiver. I stamp me foot on the ground, clench me jaw so the tendons in me neck go rigid, and ball me hands into fists.

For a moment nothing in the room moves.

Fagin and Sikes stare at one another disconcerted-like.

'Why, Nancy,' Fagin says in an oily, soothing voice like a snake might use if it could speak. 'You're more clever than ever tonight, my dear. Ha! You are acting beautifully. Beautifully.'

'*Acting*?'

The old goat stares at me, uncertain wot to do or say next.

'Am I acting?' I ask. 'Take care I don' overdo it or you'll be the worse for it. Keep clear of me, Fagin.'

Stepping back, he casts a glance, half-imploring, half-cowardly, at Sikes. He's indicating Sikes should take up where he left off, that Sikes has as much responsibility if not more to control me. And Sikes, naturally, rises to the challenge and stands over me.

'Wot do you mean by this?' he demands. 'Why you're nothing more than a three-penny-upright, and you have the gall, the gall … Oh, burn my body, Nancy! Do you know who you are, and wot you are?'

I begin to laugh knowing that if I do not laugh, I will cry—or worse.

'Keep quiet,' Sikes growls, 'or I'll quiet you for a good long time to come.'

I laugh again, but less composedly than before. For one, tears have sprung to me eyes. For another, everyone in the room has gone quiet and is staring at me. Particularly the boy. Particularly Oliver. The expression on his face is one of distress. He is embarrassed on me behalf. For Sikes has made small potatoes out of me. I twitch me skirts, turn me face away, and bite me lip till the blood comes.

'You're a nice one,' Sikes adds, with a contemptuous air, 'to take up the kind-hearted and genteel side. Imagine. Wot a pretty subject for the boy to make a friend of!'

'God Almighty help me, I am!' I cry. 'And I wish I had been struck dead in the street or changed places with them we passed so near tonight before I had lent a hand in bringing him here. He's a thief, a liar, a devil, all that's bad from this night forth. Isn't that enough for the old man without it coming to blows?'

'Come, come, Sikes,' Fagin says, appealing to him, indicating three boys all struck dumb, all avidly listening to wot is passing between us, 'we must have civil words. Civil words, Bill.'

'Civil words!' I cry, advancing on Fagin. 'Civil words, you villain! Yes, you deserve them from me. I thieved for you when I were a child not half as old as this'—I point to Oliver—'and I've been in the same trade, in the same service, for twelve years since. Speak out!' I say, when Fagin does not respond. 'Don' you know it?'

'Well, well,' he replies, 'and if I have, it's your living!'

'Ah, it is,' I agree. 'It's me living.' I go on for it seems I carnt stop. 'And the cold, wet, dirty streets are me home and you're the wretch that drove me to them long ago and that'll keep me there day and night, and night and day, till I die!'

'If you say much more, I shall do you a mischief,' Fagin threatens, glaring at me. 'A worse mischief, believe you me!'

Grinding me teeth together, me neck now like a skinny roman column, I lunge at the old man. But me wrists are grabbed by Sikes. He holds me down like a wild beast.

I struggle without success for a moment, then me eyes roll back in me head, and everything turns to black.

*

When I come to, I am lying on me side in a corner of the room. Someone, no doubt the Dodger, has covered me with a threadbare quilt. I remain still, remembering me outburst—the boy will be the death of me at this rate—and eavesdrop on the voices around me.

Charley's laughter comes from another room, no doubt at Oliver's expense, while Fagin and Sikes murmur one to another at the fireplace. I carnt hear wot they are saying. The door opens then, and Dodger enters with Betsy at his heels. Clearly he went to summon her, for Dodger would be the only one o' them who would care. Betsy's eyes fall upon me, and she rushes to me side in concern.

CHAPTER EIGHTEEN

Somehow, the time passes. The church bells continue to peal out the hours, the sky darkens, the night tumbles down around me. Then, after wot feels like an eternity of darkness, the light pads in like a grey cat, sits and stretches, and the day begins all over again.

And all over again.

And again.

I cannot sleep. I have trouble sleeping in the best of circumstances, and now there is no hope for it but to doze in odd snatches. And to wake in sudden fright.

I think about going to check on Oliver, but the sight of him will bring me to an even greater despair and the sight of me will do *him* no good. For I am lost for the moment.

Bullseye has a bone and I lie on the sofa at night and listen to him gnawing on it. It's a wonder the sound don' drive Bill mad, but he scarce seems to hear it. Bullseye's gnawing is not consistent. It's loud sometimes, a right grrr'ing noise, soft others, and still other times a faint scritching. And I lie on the sofa—the sofa because Bill's forbidden me from sleeping on the bed when I carnt sleep—I lie on the sofa and I remember the circumstances in which I left Mr Rufus. I feel certain he will return to me, that our futures are tangled up, that he will not abandon me. Not like others have done. There is too much at stake for him. Grrr. Grrr. Scritch. Scritch.

As for Oliver, I need time to think about his predicament and to think clearly. There must be a way of returning him to the old gen'leman. A way that will not jeopardise my future. I cannot simply return him to his carers, his *soft-hearted psalm singers*, as Bill calls them, for Bill would quite literally kill me and, if not Bill, then Fagin. There is too much at risk for the pair of them. Oliver can identify them. Grrr. Grrr. Scritch. Scritch.

It is a damp, chilly night, a week or so after my to-do with Fagin, Bill and Oliver, and a black mist hangs over the streets. The rain falls sluggish-like and everything is cold and clammy to the touch. I know because I been out in it. Only been home an hour or so. It was slim pickings, the weather keeping most people indoors, and I been on me feet all day. Me boots are wet through. On top of that I am morose and preoccupied, as I said, me head conflicted by wot I am to do about the boy. Me heart disturbed by the absence, the silence, of Mr Rufus.

Bill and me, therefore, been sitting round the fire not saying much of anything. I'm dead beat. I don' know wot's up with Bill—sometimes it's best not to know and sometimes it's jus' that he likes a bit of peace. Don' we all? Anyway, we hear someone coming up. There's one tread that squeaks, which is handy. Bullseye abandons his bone and growls.

'Who's there?' Bill demands.

'Only me, Bill. Only me, my dear,' Fagin says, looking around the door.

'Bring in your body,' Bill tells him, and, 'Lie down, you stupid brute,' he says to Bullseye. 'Don't you know the devil when he's got a greatcoat on?'

Fagin unbuttons his coat and throws it over the back of a chair, and Bullseye returns to his corner, wagging his tail to show he meant no harm. The poor dog don' know where he stands with Bill, and he's not alone.

'Well!' says Bill.

'Well, my dear,' Fagin replies. 'Ah, Nancy.' He glances at me. Said with just enough embarrassment to hark back to our last meeting, for I ain't seen Fagin since then.

I take me steaming socked feet off the fender, push back me chair, and tell Fagin to draw up a pew, for it's a hellish cold night and no mistake. I carry on as if nothing has come between us. And why not? I have to work with the man.

'It *is* cold, Nancy, dear,' Fagin says, warming his dry and flaking hands over the fire. 'It seems to go right through one,' he adds, touching his left side.

'It must be a piercer if it finds its way through your heart,' Bill says, and snorts. I don' know if he's being droll or if he's serious.

'Give him something to drink, Nance.'

Then, 'Burn my body, make haste!' he says when I don' jump up from the fire immediate-like. 'It's enough to turn a man ill to see this lean old carcass shivering like an ugly ghost just rose from the grave.'

I get wearily to me feet then and bring a bottle from the cupboard and two glasses, and plonk them down on the table. Bill pours out a glass—brandy, I think—and hands it to Fagin. 'Drink up,' he says.

You do recall wot I told you about Fagin and drink, don' you? The old goat only just sets his lips to it, then says, 'Quite enough, quite enough, thankee, Bill.'

'Wot! You're not afeared of our getting the better of you, are you?' Bill asks, fixing his eyes on Fagey.

'Ugh!' Bill says contemptuously and, seizing Fagin's glass, throws the liquid down his gullet. He pours himself another, and downs that, too. He's in a mood, he is.

I say nothing. I do nothing. God help me, but I am not a-going to drink tonight. I pretend I am part of the furniture. Quietly sitting down again and pushing back me chair. This may well be tedious, but I might learn something about Fagin's plans for the boy.

'There.' Bill smacks his lips. 'Now I'm ready.'

'For business, eh?' asks Fagin.

'For business,' confirms Bill. 'So say wot you got to say.'

Fagin draws his chair forwards. He glances over his shoulder at me. 'About the crib at Chertsey, Bill?' he murmurs.

'Wot about it?'

'Ah! You know what I mean, my dear,' he says. 'He knows what I mean, Nancy, doesn't he?'

'No, he don',' Bill sneers, 'or he won'. And that's the same thing. Speak out, and call things by their right names. Don't sit there winking and blinking and talking to me in hints as if you warnt the very first that thought about the robbery. Damn your eyes, wot d'ye mean?'

Fagin half-rises from his chair in agitation. 'Hush, Bill, hush! Somebody will hear us. Someone will hear us.'

'Let 'em hear!' Bill says. 'I don' care.'

But he does care, for he drops his voice as he says them words and grows calmer. I edge further forwards in my chair.

'There, there,' Fagin says. 'It was only my caution—nothing more. Now, my dear, about that crib at Chertsey. When is it to be done, Bill, eh? When is it to be done? Such plate, my dears, such plate!' The old goat rubs his bony hands and looks altogether feverish with anticipation.

'Not at all,' Bill says coldly.

Fagin is dumbfounded, leaning back in his chair. 'Not to be done at all?' he echoes.

'No. Not at all. At least it carnt be a put-up job, as we expected.'

'Then it hasn't been properly gone about,' Fagin says, growing agitated. 'Don't tell me!'

'But I will tell you,' Bill retorts. 'Who are you that's not to be told? I tell you that Toby Crackit has been hanging about the place for a fortnight, and he carnt get one of the servants into a line.'

'Do you mean to tell me,' Fagin says, softening in light of Bill getting heated, 'that neither of the two men in the house can be got over?'

'Yes. I do mean to tell you so. The old lady has had 'em these twenty years, and if you were to give 'em five hundred pound, they wouldn't be in it.'

'But do you mean to say, my dear,' Fagin says, knotting his eyebrows still further, 'that the women can't be got over, either?'

'Not a bit of it.'

'Not by flash Toby Crackit?' Fagin is incredulous. 'Think what women are, Bill,' he murmurs.

The hackles on the back of me neck rise. How dare he talk about us derogatory-like!

'No, not even by flash Toby Crackit,' Bill tells him. 'He says he's worn sham whiskers and a canary yellow waistcoat the whole blessed time he's been loitering down there, and it's all of no use.'

'He should have tried mustachios and a pair of military trousers.'

'So he did,' Bill says, 'he tried them, too, and they warnt of no more use than the other gear.'

Fagin looks blank at this information. He sinks his chin onto his chest, and I believe he is thinking. After a bit, he raises his head and sighs deeply. 'If flash Toby Crackit reported this all right,' he says, 'I fear the game is up. And yet,' he goes on, dropping his hands to his knees, 'it's a sad thing to lose so much when we had our hearts set upon it.'

'So it is,' Bill agrees. 'So it is.'

A long silence.

I sit quiet as a churchgoer with me eyes upon the fire. Fagin wrinkles his face while he ponders the situation, appearing—when I glance at him—as if he has smelled something rightly awful. Bill eyes 'im from time to time.

'Fagin,' Bill says, abruptly. 'Is it worth fifty shiners extra if it's safely done from the outside?'

Fagin rouses himself. 'Why, yes,' he declares. 'Why not?'

'Ah ha,' Bill says. 'Is it a bargain? Can we shake on it?'

'Yes, my dear, yes!' Fagin grasps Bill's hand. His face is lit up with excitement in the fire's glow.

But Bill pushes his hand aside with distaste. 'Then, let it come off as soon as you like. Me and Toby were over the garden wall the night afore last, sounding the panels of the doors and shutters. The crib's barred up at night like a jail, but there's one part we can crack, safe and softly.'

'Which is that, Bill?' Fagin leans forwards. The old goat is so eager he's hunched over like a spring.

'Why,' Bill whispers, 'as you cross the lawn—'

I clear me throat, catch his eye and he breaks off.

'Yes, yes?' Fagin says.

'Hmph,' Bill says. 'Never mind which part. You carnt do it without me, I know, but it's best to be on the safe side when I deals with you.'

Subdued now, Fagin bites his leathery lip. 'As you like, my dear, as you like,' he says. 'Is there no help wanted but yours and Toby's?'

'None,' says Bill, 'except a centre-bit, and a boy. The first we've both got, the second you must find for us.'

'A boy!' Fagin exclaims. 'Oh, then it is a panel, eh?'

'Never mind wot it is!' Bill tells him. 'I want a boy, and he mustn't be a big un. Lord!' Bill says, 'if only I'd got that young

Ned, the chimbly-sweeper's. He kept him small on purpose and let him out by the job, but then the father gets lagged, and then the Juvenile Delinquent Society comes and takes the boy away from a trade where he was arning money, teaches 'im to read and write, and in time makes a 'prentice of 'im. And so they go on,' Bill says, warming to the topic, 'so they go on. And if they'd got money enough—which it's a Providence they have not—we shouldn' have 'alf a dozen lads left in the whole trade in a year or two.'

'No more we should,' Fagin agrees. It seems to me he has let Bill bang on without paying the slightest attention. Thinking, he is.

'Bill?' he says.

'Wot now?'

Fagin nods his head towards me, and I'm still gazing inconspicuous-like at the fire. He wants me to leave the room—the nerve of him!—as if I don' know wot his game is.

Bill, to his credit, shrugs impatiently, but nevertheless asks me to fetch him a jug of beer.

'You don't want any beer,' I say, folding me arms and staying put, for I'm not about to miss out on any vital information.

'I tell you I do!'

'Nonsense,' I say, coolly. 'Go on, Fagin. I know wot he's going to say, Bill. He needn't mind me.'

Fagin hesitates, and Bill looks from me to the old goat in surprise.

'Why, you don' mind the old girl, do you, Fagin?' Bill says, at length. 'You've known her long enough to trust her, or the devil's in it. She ain't one to blab, are you, Nancy?'

'I should think not!' I say, drawing me chair up closer.

'No, no, my dear. I know you're not,' Fagin says. 'But—' and again he pauses.

'But wot?' Bill asks.

'I didn't know whether she mightn't perhaps be out of sorts, you know, as she was the other night.'

I burst into a loud laugh. 'Who me?' I say. 'Why, that's all forgotten!' This seems to do the trick, for the old goat nods his head in a satisfied manner.

'Now, Fagin,' I say, 'tell Bill at once about Oliver.'

'Ah, you're a clever one, my dear,' Fagin says, glancing at me. 'The sharpest girl I ever saw. It *was* about Oliver I was going to speak, sure enough. Ha!'

'Wot about him?' Bill demands. He is sometimes slow as a wet week.

'He's the boy for you,' Fagin whispers, and he lays one finger against the side of his long nose, and grins like a corpse with rigor wot'sit.

'*Oliver*?'

'Have him, Bill,' I say. 'I would if I were in your place. He mayn' be so much up as any of the others, but that's not wot you want if he's only to open a door for you. Depend upon it, he's a safe one, Bill.'

'I know he is,' Fagin agrees. 'He's been in good training these last few weeks, and it's time he began to work for his bread. Besides, the others are all too big.'

'Well, he is just the size I want,' Bill says thoughtfully.

'And will do everything you want, Bill,' Fagin puts in. 'He cannot help himself, he is so obliging—that is, if you only frighten him enough.'

'Frighten him!' Bill echoes. 'It'll be no sham frightening him, mark you. But take heed,' he says, raising a finger, 'if there's anything queer about him when we once get him into the work—in for a penny, in for a pound—you won't see him alive again, Fagin. Think of that before you send him!'

Me blood thickens and slows in me veins when I hear Bill's words, but I must play along at all costs. I must not protest or me and my trembling limbs will be banished from the room. It's crucial that I keep tabs on Oliver and know what it is they intend to do with the boy. I cannot think of his future if I do not.

'I've thought of it all!' Fagin says, growing excited. 'I've had my eye upon him, Bill. Close. So close. Once we let him feel he is one of us, once we fill his mind with the idea he has been a thief, he'll be ours—ours for life! Oh, it couldn't have come about better.' He draws up his shoulders and literally hugs himself for joy. It gives me a right turn, it does. Worsened by the flakes of dry skin that drift from his jacket when he drops his hands.

'Ours?' Bill repeats. 'Yours, you mean.'

'Perhaps I do, my dear,' Fagin says with a shrill chuckle. 'Mine, if you like, Bill.'

'And wot,' Bill says, scowling, 'wot makes you take so much pains about a chalk-faced kid when you know there are fifty boys snoozing about Common Garden every night as you might pick and choose from?'

'Because they're of no use to me, my dear.' Fagin looks bewildered. He cannot understand why Bill has not twigged, why Bill is not thinking along the same lines.

'Not worth the taking,' Fagin explains. 'For their looks convict them when they get into trouble, and I lose them. With this boy—this boy has a face like an angel, have you not noticed, Bill? And that's the thing, Bill, his face—with him properly managed, I can do what I couldn't do with twenty of them.

'Besides,' Fagin goes on, 'he has *us* now and we are his family and he *must* be in the same boat with us, never mind how he came here. It's quite enough for my power over him that he was in a robbery, that's all I wanted. Now how much better this is, than being obliged to put the poor little lad out of the way, which would've been dangerous, and we should have lost by it, besides.'

'When is it to be done?' I ask, changing the subject. I don' want to think of Oliver being *put out of the way*. It makes me feel ill, it does.

'Ah, to be sure,' Fagin says. 'A good question. When is the job to be done, Bill?'

'I planned with Toby the night arter tomorrow,' Bill mutters, 'if he heard nothing from me to the contrary.'

'Good,' Fagin says. 'There's no moon.'

'No,' Bill agrees.

'Then it's all arranged about bringing off the swag, is it?'

Bill nods.

'And what about—'

'It's all planned,' Bill interrupts. 'Never mind particulars. You'd better bring the boy here tomorrow night. I shall get off an hour arter daybreak. Then you hold your tongue, and keep the melting pot ready, and that's all you have to do.'

Some discussion follows, which includes me, in which it is decided that I should repair to Fagin's next evening, night-time, and bring Oliver away with me. Fagin slyly observes that should Oliver be suspicious or disinclined, he will be more than willing to accompany me than any other soul, since I so recently interfered on his behalf. Since the boy seems to have taken to me.

It is also settled that Oliver should, for the purposes of the expedition, be *unreservedly* consigned to the care and custody of Mr Sikes. And that, further, the said Mr Sikes should deal with him as he thinks fit, and should not be held responsible by Fagin for any mischance or evil that might befall the boy, or any punishment with which it might be necessary to visit him, it being understood that—to render the compact in this respect binding—any representations made by Mr Sikes on his return should be required to be confirmed and corroborated in all important particulars by the testimony of the flash Mr Toby Crackit.

I have relayed the above verbatim. Thereafter, I am convinced that Fagin has had an education and did indeed practise as a lawyer's clerk in a previous life, which he has told me, which is not common knowledge, but which he likes to boast about when he's had a few. He does have an immense vocabulary that he likes to bestow upon me when the mood takes him and it's for this reason that I speak more proper than most of me kind. For some strange reason, I remember a great deal of these words, as I said. Never let it be said that I ain't smart.

These lawyerly statements adjusted and tweaked, Bill begins to knock back the liquor at a furious rate, and to flourish a crowbar that he draws from under the bed in an alarming manner, yelling forth snatches of song mingled with wild curses—nothing I ain't never seen before.

And in a fit of enthusiasm for the job, he insists on bringing out his box of housebreaking tools, although Fagin says he has no wish to inspect them. Bill has no sooner opened the box for the purpose of explaining the nature and properties of the tools, than he stumbles over said crowbar and goes to sleep where he falls. On the floor. Snoring his head off.

I am grateful. A man can get amorous when he's had a few. In Bill's case it does take a few. In Bill's case his lust rises in proportion to his consumption, which is a thing worth remembering. There's also a tipping point, but let's not go down that road tonight.

'Goodnight, Nancy,' Fagin says, drawing on his greatcoat and taking care not to move too quickly and excite Bullseye.

'Goodnight,' I say.

Fagin looks at me hard down his long nose before he turns away, and I face his stare so he knows I am true and earnest in the matter, and I don' blink, neither.

And arter he has gone, and I have closed the door behind him and sagged against it with relief, I think that it's as much as I can do for now.

CHAPTER NINETEEN

What do I know about Fagey's past life? Not a lot.

As I said, he boasts about practising as a lawyer's clerk and I believe—from the language he uses and his talent at making ends meet—this is more than likely to be true. He has also let it slip that his father was in the shipping business, importing this and that. Mostly spices and fabrics, I believe, and the old goat does seem to know a fair bit about spices—which is where I get me knowledge of the colour of cinnamon, for every now and then when I was little he'd bring something exotic home and say, 'Here, Nancy, have a whiff of this.' He wouldn't cook with it, mind—his repertoire extends as far as sausages—the spice would only be for the purposes of sniffing at, and he'd do that and close his eyes and sigh and come over all sentimental.

Once he told me he lived in an affluent part of London as a child, and I believe that, too. But something happened to his father or to his father's business when Fagey was the lawyer's clerk, and I have a feeling that wotever it was put paid to Fagey's aspirations, and set him off on his career of dealing and stealing, scheming and swindling. Also, something worth bearing in mind: he never talks of his mother, and yet he must've had one. I have wondered wot happened to her, and why he don' mention her, and all I can think is that she either died young, or she abandoned her family. And that accounts for the fact Fagey has a soft spot for them that he finds motherless and down and out, like me and the Dodger. For he knows wot it's like to be young and not to know where your next meal is coming from or where you will sleep tonight. And not only *where* you will sleep, but whether you will sleep without being molested. And always having to look over your shoulder, for how long is it before they catch up to you and put you in the workhouse?

Things must be awful bad to reach the point of deserting your family. Or abandoning your child, as me mother did with me. For I am more than ever convinced that that is wot she did. Perhaps I showed some aptitude for looking arter meself or perhaps it was a decision she had to make. Either it were me, or one of the littler ones would go hungry, and you can see then that her decision to let go of me hand was a considered one. And then I think that maybe I am being too hard on her. She had no option.

CHAPTER TWENTY

Today I must stir meself. I must do something meaningful with me time before I collect Oliver in the evening.

I must do *something* in this window of lattice space, or I will drive meself demented. Demented and dribbling, I am of no use to Oliver. Same logic applies to Mr Rufus when he finally comes looking for me.

Bill wakes late and, by the time he has left the house to convene with Mr Toby Crackit, a man who has a high opinion of himself but is dim-witted and crass in me opinion, it is noon.

While Bill has been asleep, I have quietly gone about the place looking for a certain item, but I have had no joy. I have peered up the chimney and groped up its charred and sooty sides. I have emptied the coal bucket. I have looked behind the dresser amongst the dust and the dead flies. I have gone through Bill's mouldy pockets, and upturned his stinky slippers. All to no avail. But I do believe the item I seek is here.

Once Bill's gone, I am of course able to look more freely, but that doesn' assist in any way and after a time I sit meself down and stare into the fire. After a while me eye, in an absent way, lights upon the mantlepiece and its collection of sundries: an empty cigarette tin, Bill's pipe and a sachet of tobacco, a dried out rosebud I found somewhere that were once a beauty, a little copper jug which he holds sentimental.

A little copper jug which he holds sentimental!

I jump up, take it down, and upend it into my palm.

Ah-hah! There it is! The *bambino*! A dainty baby, fat and gold.

It has been days since I first laid eyes upon it, but it is still very beautiful. Very dear.

*

I waste no time getting meself to Mayfair and to the grey-shingled, white-washed dwelling. I waste no time for I hail a chaise-cart and pay for it with coin I found in Bill's stinky slipper, but then begins a tedious waste of time while I scout around and lurk under various trees, surveying the object of me intentions. Luckily, it is a fine but cold day, and it ain't too much of a chore to be outdoors.

The Mayfair crib appears to be as quiet as a Sunday morning without church bells. But it is often the case that *jus'* when you think it is safe to go waltzing in, something happens that derails your plans and, more importantly, puts you in danger. So, I wait further. I linger some more. And while I dawdle, I think it is strange that no-one, not even a maidservant, appears to be home. But perhaps Mr Rufus don' have servants. Perhaps he was telling a fib the other evening when he told me he had dismissed the servants. Perhaps there weren' any to start with. For how does he afford them? He told me Aunt Maud's allowance is hardly enough to subsist upon.

In genteel surroundings, a lull very often comes after the mid-day meal and before the afternoon's activities. A lull in which the upper class sometimes sleep off the effects of a hearty meal and a couple of glasses of wine. A lull in which the maids are preoccupied tidying up, and that is when I seize me chance. I move swiftly up the stairs, pick the lock—Bill taught me how to pick a lock—it's mostly jus' a matter of having an uncomplicated lock and the right implement and a sprinkle of luck. Anyway, I get the door open and slip inside. Making sure to lock it again behind me.

Inside, it's quiet and dark, as if the house has been shut up for days. I stand for a moment, letting me eyes adjust to the gloom while I insert the implement back into me cammie. The hallway still smells of furniture polish, old books and money, but not burning candles. The fancy, patterned tiles catch the light that drifts down the passage. The solemn men's and women's faces upon the walls stare down at me, but I don' look back, for surely they will judge me and find me wanting? I do survey the dark and shiny wooden table to me right. This might be a good place to leave the *bambino*, for it will be seen at first glance when someone enters. But, then again, it is vulnerable here, open to anyone's eyes. Open to anyone nicking it. Not that I've seen anyone.

I need to leave it somewhere prominent but safe. But where?

I move quickly upstairs, where the bedrooms are all closed off, make me way to Mr Rufus's room and push on the door. To me dismay, the bed is unmade, discarded clothing awry upon the floor, the cupboard hanging open, and a clutter of books and unwashed coffee cups upon the bedside tables. I carnt leave the baby here. It will be lost, never even noticed.

I am about to leave the room when a splash of colour inside the dim confines of the cupboard catches me eye.

Hanging inside the cupboard, pushed to one side, is a red coat. A soldier's uniform with glinting silver buttons and gold braid on the collar. It's similar to the one I saw previously, the uniform of the soldier who tried to have his way with me. Puzzling, is it not?

But I carnt dilly-dally. I go downstairs again. I hesitate, and then I go down the passage to the back of the house, from whence the light comes.

Sometimes, when I enter a place without permission, me instincts will tell me the house resents me. Somehow it makes me feel ill at ease, and feel unwelcome. In short, the dwelling attempts to evict me. Strange to imagine a house capable of these acts, but I do feel it. However, me point being this is not one of those times. Strangely, I feel comfortable here, as if the house and me are in cahoots, as if we know a secret no-one else is privy to.

I stop short—

Ahead of me, across a stretch of harlequin tiles, is the kitchen. Light from a big, latticed window is falling upon the kitchen's grey wooden table, and upon the wooden table is, would you believe? An orange.

And right from the start, the orange begins calling to me.

It calls to me with its scent—the fragrance that will spray into the air when I peel back the skin. It calls to me with its taste—the juice that will be sharp and sweet and will dribble down me chin as I bite into the fruit. And it calls to me with its texture—the chewy pith, the delicate globules of sunshine that will explode in me mouth.

Before I know it, I am at the kitchen table. I scarcely notice the rest of the room: the huge, blackened wood stove with its neatly packed logs in a basket beside it, the orderly arrangement of copper-bottomed saucepans—no burnt sausages here—hanging from metal hooks, the light falling upon the dresser with its display of colourful, blue Delft plates. Or observe how clean and neat my surroundings are.

Wot I do see is that there are other fruits upon the table: a banana and an apple in a bowl. The orange, however, is set apart as if someone picked it up intending to eat it, but for wotever reason left it.

Wot will be the harm in stealing it? Who will miss—?

Me thoughts are chopped in half by a key rattling in a lock.

Someone is entering the front door …

Coming through the bowels of the house …

Advancing down the passage …

Oh, Lord!

The footsteps halt in the kitchen doorway.

Someone sniffs. 'Nancy?' a voice says.

In me hiding place, crouched down beside the sink in the scullery, I am motionless. A clock ticks on a wall, another thing that has escaped me notice. A dog barks in the distance. Mr Rufus sniffs again.

Strange, that me presence can be smelt. But then I, too, can detect other smells. The owner of the voice has brought with him the crisp and the cold of the outside. The faint smell of himself. You don't lie with a person for an entire night and not remember how they smell.

The footsteps move deeper into the room. Pause, again.

Then, silence. The item I left upon the table has been found, and is perhaps being picked up and examined?

'Well, I'll be damned,' the voice murmurs. 'Nancy?' His voice is louder, as if he has lifted his head and glanced back to the heart of the house. As if he believes I am here, but not in the kitchen.

He moves off rapidly then, back down the passage. He thuds up the staircase, his footsteps as hard and as heavy as the heart banging in me chest. He is eager to find me, which fills me with gladness, which makes me blood canter through me veins.

But I carnt let him find me.

Not here. Not today. I carnt admit to stealing from Aunt Maud.

I let meself quietly out of the scullery door. I let meself into the backyard and slip across the grounds. I weave between the rhododendrons and the camellias until I reach a back fence. I hitch me skirts, hoist meself over, and then I'm away.

*

A long while back, when it were jus' me and Fagey, and I was trawling the streets, picking pockets and bringing home trinkets, I nicked an orange. I'd seen barrow boys selling them bright orange globes, I'd watched string bags of them being loaded onto ships, and I'd seen a man come out of a shop holding one in his hand. Observed him throw it up into the air and catch it again, and seen that it were something that gave him pleasure. I'd watched him bite into the skin, spit it out, then hold the fruit up to his mouth and squeeze. And I'd smelt the tang in the air, seen the look of contentment upon his mug, and the way he licked his lips.

I was intrigued. Bewitched. I had to have one.

All you need to know is that one day I nicked one and first thing I did was find somewhere private to eat it. You'll understand why I didn' take it home. So, back of an ale shop, between some casks, under the shade of a tree with leaves the size of plates, I take the orange out of me pocket. I toss it up into the air and catch it again, and that on its own gives me joy. It's not only the weight of the fruit in me palm, but a sense of liveliness, as if it's alive, and in some ways I am almost afraid to bite into it. Still, I know I carnt muck about too long cos someone is sure to attempt to take it off me.

And it's halfway to me mouth when this very thing occurs. It's whipped out of me hand. So angry am I that I jump up with me hands balled into fists, but promptly sit down again, cos the man who has me orange is not to be trifled with. Where he appeared from, I have no idea. He was stealthy. But most frightening is that he looks like a pirate. He has a beard and wears one of them cocked hats. And a scar runs clean across where one eye should be, with a black patch to obscure the damage.

'Didn't anybody ever teach you how to eat an orange!'

I shake me head. I'm too scared to speak, I am, though his voice is friendly.

'Watch,' he says.

He digs a large and gnarled thumb gently into the end that has a mark like that one in me belly, and works away at the skin. To me astonishment, the air is suddenly filled with a scent I have no name for. He produces a dangling bit of peel by and by. Like a necklace, it is. And he droops the necklace over me head and cocks his head to one side to admire his work and grins, and makes me laugh. He twinkles his remaining eye, deep blue it is, and holds the pale and unskinned orange dressed in its petticoat out to me on his palm.

'D'ye know wot to do next?'

I shake me head again, and he takes the fruit in his bear-like paws and opens it out, fanning it into two halves. Hoisting a thick and mucky boot onto the low wall alongside me, he leans his arm on his thigh, and the petticoated orange disappears into his enormous palm and, by some further trickery, he holds a single piece out to me. It's a pocket with a thin and wan covering, and I hesitate, wondering whether this layer must come off, too? Getting to the heart of this fruit is so complicated! And cos I hesitate and don' immediately take what's offered, he takes it back. Bites it clean in two. Holds out the other half.

'Go on, lad,' he says, nodding at me. I peer inside the pocket. Oozing out are glistening bits and bobs I have no name for. Each one is small and compact like a bubble, only bright orange. I look up at me new friend. He winks. But can I trust him? I close me eyes, open me mouth.

There ain't any words to describe the taste, are there?

Well, there are words like *globules of sunshine* and *bursts of candy*, but I never heard any of them strung together to do the taste justice.

I wipe the back of me hand across the juice dribbling down me chin, and open me eyes. The man has gone. I am all alone again. I almost cry out with the distress of it. But sitting neatly alongside me on the wall is the orange. *All* of the orange. He ain't taken none of it.

And I am torn between wanting my pirate back, and wanting more orange. Wanting more orange triumphs, naturally.

Now, I have known many men in my life and he is perhaps the only one that never wanted anything from me. More importantly, the only one that shared knowledge with me, and never wanted anything in return.

You can understand now why oranges are me favourite fruit, and why I have never forgotten any of this.

CHAPTER TWENTY-ONE

It's around eleven that night when I quietly enter Fagin's. I know he's not home. He's out and about, dealing and stealing, scheming and swindling. Thieves don' never do any deals before midday.

I push on the wood, but hear the murmur of a voice. I knows Oliver's meant to be alone so I pause and peer cautiously around the door.

The boy is on his knees on the floor. He appears to be praying.

'Spare me from such deeds,' I hear him say. 'Let me die at once rather than be chosen for such crimes, such fearful and appalling goings-on.'

He continues to murmur in this fashion and I wonder wot's set him off, and then I see on the table above his head the *Malefactors' Bloody Register.*

Now wot fool would give a boy of eight a book like that to read? A boy, especially, who's about to set forth to do a dastardly deed? A boy who's to be a lackey and to be involved with, and for, a known housebreaker? For the book is a history of criminals's lives, exploits and trials, and filled with dreadful things enough to make your blood run cold, of secret murders, of bodies hidden from the eye of man in deep pits and wells, of bloodshed to make the flesh creep and the limbs quail to think of.

'... And please to rescue me, to raise aid,' Oliver murmurs in a low and broken voice, 'for a poor, outcast boy, who has never known the love of friends or kin, to receive that aid now, when deserted and desolate I stand alone in the midst of wickedness and guilt.'

He stops there, but remains on the floor with his head buried in his hands.

'What's that?' he cries, starting up, as the rustle of me skirts coming through the door startles him. 'Who's there?' His voice fair quivers as he reaches for the candle and raises it above his head.

'It's only me,' I tell him, coming into the room. 'Put down the light, love,' I say, 'it hurts my eyes.'

He does as he's told. He looks at me. 'Are you ill, Nance?' he asks.

'Why?'

'You look very pale.'

I throw myself into a chair and bite my lip. 'God forgive me!' The words escape before I can stop them.

'Has anything happened?' Oliver asks, leaning towards me. He puts his small hand upon my arm. 'Can I help? I will if I can, I will indeed.'

I rock back and forth, my hands clasped about my arms, my boots beating upon the floor. Now that I see the boy, see his innocent face and hear his humble entreaty, now that I am *with* him, the enormity of wot I am a part of, wot I have knowingly committed him to, is too much for me. I cry out, struggle and gasp for breath. Ah, God forgive me.

'Nancy!' Oliver cries in alarm. 'What is it?'

I do then wot I always do when I need to shock myself out of dark places and dismal thoughts. I burst into a fit of bright laughter and beat my hands upon my knees. And just as sudden, I stop, shiver with cold, and draw me shawl around me.

Oliver rises to stir the fire, to distract himself. I believe he does not know wot to do or wot to say, and who can blame him?

'I don' know wot comes over me sometimes,' I say, rearranging the folds of me skirt. 'It's this damp and dirty room, I think.'

'Most likely,' Oliver says, turning to look at me. 'Are you all right now, Nance?'

'I am.' I nod. 'Now, Oliver, dear, are you ready?'

'Am I to go with you?' he asks. His little voice wavers, and a pulse catches the light and thrums at the base of his neck.

Oh, how I wish I didn' have to do this.

'Yes,' I tell him. 'I have come from Bill, and you are to go with me.'

'What for?'

'Wot for?' I echo. I raise my eyes and avert them again the moment they encounter the boy's face. 'Oh, for no harm,' I say airily.

'I don't believe it,' Oliver says. He has been watching me closely.

'Have it your own way,' I say, trying to laugh and make light of the matter. 'You are to come with me for no good, then. Is that better?'

It seems I have said the right thing. Either that, or he is facing up to his future. For he steps away from the fire and says, yes, he is ready. And I look at him and narrow my eyes, and let him know by my expression that I understand at least something of wot has been passing through his mind.

'Hush,' I warn him, rising and gazing cautiously around. I believe we are alone, but it's always good to check a second or a third time. I point to the door, indicating we are on our way. 'You carnt help yourself,' I whisper to him. 'You are hedged round and round, and if ever you are to get loose from here, this is not the time.'

Oliver looks earnestly up at me. He seems surprised by me words.

'I have tried hard for you, but all to no purpose. I have saved you from being ill-used once, and I will again, and I do now. For those who would've fetched you if I hadn' would've been far rougher than me. I have promised for your being quiet and silent—if you are not, you will only do harm to yourself and to me, too, and perhaps be my death.'

I pause, and still he continues to gaze sombrely into my face.

And it is altogether unsettling, let me tell you, to be looked at with such innocence and beauty, to be gazed upon by one who bears the face of an angel. To be entrusted to safeguard the life of a child!

'I have borne all this for you already, as true as God sees me show it,' I say, and tilt my neck and point to the bruises upon it. That are the result of an incident I have not yet brought meself to talk about.

'Remember this, and don't let me suffer more for you just now. If I could help you I would, but I have not the power to do so. They don't mean to harm you, and wotever they make you do is no fault of yours.

'Now give me your hand,' I say, reaching for it, 'and let us make haste.'

I blow out the light, and draw him after me through the doorway and up the stairs. The door at the top is opened by someone shrouded in darkness—I don' ask—and closed when we have passed out.

The cabriolet is still waiting, thanks be, and I pull Oliver roughly in with me and draw the curtains. Without an instant's delay we are gone, the driver wanting no instructions, the horse being lashed into full speed and knowing where to go.

I draw Oliver to me side and keep him close, and continue to hold his small hand.

'Tell me,' I say, to distract him, 'why you speak so properly? Where did you learn, and why do you persist in speaking proper-like?'

He looks up at me, his little brow creased with concern. 'Well, miss,' he says. 'All the people I have met who have money, or titles, speak like that, don't they?'

I nod. 'They do, indeed.'

'So, shouldn't it stand to reason that if I want to get ahead, I must speak like them?'

I nod again.

'And see, Nancy,' he says, confiding-like, 'I believe my mother was educated, was someone, and it's out of respect for her that I do this …' He trails off, clutches me hand tighter.

'Are we nearly there?' he whispers, his fingers going rigid.

'Not far now,' I say. And I pour out warnings and reassurances such as I have already imparted, and very soon we have arrived and are stepping out of the carriage into the street.

The boy casts a hurried glance around him. Perhaps he wants to cry out, but there is no-one around.

The street is empty. The wind chases the brittle leaves along the gutter. The signboard above our heads creaks and the gas lamps flicker. In the distance, a black cat, silhouetted by the streetlight, pauses to look at us with one front paw raised in the air, then skitters away.

I push Oliver forwards and into the house and shut the door behind me.

'This way,' I say, releasing me hold on him. 'Bill?'

He appears quick smart at the head of the stairs with a candle. 'Oh, that's the time of day, is it?' he says. 'Come on!' An uncommonly hearty welcome from a man of Bill's temperament, I have to say.

'Bullseye's gone home with Tom,' Bill says as he lights us up the stairs. 'He'd have been in the way.'

'Quite right,' I say.

'So you've got the kid,' Bill says, when we all reach the room, closing the door as he speaks.

I think it's bleedin' obvious I got the kid, so I say nothing.

'Did he come quiet?'

'Like a lamb.'

'I'm glad to hear it,' Bill says, looking grimly at Oliver, 'for the sake of his young carcass as would otherwise have suffered for it. Come here, young 'un, and let me read you a lectur', which is as well to be got over at once.'

Oliver, all this time, has said naught. But I am standing so close to him that I feel him tremble. He is frightened of Bill and who can blame him?

Bill pulls off his cap, throws it into a corner and, taking the boy by the shoulder, sits himself down by the table and stands Oliver in front of him.

'Now, first, do you know wot this is?' Bill takes up a pocket-pistol which lies upon the table.

'Y-yes, sir,' Oliver says.

'Well, then, look here,' Bill goes on. 'This is powder, that there's a bullet, and this is a bit of old hat for waddin'.'

'Yes, sir,' Oliver says again.

Bill proceeds to load the pistol, doing it with deliberation and a nicety I didn' know he was capable of. He seems to want the boy to like him. Oliver's fingers, meanwhile, have caught at the hem of his jacket and are rubbing at it to and fro.

'Now it's loaded,' Bill tells him when he's done.

'Yes, I see it is, sir,' Oliver says. His voice quivers again.

'Well,' Bill says, suddenly grasping Oliver's right wrist tightly and putting the barrel close to the boy's temple, so close that it touches the skin, at which point Oliver shrieks, but like a mouse.

'Bill,' I say, warningly.

'If you speak a word,' Bill continues, ignoring us both, 'when you're out o' doors with me, except when I speak to you, that loading will be in your head without notice. So, if you *do* make up your mind to speak without leave, say your prayers first.'

Bill scowls at the boy, as if he's looking inside his head.

'As near as I know,' he says, 'there isn't anybody as would be asking very partickler arter you, if you *was* disposed of. So I needn't take this devil-and-all trouble to explain matters to you if it warnt for your own good, d' ye hear?'

'The short and long of wot he means,' I say to Oliver, 'is that if he's crossed by you in this job he has on hand, he'll prevent you ever telling tales afterwards by shooting you through the head, and he'll take his chances of swinging for it as he does for a great many other things in the way of business every month of his life.'

'Ha!' Bill says approvingly, putting down the pistol. 'That's it. Women can always put things in fewest words, except when it's blowing up, and then they have to lengthens it out.

'Now that he's thoroughly up to it,' Bill says, turning away, 'let's have some supper and get a snooze afore starting.'

I lay the cloth on the table, then, and leave them and go downstairs to old Mother Hubbard, and bring back a pot of porter and a dish of sheep's heads.

Bill drinks all the porter at a draught and digs into the meat, but Oliver and me—we've got no appetite. Bill tries to jolly us into eating, telling the boy he needs to plumpen up, as if he was taking him to market to sell. He does not utter, on a rough calculation, more than fourscore oaths during the entire meal, which is something.

Afterwards, Bill has some spirits and water and finally throws himself upon the bed, ordering me to wake him promptly at five, with no end of the consequences of failure.

'Yes, Bill,' I say, patiently, and he tells me not to be cheeky or he will put me over his knee and smack me bottom. This is for the benefit of Oliver, but I do not think he finds the image the words bring to mind amusing. He stares at Bill, his little hands clenched at his sides, and I believe that if he were older he would take his fist to Bill in me defence.

I lay a mattress upon the floor for the boy and tell him to try to sleep, and he gets down there and stretches out upon his back in his clothes, but every time I look over, his eyes are wide and fastened on the ceiling.

For me part, I sit alongside the fire without moving, save now and then to trim the light, and brood, and wonder wot the boy sees there upon the ceiling boards and where his thoughts roam.

Does he think of his mother, I wonder? Or the people that cared for him? Does his mind go over and over how he might have done things differently? Eventually, he sleeps. His eyelids close, his lips part, his chest rises and falls like a sparrow's. One of his small hands is laid across his chest and now and then his fingers twitch or clutch at nothing. I half expect him to cry out, but he never does.

I half want him to cry out, so that I may comfort him.

As I sit, I wonder how I can best help this boy. And how anyone can do the cruel and despicable things they do to children? How do they live with themselves arterwards?

At around four, moving quietly and softly, I lay out the tea things, and then I wake Bill.

He is in a muddle, he is, when he wakes. He catches at me, pulls me to him and kisses me full on the mouth. 'Bill,' I murmur, 'the boy's here,' and then he remembers. His face grows sober and his eyes dark.

'It'll be all right,' I whisper.

'Will it?' he says.

By the time the boy wakes, Bill is getting ready. I am preparing breakfast. It is still dark outside, and a sharp rain beats against the windowpanes like several people wanting to come in out of the wet. I looked out earlier to see a black sky aswirl with clouds like the wings of ravens. It looked ominous but I would never have said.

'Now then,' Bill growls at the boy as he starts up from the mattress, 'half-past five! Look sharp, or you'll get no breakfast.'

The boy sits at the table without a word, only a glance in me direction, and I force myself to give him a wink and touch his shoulder as I place buttered toast and a mug of coffee before him.

Bill drinks his coffee as he makes preparations, thrusting various articles into the pockets of his greatcoat that hangs over the chairback, checking his toolbox.

It is while he is thus engaged that I step forwards and place something I been carefully carrying since I left the Mayfair crib, something that has been burning a hole in me pocket, in front of Oliver.

His eyes grow big. He glances from it to me, and back to it. He seems struck dumb by the beauty, the surprise, of the thing.

'An orange, Oliver,' I murmur. 'Have you never eaten an orange before?'

He shakes his head.

I lift the fruit and put it in his hand.

'But how?' he says.

'How do you think?'

He glances at me once more, bites the edge of his lip, and digs his thumb nail into the skin and all at once the air is filled with the scent of orange peel. Even Bill stops wot he's doing to sniff.

'Where'd you get that, Nance?' he asks, but I tap one finger against me nose.

'Now,' I say to Oliver, when the skin is in bits and pieces on the table in front of him. He ain't managed one long entire piece without stopping, but it's early days, the boy will learn. 'Put two thumbs into the top opening together-like,' I say, leaning over him, my hand on one of his little bony shoulders, feeling the soft warmth of him, the fragility that lies beneath his bones, 'and gently break it open.'

He turns to look up at me. This boy with the face of an angel.

I understand that he seeks reassurance, wants to be shown how best to respond to life, desires to learn from me—as if I were ever an expert! And I smile down at him. I smile as if we ain't here in this dump of a place, and he ain't about to be sent away. I smile as if he might be me own son.

'Like I would if it were a rose bud or something precious?' he asks.

I nod. 'Exactly,' I say.

He does wot I ask. He does wot I ask, but he glances at me all the time as if to say, Am I doing this right?

He breaks the orange apart, into two pieces, and stares down at the two halves in disbelief.

'Good lad,' I say. 'Not a drop o' juice wasted.'

'Now what, Nance?' he asks.

I want to tell him that I don' know, that I carnt foretell the future, that I can only hope and pray and try to work things in his favour.

'This bit's even trickier,' I tell him, moving forwards to show him how the segments lie like babies one against t'other. 'You have to get your thumb between them and, ever so gently, winkle them apart—'

'Hurry up, you two,' Bill growls, coming over. 'We ain't got all day. Look,' he says and he reaches over and picks up one half of orange and before I can stop him, bites it clean in two.

'Bill!'

'Wot?' he says, juice running down his chin.

'Here,' he says to me, 'open wide.' And he stuffs the other half into me mouth. When I look back down at Oliver he has done the same. Only his cheeks are bulging. Oliver has stuffed the *entire* half an orange into his mug—probably because he is afraid of Bill stealing it, too.

For a moment none of us speaks. We are all in heaven, chewing, savouring the juice and the popping of the little globules of sunshine.

'Right,' Bill says, swallowing, and licking his fingers.

I go to me box of things and find the boy a handkerchief and have to stop meself from mothering him and tying it round his throat, and simply hand it to him.

Bill gives him a large cape to button over his shoulders. It will be cold where they are going. It will be cold, but the air will be fresh and clean, the ground frosty, the stars bright. I half envy them.

Bill announces, all of a sudden-like, that he is ready. He pats his side to show Oliver the pistol is in a pocket of his greatcoat, and takes the boy's hand firmly in his own. He takes the boy's hand, then lets it go again.

'Sticky,' he says with distaste. 'Give us a cloth, love.'

Oliver wordlessly wipes his fingers on the cloth that I produce and hands it back to me. Reaches up for Bill's hand.

Bill dips his head to me and says 'Nance'—he's not one for sentimental partings—and leads the boy away.

I turn abruptly before the child sees me eyes and sit down heavily in front of the fire. I carnt bear to look. I carnt bear to watch the lad walk out of me life.

CHAPTER TWENTY-TWO

Me thoughts will not leave them.

I think about where they will go, and how …

A cheerless morning when they get into the street, blowing and raining hard, and Oliver perhaps clutching tighter at Bill's hand. The night having been wet, for large pools of ruffled water lie over the road. A faint glimmering of the coming day in the east, and the windows of the dreary houses all shuttered closed, and the streets through which Bill and the boy pass noiseless and empty, their footsteps echoing.

Then, by the time they turn into Bethnal Green Road, the day beginning to break—like a cat arching its back. The gas lamps mostly already gone out, and a few country wagons slowly toiling on towards London. The public houses, with gaslights burning inside, already open, and a few scattered people about. Then straggling groups of labourers going to their work, then men and women with fish-baskets on their heads, donkey carts laden with vegetables, chaise-carts filled with livestock or whole carcasses of meat, milk-women with pails, and people trudging every which way.

Approaching the city soon, and the noise and the traffic and the smell and swell of humanity, then turning down Sun Street into Crown Street and crossing Finsbury Square, then Chiswell Street into the Barbican and into Long Lane, and so into Smithfield with its tumult of discordant sounds. And its smells. And the ground covered nearly ankle-deep with filth and mire, and a thick steam rising from the reeking bodies of the cattle, and the pens all filled with sheep, bleating and blaring, and tied up to posts by the gutters, long lines of beasts and oxen three or four deep … three or four … three or ...

My eyes glaze over and at last I sleep.

When I wake with a start, it is after twelve. I know, for it is the peals of St Paul's that wake me. It's the wind that blows them to me.

*

The floor, tiled in black and white, seems never-ending and hypnotic, pulling me forwards, and I slide into a pew at the back of the cathedral and sit tight.

St Paul's is that ornate, that fancy, I am half scared out of me wits to venture any further. It's me eyes that venture, always gazing up, always being drawn heavenwards. The marble walls soar above me head and looking up at them makes me right queasy, as if me head might fall off me shoulders and roll away between them pews.

Fagey has told me that the dome is one of the largest and tallest in the world. I would love to stand underneath it and be blessed by the hallowed light drifting down, but the chances of me getting that close are slim. This is only me second visit—it took me years to pluck up the courage—so I remain where I am, hard upon the wooden pew.

After a bit, when I have thought of matters of all kinds: of Bill and the boy making their way to the country, of traipsing over the mucky roads, and whether Oliver will do as he's told for his survival depends upon it, I remember yesterday evening when I arrived home from me outing, me cheeks flushed with excitement and a smile upon me mug after the escapade of the return of the *bambino*, and I murmur, 'Dear Lord, please forgive Bill—Mr Sikes—for he knows not wot he does. Please forgive him, dear Lord.'

I carnt help touching me neck. It's still tender. It's still bruised and purple as I showed Oliver, and all from Bill's boot. For he had me down on the floor with his boot pressing upon me neck.

'Where you bin, you tart?' he growled when I came in. 'I know you bin with someone cos o' that silly grin upon your plate. Now you tell me or it'll be the worse for you.'

'Bill,' I croaked. 'I carnt speak.' Well, I couldn't.

'Do I care?' he muttered.

He hopped forwards on his t'other leg to be all the closer to stare into me face, and in so doing cut off me air completely. I think I went bright red. I know I clawed at his boot. I know when he eased his foot, I were gulping, mechanisms clicking in me throat. 'Give over,' I managed to get out.

He let me sit up, then. But he didn' let it alone. He stood over me and waited, waited for me to explain meself.

'Wot's this?' I croaked. 'A girl carnt take pleasure in a walk in the park without having to account for her every movement?'

'A walk in the park?' Incredulity in his voice.

'Tell you wot, Bill,' I ventured. 'Let's say I make it up to you … Afore I go and fetch the boy? With you being away from tomorrow with Oliver and on the job and all, it'll be a while, maybe a week afore—'

'Hmm,' he agreed. 'That it will.'

He put out a hand to help me to me feet then, as if he hadn' just two minutes ago been forcing his boot down upon me throat.

He's like that. Betwixt and between. One minute so dark he's contemplating murdering me, the next as frisky as a lamb.

And he were frisky, let me tell you. At least to start with. But then something—I never know wot it is—changed his mind. He began to cry, to weep as he were going at it, which naturally undid him. He collapsed on top of me eventually and fell into a deep sleep. I eased meself out from under him, then, and set about getting things ready to fetch Oliver.

After a bit, the pew under me arse becomes too hard and I stop thinking about Bill. And Oliver. I carnt do much about either of them. They are out of me hands. And I carnt do much about the fact that the Lord is consistently refusing to give me any signs.

I rise from me feet, curtsey, and leave St Paul's.

CHAPTER TWENTY-THREE

I am *perambulating* past The Cripples, on me way to Fagin's since I'd better see if he has work for me, when someone calls out, 'Nancy, my girl,' and, turning, I see Fagin standing in the doorway.

'I've been keeping a lookout for you, my dear,' he says, stepping out when I draw close. 'Where've you been?'

'Only to church,' I say shortly, which shuts the old goat up.

He holds out a slip of paper. 'That client you saw a while back, Mr Rufus Somebody. This here's a note from him. He wants to see you again. You have no objection to going without Bill?'

I feign indifference. 'No objection.'

'He treated you all right, didn't he, Nance?'

'He treated me jus' fine.'

I reach for the note, and me fingers are trembling. I don' open it in front of Fagin. 'Where's Barney?'

Fagin tips his head. 'At the Chertsey crib,' he mutters, 'waiting with Toby Crackit for Bill and the boy.'

'I see,' I say.

'Right, my dear,' he says, wringing his dry and bony hands together. 'You'd best be on your way. I'll expect you in the morning, then.'

He turns back to The Cripples, and I set off hastily towards home to tidy meself up and for me pessary, for you never know when you might need it, and as I walk I peel open the note—

Oh, woe!

It's all script! Handwriting. Two lines of it. No day of the week that I can make out, no numerals showing the hour. I carnt understand a word.

I decide to go, anyway. Though I am in two minds about whether to go to the Mayfair crib or t'other one. But it don' seem right to front up to Mayfair, not in me own clobber, so I set off for the ramshackle tenement at the end of the lane.

It's now around four and them streets are busy, but not as busy as they soon will be, and I make good time. I have jus' turned into the road that leads to Mr Rufus's lane when I spot a man further down standing alongside a carriage. He is dressed nicely: a cane, a top hat, a waistcoat and overcoat. But he fidgets. He takes two steps forwards, stops, and turns back again. He glances at his watch, stamps his foot as if he is cold—or annoyed—then raises his face to the driver to say something. Then, tipping his head, the man gives one last look up the road, as if that might help him to see further.

It does. 'Nancy,' he roars at me, and I break into a run.

'Sorry, sir,' I say, when I arrive breathless.

He glares at me with them deep-brown horse's eyes, a curl of cinnamon falling over his forehead. 'What kept you?'

'They lost me note,' I lie, crossing me fingers behind me back. 'All I knew was you'd sent a note.'

'So it's a miracle you're here at all?'

'A miracle,' I agree.

'Well, get in,' he says, opening the door.

I get in and seat meself. I carnt help but remember the last time we were in the carriage together—I believe it is the same one—and he kissed me. Kissed me with such ardour it makes me blush to remember.

He gets in arter me, seats himself across from me, and the carriage moves off, and for some time he says nothing. He taps his cane upon the floor, avoids looking at me and gazes out of the window as we trundle along. The noises of the outside, the flower sellers, the barrow boys, are all muffled. He seems to be in another world and, in some strange way, he reminds me of Oliver lying upon the floor and gazing up at the ceiling.

I told you before, didn' I? How the two are inextricably linked in me mind. How they seem to be similar in nature, and yet are vastly different in looks. The one fair, innocent and angelic, the other darkish and troubled, yet kind.

'Where are we going, Mr Rufus?' I ask arter some time has elapsed.

'Why, the Mayfair house to get you washed and dressed, of course,' he says, bringing his gaze back to me. 'Aunt Maud is expecting you at six, hence the rush.'

'Aunt Maud? At six?' I hadn' thought I would see the old lady again.

Mr Rufus puts both hands on his cane and leans forwards confidingly. 'Yes. She has decided she wants to see more of you. She wants to spend time with you without me. Ha!' he says. 'I don't know what she hopes to achieve by that considering you are mute. You must remember, Nancy, that my future—*our* future—is dependent upon your remaining mute, upon your keeping up the façade. You *will* remember that, won't you?'

I nod me head vigorously, as if to illustrate I am already in character. And he smiles. He has such a nice smile. It is kind and warm and sincere, and it lights up his whole face.

'So you are to leave me there?'

He nods. 'I will be going to the club—the club for which she pays—while you are with her. I believe she is hoping that in my absence you might speak. Ha!' he says again. He looks steadily at me. 'You won't double-cross me, will you?'

'I have no reason to, sir.'

'Quite.' He looks away from me and out of the window, as if looking at me pains him in some way.

'I had thought,' I begin, but I trail off. Do I really want to broach this subject?

'You had thought what, Nancy?' he asks, as if he is genuinely concerned. He leans forwards again, so close that if I wanted I could put out me hand and touch his cheek, run me fingers through his cinnamon curls, smooth down the ends of his moustache.

'I had thought I done something wrong, Mr Rufus.'

'And why's that?'

'It's been an age since I saw you,' I murmur.

'Indeed it has.' He looks away from me again and taps the cane agitatedly on the floor. 'There were,' he says. 'There were some matters I had to settle.'

'And have you settled those matters satisfactorily?'

He glances at me. He is taken aback by me interest.

'Why, yes,' he says. 'I believe so. The *bambino* has been returned—' He breaks off to widen his brown eyes in mock surprise and grins faintly.

'Sir? Sir, may I ask a question?'

'What is it, Nancy?' He tilts his head to one side.

I shouldn' broach this subject. It may not be the right time, but I don' want him to stop talking to me, to stop looking earnestly, seriously, at me, to stop fixating upon me. I don' want him to stop. I like it. I like all those things. I don' know a man who's made me feel like he's making me feel right now. Right this minute. I don' know a man who's made me feel I'm someone worth talking to, that I'm someone who has something to say, to offer. I don' know a man like this one.

'Have you ever been a soldier?'

'A *what*?'

'A soldier, sir. A man who goes to war, who—'

'Yes. Yes. I know what a soldier is,' he mutters. 'Why do you ask?'

I shrug. I carnt tell him wot I found in his cupboard. He'll wonder when I was in his bedroom, and wot I was doing there.

'Something about … about …' I pause, thinking wildly. 'About your moustache, sir. See, it reminds me of a soldier's moustache.'

'Hmm,' he says. He stares out of the window, blinking rapidly, changes the grip on his cane from his right to his left hand. Perhaps I shouldn'a said anything?

'Once, long ago, I thought … I thought I might be a soldier.' He turns and fixes his eyes upon mine. A flush has appeared upon his cheeks and a nerve jumps along his jawline.

'But …' he goes on forcibly. 'I found I could not. I could not, Nancy. I could not be a soldier.' He almost spits out the words. Taps his cane agitatedly upon the floor. 'There,' he declares. 'I've said it. I've never told anyone this before.'

He glances away, then returns to me. His cheeks have gone quite pale. He says, 'It didn't suit me or, rather, *I* didn't suit it.'

'There's naught wrong with that, sir—'

'Oh, yes, there is! It's unmanly, cowardly. Lily-livered! But I couldn't do it. Couldn't even *think* of killing another, let alone carrying out the deed.'

He sniffs. 'Quite frankly I do not approve of soldiering. It seems a profession at war with itself. On the one hand is all civilised pomp and ceremony, and on the other all savage brutality.'

He glances out of the window again. 'But the other night … The other night the soldier in the lane disturbed me. He unsettled me. I thought I had put it all behind me. You were right to ask me what was troubling me.

'Because I found myself wanting to kill the man. Stab him! Throttle him! Which didn't make any sense. Which isn't logical, or reasonable, after what I've told you. Anyway, it alarmed me. Frightened me, if you must know. That I could have such barbaric thoughts.

'Now I've told you too much.' He sighs and gazes at me. 'You won't tell anyone, will you?'

'Who am I a-going to tell?'

'Oh, I don't know. Your people?' He raises one eyebrow, but I say nothing. 'Why I tell you too much, I don't know. You seem to have that effect upon me.

'Oh, look,' he exclaims, glancing out of the window for the hundredth time, 'we have arrived. At last,' he adds. 'Now'—he taps the cane on the floor again—'remember how we did this last time? Quickly out, and in on the other side?' He puts his finger to his lips. 'And not a word from now on.'

I nod, and smile.

'This is not a game, Nancy,' he murmurs, as we alight from the carriage.

*

There follows procedures—bathing, hair-washing (coming up for air a-splutterin') and drying, and dressing—much the same as the first occasion.

In the kitchen, another orange is upon the table. In the fruit bowl. I see it when I return my soup dish and before I put on my finery. I do not steal it. But I carnt help but think of Oliver. He was like a squirrel with his two cheeks bursting with acorns, his eyes popping from his head, when he ate that orange. I carnt help but worry about him, wonder wot he's doing, and how he's faring with Bill? Wot am I a-going to do about him?

We set off for Aunt Maud's at six o'clock. We are running late, but it carnt be helped, Mr Rufus says. I wear a different dress and other shoes, which are still on the small size. He went away to another room to fetch these things. The dress, this time, is a deep blue sateen with a low bodice ending in a stiff V. The skirt flounces out around me, and the cuffs and neckline are edged with lace. The shoes are a matching blue. Whoever these clothes belong to, they have been well looked arter and fit me to a tee, except for the shoes which pinch. Me hair is hanging loose on me shoulders today, as we ran out of time to put it up.

Foxley greets us at the door and ushers us in. The drawing room is much the same as it were the first time. Stiflingly hot, a fire burning in the grate, et cetera.

'You're late!' Aunt Maud says.

'I do apologise, Aunt.' Mr Rufus reaches for her hand. 'I will not bore you with the details. Let me just say the circumstances were out of my control.'

This is me he is referring to, of course. I am 'circumstances'.

'I see,' she says, raising the lorgnette to her eyes. Like me, she is wearing a blue dress this evening, but everything else about her is the same: the grey shawl, the rings on her fingers, the silver hair plaited and wound up behind her head. 'Good evening, Miss Richardson,' she says, peering at me.

I curtsey politely and give her a smile.

'My goodness,' she says, still gawking at me. 'I cannot get over your resemblance to poor, dear Juliet, especially in that dress. Isn't she the spitting image of her, dear boy?'

Mr Rufus turns to me. They both stare. I feel me face flushing furiously.

'And even prettier when there is a bloom in her cheeks,' Mr Rufus murmurs to his aunt.

'Now,' she says, putting down the lorgnette. 'I understand you are leaving us and going to your club?'

'I am, dear Aunt. If that is still in accordance with your wishes?'

'Quite,' she says. 'Foxley will see you out, and I expect you back around nine. Do not be late this time, boy,' she warns.

I wonder wot sort of punishment she might dish out if he is?

'Sit down, child,' she says to me after Mr Rufus has left the room. She reaches over to pat the seat of the sofa where Mr Rufus and I sat before.

'Foxley, please bring us the refreshments,' she instructs, waving a hand and making the rings on her fingers tinkle, and I turn me head to see the man hovering in the doorway.

'Now, Miss Richardson,' she says, 'I am going to call you Titania. It is less of a mouthful.'

She reaches for a slate and a piece of chalk, conveniently placed upon the small table at her side, and passes them to me.

'Let us converse this way, Titania,' she says. 'I will ask a question, and you will write down the answer.' She gives me an attempt at a smile, pursing up her withered rosebud of a mouth like it is being gathered with thread, but her eyes remain cold.

I take the slate and the chalk from her. Wot else am I to do?

'How old are you, child?'

This one I can answer. I write 18—that extra year will make a difference—on the slate, and show it to her.

'Good,' she says. 'Round about what I guessed,' she murmurs.

We pause there, for Foxley returns with the silver tray of refreshments. They are exactly as they were before: the dainty glasses of sherry, the delicate pastries, and I put down the slate and chalk and help meself to both.

Aunt Maud raises her drink as before, only this time we do not toast anyone. We sip and place our glasses back down. I try to mimic wotever she does to keep me on the straight and narrow. Taking a ladylike bite of her pastry, she replaces it on the plate, and I follow suit.

She points to the slate and chalk and I pick them up again. 'Where were you born, child?' she wants to know.

Again, this is something I believe I can write. But when I come to form the letters, it's as if me mind has been scrubbed clean of any knowledge of how they should look, how I should shape them. It takes me a while. I know there is an *L* and an *O* and an *N* but I am not clear where they stand in relation to one another. I begin to write something, but rub it out with the butt of me hand. I start again, conscious that the tip of me tongue is tapping against me front teeth. Conscious that she is watching me and waiting for me response. But, to her credit, she does not appear impatient.

Eventually, I show her me word. It's not wot I wanted to write, but it's the best I can do for now.

'Really?' She looks askance. 'What terrible handwriting you have, child. Is that the best you can do?'

I nod meekly.

'Let's try again,' she says. 'Did your father have a title?'

No, I write.

'Hmph,' she says. I am not sure whether it is my writing giving her displeasure or my answer.

'Are you in love with Mr Rufus?' she asks next, but quietly, as if she knows it's not any of her business whether I am in love with her nephew or not.

Yes, I write. But I frown quietly to meself for I am not sure whether I am or not.

'Excellent,' she says. She sips once more from her sherry glass, and so do I.

'You have an inheritance?'

This time I nod. Lying through me teeth, of course.

'And what will you bring to the marriage?' She raises one eyebrow.

Wot will I bring to the marriage?

I do not know wot she means. She carnt jus' be meaning me. I mean, it is obvious I bring meself. Innit?

I do not know wot to write upon the slate and I stare down at the board in consternation for a long time.

'Come, child,' she says, growing agitated, for a pocket of skin under her jaw wobbles. 'Titania, you must be bringing something? Do you have property, assets?'

Aah. So that is wot she means.

I have two choices. Three, actually. I can shake me head, nod it, or I can do nothing. Which will only annoy her, which will only make the situation worse.

I nod me head. Tentatively.

'You don't seem sure,' she says. 'Why are you not certain?' She points to the board. 'Write it down. Tell me,' she demands.

I look from the slate to her—the fingers of one hand now drum impatiently on the arm of her chair, the rings tinkling—and back again.

Rising, I place the slate and chalk back down on the sofa alongside me. I curtsey and make to leave the room.

'Ask Foxley, in the kitchen,' she instructs, jumping to the right conclusion, the call of nature being a perfectly understandable one.

Only I ain't had a call of nature. Only all I desire is to escape me predicament.

Passing the enormous precious-looking vases standing like sentinels in the entrance hall, I head down the passage, in time reaching a staircase. I peer down it. The edge of a wooden table stares back up at me. Assuming this is the kitchen, I go down the stairs. Quietly.

The room is empty. No signs of maids or cooks. However, there are signs—a chair pulled out from the table, a cup of tepid tea—that Foxley was here, but he ain't here now. The kitchen is altogether different to Mr Rufus's one. It is gloomy and dark with a mere flicker of a flame in the stove, and a fierce draught coming from somewhere.

The scullery door is ajar. The scullery door is ajar, letting in cold air and cigarette smoke. Foxley is out there, then, having a quick one.

I go back up the stairs. When I reach the landing I notice another set of stairs leading upwards. To the bedrooms? I don' have time to inspect them now.

I return to Aunt Maud, me conclusions being that no maids have quarters on the premises. Foxley does, however, his bed being off the kitchen. I did have time to locate his quarters, but not time enough to do much else. Still, it's a start.

I carnt believe this! Am I seriously considering telling Fagey and Bill about this crib? I must be. Why else would I be investigating?

Old habits die hard is all I can say.

Aunt Maud has dozed off in her chair when I return, her head sunk to her chest. A faint whistlin' sound comes off her, setting the hairs on the end of her chin all aflutter. I take me place quietly, sip at me sherry, and look around as before.

The *bambino* is back in the gold-rimmed dish containing knick-knacks. The dear little clock in the gold case continues to tick and to tock. I take the opportunity to make the slate and the chalk do a vanishing act and shove them under the sofa, should they be wanted again. I lean forwards and study Aunt Maud's rings. There are five altogether, one a large emerald, another a plain gold band encrusted with wot I believe are diamonds. Sadly, there's little chance of getting me hands on these, since in each case it is obvious the arthritic knuckles prevent them travelling anywhere. Wot a pity!

When I hear Mr Rufus's light tap upon the front door, I get up quietly.

'Hallo!' he says at the door, somewot startled by me answering his knock. He looks pleased to be back, and I am glad to see him return. I don' think I could stand no more interrogation.

I put me finger to me lips, then fold me hands sideways and lay me head on them and mime sleeping.

'I see,' he murmurs.

He enters the drawing room. 'Aunt Maud?' he says gently.

But lo and behold she is awake and sitting up perkily, like she never was asleep. 'Yes, my boy,' she says. 'You are back, I see.'

She tilts her head to peer sideways at me. 'Call Foxley, would you?' she instructs. This is in spite of the brass bell at her elbow that is normally used to alert Foxley.

She wants me out of the room.

She wants to discuss something with Mr Rufus in private.

I nod. I don' know wot else to do, how to escape me situation, and I feel meself grow pale at the prospect of Mr Rufus knowing I carnt write. His opinion of me will be lowered even further. Oh, woe!

Foxley is sitting at the kitchen table, reading the paper, and I beckon to him to follow me.

We return to the drawing room and Mr Rufus looks steadily at me.

I carnt fathom his expression.

Oh, dear! Oh, dear!

As we exit the house and go down the stairs, he murmurs, 'She wants to see you again.'

But I don' think this information is wot caused him to look at me the way he did.

CHAPTER TWENTY-FOUR

Our journey back to Mayfair is a quiet, reflective one.

Mr Rufus says nothing about being illiterate. He says nothing about me handwriting. He says nothing full stop.

He seems, if I may say so, to be out of sorts.

'When is it she wants to see me again?' I ask, after some time.

'Tomorrow,' he says.

'*Tomorrow*?'

'That's what I said.'

He edges forwards. He looks down at his cuffs and straightens them. Adjusts the upholstery. Places his cane one side of his legs, then t'other, then back the way it were in the first place.

'Wot is it?' I burst out when I carnt abide any more. 'Wot did she say to you?'

'Oh, Nancy,' he says ruefully. He seems full of sadness.

'I carnt help it,' I burst out again. 'I ain't never had the opportunity to—to—' I break off for he is frowning.

'You *ain't* had the opportunity to do what?' he says, teasing gently.

'Oh, never mind,' I say, biting me lip. 'Never you mind.'

We are not thinking along the same tracks. Wotever Aunt Maud said to him, it's not wot I think. She hasn't told him I carnt write. If she had, why does he seem regretful—for surely he already suspects?

This is not the expected reaction to learning some chit off the street carnt write, is it?

Wot *did* she tell him, then?

*

In the morning when I wake, I don' know where I am for a second or two. I am not in me own bed. I am in some fancy four-poster and the light has woken me, peering and winking at me between the velvet drapes, saying, 'Get up, Nancy!'

I remember I am at Mr Rufus's Mayfair house, in the guest room. That he suggested I stay over. If I liked. To save to-ing and fro-ing, he said. It were only the two of us and it would not be an inconvenience. And since Bill is away with the boy—oh, poor Oliver!—it seemed like a good idea.

We were still in the carriage, paused out front, at the time Mr Rufus made the suggestion.

'Are you, in a roundabout way, asking me to sleep with you?' I asked.

'No. I am not.'

He rose and pushed his way out of the door like he didn' want me to see his face. And I wondered where that man, that man who had kissed me so passionately here in this very carriage, and that first occasion held me close to him all night, had gone.

'Come on, let's go in,' he said, turning to hold out his hand for me.

I looked at him, but he would not meet me eyes. I took his hand and we went in without another word between us.

Something has changed there, too, and I don' know wot it is.

I find a dressing gown now in the clothes closet and put it on, and go down the stairs to the kitchen.

The wooden table still contains the orange, but I try to put it from me mind and leave it be. When you ain't got much, when you are always envying wot others have, it is not a difficult thing to learn—to put things from your mind. You *have* to, or you don' survive.

The air is still and cold. I set a fire in the woodstove and light it, and look in the pantry. I find a dish holding eggs, some butter, a half-loaf of bread and some rashers of bacon, but not much besides.

When Mr Rufus comes down—drawn most likely by the smell of sizzling bacon—I have carefully taken down two of them pretty, blue plates from the dresser and placed them on the table, and am frying up them eggs, keeping the bacon warm.

'Good morning, Nancy.'

He pauses in the kitchen doorway to give me a faint smile. His hair is all rumpled and his dressing gown askew, hastily flung on over his nightclothes. But for all that, he is a sight for sore eyes, if I may say so.

'Morning, sir,' I say, breaking an egg into the pan.

'Smells good.' He sniffs the air. 'It's time you stopped calling me *sir*,' he says, coming into the room and pulling up a chair at the table.

'Wot you want me to call you? Rufus?'

'It is my name.'

'I'll consider it,' I tell him. 'How do you like them eggs, sir—Mr Rufus?'

'Runny, please.'

'Is there any coffee? I carnt find any.'

'There will be tea, but it'll have to be black. I am sure there is no milk, either. Did you sleep well?'

'I did, thankee. Did you?'

'As well as can be expected,' he says.

I think about the matters preventing him from sleeping like a baby: his financial situation, Aunt Maud's stipulation that he marry. When you look at it, almost everybody has something niggling at them, something keeping them awake all hours. It's jus' a case of how severe it is, innit?

Reaching past the orange, I place a plate of eggs and bacon in front of him. Set the toast out in the rack.

He makes a sound of appreciation and says, 'I can't tell you how nice it is not to have to cater for myself.'

'Why is that? Why are there no servants?'

'I can't afford them.' He picks up his knife and fork. 'Aunt Maud's charity extends to housekeeping costs, but not to servants. Although every now and then, she sends over Foxley and a hired hand to give the place a thorough going over. But I do know how to fend for myself.'

'I gathered as much,' I murmur, putting down me plateful and sliding into the opposite chair.

'What gave you that idea?' he asks around a mouthful of toast.

'T'other crib,' I say, cutting into me egg and watching the yolk ooze out prettily over the blue, patterned plate. 'The first day I met you. You seemed quite at home there, like you know wot it is to be poor. Why is it you have two residences?'

He breaks off a bit of toast to mop up his egg and says, 'Full of questions, you are this morning, Nancy.'

For a while, there's no sound but the noise of us eating. There's no sound but the orange stares at me. Watches me fork up egg and bacon and put them into me mouth.

Me eyes carnt help but stray towards it.

He finishes before me, pushes back his chair, goes to the pantry and returns carrying a tea caddy.

'I didn't mean you to stop talking altogether,' he says, pausing behind me chair. His voice comes over the top of me head. I carnt see him without turning around. He must be standing directly behind me, staring down, and the hairs on the back of me neck stand up. I'm not afraid, but I am on edge. I don' know with what. Excitement? Anticipation?

'You want me to talk, then?'

'It … It feels very lonely when you don't. As if you are cross with me about something. Are you cross?'

I shake me head.

'But something is bothering you?'

I nod me head.

'What's bothering you?'

I do wot I carnt help doing. I turn and gaze up … And find him gazing thoughtfully down at me with his deep-brown eyes.

'Mr Rufus?'

He turns abruptly back to the stove and the moment, fraught with unsaid words, passes.

I look across the table and the orange tells me if I'd picked it up earlier and were eating it, I would've been distracted, and this moment wouldn' have occurred. I don' know that the orange is right and, in any case, whoever heard of a talking orange? I believe it would've still occurred, but maybe in a different, less awkward, way? It's like that game you play in your head: wot if I had done this instead of that? And then *that* instead of this. It can drive you to insanity, it can.

Go away, orange, I think. Who said you could speak, anyway?

Mr Rufus pushes a cup of tea in front of me.

'Thankee.'

He appears to have forgotten he asked me wot was bothering me. A good thing, I think. If he asks me right now I might very well say—an orange!

At the door he turns to me, tea in one hand.

'I'm going upstairs,' he says. 'You have no need to dress. Stay as you are until it is time to return to Aunt Maud's at four. There is a library down the passage. You might like to light the fire and read while I work?'

'You are employed?' I pause with me cup halfway to me mouth. 'What is it you do?'

'Always the questions,' he says.

He disappears down the passage then, and I hear his footsteps going up the staircase.

I clean up in the kitchen arter I finish me tea, and put everything away jus' as I found it, taking one last lingering look at the bright orange ball before I leave the room.

You'll be wondering why I don' eat it.

I believe it's a test, see. I believe Mr Rufus knows I took the orange before and he's put this one out here to test me. If I take it, he will know it were me that returned the *bambino.*

*

I find the library but I am not convinced I can occupy meself in it for too long a time. It is full of books, of course. Books full of pages containing words. Words that I carnt read!

I open the drapes, letting in the light, and then I put a match to the kindling and feed the fire. Stepping back, I gaze up at the shelves that extend along two walls from floor to the ceiling. They are, naturally, crammed with books. Mostly brown, mostly leather. I move forwards hesitantly, as if they might snap and bite, and, with the tip of me index finger, hoick out the nearest dusty volume. I carry it over to the dark, wooden desk that is topped with leather, that is under the window, and open it out and turn the pages. There are no pictures.

I take down another dusty tome and open it up as well, but same outcome.

I take down further copies, adding to me collection, and open *them* on the desk and, very soon, a variety of dusty open-paged books all filled with print, all yellowed with age, all pictureless, lie in front of me.

Oh, if only I knew wot they said!

I am considering putting them all back, for it will never do for Mr Rufus to find me (and the books) like this, when the door creaks.

Too late!

'Ah, Nancy,' he says entering, as if he has been gone for hours when in actual fact I believe he has been upstairs for less than one.

Why is he suddenly awkward with me? Is it because he has sought me out? Is it because he said he would be *working* and clearly whatever was preoccupying him hasn' taken very long? Or is it because he couldn' stay away?

He tightens the cord of his dressing gown. He takes in the books strewn on the table. He looks at me in puzzlement.

Picking up a volume, I bang its edge on the desk and blow hard on the cover as dust particles rise into the air.

'Filthy,' I say.

'Indeed, they are,' he agrees.

'Do you have a rag I can dust them with?'

'You won't object to cleaning them?'

'Why should I mind?'

'You are meant to be a lady while you are here—'

'Pffft! And who's to know that I ain't?'

He smiles. 'Let me see,' he says, and disappears again.

When he returns, I have hauled out a great many more books and stacked them upon the desk ready for dusting.

He places a bowl of warm steaming water upon the desk and hands me an old cloth—a remnant of a man's shirt—and from his pocket withdraws …

The orange!

Ta-dah.

Without a word he begins to peel it.

I shuffle the books around and start shaking out the pages, and then I immerse me rag, squeeze it out, and begin wiping down the covers, but I can scarce keep me eyes on me task.

A citrusy tang fills the air. Out of the corner of me eye, I see a long S-shape of skin beginning to trail from his hands. He knows how to peel an orange, then. I imagine the juice, tart and fresh, in me mouth, and me mouth begins to water.

He breaks open the fruit with two thumbs and hands me half. I take it carelessly—as if I don' really care either way—but I don' think he is fooled, for he bites into a segment and watches me as I pop one into me mouth.

'Nice, innit?' I say, around the fruit.

'Very,' he agrees, swallowing. He pops another piece into his mouth. 'What is it with you and oranges?'

'*Me*?'

He smiles. 'Your fascination hasn't failed to escape me. All through breakfast, you could hardly keep your eyes off it.'

I glance away, chew slowly. I am not about to tell him that this is only the third time in me life I have eaten an orange, am I?

I wonder how many times he's eaten an orange? Possibly so many he carnt remember. I wonder wot stories he has? There's a great deal I don' know about him. There's a great deal I don' know and yet I trust him implicitly. Why is that?

He pushes the peel to one side then, and begins—for he has brought a cloth of his own—shaking out the pages of the books and wiping down the covers.

We place the books we've cleaned to one side and, while we work, I glance up every now and again at the shelves. There's a pattern to the way they stand upon the shelf, I've noticed. Mostly, the words—the print—appears in the top third of the book's spine. This is important to know, for if I replace them the wrong way—upside down—Mr Rufus will realise it is because I carnt read.

So I begin to return them to their shelves, taking care that the writing, the print—is it the book's title?—is always in the top half.

And he glances at me, and at the books, every now and again, in between wiping, and he doesn' say anything, only wears a faint smile, so I must be doing it right!

We continue to work until we have done all the volumes except for those that are too high for him to reach. The water is cold by now, anyway, and the fire burnt down to embers, but I am not chilled for I have been usefully employed.

'There was a little ladder once,' he tells me, glancing up to the top shelves, 'but it is long gone.'

'Does the library belong to Aunt Maud?' I ask, starting with the questions again.

'Uncle Bernard. He was Aunt Maud's husband.'

'Aunt Maud was married!'

'Yes. Why do you sound so surprised?'

'I didn' think. It hadn' crossed me mind. She *looks* like she has never married, is all.'

'Ah, but we know looks can be deceiving, don't we, Nancy?'

'We do,' I say, and grin. The grin seems to please him and he grins back.

'You are easily made happy,' he remarks.

I glance away. 'No point dwelling in the dark about things you carnt change,' I say.

'I agree. It is a good philosophy. Now,' he says, picking up the cloths and the bowl, and glancing at me, 'I have a surprise for you. Would you follow me, please?'

We go back to the kitchen first, to return the cleaning materials, and I wonder if the surprise has anything to do with them little foxes? I often wonder wot has become of them. I do mean to ask when the time is right.

But he leads the way upstairs and, hitching up me dressing gown, I follow.

Halfway down the passage to his room, he pauses outside a closed door. He takes a while to speak, like he don' have the words and must pluck them out of the air and arrange them in order. And it starts me thinking of them words on the backs of the books again. How mostly there were one, two or three words together in a bold print, then a gap, then another two or three, but seldom one, close by in a smaller print. And how sometimes I recognised the first letter of the first word, because not only were it big and clear, but it were a letter I knew, like *N* for Nancy, or *B* for Bill. And then I start to wonder whether them books should have been put back in an order of some kind, like the *B* should've come before—?

'This … This was my mother's bedroom,' he says at last.

'We don' have to go in if you don' want to,' I say.

'I do want to,' he says, his hand on the doorknob. 'The room is untouched, but there are dresses, outfits, that might fit you, that you might like to have. Someone may as well put them to good use.'

'*Me*?' I put me hand on me chest. 'That I might like to have? Are you sure, Mr Rufus.'

'I'm sure. I have thought this through, Nancy.'

'But wot about Aunt Maud? Wouldn' she have something to say?'

'Aunt Maud was not particularly attached to my mother,' he says, opening the door. 'She … She …' But he trails off and gazes away. There's obviously more to tell, but perhaps not today.

'I see,' I say, and follow him in.

At first, the room is gloomy for the drapes are closed. But then he moves across to open them, letting in the light and a sprinkling of sunshine, and I see the furnishings are sumptuous. A big bed with a brocaded and colourful cover, all blues and greens, occupies one half of the room, and the other half is taken up by a small sofa with matching armchairs, and a bookcase. The fireplace is laid with kindling. Mr Rufus bends to light it while I gaze around …

The walls are hung with paintings, but not of solemn and sombre folk as they are downstairs, but of a variety of natural subjects. Of sheep grazing in a daisy-dotted meadow. Of a vase of full-blown, pink roses with petals falling to the floor. Of horses running wild in a field.

A writing desk with a lamp upon its surface stands in another corner. There is paper with curled up edges upon the desk, a quill and an open inkpot, as if the writer were called away, had laid down her pen and stepped outside for a moment. As if her presence were still lingering. As if she were still somewhere in the house. I carnt help feeling something happened in this room, something significant—

'It is very pleasant in here, is it not?'

Mr Rufus leans against the wall, his thumbs hooked into the cord of his dressing gown. He gazes intently at me in—I hesitate to say it for I don' intend to sound vain, but he gazes at me in *fascination*.

I understand, then, wot it is. Wot he is looking at.

He is not seeing me, not seeing Nancy here in this bedroom …

He is seeing his mother. *His mother.*

Pain appears in his eyes, like he is slowly realising, like he knows I ain't her but don' want to accept it. That for all his wanting me to be his mother, I am *not* her.

And I don' want to be her!

I'm already a mother, after a fashion, to Oliver, Dodger, and the boys, and sometimes even Bill, Lord help me. I certainly don' want to be a mother to Mr Rufus, too!

I want to be Nancy. Me. Myself.

I want Mr Rufus to know me for wot I am.

For who I am.

I want him to love me for who I am.

Is that too much to ask?

CHAPTER TWENTY-FIVE

I step forwards. I walk across to Mr Rufus and take his hand, and I lead him from the room.

I lead him from the room and down the passage, and he lets me take him, like he is sleep-walking.

I lead him down the passage and into his bedroom, and I close the door.

Here, the sun is falling like slices of butter through the gaps in the curtains, and I let go of him for a moment and move to open them, to let the warm buttery light lie upon the bed and upon the floor.

Then I return, and pause before him and undo me dressing gown and let it slide off me shoulders. I do the same for him, and he stands and allows me to, like I have cast a spell upon him. Then I start upon me nightclothes and let them fall from me body, too …

And I start upon his nightclothes until we are both like Adam and Eve.

Like Adam and Eve, but shivering. With cold or anticipation, I ain't sure.

I move me face against his. His eyelashes bat softly against me cheek. I open me mouth to him, let me tongue brush against the warm wetness of his— he tastes of orange—and hear him breathing. His breath is not regular. His breath is jagged. And under me hand, his heartbeat is racing. He says me name, he says, 'Nancy.'

'That's right,' I murmur. 'Nancy. I am Nancy.'

Then I carnt speak no more, for I am lost …

Or maybe it is that I am found? For I am made to feel that me body and the pleasuring of it matters. I am made to feel that *I* matter.

He does take his time, he does shilly-shally to get there. I were right about that. But I am taken aback. I ain't never been treated like this before. For he takes me on the rug buttered by the sun, he folds me up gentle-like into himself, he gazes into me eyes, and seems to look into me *soul*. He touches me, caresses me, moves against me, opens me up like a flower to light. And when he does get there …

Ain't nobody ever done that for me before.

*

We come to our senses when the knocker-upper bangs ferociously on the front door. For me, that's a first—being woken by a knocker-upper. Not woken exactly, but brought back to earth. Mr Rufus has to leave me side and throw on a shirt, and move to the window and open it, yell out, 'Thank you!'

It occurs to me to wonder at this. Why was a knocker-upper engaged to come to the house? Surely Mr Rufus didn' predict our liaison? Am I that easy to read? (Ha ha. When I carnt!) Or was it merely that he thought we would get distracted by, perhaps, the showing of his mother's room to me?

'Now we have to make haste, Nancy,' he says, turning to me and running one hand through his tousled hair.

We scramble around like a married couple—it don' half feel strange—passing each other in the bathroom, running back to his mother's room to get me dress from the closet—the first one I wore, the pale blue. On the way, bumping into Mr Rufus going t'other direction, and Mr Rufus catching me to him and kissing me quickly on the mouth, then letting me go, but his eyes smiling and lingering on mine. And I don' want this moment to end, I don' want any of it to end. Then Mr Rufus is fastening me buttons and doing me hair, and somehow we manage to get into the carriage just before four.

'Are you hungry?' he asks as we careen along the streets, the horses's hooves beating a tattoo, for he gave instructions to make haste.

I nod for we ain't had anything to eat, apart from the orange, since breakfast. I am attempting to remain silent, to get into the habit of being mute again. Trying also to remember I am Mr Sikes's Nancy, Nancy from Bethnal Green, and afore that, Nancy from the crib of Fagin, and not to let the recent events go to me head.

Reaching for me hand, he squeezes it, and glances at me, and then away again. I wonder wot he is thinking?

At Aunt Maud's, he doesn' come in. He tells me in the carriage she is not expecting him and he will go straight on to his club, and that I am to remember to—he puts one finger to his lips—and I nod again.

Foxley lets me in at the door, and Aunt Maud looks pointedly at the dear little gold clock and says to me, by way of greeting, 'I see you got here at last.'

I have to lower me eyes and appear contrite. I know me cheeks are flushed, that I am still damp between me legs. I wonder if she guesses why I am late?

I admit I have an altogether different view of her, now that I know she were once married. I don' know how to explain it, 'cept to say that I no longer think of her as being so rigid and impenetrable.

Impenetrable! Hah!

That were not a ladylike thing to say, I know, but then I ain't a lady, am I?

I sit down in me usual spot. Everything is the same as before: the heated room, the bright lights, the roaring fire, Aunt Maud with her silvery hair atop her head and wearing her forest green dress and grey shawl, Foxley sent away to fetch the refreshments.

After he has left, without any ado Aunt Maud reaches for a long, slim jewellery box on the table alongside her.

'I want you to have this, my dear,' she says, opening up the box. She takes out a gold chain with some baubles hanging from it and it's as much as I can do not to cry out. As it is I raise my eyebrows.

She holds the necklace up to the light. Dangling from a gold chain is … is … an amethyst, I do believe—here Bill would be good for confirmation—together with two clusters of pearls, one to each side of the stone.

I put me hand in front of me mouth. Attempt to mimic being struck dumb, although part of me attempt is precisely how I feel—I am struck dumb! She carnt be serious?

I move me hand to me chest, like I did with Mr Rufus. *Me*?

She nods. 'Here, child.'

I rise and take the chain from her, hold it in me hand, half afraid I will drop it. It is exquisite. The amethyst glitters between me fingers. Sparkles, like I have reached up to the heavens and gathered a bunch of stars in me fist.

'Foxley,' she says, for the man has just entered the room. 'Help Miss Titania with the necklace, please.'

I stand still while he threads it around me neck and fastens it at the back—he has done this before, I think. He seems practised at it. He must do it for her—and then I step forwards to show Aunt Maud.

'Very nice,' she says. 'As I suspected. Go and look in the mirror,' she instructs, waving her hand at me.

The mirror is in the hallway. It is, of course, gold-rimmed, large and opulent. I stand in front of it, and gaze at meself. It is hard to accept that the young lady I see before me is Nancy from Bethnal Green. The thought that runs uppermost in me mind is, Thank the Lord, Bill is not home right now. For he would demand to know how I came by such a fine piece of jewellery. In fact, I don' believe I should return home with it. I carnt risk having him find it.

Bill ... Oliver … The crib at Chertsey.

I have scarce thought of them all day. And I carnt help but have a pang of despair. Oh, that there was something I could do for the boy! Something to save him.

I leave the mirror and return to the living room and Aunt Maud. Would the old lady help me with Oliver? Is it possible? But that would mean speaking!

We proceed as usual. Sherries, pastries. Foxley leaving us. I wonder whether I am going to have to write again on the slate, but I don' see it or the chalk. Instead, Aunt Maud wipes her fingers on a linen napkin and picks up a pack of cards.

'You play whist?'

I nod. This is something I can do!

She shuffles expertly, deals out thirteen cards each on the coffee table between us, flips over the trump card, and we begin.

'Oh, it is so annoying that you cannot speak!' she blurts out and, I must say, I have to agree.

She moves the last trick we played to one side, examines her cards, then leads with another Ace, this time of Diamonds. There's no doubt I am going to lose this round, too, if me luck don' change soon. But after I have played me card, she puts hers face down on the table between us and reaches for her half-eaten pastry on the plate. I pause too, naturally, and do the same, and then we sip from our sherries and replace our glasses at our sides.

I move to pick up me cards again, but she starts to cough. At first politely with her hand in front of her mouth. Perhaps a flake of pastry is caught in her throat? But then she splutters, coughs harder and harder, and her face grows red and still she doesn' stop and I sit forwards in concern.

There's no indication she's going to stop coughing anytime soon!

Wot should I do! Oh, if only Mr Rufus were here!

Her face is puce now, her eyes watering. I rise from me seat and reach for the bell alongside her, and shake it hard. As I do so, Aunt Maud pitches face forwards onto the floor, narrowly missing the coffee table.

Oh, Lord! Oh, Mary, Mother of God! Oh, sweet Jesus!

Where is Foxley! Where *is* the man?

I cry out. I carnt help it.

'Aunt Maud!' I say, frantically, 'Aunt Maud!'

I reach for her, then pull back nervously. It is not me place to touch her! Is it? She being a lady and all.

But if I don' help her, who will? She has stopped coughing, which makes me even more anxious, for she is lying very still upon the rug.

Has she fainted? Is she still breathing? Oh, sweet Jesus, wot if she has died?

Hastily I push away the table, get down on me knees, and take her shoulders.

Gently—she is not heavy, thank goodness, more like a small bird in me hands—I turn her over onto her back and cradle her head in me lap.

Her lined face gazes up at me.
Her greeny gold eyes are wide open.
She's not gasping for breath. She's not dying. She's not ill at all.
She's triumphant!
'Ah ha!' she says, smiling wickedly. 'You spoke.'

CHAPTER TWENTY-SIX

Aunt Maud sits up.

'Now, let us hurry,' she says, glancing at the dear little gold clock. 'For there is a great deal to say, and not a lot of time.'

I hold out my hand and help her to her feet. I don' know wot to say. I am without words. How could she, a lady, have tricked me like this? She has wounded me to the quick. It were not a nice thing to do. Not ladylike at all.

She looks dubiously at me as she rises, for I believe the blood has drained from me face. 'You are cross with me? Well, it can't be helped.'

'But … but how did you know?'

She smooths down her dress and pats her silver hair. 'Well, where is your companion, Miss Tweedles, for one? You and Rufus seem to have forgotten her existence. For two, your fingernails, my dear, are bitten down to the quick. No lady would have fingernails like that. For a third, I know that dress. It's one of Juliet's. What are you doing wearing Juliet's clothes, and while we are about it, what *is* your name? Your real name?'

'Nancy,' I murmur.

'Pretty name,' she says. 'I suppose some of what Rufus told me is true? You are an orphan?'

'I am. I—'

'No,' she says sharply, 'I don't wish to know any more.'

She settles herself back in her chair and pats the arms impatiently, making her rings jingle. I have a mind she is thinking. 'Now,' she says. 'You know I can't *really* let you marry Rufus? A hare-brained scheme, anyway! If I may say so.'

I nod, taking me place again on the sofa. 'It weren' going to be real, anyway, dear lady. We were only going to pretend … Forge them papers. For the sake of the money, the inheritance.'

'I see. But you love him? You told me you did.'

I glance away. I feel meself flushing.

Is this love that I feel?

'I think so,' I say timidly.

'So two broken hearts,' she murmurs, and I wonder wot she means. She carnt really mean he is in love with me, too?

'Let me tell you what I want you to do,' she says, more brightly, 'and there may be something in it for you. Incidentally, you may keep the necklace. It is not one of my more valuable pieces.' She clears her throat. 'I beg your pardon, but all that forced coughing did me no good.'

I begin to realise that perhaps even yesterday when I were here and Aunt Maud *fell asleep*, it were all part of her trying to get me to talk.

She says nothing for a bit, merely drums her fingers against the arm of the chair, making them rings tinkle.

Then, 'All right,' she says, as if she has made up her mind about something. 'Let us go ahead with the fake wedding—I know, I know, I said I couldn't, but at least this way Rufus abides by my wishes and the inheritance comes to him—'

'Are you sure?'

'Do not interrupt me, child. I believe he deserves it. He is, by all accounts, a good and kind man. Tell me, is that what you believe, too?'

I nod.

'You have no reason to think otherwise?'

'No,' I say.

'Something does concern me, however,' she continues, picking up her lorgnette. 'He seems to be able to survive on the allowance I give him, which is not much. And I wonder if he has some other income he is not telling me about. I want you to find out if he is gainfully employed. Can you do that?'

'I can,' I tell her, but I glance away.

'What is it? Speak out, child.' She looks at me steadily through the thick lenses that make her eyes bulge. 'We need to be open with one another.'

'I—I am not always me own mistress. Sometimes there are matters, business, I have to attend to …' I trail off, thinking of Oliver, and of Bill. And of Fagin.

'I see,' she says.

But I wonder if she does? I wonder if she has any idea wot me life is like? Do any of these people in their fancy mansions have any idea wot our wretched lives are like? Do they know wot a struggle it is merely to exist?

'I want you to come alone and see me again next week—I will inform Rufus of the date and time when he comes—for the purposes of letting me know what you have discovered, obviously.'

She glances back up at the little clock. 'Now let us pick up our cards again and continue with our game, and with your silence, so that when he turns up, everything appears as it should. I believe I was winning. Have you always had such poor luck at cards?'

'I—I have a question,' I blurt out.

She stops to look across the coffee table at me. 'There isn't much time,' she says, when I don' speak. 'What is it you want to say? Quick, before he arrives.'

'Wot did you tell him yesterday? Wot did you say, did you tell him I carnt write or were it something else?'

She smiles, picks out a card from her hand and lays it on the table. The King of Hearts this time, leaving me no option but to play me Knave. To lose again.

'I told him it was clear you were in love with him,' she says. 'Very much in love, I believe. Would this be correct?'

'I don' know,' I say miserably. 'I ain't never been in love. I don' know wot it is.'

'Oh, you'll know,' she tells me. 'Believe me. Maybe not at first, but it will come to you. Take my word for it. Now, let us be silent,' she instructs.

And we resume our game, and when Mr Rufus arrives I believe nobody would know wot has come before.

It is only in the carriage, on the way home, that he says to me, 'You are very quiet tonight, Nancy. Did everything go well?'

He is sitting across from me, and he leans forwards and puts his hands on his knees and looks at me in concern.

I *am* very quiet. Everything is *not* going well. Oh, Lord!

'I am merely tired,' I say, forcing a small yawn, as the carriage rumbles over a bump. 'It ain't easy to pretend to be mute.'

He blinks at me, then leans further forwards. 'What *is* that you are wearing?'

I put me hand upon the necklace feeling the cold amethyst and the cool slippery pearls under me fingers, and smile. It does bring me joy. 'Oh, jus' something I picked up,' I say airily.

'Nancy!' He is aghast. Appalled.

I burst into laughter. 'It's all right, sir,' I say. 'Aunt Maud gave it me.'

'Aunt Maud gave you her amethyst?'

I nod.

'What did she want in return?' he asks, slyly.

'In return?' I shake me head. 'Why, nothing. Wot would she want in return?'

'Well, well,' he says, leaning back, and patting down his moustache. 'Fancy that. The old dear must be growing fond of you.' He looks at me keenly across the distance.

I *know* he is suspecting something!

Wot can I say?

'It's me appealing nature,' I say, cheekily.

He grins at me. 'Well, I hope that's all it is. You aren't—'

'Would I do something like that, Mr Rufus?'

'Rufus,' he murmurs, correcting me.

He places his hand upon me knee, and looks into me eyes with his deep-brown, horsey ones. 'We are growing quite familiar, are we not?'

I nod. I don' believe I can speak when he looks at me like that. I don' believe I am rightly in control of me senses.

'Can you—' He pauses, and a small nerve on his cheekbone jumps. 'Can you stay over again tonight, Nancy?'

'I can,' I say, 'but tomorrow I need to get home. There are matters needing attention.'

'I see.' He sits back, but now he looks worried, creasing his brow. 'You are not …?' he trails off.

I think he means, am I sleeping with any other gentlemen? Wot else can he mean?

I shake me head. 'No, I am not.'

'Good,' he says. 'I don't want you to. Is that too much to ask? I will, of course, pay you extra.'

'Thankee,' I say. I do need the money. I ain't done any other work since I been with him. No need to let on, of course.

*

In the morning, Mr Rufus offers me the carriage—I don' understand how he has a carriage, horses and a driver at his disposal, but no maid or manservant. It don' make sense—but I tell him I would rather walk. For one, I don' want anyone to see me arrive home in a carriage and start asking questions. For another, I need the time to think.

Mr Rufus seems downhearted when I take me leave, and it worries me that he appears to have no friends, that he is knocking about the big house all alone.

Outside, spring is coming and although it's not exactly warm and cheerful, the sun is shining and no chilly winds rattle me bones on me walk. I take me time. I am in no hurry. Only the empty and cold crib awaits me. I am not expecting to hear anything from Bill, or from Fagey, for days.

It bothers me that Aunt Maud sees the marriage proposal as *hare-brained* for I believe she is right. It *is* a hare-brained endeavour. Mr Rufus must be desperate to believe he can fool his aunt. And why is it so important? The man is not dim-witted. So, is there something going on, something *other,* over which he has no control? And has it something to do with his dead mother?

How will I find out?

By stalking him? As Aunt Maud requested?

CHAPTER TWENTY-SEVEN

I bump into Dodger not far from the crib. Naturally, I ain't seen him for days.

'Nancy!'

Stepping aside, he raises his eyebrows. Evidently, he has knowledge he wishes to impart. About time, too!

He glances about, but we are in the thick of hordes heading home after a long, filthy day at the factories and wot not. People bump and press against me and say wearily, 'Excuse me, miss,' or they growl and push between Dodger and me without so much as a by-your-leave.

The Dodger flicks his head. I know wot he means. The Cripples.

We each make our own way there, for it is well-nigh impossible to walk together in that scrum, and when I reach the establishment, I find him already inside. The landlord—still no Barney in evidence—nods to me at the door, and flicks his head towards one of the out-of-the-way tables in a back room, one with its chairs to the wall.

There I find the Dodger with a pint of ale in front of him—more for show than anything else. He offers me a sip from the glass, which I do partake of, and while me head is bent over towards him and the drink, he murmurs, 'I have news.'

'Go on,' I murmur in return.

'The crack failed—' he says.

'Wot!' I say, jerking up me head.

'Lemme finish,' he says. 'The crack failed. The other party fired and hit Oliver—'

'No!'

'Shh,' he says, looking hastily about. 'Someone might hear you.'

'How do you know this?' I whisper.

'I bin listening outside the door, ain't I?' he says. 'Toby Crackit and Fagin?' he says, as if that's self-explanatory.

'Go on,' I say again, and bend over the ale once more, taking sips of the bitter liquid.

'Bill had him on his back arterwards, the boy, lugging him arter the shooting,' Dodger says. 'But they—t'other party—were on their heels. Every man for himself, Bill said. So he and Toby Crackit parted company, and left the lad lying in a ditch. They don' know if he were alive or dead, but they left him. They left Oliver—'

'No,' I whimper. 'No.'

'That's all I know, Nance,' Dodger murmurs.

I carnt hardly take it all in. Oliver shot and abandoned? Left in a ditch like a dog? Alive, but more than likely dead. I carnt believe it. Oh, me heart!

'Shh!' he says abruptly, nudging me, and putting his finger to his lips for I have begun to rock to and fro and keen with grief.

'There's something more,' Dodger mutters after a bit.

'Wot?' I say. 'I don' think I can stand to hear much more.'

'Bill,' he says. 'Mr Sikes,' he says. He turns to me. His eyes are big. 'He ain't returned. He ain't returned and Toby Crackit don' know where he's at.

'Nance?' he adds urgently, 'are you all right?'

I have gone pale. I feel rightly ill. I think I might faint.

'Here, put your head down,' Dodger instructs. 'Get some blood back into it.'

I do as I'm bid. And hear Dodger leaving the table. I do hope he has gone to get something to revive me!

I shut me eyes. It's a nightmare, it is. The boy wounded *and* Bill missing. And Toby Crackit, home and dry, of course, *and* knowing nothing. He would be!

When Dodger returns, I reach for the tumbler of brown liquid and knock it back in one go. It makes me eyes water. But it steadies me nerves.

'You going to be all right, Nance?' Dodger murmurs.

I nod me head. 'I think so. Let me know if you hear anything more, there's a dear,' I say.

''Course,' he says. He leans back on the bench, sticks out his boots and drums his fingers against the pint of ale. 'Got a feeling that boy's a-going to be just fine though, Nance,' he murmurs. 'Wotever life throws at him.'

'It's that face of his,' I say. 'Innocent, it is. Sweet and good and kind, he is. And yet … And yet I also feel his life could go either way. That the angels are watching over him, but they also wouldn' object to making him one of them. One skid in the wrong direction on a dismal and dreary night and he's—he's—' Tears come to me eyes.

'There, there, Nance,' Dodger says, patting me hand, while I sniff. 'Don' worry your head about things that haven' happened.'

I don' stay much longer. See, Dodger's relationship with me works cos people don' suspect us of conniving. Don' suspect he may be passing on information to me and vice versa. And we need to keep it that way.

*

The crib is cold and empty, as I said it would be, when I drag me sorry self home. And my heart is jus' as chilled and hollow. Even if I light the fire now, it will take a couple of hours to warm things up, since I been gone for so long. But I do light it.

I wash me face, then, standing in front of the fire for wot warmth I can get, remove me pessary, and I rinse that, too, as well as me nether regions.

Then I plonk meself down at the table in front of the fire. There's a very real danger I may start drinking. And, indeed, I reach for Bill's bottle and pour meself out a small quantity of spirits and sip at the tumbler. I tell you, it feels wrong to be sitting around a cosy fire when the boy is lying somewhere in a ditch!

How long afore Fagey comes knocking at me door with bad news? Can it get any worse?

Why, my dear, yes, it can. Why don't we run through the scenarios? Let me see now, the boy dying, and Bill making it out alive. Or would you prefer the boy dying, and Bill making it out alive but being incarcerated. Then there's also the possibility of the boy dying *and* Bill dying—

Stop it, Nance! Stop before you drive yourself to the mad house.

I go out. I ain't going to work. I ain't in a fit state.

I go out and get some sustenance from old Mother Hubbard with leftover blunt from that which I found in Bill's slipper, and bring back the watery soup and the crust of bread and sit meself down at the table with it, but my nerves are that frayed I can only manage to eat half before I lay me head down and go off thinking over and over about wot I know.

CHAPTER TWENTY-EIGHT

This is where Fagey finds me—laying with me head upon the table in front of the fire, half comatose, half dead with disquiet. The tread on the stair squeaks. I glance around. Fagin, coming in the door without so much as knocking. Rude he is, sometimes.

I sit up, push me hair out of me eyes, and gaze at him. He has a crafty look about him, as if he's been thinking and has reached a decision.

'Any news?' I ask, rising to feed the fire.

'Ah, yes, my dear,' he says.

I know it ain't good news, of course. And even if I didn', Fagin's face is so mealy, so lined with worry, it's like a piece of parchment folded over and over and over again and stuffed into someone's back pocket.

I sit down again and he proceeds to tell me Toby Crackit's story. Like the Dodger told me, only I get more details. And I ain't going to interrupt him, or let on, or tell him I already have half the story.

Naturally, first thing, Toby Crackit went round to the old goat's, which is obvious. That he was starved and ate wotever eatables Fagin put out, is also obvious and the second thing. That Fagin, in an agony of impatience, watched every morsel the man put into his mouth, meanwhile pacing up and down, is the third, and a given. Then the story really begins, and I tell it as if I were there.

'First and foremost, Fagey,' Toby says, after he's mixed a glass of spirits and water, and Fagin has drawn up his chair—but he goes no further. He stops there to take a draught of the mix, declares the gin is excellent, and stretches out his legs, placing his boots against the low mantelpiece. Causing the old goat to be half beside himself with anxiety.

'First and foremost, Fagey,' Toby says all over again, 'how is Bill?'

'What!' Fagin screams, starting from his seat.

'Why, you don't mean to say—' Toby begins, turning pale.

'Mean?' Fagin cries, stamping on the floorboards. 'Where are they? Sikes and the boy—where are they! Where have they been? Where are they hiding? Why have they not been here!'

'The crack failed,' Toby says faintly. 'Don't you know it?'

'I know it,' Fagin replies, tearing a scrap of newspaper from his pocket and pointing to a report upon it. 'But what more?'

'They fired,' Toby says, 'and hit the boy. We cut over the fields at the back with him between us—straight as the crow flies—through hedge and ditch. They gave chase. Damn me! The whole country was awake, and the dogs upon us.'

'The boy!' Fagin gasps.

'Bill had him on his back, and scudded like the wind. We stopped to take him again between us. His head hung down like he were cold, like he were dead. They were close upon our heels, every man for himself, and each from the gallows. We had no option but to part company and leave the youngster lying in a ditch. Alive or dead, that's all I know.'

I rise from me chair in agitation here—*Oh, Oliver, Oliver*! Even though I already know the old goat's story, I carnt help but be moved. I want to cry out, I do. Wail. But I sink back down into my chair and lay me head again upon the table. I've no sooner done that, than I lift it again. The candle is too close to me hair. I push it away. Shuffle me feet. For the life of me, I carnt sit still. I have pins and needles. Every part of me is on fire, burning and sparking, me veins running with molten liquid. I feel I must burst.

Fagin coughs politely. He's waiting for me to say something. He's waiting for me to tell him where Bill is. As if I would know. Wot I do now know is that the break-in were reported in the newspaper, that more than likely Oliver is alive—or the newspaper would've reported the crime being linked to a boy's death and Fagey would've admitted as much—and that nobody, well, none of the gang, know where Oliver is.

Nobody knows where Oliver is. I repeat it, for it seems a good thing. Though whether it is or not is anyone's guess. But for the time being, he is out of the clutches of Fagin and Mr Sikes.

'Ah, Nancy,' Fagin says in the silence. 'I wonder, Nancy.'

And still I say nothing.

'And where should you think Bill was now, my dear, eh?' he says at last.

I don' know wot I say. I moan out some scarcely intelligible reply and push me face into the wood of the table.

'And the boy, too,' the old goat goes on. 'Poor leetle child,' he says. 'Left in a ditch, Nance, only think!'

I look up sudden-like.

'I do think!' I burst out. 'The child,' I exclaim, 'is better where he is than among us. And I hope the boy lies dead in the ditch and that his young bones rot there.'

'What!' Fagin cries.

'Aye, I do,' I say, meeting his gaze. 'I shall be glad to have him away from me eyes, and to know that the worst is over. I carnt bear to have him about me. The sight of him turns me against meself and all of you.'

'Pooh!' Fagin says scornfully. 'You're drunk, girl.'

'Am I?' Tears well up in me eyes. 'It's no fault of yours if I am not. You'd never have me anything else if you had your will, except now! My humour don' suit you, do it?'

'No, it does not!'

'Change it, then,' I respond with a bark of laughter.

'Change it?' Fagin exclaims.

He makes fists of his hands and pumps them furiously up and down. 'Listen to me, you old drab! Listen to me who with six words can strangle Sikes as surely as if I had his bull's throat between my fingers now. If he comes back and leaves that boy behind, if Sikes gets off free and, dead or alive, fails to restore that boy to me, murder him yourself and do it the moment he sets foot in this room or, mark my words, it will be too late!'

'Wot is all this?' I cry. 'What are you on about?'

'This!' Wild with rage, Fagin's foaming at the mouth. 'This! That boy's worth hundreds of pounds to me! Hundreds! And I'm to lose that, all through the whims of a drunken gang that I could whistle away the lives of. I'm to lose what chance threw me—and there's me bound to a born devil that has the power—the power—to—to—'

Panting for breath, he's begun to stutter. And in this instant, he checks his torrent of words and changes his whole attitude. Like a volcano gone cold, he is, all the fire gone out and dribbling wet mush. He shrinks into his chair and cowers. He trembles with apprehension that he's given away some hidden part of himself. It's got me right puzzled, it has.

After a short silence, he looks round, and seems satisfied to find me in the same listless mood from which he first roused me.

'Nancy, dear,' he croaks. 'Don't mind me, dear.'

'Don' worry me now, Fagin,' I murmur, raising me head. 'If Bill has not done it this time, he will another. He has done many a job for you, and will do many more when he can, and when he carnt he won', and so no more about that.'

'Regarding the boy, my dear?' The old goat rubs his dry flaky hands together, but he's nervous of me, now. Having said too much.

'The boy must take his chance with the rest,' I say, 'and I tell you again, I hope he's dead and out of harm's way, and out of yours. That is, if Bill comes to no harm. And if Toby got clear off, he's pretty sure to, for he's worth two of Toby any time.'

'And about what I was saying, my dear?' Fagin says slyly, keeping his mucousy eye upon me.

'You must say it all over again if it's anything you want me to do,' I tell him, and wave one arm in the air like I'm only half here. 'And if it is, you'd better wait till tomorrow. You put me up for a minute, you did, but now I'm stupid again.'

I lay me head down again on the table and close me eyes. And after a bit, Fagin gets up and leaves as quietly as he arrived.

The poor boy. Wot am I to do? How am I to save him? If he is still alive, that is.

I sit up abruptly. For a start, I can get off me backside and follow the old goat.

See, I am not drunk at all. I do admit to having a glass or two, but on the whole I am perfectly sober, merely pretending.

When I get outside, St Paul's tells me it is within an hour of midnight.The weather is dark and piercing cold. A sharp wind scours the streets and has cleared them of pedestrians, which makes keeping out of sight difficult. But Fagey doesn't loiter. The wind is behind him, blowing him trembling and shivering, and rudely on his way, and he don' suspect a thing.

He reaches the corner of his own street and pauses to fumble in his pocket for the door key, I think, when a dark figure steps out from a nearby entrance lying in deep shadow, and crosses the road and glides up to Fagey unsuspected. The man must say something, for the old goat turns in alarm. They converse and then Fagin unlocks the door, goes in, and the man follows. All in darkness.

This suits me. I hitch up me skirts and, quick as I can, bolt down the street. The door's still standing open, and I hear the man say from inside, 'It's as dark as the grave. Make haste. I hate this!'

I step in the doorway quickly and, as I do so, Fagey says from the end of the passage, 'Shut the door,' and I let it slam shut behind me with a loud bang.

'That wasn't my doing,' the other man says, pausing. 'The wind blew it to, or it shut of its own accord, one or t'other. Look sharp with the light, or I shall knock my brains out against something in this confounded hole.'

We wait, him and me—me keeping still as the dead—while Fagin descends the kitchen stairs and, after a short absence, returns with a lighted candle. He tells the man Toby Crackit is asleep in the backroom below, and the boys in the front one, and he leads the stranger up the stairs.

I follow, quiet as a church mouse.

Fagey says, 'We can say the few words we've got to say in here, my dear,' and a door opens on the first floor. 'And as there are holes in the shutters, and we never show lights to our neighbours, we'll set the candle on the stairs. There.'

Leaving the candle on the landing, the men enter the room, and I hear the creak of the sofa as the stranger flings himself upon it, and the scritching scoring of the armchair's legs upon the floor as Fagey draws it up.

Paused at the bottom of the flight of stairs, for some time I carnt hear nothing more than whispers, but I can hear the man is in a state of considerable agitation. I can also hear he speaks well, as if he has had an education.

Little by little, I manoeuvre meself up the stairs until, quite clearly now, I hear the man say, 'I tell you, it was badly planned. Why not have kept him here among the rest and made a sneaking, snivelling pickpocket of him at once?' Fagin says something in response but I carnt make it out.

I creep closer.

'Why?' the man says. 'Do you mean to say you couldn't have done it if you had chosen? Haven't you done it with other boys scores of times? If you had the patience for a twelvemonth or most, couldn't you have got him convicted and sent safely out of the kingdom, perhaps for life?'

I believe I know now about who they speak. Oliver.

'Whose turn would that have served?' Fagey asks.

'Mine,' replies the other man.

'But not mine,' Fagey says. 'When there are two parties to a bargain, it is only reasonable that the interests of both should be consulted, is it not, my good friend?'

'What then?' the stranger says sulkily.

'Look,' Fagey says, 'I saw it was not easy to train him to the business. He is not like the other boys in the same circumstances.'

'Curse him, no!' the man mutters. 'Or he would have been a thief long ago.'

'I had no hold upon him to make it worse,' Fagey goes on. 'His hand was not in. I had nothing to frighten him with—which we always must have in the beginning, or we labour in vain. What could I do? Send him out with the Dodger and Charley? We had enough of that at first. I trembled for us all.'

'*That* was not my doing,' the stranger says.

'No. Quite. And I don't quarrel with it now, because if it had never happened, you might never have clapped eyes upon the boy to notice him, and so led to the discovery that it was *him* you were looking for. Well, I did that. I got him back for you by means of the girl.' He pauses—he means me. 'But then, my dear, *she* begins to favour him—'

'Throttle the girl!' the stranger says. Me blood runs cold. I put me hand in front of me mouth in case I should cry out.

'Why,' Fagey goes on, 'we can't afford to do that just now. And, besides, that sort of thing is not in our way, or one of these days I might be glad to have it done. I know what these girls are, Monks'—*Monks!* This is the man's name!—'and as soon as the boy begins to harden, she'll care no more for him than for a block of wood. You want him made a thief? If he is alive, I can make him one from this time. And if—if—it's not likely, mind—but if the worst comes to the worst, and he is dead—'

'It's no fault of mine if he is!' the man named Monks interrupts. 'Mind that, Fagin!' he says. 'I had no hand in it. Anything but his death, I told you from the first. I won't shed blood. It's always found out, and haunts a man. If they shot him dead, I was not the cause, do you hear me? Fire this infernal den! What's that—?'

'What!' cries Fagin, and I hear him spring to his feet. 'Where?'

By degrees I have been edging up and up the stairs and I know as soon as Monks says it, I am too close.

'Yonder!' Monks cries. 'A shadow—I saw the shadow of a woman in a cloak and shawl pass along the wainscot like a breath!'

Silently and stealthily, like the ghost I can be, I slip back down. And by the time I hear them springing to their feet, I am easing meself out of the door. I close it softly behind me, and flee down the street.

Throttle the girl?

One of these days I might be glad to have it done? I know what these girls are? If he is alive, I can make him one from this time?

Arghh!

Me hands are clenched into fists. I am as angry as … As angry as … But I carnt find a thing to compare me feelings to. I jus' know I want to hit something, kick something, lash out … And the Lord help anyone who gets in me way tonight.

It is just as well it is after one and the streets are deserted. Just as well. For I think if I met another man coming t'other way I might jus' throttle *him*.

We'll soon see about that, Mr Fagin. And Mr Monks! I may not know you, Mr Monks, but I have heard of you and it ain't nothing but bad words.

CHAPTER TWENTY-NINE

Wot happened to Oliver weighs heavily on me mind. Though wot really weighs heavily on me mind is where the boy is now and who is taking care of him? Is he even alive? I must believe so, for Fagey has the newspaper report of 'a failed break-in at Chertsey', but which contains nothing of the boy. I must believe, then, that he has survived or the newspaper would've said.

I can see only one way to solve me dilemma: I must go there meself and find out the truth. But *when* am I to go? If I go now, there is the danger of Bill arriving back and not finding me here, which is taking an awfully big risk. But, on the other hand, Bill may be lying low and it may be days before he is back. Days in which I will go half-demented with worry for the boy.

I am half-demented already. I will only get worse as more time passes.

With that thought uppermost in me mind, I make a decision to set off at first light. I would go *now*, but it won' help me. The night, as I've said, is piercing cold. The icy wind scrubbing the streets clean of folk and trying its best to wheedle its way into any orifice, and whistling cheerful-like while it's about it. I have no option but to return to the crib and try to get some rest.

Up before light, I dress warmly. I force down some coffee, pack some bread and cheese into a red handkerchief and slip that into me pocket, then make me way quietly down the darkened stairs.

I follow the same route Bill and the boy would've taken, the one that passes the beasts at Smithfield, and I move quickly for the cold. By the time I pass Hyde Park corner and am on me way to Kensington, it's almost light and people are scurrying to work, their collars turned up, their coats firmly fixed about them. I part with some of me coins and get a lift on an empty horse-drawn cart and snuggle up against a heap of coarse sacks out of the wind behind the driver, and bite me lip and watch the great city of London, wreathed in smoke and fog, slowly disappear from view. If I weren' so beside meself with worry, this could be a nice little adventure, it could. We pass Kensington, Hammersmith, Chiswick, Kew Bridge, and Brentford, and although I see every one of them milestones, I don' know wot they say until the driver yells out their names like he has a duty to keep me informed of me whereabouts. At length, we pass a public house with a signboard depicting a coach and horses, a little way beyond which another road appears to turn off, and here the cart stops. By now it's about midday.

'Far as I'm going, miss,' the driver says.

I raise meself onto me shaky legs—it's that cold they've gone stiff under me—and look at me surroundings. The road is lonely, the clouds grey and swollen, and the wind moans through the trees. 'Which way to Chertsey?' I ask, reluctant to alight, and hanging onto the back of the driver's seat and stamping me feet.

'Thataway.' He points to the left with his whip. 'Then take a right-hand and walk for some time until you reach a bridge that'll lead you into Twickenham.'

'Thankee,' I say. I lower meself from the wagon and draw me cloak around me.

'Miss?'

I gaze back up at the driver and he tosses me coins back down to me. 'Looks like you could use 'em,' he says.

Grateful for any mercies, I pocket me savings and head off in the direction he's given. I find the bridge that leads me into Twickenham, and walk on until I reach another town in which I see, written up in pretty large letters, the name of the town, beginning with a H. There's another public house, this one bearing the sign of the Red Lion and looking too posh for the likes of me, and I keep on by the river. The current is moving swiftly and making a pleasant sound and, across the water, a man is working with a horse and plough, a scattering of black birds following behind, squawking one to another.

By and by, I meet an old woman coming t'other way, balancing a heavy load of something in a basket upon her head.

'Excuse me, love,' I say, 'but where can I find a place to eat?'

She says something, but her teeth are so blackened and her accent so countrified I have no idea wot she's on about, and I must stare vacantly, for she points over her shoulder. In the distance, further ahead, I see another public house with a crooked sign board. She pats me hand, nods at me and sends me on me way, and I think that people in the country must be altogether kinder and more tolerant than those in the city.

The kitchen is an old, low-roofed room, with a great beam across the middle of the ceiling and thatch for a roof, and benches with high backs to them by the fire. Several rough-looking men in smock-frocks are seated there, drinking and smoking. They glance around at me when I come in, but I slip into a seat in a corner and pay them no further heed.

I ask for whatever's cheapest, and a man brings me a glass of warm ale, and plonks a plate of cold mutton down in front of me and soon, wot with the warmth of the fire, the food, and me weary bones, I am close to falling asleep. And I think I do doze off for a bit. But I carnt afford to, and I get to me feet, settle me bill and, drawing me cloak around me, head out into the evening gloom. I walk as if I am sleep-walking, pinching me cloak tight around me to ward off the teeth of the wind, and putting one foot in front of the other. And all I can think of is Oliver, and wot Bill might do to me if he knew where I was.

I been walking a while when I hear the clip-clop of horses's hooves behind me, and I turn to see a wagon drawing up level. 'Get in, love,' a voice says, 'it isn't a night to be out and about.' In the dark, I can jus' make out the features of one of them frock-smocked farmers that were smoking in front of the fire, and he reaches down a hand and hauls me up onto the seat. 'Get behind me, out o' the wind,' he says. 'Where you going?'

'Chertsey,' I say.

'Well, I ain't going that far, but I'll as take you as far as I am, all right?'

I mumble me thanks, and sink down behind him onto the dray. The night is like the inside of a closet, and a damp mist rises from the river and the marshy ground and spreads itself over the dreary fields. All is gloomy and black. The driver don' say another word—I reckon he's as sleepy as me—and I watch the gaunt trees go by and the branches waving grimly to and fro as if they would have me wave back to them.

We come, finally, to a church and the clock striking the hour of eight, and light in the ferry-house window opposite streaming across the road, and showing me a dark yew tree with graves beneath it. There is the sound of water falling not far off, and the leaves of the old tree stir gently, and it seems like a pleasant enough place to lay a dead body. And I think we must be going to stop here, but we go on again, the horses' hooves striking the ground rhythmically.

We come to another town where all is silent and sleeping, and then we are once more upon the lonely wind-blown road. A few miles further on, the cart stops and the farmer tells me this is as far as he is going. 'You'll find naught but mud and darkness, and cold open wastes now, until you reach Shepperton, and after Shepperton it's not much further to Chertsey. But if I were you, lass, I'd take shelter in that there barn'—he rises up in the cart and points over a hedge—'it's me own, and I don't object to you spending the night there, and head off again at first light.'

'Thankee,' I mumble. 'Much obliged,' I say. And he reaches out a hand again and helps me dismount from the cart. 'Bless you, sir,' I say. But he does not respond, which I take for not knowing wot to say.

I scramble over the low hedge, and see the lights of a farmhouse in the distance where he must be heading, and they light me way until I come to a great shadowy thing that must be the barn, and fumble to gain entry. Inside, I stagger up against wot feels like a pile of hay, and fall to me knees. Then, curling meself up into a ball, I try to sleep, and for once it comes easy and I know no more.

In the morning, I am awoken by a young girl staring at me, and it takes a bit to recall where I am and why. It seems the farmer has sent her, for she places a steaming mug of tea upon the ground. She tells me there's breakfast in the farmhouse if I want, and also a privy and fresh water, but I don' much like the way she looks at me—like I'm vermin or something—and arter I've had me tea, I move on. Only later does it occur to me that the straw and such that's in me hair would've been giving me a wild and half-crazed look.

The farmer ain't wrong about them cold and open wastelands and the dank smell of water. The mist loiters about until I feel I am trudging through a dream, on and on, with the occasional cow lowing. Finally, I reach Shepperton and get through, and then the weather clears and turns into a sunny day. Cold though. But I am ever so grateful to see the sun.

Great big stretches of water lie alongside Chertsey, and I cross a bridge over a river that leads into the village, and I wonder if it's possible that this river is the same one I see every day in London town? I dawdle for a bit, looking down into the water, wondering how I'm to find out which house is where the break-in occurred, without it looking suspicious-like. But then a horse and carriage comes over the bridge and I follow it with me eye, and see it pull up in front of a house standing alone and surrounded by a wall, and someone gets out of the carriage and goes into the house. I walk over there, and find a hedge from where I can observe both the carriage and the house, and sit down in front of it and wait. And it ain't long before an elderly gent carrying a doctor's bag of sorts emerges, gets back into the carriage, and off it goes.

Which solves one dilemma—I now know there's someone poorly in the house—but it don' exactly tell me whether it's Oliver.

Before I know wot I am about, I find meself pushing against the garden gate of the house. It is unlocked and swings open upon its hinges. I slip across the grass, climb the steps and knock faintly at the door. I have time to register that the house has two levels, is neat and tidy—the doorknob is polished brass and no leaves are scattered about—and that there is a pot of pink geraniums in the entranceway, and then me entire heart begins to knock, not faintly but heavily against me ribs. Wot am I doing!

I hear footsteps advancing and dogs barking, and I cling onto one of the pillars of the little porch for support and courage. Then, the door is opened and the faces of two men appear around it. One is middle-aged, whiskered and jowly, and could be a butler of sorts, and the other is younger and more sprightly.

'Yes?' they say in unison, then look one from t'other and widen the door.

I curtsey with as much charm as I can muster, given me knocking heart (and knees), and say, 'I beg your pardon for disturbing, kind sirs. But you wouldn' be needing help of any kind, would you? A maid, or such-like?'

The younger one gazes up at the older. 'Mr Giles, are we needing anybody extra? What with our sitiwation and the boy and his being poorly?'

'I don't believe so, Brittles,' Mr Giles, the jowly butler, says. 'But I will check with Miss Maylie. Would you wait a moment, please, miss,' he says to me, and he disappears from sight and leaves me with Brittles. Brittles, it must be said, can scarce take his eyes from me face. I don' know what it is with him.

'Wot boy?' I ask, softly.

He points upstairs. 'One that came with the break-in, miss. One that we apprehended. I believe his name is Oliver.'

'And how is the boy?' I ask, not believing me luck. 'You said he were poorly.'

'He's been seen by the doctor, miss. And I believe he will be arright. He only needs rest and 'cuperation.'

'I see,' I say. 'And whose house is this, if I may ask?'

'Oh, you may ask, miss. It's Mrs Maylie's. And Miss Maylie, she lives here as well—' He breaks off, for Mr Giles reappears.

'Brittles!' the butler says, warning-like. 'What are you doing?'

'Oh, I'm only a telling about the boy—'

'That's what I mean!'

Mr Giles shakes his head and rolls his eyes, as if Brittles is beyond hope.

'We don' require the services of anyone at the moment, thank you, miss,' he says, and shuts the door. Firmly. In me face.

Clearly, he is concerned that Brittles will tell me even more, given half the chance.

Still, it warms me heart knowing the boy is somewhere in a room not far above the top of me head. It warms me heart knowing I have wot I need, wot I have come for. A weight is lifted from me shoulders. The boy is poorly, but alive.

Oliver is alive.

CHAPTER THIRTY

All right, then. After a long and tiring journey, I am back at the crib in the early hours of the following day. And although me mind still dwells on Oliver, it is altogether lighter. For now, I believe he is safe where he is. Of course, once Fagey finds out where he is he will no longer be safe. But by then, things might've changed. For I have no doubt that once Oliver is well, he will be trying to find the elderly gentleman wot looked after him before.

I manage to get a couple of hours of sleep, before I get up. Go out. I have things to do.

This time o' the morning, the inside of a church is icy cold, but it's silent and peaceful, too. I slide into a hard wooden pew near the back and look up at them particles of dust drifting down in the pearly light. How far away the pitched roof is. So high it's almost out of focus. How insignifican' I feel. How humble.

And I think how the space between me and the roof beams could be a heavenly one. And if only I could rise above everything and float up, I would be right hallowed and might be a better person for it, and know wot decisions to make … But instead I grovel here on earth, trying to make sense of things.

A clattering noise startles me clean out of me daydreams. An elderly woman is down the front with her maidservant. She's been on her knees, praying, I believe, but has dropped her walking stick as she rose, for the maid is retrieving it and handing it back to her. They turn to walk up the aisle, which is when they see me, and the old lady stops and spends an inordinately long time staring at me. Then she glances around agitatedly as if looking for someone—probably someone to report me to—and, finding no-one, takes her maid's arm and advances.

Oh, Lord!

I get up to escape, but I'm caught between two forces, for approaching from the opposite direction is the priest. I sit down again and slide into the furthest corner of the pew, try to make meself invisible. Then I have a better idea and, fumbling for the cushion, go down on me knees, and pretend to pray. Well, I do pray, actually. I pray the old woman leaves me alone.

Something rustles past upon the flagstones, and I squint through half-closed eyes to see the priest hastening down to meet the old lady and her maid.

'It's outrageous,' she says. She don' even attempt to whisper. 'It shouldn't be allowed!'

The sound in churches is very good, you know that, don' you? They are built special that way.

'M'lady, forgive me,' the priest murmurs, 'but why should she not be allowed? Her soul,' he goes on, 'more than anyone else's, needs to be saved. Would you not agree?'

'Her sort doesn't have a soul!'

'I don't know about that, m'lady—' he says, hedging.

Spineless man!

'Well, I do,' she declares, banging her stick upon the floor. Which begs the question—how does she know about me sort? 'I don't want to see it again. Is that understood?'

'Yes, m'lady,' the priest says. He bends his head and puts his hands together in a praying gesture.

The old crone and her maid proceed. They stop at the end of me pew. Where I am still on me knees, praying frantic-like. 'Jesus, Mary, mother and child,' I mutter.

'Filth,' she says. 'Naught but filth.'

In spite of everything, in spite of me being accustomed to her kind, I feel meself reddening behind me closed palms. I feel meself turning ashamed and despairing.

Wot hope is there for me? Wot hope is there for Oliver, for Bill, and the Dodger? Wot hope is there for anyone never given an opportunity to rise above their situation?

She sweeps out, her stick tap-tapping on the floor, and I stay where I am, try to pull meself together.

'I am sorry, my child,' the priest murmurs, as he passes by.

*

I undertook to keep an eye on Mr Rufus, and I have done nothing for days, being otherwise engaged, and by the time I get to the ramshackle crib, the day is beginning to warm up. It is, after all, spring, and the first small pink and white blossoms are beginning to sprout from them trees like coy little newborns. But I don' have a spring in me step, I don' feel inspired by the change in them seasons although, admittedly, the coming of summer does make me life easier. It's not only the warmth, but also that men seem to have a renewed urge to get out and about, to gird their loins, you might say, though I prefer the idea of them having renewed urges. Ha ha.

A glow is behind the curtains of the last tenement so I knows someone is home, and I mount the stairs with due caution. It seems a lifetime ago that I found them fox cubs in the shrubbery just here. I wonder wot happened to them, whether they made it out alive, or whether they made it out alive only to be hunted and torn to shreds by dogs. Oh, God, forgive me. Me mind is not right. It is on the path of self-destruction.

I edge right up to the door. I am taking a chance, for if someone opens the door I have no time to hide.

I perch on the threshold and the light that comes from under the door flickers, indicating someone inside walking about.

I duck behind the rhododendrons and sit tight, pretend to the passers-by that I am waiting for someone, and when Mr Rufus eventually emerges, he turns to lock the door behind him and walks off and does not notice me. He is not suspicious like me, Bill, Fagey and the boys are all trained to be—looking here, there and everywhere, every time we go somewhere—and having eyes in the backs of our heads.

Today, Mr Rufus walks purposefully, and I follow as before at a discreet distance, and again he heads for The Horse & Groom and disappears inside.

I wander up the alley at the side of the establishment, deliberating how to spy on him since I cannot enter the place, not without drawing unwanted attention to meself. The alley is murky, muddy, and reeks, but it's quiet and out-of-the-way, and I lean against the wall. And while I am thinking, I overhear snippets of muttered conversation floating from out the window that's above me head.

Something about a horse race … *ten to one* … that's the odds … And something about wot's going to be used for blunt … *I need coin, my man*!

And standing there, I start to wonder if this is perhaps how Mr Rufus's father lost his fortune. Aunt Maud talked of his parents not being *prudent*—I think that means not looking after their money. Was Mr Rufus Senior a gambler, perhaps? And does Mr Rufus gamble, too?

I wander back down to the front of The Horse & Groom and, as I pass the front door, I peer in, but I carnt see nobody. I cross the road, then, find a sunny patch against a doorway and prepare to wait. Two things I am good at in me line of work and one of them is waiting. And in due course, Mr Rufus appears. He gazes up the street as if he is deliberating whether to hail a horse and carriage or not, and then he pulls on his gloves, and sets off, swinging his cane in one hand.

We walk for some time, heading north, passing near me old place of residence in Whitechapel. Then, jus' when I think we must be going all the way to The Angel and Islington, Mr Rufus disappears into a burial ground! It is named some word beginning with *B*. I pause outside and, after a bit, follow again. I need to keep me distance.

The graveyard is a lonely, wild place. The grass is overgrown, the pathways criss-crossed with knotted roots, and the tombstones blackened and stained with mould. Many of the headstones are like drunken men tottering on their feet, but they do offer me protection. The area is open so that, from where I stand half-hidden behind a tablet, I can watch Mr Rufus as he roams further afield. He knows where he is going, that much I can say. He pauses at last, his back to me, and stands for an age looking down upon someone's grave and I see him put one hand to his face, and wonder if he's wiping away tears. Finally, he moves away. He does not return the way he came. He takes a sideways route and disappears from view.

The gravestone is fairly new and the words on it, simple. I mean, they are three lines. I believe I see the word *Rufus,* but I am not convinced. I gaze around to see if there's someone I can ask for help and, out beyond one of them gates, I see a lad selling flowers from a basket. 'Can you read?' is wot I first ask before I give him a coin. 'Of course, miss,' he says indignant-like, as if I must be stupid if I carnt. I take no notice and lead him back to the grave.

'*Juliet Walker*,' he reads out, '*dearly beloved wife of Redfern, and mother of Rufus*. There, miss,' he says. 'Will that be all?'

I walk home in a daze. This is nothing more than a man mourning his mother. Now, how many men do you know that regularly visit their mothers's graves? Not a lot, I warrant. And it starts me thinking that Mr Rufus is not your average man. It's touching, it is, his behaviour, causing me to feel teary. And it all brings back to me how I never had a mother, a mother that cared, a mother I could have loved, and who loved me in return, and I carnt help thinking how lucky Mr Rufus is. Yes, *lucky*.

He has had a mother, and I believe she were with him for most of his life. He has loved her, but more importantly, he has known her love. She has loved him. This, most of all.

*

I am as hungry as a growing boy who's caught a whiff of roast meat when I near home, but there ain't any food. This I know. So I go to The Cripples to see if Barney is back and whether I can beg, borrow or steal something off him.

Barney won' talk to me. He pats one side of his *dose* with one finger and glances away. But he does bring me a plate of onion soup and a crust of bread.

'Wot do you know?' I whisper.

He shakes his head. 'Bill,' he says. 'Midder Sikes,' he says—in case there's a misunderstanding. But that's all. And wot I am to infer by that I do not know.

CHAPTER THIRTY-ONE

Wot I was intended to infer is that Bill's on his way home.

For the next thing that happens is he arrives in wot feels like the middle of the night, and hauls me out of bed by throwing back the covers and yanking on me cammie.

'Where you been?' I mutter, only half coherent. 'Are you all right?' and 'Wot happened to the boy?' I ask, remembering in spite of me dazed state that I am meant to know nothing. I push the hair out of me eyes, hug meself for warmth.

'No time for idle chatter. We got to go, Nance,' he tells me, moving around. He's at the mantelpiece sweeping everything on it—including the little copper jug—into a large portmanteau, then peering over his shoulder at the door like he's expecting the Grim Reaper. His face is haggard and gaunt in the light of the dying fire, his smoky eyes deep in his skull like he ain't eaten for days, like he ain't had a drop for nights.

'Now! Move your arse, woman,' he says, glaring at me.

'Bill,' I say, going to him and asking again. 'Wot happened? Are you all right?'

'No, I ain't bleeding all right,' he spits out, 'but we ain't got time to talk about it. We have to go.'

Where we might be going at this time of the night, I have only a vague idea, but I know better than to argue. Arter I've dressed, the first thing I do is locate me pessary and slip it into me cammie. It's me most valuable possession. Arter the amethyst necklace, of course. But I ain't brought that home, see. I left that, nicely hidden, at the Mayfair crib—

'No crockery,' Bill says, finding me in the kitchen and interrupting me train of thought, which isn't wot he thinks it is. 'We ain't got time for that, it's too cumbersome—'

'All right,' I say, 'so just me clothes?' I glance at him. He looks altogether less of a man, as if whatever happened out there has taken the stuffing out of him. 'Bill?' I say gently, moving to him. But he pushes me away.

'Later,' he says. 'I ain't feeling too good now.'

*

Where we end up is no great distance from our former lodgings, but in appearance not nearly so desirable. I have stayed here afore, but only once or twice when we had to urgently vacate t'other crib for one reason of security or another, the least talked about the better, and it is a mean and ill-furnished room of limited size. It is lit only by one small window in the shelving roof, and abuts a close and dirty lane. A total absence of comfort, no linen or such, completes the picture. And it is as cold as a witch's bum when we creep up the stairs in the dark, Bill lugging the portmanteau, and push upon the door.

Bill glances around, wild-eyed. I think he's half afraid others might've taken up residency in his absence, but once he's drawn a candle from his pocket and lit it, and assured himself it's only him and me, he shuts the door and bolts it quick smart.

In the meantime, I have found a stack of kindling and am engaged in getting the fire going, and next time I turn to Bill he has lain down on the bed and seems to have near fainted from exhaustion. At any rate, he is out to it. I cover him with a raggedy quilt that I find, but there is little point in me trying to sleep.

I sit in front of the fire and think about how I'm meant to be turning up at Aunt Maud's soon, with information on Mr Rufus, and how I need to find Bill some sustenance when I don' have any blunt. (Well, I do, but it's *my* blunt and I am reluctant to part with it.) And I think about how much I want—*need*—information of Oliver, but must tread carefully. Bill is already jealous. He knows I have feelings for the lad. He'd be stupid if he didn'.

By the time the grey day has padded into the room, I know Bill's not well. He has cried out in his sleep, and when I've gone to wake him, to hold him close, he's been delirious. Muttering, shouting at one point. One minute he's been hot and sweaty, perspiration pooling in the hollow of his neck, and the next he's been all a-tremble with cold, calling out. And when I've tried to placate him, he's pushed me away and cried, 'Get orff me, get orff!' And not responded to anything I ask of him.

As soon as the day is upon us, I set out for Fagin, but he's a wily one. He's not where he's supposed to be, and neither is he at t'other crib. Or at The Cripples. And Barney, while he's there, ain't answering any of me questions. I carnt find any of the boys—Dodger, Charley—neither, which is when I begin to suspect they're all lying low. See, they don' know that I know where Oliver is, and none of them—except for Dodger—has got the courage to tell me wot they do know. *Oh, Oliver!*

But me first obligation is to Bill. He needs sustenance. On me way back from seeking out Fagey, I go down to old Mother Hubbard and ask her sweetly if she will put it on the tab, but she pulls a much scribbled-upon slate out from under a heap of other slates and thrusts it in front of me nose. 'This here,' she says, 'is Mr Sikes's. Do you see how long it is? Do you see how I've run outta space to write anything more? Do you understand wot that means, sweetheart?' She's being sarcastic, of course. I ain't her sweetheart, never have been—she tolerates me. She tolerates me because of Bill.

All right, I think. Needs must when the devil drives. I turn away to the wall, dig down deep into me cammie, and turn back to her flourishing a crisp note. Her eyes grow big.

'Phwoar,' she says, putting her hands on her ample hips. 'Is that yours, or someone else's? Where'd you get that, girl?'

'Never you mind,' I say. 'Now can I have some o' the sheep heads, please?'

She takes the note out of me fingers and begrudgingly obliges, bringing me back a steaming dish. 'I ain't got no change,' she tells me.

I know she's lying. 'Course she's got change, but I ain't going to waste time arguing. 'Well, put it against wot he owes. Let me see you do that,' I say, and watch while she rubs out some figures with the heel of her hand.

'There,' she says, more kindly, 'now get along before that lot's cold.'

Back at the crib, I try feeding Bill. I have some success. He has some mouthfuls, but then he pushes the plate away, almost spilling the lot on himself, and falls back onto the bedding. Disappears to some place I carnt reach him.

He's hot to the touch and ain't smelling too wholesome and I build up the fire, then strip him of wot gear I can and wash him down with a damp sponge. I cover him with his great, dirty, white coat, draw up the quilt, and soon he's breathing heavily through his mouth once more, like you do when your *dose* is blocked.

Time for me to get going.

*

I'm on me way when I hear someone calling me name.

'Nancy? Nance!'

I pause and peer across the street, over the drivers' whips egging on the horses and cutting the air, between the barrow boys with their potatoes, and avoiding the eye of the begging woman with the withered leg on the corner, and jus' stepping back in time from the sooty muck spraying up from them carriage wheels.

The Dodger is standing t'other side of the street, gazing back at me. His cap is pulled low over his face, his hands in his capacious pockets, and he looks downright forlorn.

'Wot?' I yell.

Before I can think how to put him off, he's darted across the street, narrowly missing a wagon of coal and receiving a tongue lashing from its driver.

'Hallo,' he says breathlessly, bobbing up against me.

I carnt help smiling. 'Wot?' I say again. 'I got places to be, sweetheart,' I tell him.

He looks crestfallen.

'Wot's up?' I say, more kindly.

'The old goat's mad as hops,' he says.

'And …?'

He glances away. 'You couldn' … '

'Couldn' wot? Spit it out, Dodge.'

'Lend me a kiss and give me a coin,' he says cheekily, grinning sudden-like. He's like me, see. Hard to keep down.

I smile. 'Come here,' I say.

I pull him to me and give him a smacker on the cheek, which turns his skin pink and makes them passers-by smile, too. 'Watch out, son,' one says. 'She's on to you!'

Reaching into me cammie, I pull out a piece of blunt, and slip it to him. 'Here.'

It's more than I'd normally hand over, but I'm feeling kindly, and he raises his eyebrows. Kind of like I do when I'm taken aback.

'Thankee, Nance,' he says. Relief is in his face, and I wonder wot bother he's got himself into now with Fagin.

'Tell you wot,' I add, jus' remembering, 'you couldn' look in on Bill for me, could you? He's not up to dick.'

He nods. Waits as if there's something further he needs to say. But like I said, I'm in a hurry.

'Got to go,' I say, blowing him a kiss, and turning away.

'Be careful, Nance,' he calls arter me.

I'm halfway down the road when I remember I should've asked after Oliver! That's why the Dodger were waiting—patient-like—for I should've asked after Oliver—and he'll be wondering why I didn'.

Oh, Lord! Two people in me life now I half forgot about! What is wrong with me?

I did get up to some larks with the Dodger when we were both still small, I can tell you. One time, soon after he arrived and I ain't had much success workwise, to the degree we were going to bed hungry and Fagey knocked me down the stairs shouting that I were idle and lazy, which I objected to, but I digress. One time, I took Dodger out with me. Fagey warned me to treat him with caution, and advised him to follow me lead, until we knew each other's ways and I knew wot he were good at and wot he were not.

We strode along—see, it's no good sauntering; sauntering only brings you suspicion—anyways, we were like two boys who had a purpose or an errand to run. The Dodger was dressed like any other urchin, but on account of the day being a breezy, chilly one, he kept complaining of the cold. Fagey didn' have anything to give him to wear except for one of his own coats, which the Dodger would've drowned in.

'Nick a coat, then,' I said at last when I were tired of his whining.

'All right, I will!' he declared, and paused outside an apparel shop of sorts where coats and jackets were hanging from hooks on a railing outside. 'Be prepared to leg it,' he whispered.

I thrust me hands into me pockets and leant back on me heels and waited. A gent, a respectable-looking but portly personage attired in a fancy cravat and dresscoat, was at the front end, the part nearest the shop entrance, and was going through the jackets, pulling them from them hooks and holding them out for size. All of a sudden-like, I see the coat in his hands being wrenched from his grasp, and him being yanked off his feet. I turn to see the Dodger disappearing up the street with a string of coats following behind him. All connected one to the other on string they were, for the very purposes of preventing those like the Dodger pilfering them. Next thing, the gentleman has fallen face-first, flat upon the coat in his hands, his not inconsiderable weight causing the string to snap. And the Dodge is gone, fleeing with all them coats flagging behind him. Only now, some of them coats are being grabbed at by people in the street, on account of the shopkeeper—a man in a waistcoat with a bevy of pins decorating the front—appearing in the doorway, shouting, and gesticulating. 'Stop thief! Stop thief!'

Where am I? I am helping the elderly gent to his feet, and asking after his health and at the same time putting me hand in his pocket and lifting his handkerchief, but looking concerned, and dusting off his front, and telling him that the young of today are not to be trusted. No, sir, the young of today are not to be trusted!

So that first day Dodger were out with me, he got his trademark coat that falls to his heels and has the sleeves folded back several times over. He also pilfered a soft cap. He was in the habit, whenever we were out and about, of pulling the caps off the heads of smaller boys and tossing them places for fun, and so quick was he that when the little 'uns turned, he would gaze at them innocently and say, 'And good morning to you, too, young master,' and doff an imaginary cap.

I believed *I* was going to be the one teaching him things, and instead it were the other way around.

I wish I could tarry and talk some more about the Dodger and me, and some of the scrapes we got up to when we were little, but I got to move on.

*

Mr Rufus is waiting for me in the afore-arranged place. Where we usually meet, near the ramshackle crib. I turn the corner, hitch me skirts to dodge a little chimneysweeper as black as the Ace of Spades, only the whites of his eyes and them pale moons of fingernails showing, and see Mr Rufus waiting outside the door of the carriage. He carnt keep still, that one. He's got his cane in one hand and is tapping it on the cobbles and glancing in me direction. But he ain't see me yet. I have an opportunity to study him from afar.

He is a handsome man. I carnt say it too many times. The curly, cinnamon-coloured hair, the deep-brown eyes, the way he holds himself—and yet these are nothing, really, against the man I know when we are abed together. His gentleness, his quiet passion, his desire to pleasure me as much as himself—these are the things I value about him.

Mr Rufus sees me now and raises his hand in greeting, and I hasten me footsteps. And when I reach him, me cheeks flushed from hurrying, he says, 'Ah, there you are, Nancy,' as if he hasn' been impatiently waiting, and he smiles that smile that reaches his eyes.

How happy that makes me.

When we are seated in the carriage—he always sits across from me so he can look at me, I believe—the first thing he does is lean forwards, put his hand over one of mine, and say, 'Please tell me you can stay the night?'

'I can,' I say, and he breaks into another smile.

*

Mr Rufus accompanies me inside to greet Aunt Maud. I smile mutely and do me curtsey.

'Miss Titania,' she says, nodding her silvery head. She gives her nephew her hand. 'Rufus, how nice to see you.'

She asks him something about his club, but it sounds as if she is being polite, is all. She don' really want to know whether he will get supper there or not. Then she tells him, in her forthright way, to get going for we—she means me and her—don' have long together. She don' beat about the bush, this one. And as soon as he is on his way out and his back is to us, she gives me an exaggerated wink, which almost makes me laugh out loud. I believe she is taking pleasure in the little game of deceit we have going on.

Fortunately, he does not glance back at us as Foxley lets him out.

I feel bad for deceiving him.

But I believe I am doing the correct thing. That it will all be right in the end. Me instinct tells me this.

Me instinct better not be wrong!

Aunt Maud instructs me to sit, and sends Foxley away to fetch the refreshments. All as per usual.

'Now, my child,' she says, as I perch on the sofa. 'What do you have to tell me? Have you discovered anything?'

I say nothing. I twirl one finger in the air, then put it across me lips. 'Foxley?' I whisper.

She waves a hand. 'You need not concern yourself there. I can trust him with anything. You will have noticed that I do not have a maid, or a companion. Foxley has been with me since I was a child, and he was not much more than a child himself.'

'I see,' I say. I had thought as much.

Aunt Maud looks expectantly at me. The fingers of one hand tap softly upon the armrest, making them rings jingle.

'To be fair,' I say, 'I ain't found out much at all. In all truthfulness, I don' think you have anything to be concerned about. There's nothing secretive going on.'

'But how does he spend his day? Where does he go?' she blurts out. 'What does he do?'

'Nothing much. He goes to an establishment called The Horse & Groom most mornings for breakfast.' I pause here, but decide I ain't going to tell her about the possible gambling until I have proof. 'One time I saw him with a bunch of papers at his side and a pen in his hand, making notations, but I don' know wot that's about. And yesterday,' I go on, 'he went to visit his mother's grave in B … B …' I stop, hoping she will fill in the rest, and she does.

'Bunhill Fields,' she says. 'He was awfully fond of her,' she says and gazes away as if recalling memories of her sister-in-law.

We play cards for a while, then. In silence. Well, I am silent, mute, in character. Aunt Maud occasionally says things like, 'Play a heart, would you, Miss Titania? We'll see about that!'

She seems altogether more at ease with me. It makes me heart glad, it does. In me lifetime, I have not known many older women and most of them wot I have known, like old Mother Hubbard, are not particularly nice to me. I know it's on account of wot I do.

But strange that other women should be so uppity regarding me profession. You'd think they'd be grateful, wouldn't you? I mean, there I am, slaving away to make their lives easier.

'You know the story of Titania, don't you?' Aunt Maud asks.

'Yes,' I whisper. 'Mr Rufus told me.' I pause, uncertain of whether I really want to know the answer to my question. 'But wot happens to the boy, to the changeling?'

'They, Oberon and Titania, fight over him,' Aunt Maud says airily, putting down a card.

'Who's Oberon?'

'Titania's husband. He's the king of all the fairies. Oberon wants the boy—'

'He does?'

'Yes.'

'And does he get him?'

'Eventually. But not without playing a trick on Titania—'

'A trick? What sort of trick?'

'He gives her a potion while she's asleep and, when she wakes, she falls in love with the first thing she sees, which happens to be a man with the head of a donkey—' She breaks off. 'It becomes very complicated after that,' she tells me, peering at her hand.

I put down a card, but I'm not even looking at wot I've put down and Aunt Maud says, 'Ha!' and trumps it.

'Tell me wot happens to the changeling, to the boy, please? Does he survive?'

'Oh, yes.'

'He does?' I breathe out.

'Yes.' She looks at me sharply with her bulbous eyes. 'Why? Why are you so interested in the boy?'

I shake my head. 'No matter,' I say.

The changeling survives.

I know there must be more to this story, to the play, but I don' want to know anything further. It might turn out to be so much like me own life that I carnt bear it.

When I hear footsteps on the outside stairs indicating Mr Rufus has returned, I reach across the table, put me hand on Aunt Maud's arm, and tilt me head towards the door.

'Oh,' she says, and seems disappointed that our time together has come to an end. She peers hastily at the cards in her hand, slaps down a King of Clubs, and juts her hairy chin out at me. She does like to win, does Aunt Maud.

The dear little gold clock takes that moment to decide to strike, and I realise I ain't thought about how much I would like to have one of Aunt Maud's rings. I ain't reflected on the clock, or the *bambino*, or considered exploring the house for possible artefacts I could lift. Or debated whether the house is something I should tell Bill about. Not for the entire duration, either. Not, in fact, for some time.

Wot is happening to me!

Fagey would say I am losing me touch, and he'd be right.

CHAPTER THIRTY-TWO

Things are uneasy between me and Mr Rufus in the carriage. Or, rather, I am awkward with him. I want to tell him wot I have done—spoken to Aunt Maud. But I must not.

I have also begun to worry about Bill. Wot if he should wake, miraculously be better, and not find me by his side? He will half kill me when I get home. And wot of Oliver? *The changeling.* Is he even still alive? And if he is alive, how am I to get him out of his predicament?

All this talk with Aunt Maud, which is wrong, is making me nervous. And when I get edgy, I think of all the issues—and I mean *all*—that could go wrong, that have gone wrong, that I made mistakes in the past with. It's like quicksand—the more you struggle, the worse it is, the deeper you sink—

'Penny for them?' Mr Rufus looks at me with concern, and how long he has been looking at me for is anybody's guess.

He sits forwards, runs one hand through his hair, lifts the tails of his jacket from under him and reaches for me cold hands with his own warm ones. 'What's the matter, Nancy? You look like you've seen a ghost.'

I want to say that if I have seen a ghost, that spectre is me! But I carnt. I carnt say anything. I am afraid if I open me mouth everything will come out. *Everything.*

'Nancy?' he says again, softly.

I bite down hard on me lip and stare out of the window. Blurred forms and shapes bump through the night and muffled cries echo. The carriage sways, rumbles beneath me, and the soft lights of the gas lamps go by and flash upon Mr Rufus's face. Lighting his features like he is some kind of noble being. Darkness. Then light. Then darkness again. This is like me own life, I think. I am in the dark when I am not with him. And I know that if I have to look at him, look into his gentle, kind eyes, it will be the undoing of me.

I think of Oliver and the hard nubbles of his shoulders and the softness within the boy, and how I told you I were as taut as a skein of wool and if he pulled at the thread it would be the unravelling of me, and I think to meself that this has begun. The unravelling has begun—

'Nancy.'

Mr Rufus touches me face, turns it towards his, towards his dark eyes and the shine within them, the shine of kindness. And perhaps even love? And I have to look into his eyes.

God strike me dead, but I carnt look away any longer!

And then I am crying. Sobbing. In his arms.

He is kissing me face and kissing away the tears, and saying, 'There, there,' like I am a child.

He don' ask me why I am crying. He don' ask me at all. Not then. Not later when we lie in bed together, folded up in each other. Not when he wakes in the night and finds me unable to sleep and holds me, snuggling me head under his chin. 'Nancy, Nancy,' he murmurs, 'what am I to do with you?'

'Tell me a story, please?' I whisper.

'A story?'

'Wot happened to them little fox cubs?'

'Ahh,' he says. 'That's the mother in you coming out, wanting to know—'

'The mother? I ain't no mother—'

'I know that, Nancy. But if you were … If you were a mother. Because, as a matter of fact, I think you'd make a fine mother. You have a caring nature.'

'Do I, now?' I say, sarcasm in me voice.

'Why is it,' he says, thoughtfully, stroking me hair away from me face, 'that you cannot accept a compliment gracefully?

'Do you know why I think it is?' he goes on, when I don' reply.

I shake me head.

'I think it's because nobody has ever given you compliments before and you don't know how to respond when they do. Would I be right?'

'I expect so, sir. You're pretty much right about everything else, ain't you?'

'Don't flatter me, Nancy.'

'I'm not, sir. I'm simply telling the truth.'

'Is that so?'

'Mr Rufus?' I look up at his dark eyes.

'Yes, Nancy?'

'Them foxes, please. What happened to the cubs?'

He shakes his head. 'You don't want to know,' he tells me.

'Why, is it bad?'

'You could say that. They never stood a chance. No mother, no father. Born in the wrong place at the wrong time,' he says, and I think to meself he could easily be talking about me.

'I see,' I say.

He studies me in the dark, and I believe he knows he could be talking about me. 'How do you usually go back to sleep?' he asks.

'I don't.'

He leans over me then, and kisses me gently on the mouth. And the Lord help me, but I respond.

'There,' he murmurs, 'that's one way we can get you back to sleep. Now lie quietly,' he says, his mouth working its way down me neck.

There are men who blather a great deal, but in the end do very little, and there are men who speak very little, but achieve a great deal. This man with his head between me bosoms is, I believe, one of the latter.

*

In the morning, I am awake afore Mr Rufus. I shift me head on the pillow to look at him and his eyes are closed, and while he ain't snoring—I ain't heard him snore, he's too handsome to snore—his chest rises and falls as if he's in a deep sleep.

I indulge meself and lie for a bit and think about the fox cubs and how they are like me. No mother, no father. Born in the wrong place and the wrong time. Does Mr Rufus mean I could've been someone if things had been different? Perhaps I could've been a lady? How much different me life would've been. I tell you one thing, I wouldn' have had so much freedom, would I? So there are some favourable things to be said for wot I am, ain't there?

I push the bed covers aside and swing me legs over the side of the bed, and still Mr Rufus doesn't stir. But I must get on. I must get back to Bill.

I find me own clothes, dress hurriedly, and take one last look at the man in the bed. He looks so warm and comfortable, and so relaxed lying on his belly with one hand above his rumpled hair, truly, I don' want to leave him. But I must!

I slip out the door then, and hasten down the passage.

CHAPTER THIRTY-THREE

Bill don' seem to have moved since I left the day before. But he must've, for the chamber pot needs emptying. The fire is still burning, too, which means Dodger has been. He's a good friend, the Dodge is.

I go down to old Mother Hubbard again and this time she ain't half as nasty—somehow she knows Bill's ill—and I return with broth and manage to get some of it into him.

I have to wash meself, and remove me pessary in front of him but I don' think he's of this world at the moment.

I stay put for a bit. I stay put, sit by his side, and attend to his needs.

But me mind's all over the place. Now with Mr Rufus, now with Aunt Maud, then scuttling back to Bill, then the boy, and wondering where he is, and wot's to become of him. And how I can save him. And reminding meself that *the changeling survives.*

Occasionally thinking of Fagey. Where is the old goat in all of this?

Why hasn' he been to check on Bill, on us? To show some concern and charity? I am not best pleased, I can tell you.

By the end of the day, I think Mr Rufus is right—I am going mad.

By the end of the day I know wot I need.

*

I been to this church before, and it's still open when I get there. It stands near London Bridge, and were built a very long time ago with a spire that sticks out above the gloom, above the muck and mire, above it all—one reason why it appeals to me.

I've been told the church was partially destroyed by the Great Fire of London in 1666, since it ain't far from the bakehouse in Pudding Lane where the fire first began, and that it were rebuilt under the direction of Sir Christopher Wren, him that built so many of London's beautiful buildings. He designed fifty-something churches, and were also an astronomer, *and* lived to be ninety. He must have been a nice man, is wot I think.

Inside, all is quiet. And cold. The air is heavy and damp and weighs on me like cold, lumpy porridge, and within minutes I am shivering like a fragile and desiccated leaf on a tree.

But stay I do. I sit. And stay still. I try to think of me sins, but me mind is in turmoil. Thinking of Sir Christopher Wren, of the church's history, of how ancient it is, helps a little, but very soon me mind is going round and round again.

Oliver—Mr Rufus—Bill—Fagin—The Dodger—and now *the changeling* who survives ...

The calm and the tranquillity that normally fill me ain't to be found here today.

Have you been a good girl, Nancy?

I must find another way to quell me spirit.

Spirit being a strong reminder of that other remedy.

On me way home, I near the beggar woman with the withered leg that I have mentioned before. We are not on speaking terms, but as I pass her almost every day, she's aware of me, and me of her. Once or twice, I have stopped to give her a donation, but it ain't often, and I almost always feel that she resents me gift, that she would rather not take anything from the likes of me, but beggars carnt be choosers, as I have said before.

She is not that old, perhaps in her thirties? And I don' know why her leg is shrivelled and as thin as a rail, but she has had the leg and the street corner for as long as I can remember, and must use a battered and rickety crutch to get around. Anyways, as I draw near, she lurches from her corner to look at something lying in the gutter—perhaps a coin?—and at the same time a horse and carriage, travelling much too fast, comes hurtling around the corner. I don' see wot happens—the carriage blocks me view—but I hear someone scream and scream, and they are still screaming arter the carriage has driven on. The beggar woman is down in the gutter, but it ain't her screaming. It's another woman, who has dropped all her belongings and has her hands up to her face and is struck dumb by wot has happened. Dumb, but not mute. I run over. 'Be quiet,' I tell her, and hastily pick up her basket and take her elbow and lead her out of the way to rest against a shop front, and then I turn to the beggar woman.

A crowd has began to gather around her, but I don' see anybody actually kneeling alongside her, helping. And when I get through, I see why. Her leg—her good leg—has been severed almost in two by the carriage's wheel. There is a lot of bright blood and a bone protruding from the mangled flesh, and to distract meself I look at the crutch, shattered and flung to one side, and one of the beggar woman's pale hands with the fingers spread out and flecked with mud, quivering alongside her. I stoop down and pick up her hand and hold it in mine, and it is like Aunt Maud's, icy cold. The woman's eyes are open, her lips pulled back in a grimace, in a cry that refuses to come out. The inside of her mouth is dark like a crypt. I lean over. I say, 'Hold on, love. Someone will come to help.' And then I look up into the crowd and ask if someone has called for help, and a man gazing down at us with his hands in his pockets says, yes, someone is coming.

I hear snatches of conversation from above—how fast the carriage was going, how the woman had no hope of getting out of the way, how dreadful it is that the driver never stopped. The beggar woman's hand continues to tremble in mine, and I carnt help it, but I must gaze down at the maimed leg throbbing with blood, at the blighted mud, and again I murmur, 'Hold on, love, someone is coming,' but by and by the onlookers begin to drift away, the hand in mine becomes motionless, the head lolls to one side, and I know the beggar woman is dead.

And still no-one comes, and no-one cares. And I reach over and gently close her eyes.

*

When I get back to Bill—and it takes me ages, for me legs tremble so violently they barely hold me up—he's lying on his back, breathing heavily through his mouth, and at first I think he's still poorly. Then I notice the half empty bottle of spirits on the table.

I don' disturb him. I creep up onto the sofa and cover meself quietly with his greatcoat, which he has flung off, and try to sleep.

I try to think about wot the morning will bring. Whether Bill has any idea how long I've been gone? If he will be in one of his moods when he wakes? And wot of the boy, of Oliver? Wot has become of the lad? I ain't heard nothing to the contrary so I must assume he is still alive. And still in the country. And then me mind wanders to the beggar woman, and I carnt escape the vision of the blood, the gaping wound, the woman never uttering a word of complaint, the pale, mud-flecked hand—and eventually, the Lord help me, but I sit up and reach for the bottle of spirits. I gulp at it several times, and when I finally lie back down, me world turns to black.

CHAPTER THIRTY-FOUR

I carnt tell anymore—he's been ailing that long—if Bill's lying there sleeping or merely thinking. Or somewhere in-between.

I ain't been anywhere for days. I been more or less housebound, minding Mr Sikes.

I ain't been anywhere and we ain't had proper sustenance. No work, and no blunt as a consequence. Wot coin I got from Mr Rufus, I have put safely away and won' touch. I got this instinct I'm a-going to be needing it.

Bill lies on the bed, wrapped in his dirty, white greatcoat. He is a sight, believe you me. Unshaven, and his face gaunt and haggard. The only one of us that looks slightly better is Bullseye, a-laying on the floor with his ears pricked and growling every now and then when some noise elsewhere attracts his attention. He's hungry, too. But he knows his place and won' complain.

Right now, I am quietly minding me own business, patching an old waistcoat of Bill's in the fading light of the window. Not feeling too good meself, but trying to make the best of it.

'Wot time is it?' Bill wants to know, suddenly rousing himself from the bed.

'Not long gone seven,' I tell him. 'How do you feel tonight, Bill?'

'As weak as water,' he says. 'Here, lend us a hand, and let me get off this thundering bed, anyhow.'

Illness has not improved his temper, I can say that. I help to raise him up and lead him to a chair, and out of the blue he mutters something and gives me a back hander across the head, making me flinch.

'Whining, are you?' he says. (I swear I didn' say a word.) 'Come, don't stand snivelling there,' he says—cross me heart I did not think I were crying, neither—'if you carnt do anything better than that, cut it off altogether. D'ye hear me?'

'I hear you,' I say, and turn aside and force one of them bright laughs, for if I don' laugh I really will cry. 'Wot fancy have you got in your head now?'

'Ooh, you've thought better of it, have you?' he growls, seeing the tear which trembles in me eye. 'All the better for you, you have.'

'You don' mean to say you'd be hard upon me tonight, would you?'

'No?' Bill cries. 'And why not?'

'Such a number of nights,' I say, making me voice sweet and tender, 'such a number of nights as I've been patient with you, nursing and caring for you as if you had been a child and this the first I've seen you like yourself. You wouldn' have hit me as you did just now if you'd thought of that, would you? Come, say you wouldn'.'

'Well, then,' Bill says, 'I wouldn't. But why, damn, if you're not whining again!'

'It's nothing,' I say, falling back into the other chair. 'Don't you mind me and it'll soon be over.'

'Wot'll be over?' Bill demands savagely. 'Wot foolery are you up to now, woman? Get up and bustle about, and don't come over me with your woman's nonsense ...'

His voice fades into the distance and a kind of darkness comes over me. I am worn out with worry about Oliver, and about Mr Rufus, and for a bit I absent myself and go I know not where ...

I come to because I'm choking.

'Leave off,' I get out, clutching the arms of the chair and gasping for breath. For someone has opened me mouth and is pouring spirits down me throat.

I heave meself out and stagger to a perch by the fireside—I've come over all cold—and look away from them who administered assistance. It's the old goat and the Dodger. And Charley Bates, I think.

'Why, wot evil wind has blowed you here?' Bill asks Fagey.

'No evil wind at all, my dear,' Fagin replies, 'for ill winds blow nobody any good, and I've brought something good with me that you'll be glad to see. Dodger, my dear, open the bundle, and give Bill the trifles that we spent all our money on this morning.'

Out of the corner of me eye, I watch as Dodger unties his bundle of old tablecloth and hands the items contained therein, one by one, to Charley Bates, who places them on the small, rickety table.

There's a pie of sorts—rabbit, I hear Charley telling Bill, a delicate creetur with such tender limbs, he says—and green tea, and butter and Glo'ster cheese and sugar and a bottle of wine, and I want to fall upon these luxuries and gorge meself, stuff me mouth full, and yet I cannot. I thought I was so hungry I could eat a house. I thought me belly was so empty I could house a family in it, too.

'Ah,' Fagin says, rubbing his hands together. 'You'll do now, Bill. You'll do.'

'Do!' Bill says. 'I might have been done for twenty times over afore you'd have done anything to help me. Wot do you mean by leaving a man in this state three weeks and more, you false-hearted vagabond?'

'Only hear him, boys,' Fagin says, shrugging his shoulders, 'and us come to bring him all these beautiful things.'

'The things is well enough in their way,' Bill says, glancing over the table's contents, 'but wot have you got to say for yourself, why you should leave me here, down in the mouth, health, blunt, and everything else, and take no more notice of me all this mortal time than if I was that 'ere dog. Drive him down, Charley.'

'I never seen such a jolly dog as this,' Charley cries, smacking Bullseye on the nose. 'Smelling the grub like a old lady a-going to market! He'd make his fortune on the stage, that dog would, and revive the drama besides.'

'Hold your din,' Bill cries, as Bullseye growls and retreats under the bed. 'And wot have you got to say for yourself, you withered old fence, eh?'

'I was away from London a week and more, my dear, on a plant,' Fagin says.

'And wot about the other fortnight?' Bill demands. 'Wot about the other fortnight that you left me lying here like a sick rat in his hole?'

'I couldn't help it, Bill,' Fagin says. 'I can't go into a long explanation before company, but I couldn't help it, upon my honour.'

'Upon your wot?' Bill growls with disgust. 'Here, cut me off a piece of the pie, one of you boys, to take the taste of that out of me mouth, or it'll choke me dead.'

'Don't be out of temper, my dear,' Fagey murmurs all humble-like. 'I have never forgot you, Bill. Never once.'

'No, I'll pound it, that you hadn't,' Bill replies with a bitter grin. 'You've been scheming and plotting away every hour that I've laid shivering and burning here. Bill was to do this, and Bill was to do that, and Bill was to do it all dirt cheap, as soon as he got well, and was quite poor enough for your work. If it hadn't been for the girl, I might have died.'

'There now, Bill,' Fagey says, glancing in me direction. 'If it hadn't been for the girl! Who was the means of your having such a handy girl about you, but me?'

'He says true enough there, God knows!' I say, coming hastily forwards. 'Let him be, let him be.'

Dodger nods at me and pours me a small tumbler of the spirits, but I ain't going to have any, and I shake me head at him. I'll fall down if I do. Instead, I reach for the cheese, break off a bit and nibble upon it, and pretend I'm only half here, but of course I ain't, I'm listening intently for word of the boy, aren' I?

'It's all very well,' Bill says, after some time in which they have laughed a bit and drunk a bit, and the old goat has indulged me lord and master, and grovelled and wormed and wheedled his way back into his favour. 'It's all very well, but I must have some blunt from you tonight.'

'I haven't a piece of coin about me,' Fagin replies.

'Then you've got lots at home, and I must have some from there.' Bill's voice is firm.

'Lots!' Fagey cries, holding up both hands. 'I haven't so much as—'

'I don't know how much you've got,' Bill interrupts, 'and I dare say you hardly know yourself, as it would take a pretty long time to count it. But I must have some tonight, and that's flat.'

'Well, well,' the old goat says with a sigh. 'I'll send the Artful round presently.'

'You won't do nothing of the kind,' Bill says. 'The Artful's a deal too artful, and would forget to come, or lose his way, or get dodged by traps and so be prevented. Or anything for an excuse if you put him up to it. Nancy shall go to the crib and fetch it, to make all sure, and I'll lie down and have a snooze while she's gone.'

There proceeds to be a great deal of haggling and squabbling between Bill and the old goat as to the required advance of blunt, and while they are at it, I break off some pastry from the pie and squirrel out a piece of meat and nibble at that, and start to feel more like meself. Bill eventually yields to Fagey and says if he carnt get any more coin, he must be content. And he throws himself on the bed and immediately begins to snore.

Meanwhile, I find me shawl and accompany Fagey and the boys, and in due time we arrive at the crib where Toby Crackit and him that I know as Mr Chitling have been playing cribbage and keeping guard.

Fagey claps his hands together in impatience, as if the sight of them two has riled him. 'Come, come, now, it's time you were all on the lay. Dodger, Charlie, it's near ten and nothing done yet!'

They all nod to me, take up their hats and leave the room. Not without some banter and bickering between them, of course, but wot a relief that is for me, having unobtrusively sat down at the table, to have the crib once again silent and quiet. I am not meself, I tell you.

'Now,' Fagin says, 'I'll go and get you that cash, Nancy. This is only the key,' he says, holding it out to the light where it glints, 'of a little cupboard where I keep a few odd things the boys get, my dear. I never lock up my money for I've got none to lock up, my dear, none to lock.' He laughs, and I wonder just who he thinks he is fooling. Certainly not me. 'It's a poor trade, Nancy,' he goes on, 'and no thanks, but I'm fond of seeing the young people about me, and I bear it all. I bear it all—' He breaks off.

'Hush!' he says, hastily concealing the key in his breast. 'Who's that? Listen!'

I cock me ears and hear the murmur of a man's voice, a voice I recognise and, hastily tearing off my shawl and hat, I thrust them under the table. Fagin's not looking, luckily, his back is to me. He's standing quite still and listening.

'Bah!' he whispers, clearly rattled by the interruption. 'It's the man I expected before. He's coming downstairs. Not a word about the money while he's here, Nance. He won't stop long, not even ten minutes, my dear.'

Laying his skinny forefinger upon his lip, Fagin carries a candle to the door as a man's step is heard upon the stairs. He reaches it at the same time as the visitor, who steps hastily into the room, and is almost upon me before he realises Fagey is not alone, and startled, steps back.

It is Monks. As I suspected.

I glance at him and then I avert my face.

'Only one of my young people,' Fagin says, reassuring the man. 'Don't move, Nancy.'

I don'. I keep me face turned towards the fire. I don' want the man—Monks—to see me features. To be able to recognise me again.

'Any news?' Fagin asks him.

'Great,' Monks replies.

'And—and good?'

'Not bad any way,' Monks says. 'I have been prompt enough this time. Let me have a word with you.'

I hunch over the table and try to make meself invisible, and I don' know wot happens behind me back but they—the pair of them—leave the room. As they go upstairs, I hear Monks say, 'Not that infernal hole we were in before?' and Fagin makes some reply, and by the creaking of the boards, I know he is taking Monks to the second storey.

I slip off me shoes, draw me shawl loosely over me head and around me arms, muffling me movements, and then I tiptoe to the door and stand listening. As soon as there is quiet, I glide upstairs into the gloom, treading ever so faintly on the edges of the stairs, and follow them up.

For some fifteen minutes I stand in the darkened stairwell listening to their conversation. For some fifteen minutes I carnt believe wot I am hearing. For some fifteen minutes I must clench meself into a tightness, must do all I can do to control every emotion I have. To stop meself from crying out loud.

Then somehow, I manage to glide back down with the same unearthly tread, discard me shawl, and sit at the table as before. Stare into the fire. As if I have not moved in their absence. As if, awaiting Fagey's return, I may be dozing. Which is hard, which is difficult, considering how agitated I am! Considering how me poor body shivers.

I hear them descending, Monks at once continuing on into the street.

Fagey pokes his head in at the door—it squeaks—and sees me there, and returns upstairs. I know he has gone to get the cash, and I pick up me shawl again and replace me shoes and prepare to go.

'Nance,' he says returning with the candle and putting it down. He glances at me in consternation. 'How pale you are, girl!'

'Pale?' I say. Oh Lord, I cannot help the state of me skin!

'Yes, pale. Quite horrible. What have you been doing to yourself?'

'Nothing that I know of except sitting in this here close place for I don' know how long and all,' I say carelessly. 'Come, let me get back, that's a dear.'

I put out me hand for the coin, and have to support it with t'other to stop it trembling.

Fagin counts it out, piece by piece. He sighs all the while as if he is parting with his own flesh and blood. Funny how some are about coin. Coin is necessary. We carnt survive without coin. But it ain't the be-all and end-all of life.

I stash the money away and take me leave. I say, 'Goodnight', and head smartly out the door. Make it seem like it is Bill needing me that sends me away in a hurry.

But when I get out onto the street, I am all a-wobble and have to clutch the doorway. Me legs won' hold me up, and I must sag upon the dark and dismal doorstep to collect meself.

Arter some time, I make a decision. It is the newfound knowledge I have that forces me to make a decision.

For Oliver is still alive!—this much I have gleaned. I have no alternative now. I will go and see them *soft-hearted psalm singers* that provided shelter and care to Oliver. And, rising to me feet, I set off quickly and half-walk, half-run to the residence in Claremont Court where I stood watch before, all the time thinking I must make haste, I must hurry, I *must* tell them, and finally stopping to get me breath, and realising it is too late, it is long gone the decent hour of calling, if I turn up now on their doorstep, I will be chased away. Or end up in The Office. I must, instead, *reflect on* how to solve this and not act rashly, and then I burst into tears with the worry of it.

I turn back and, sniffing and snivelling, go home to Bill. Me heart is heavy and it takes me twice as long to walk back. I seem to be at a loss to know how to put one foot in front of the other.

I get in and Bill lifts his head from the pillow to ask if I have the ready and, satisfied with me reply, lays it down once more and returns to the Land of Nod. Just like that.

Oh, if only sleep came so easily to me!

CHAPTER THIRTY-FIVE

It is fortunate for me the old goat gives Bill his blunt, for he spends the day out, eating and drinking, the effect of which is to turn him altogether. By the time he returns to me in the evening, he is saying nothing hard about me or me behaviour, and is gone to bed fairly soon. The drink has made him blind to the fact that I am distracted and nervous, apprehensive of wot it is I must later set out to do.

I am sitting close by him with me needle and cotton, darning, and he is laying there still weak from the fever, when he sits bolt upright sudden-like and stares me in the face. 'Why burn my body! You look like a corpse come to life again. Wot's the matter?'

'Matter?' I say, wondering wot has changed about me looks that Bill's picked up on. Maybe I been talking to meself? Maybe there is fire in me eyes? God help me, it ain't my fault if there is. 'Nothing,' I tell him. 'Wot do you look at me so hard for?'

'Wot foolery is this?' he demands, grasping me arm and shaking me. 'Wot is it? Wot is wrong with you?' And when I don' respond, he says, 'I tell you wot it is. If you haven't caught the fever and got it comin' on now.'

Then he says, 'Or there's something more than usual in the wind. You're not a-going to—No, damn! You wouldn't do that!'

'Do wot?'

'There ain't,' Sikes mutters, fixing his eyes upon me and I have to force meself to coolly stare right back at him. 'There ain't a stauncher-hearted gal going, or I'd have cut her throat three months ago. She's got the fever coming on, that's it.' And draining his glass of hot water and gin, and swearing and cussing, he asks me for his nightcap.

I jump up and go over to wot passes for the dresser. And, with me back to him, I pour out his medicine quickly and carry it over, being careful not to spill a drop, and hold it to his lips while he drinks it off, and continue to hold it there until it is all gone. All gone! Wot a relief that is. Me hands are shaking by the time I withdraw the glass and I pull them hastily down to me sides.

'Now,' Bill says, 'come and sit aside of me, and put on your own face, or I'll alter this one you got so that you won't know it again when you do want it.'

I do as I'm told, grateful that he doesn't want the other, and he reaches for one of me hands and holds it in his, and falls back upon the pillow, his eyes upon me face. They close, open again. Close once more. Open again as he shifts his position, then close again.

And just when I think he's gone off, he springs forwards with a look of terror, says, 'Nancy!' and then just as quickly falls back upon the pillow. The grasp of his hand relaxes, and he lies like one in a profound trance.

'Bless me,' I murmur. 'The laudanum has taken effect at last.'

I rise from the bed and rapidly draw me shawl around me shoulders, glancing fearfully round, for I keep expecting to feel the pressure of his heavy hand upon me shoulder. Or worse. Stooping over the bed, I softly kiss him—you never know this may be the last time I see him—and hurry from the house.

A watchman is crying half-past nine in a dark lane.

'Has it long gone the half hour?' I ask.

'It'll strike the hour in another quarter,' he says, raising his lantern to me face.

'Thankee,' I call, over my shoulder. I cannot get where I am bound in less than an hour and a bit, and I pick up me skirts and quicken me pace.

Many of the shops are already closing as I rapidly make me way, but there are plenty of people still out and about, hampering my progress. A flower-seller, with a filthy apron and nothing but drooping carnations left clutched in her hand at this hour, announces to anyone with half an ear, 'That woman is mad,' after I have to elbow her out of the way. But nobody takes any notice. And I may well be mad, I tell you.

If I am late, if I do not reach my destination within the allotted time, it will all be to no avail.

Gradually, as I reach the richer part of town, the streets quieten, and I am able to make headway and, by the time I arrive at my destination, I am alone.

It is a quiet and handsome street near Hyde Park. And the clock strikes eleven as I pause outside a hotel. I have made good time, then. The hotel is a welcoming-looking place, with a warm light burning before the entrance. Not too grand so's I'd be frightened of entering, but all the same I hesitate before I climb the stairs.

Inside, the night porter's seat is vacant. I glance around. At the opulence. At a gigantic fern in a copper pot. At the shiny wood panels and burnished gold ornaments. At the marble staircase. *A staircase.* I head towards it.

'Now, young girl,' a woman appearing from behind a door says, checking me in me tracks, 'who do you want here?'

'A lady who is stopping in this house,' I say.

'A lady!' she says scornfully. 'What lady, pray?'

'Miss Maylie.'

The woman looks me up and down, calls to a waiter who has appeared out of nowhere, and flicks her finger at him as if to say, *Deal with it. Deal with* her.

'I need to speak to Miss Maylie,' I tell him.

'What name am I to say?' he asks.

'It's no use saying any,' I tell him.

'Nor business?'

'No, nor that neither. I must see the lady.'

He takes me by the arm. Pushes me towards the door. 'None of this, miss. Take yourself off, will you?'

'I shall be carried out if I'm to go!' I say violently. 'And I can make that a job that two of you won' like to do. Isn't there anybody here,' I plead, gazing around, 'will see a simple message carried for a poor wretch like me?'

Staff dribble into the hall now, come from out the kitchen because of the ruckus. One steps forwards and says, 'Take it up for her, Joe, carnt you?'

'What's the good?' the waiter replies. 'You don't really suppose Miss Maylie will see such as her, do you, now?'

I am accustomed to being treated like something nasty underfoot, but clearly those here are not accustomed to the likes of me in their presence, for there is an outcry.

'You're a disgrace!' one of the housemaids cries.

'Throw her into a kennel,' says another, and dusts off her hands as if I were vermin.

'Do wot you like with me,' I say, 'but I ask that you give this message first, for the love of God.'

I ain't going to go on relating the bickering and the backbiting and the calling of names, but, finally, the man runs up the stairs with me message to Miss Maylie, while I wait breathless and trembling. Everyone else waits breathless and trembling, too, but for different reasons. When he returns and tells me I am to come up the stairs, I take no heed of the last of the scorn and derision sent me way and follow him.

He leaves me in an antechamber, lit by a lamp from the ceiling, and I stand close to the entranceway as if it can disguise meself and hide me shame at being wot I am.

A figure, which has the form of a slight and beautiful girl, presents itself in the far doorway. She is probably no older than me, but wot a wealth of years and experience divides us. Wot a wealth of opportunity divides us.

'It's a hard matter—' I begin, but she puts up a hand and silences me.

'I am very sorry if anyone has behaved harshly to you,' she says. 'Do not think of it now, but tell me why you wished to see me. I am the person you asked for. I am Rose Maylie.'

I swallow. The kindness in her voice is almost more than I can bear. 'If there were more like you here'—I have to break off to get me breath—'there would be fewer like me. There would! There surely would.'

'Sit down,' she says, indicating an armchair to her right. 'You distress me. If you are in poverty or affliction, I shall be truly happy to relieve you, if I can. Sit, please.'

'I carnt,' I say. 'Let me stand, and do not speak so kindly until you know me better. It is growing late. Can I shut this door?' I ask, indicating the one I have come through.

'Yes,' Miss Maylie says, 'but why?'

'Because,' I say, closing the door softly behind me, 'because I am about to put me life and the lives of others into your hands. I am the girl that dragged the boy—little Oliver—away. Back to Fagin's. On the night he went out from the house in Pentonville.'

'You!'

'Me, lady,' I say. 'I am the infamous creature you have heard of, that lives amongst the thieves, and that never from the first moment I can recollect me eyes and senses opening on London streets, have known any better life, or kinder words than wot they have given me, so help me God!'

'I pity you,' Miss Maylie says. 'It wrings my heart to hear you.'

'But never mind that now. If you knew wot I am sometimes, you would pity me, indeed. But I have stolen away from those who would surely murder me if they knew I was here, and wot I am to tell you. Do you know a man named Monks?'

'No,' Miss Maylie says.

'He knows you,' I tell her. 'And knows you are here, for it was by hearing him tell the place that I found you out.'

'I never heard the man's name.'

'Then he goes by some other amongst us,' I say, 'which I more than thought before. Some time ago, and soon after Oliver were put into your house on the night of the robbery, I—suspecting this man—listened to a conversation held between him and a man known as Fagin. I found out that Monks'—and here I glance over me shoulder and check the door is still closed—'that Monks had by happenstance seen Oliver on the day we first lost him, and had known him to be the same child he was watching for, though I carnt tell you why. I do not know why. A bargain was struck with Fagin, that if Oliver was got back, Fagin should have a certain sum, and he was to have more for making Oliver a thief, which Monks wants for some purpose of his own.'

'For what purpose?' Miss Maylie asks, whispering. She is wide-eyed.

'He caught sight of me shadow on the wall as I listened in,' I say, 'and there are not many besides me that could have got out of the way in time to escape discovery. But I did, and I saw him no more till last night.'

'And what occurred then?'

'Last night he came again,' I say. 'Again they went upstairs and I, wrapping meself up so that me shadow would not betray me a second time, listened at the door. The first words I heard Monks say were that "the only proofs of the boy's identity lie at the bottom of the river, and the old hag that received them from his mother is rotting in her coffin". They laughed then, and talked of his success, and Monks said that though he'd "got the young devil's money safely now", he'd rather have had it the other way, for wot a game it would've been to have drove the boy through every jail in town and hauled him up for some capital felony, which Fagin—if you know Fagin—could easily manage.'

'What is all this?' Miss Maylie says, her eyes still as big as plates.

'The truth, lady,' I say. 'Then he said with oaths I won' repeat that if he could gratify his hatred by taking the boy's life without bringing his own neck into danger, he would. But as he couldn' he'd be upon the watch to meet him at every turn in life, and that he might harm him yet. And then he said, "In short, Fagin, you never laid such traps as I'll contrive for my young brother, Oliver".'

'His brother!' Miss Maylie exclaims, clapping her hands in consternation.

'Those were his words,' I say, glancing round again at the closed door for, so help me, I am imagining a vision of Sikes as coming through that said door. Haunting, it is. 'And when he spoke of you and the other lady, he said it seemed contrived by Heaven, or the devil, that Oliver should come into your hands, and he laughed and said there was some comfort in that, too, for how many thousands, and hundreds of thousands, of pounds would you not give to know who your two-legged spaniel was.'

'You do not mean,' Miss Maylie says, turning pale, 'that this was said in earnest?'

'He spoke hard and angry, if a man ever did,' I say. 'He—Monks—is an earnest man when his hatred is up. I know many who do worse things, but I'd rather listen to them all a dozen times than to Monks once.' I glance at the closed door again. 'It is growing late, my lady, and I must reach home without suspicion of having been on such an errand as this. I must go now.'

'But what can I do?' Miss Maylie cries in a whisper. 'To what use can I turn this communication without you? Why do you wish to return to your companions? If you repeat this information to a gentleman I can summon from the next room in one instant, you can be taken to some place of safety without delay.'

I sniff. Straighten me shoulders. 'I wish to go back. I must go back. Because …'

I stop. I am all a-tremble again. 'How can I tell such things to a lady like you? Among the men I have told you of, there is one who is the most desperate, but I cannot leave him. I carnt,' I say and the anguish in me voice is real. 'No, not even to be saved from the life I am leading now.'

'Your coming here,' Miss Maylie says, 'at such great risk to tell me—'

'You do not understand, lady,' I say. 'I cannot leave him now. I cannot be his death.'

'Why should you be?' She looks appalled.

'Nothing can save him,' I tell her. 'If I told others wot I have told you and this led to their being taken, he would be sure to die. He is the boldest, but he is also the cruellest.'

'This is madness,' Miss Maylie says.

'I don' know wot it is,' I say. 'I only know that it is so, and not with me alone, but with hundreds of others as bad and wretched as meself. Whether it is God's wrath for the wrong I have done, I do not know, but I am drawn back to this man through every suffering and beating, and I believe—I believe that I will die by his hand at last.'

Will I? I am thinking. Why do I have the feeling that Bill will kill me? Is it because he has almost done for me several times? Miss Maylie is looking at me strangely. I must stop thinking like this.

'Now,' I say, firmly, 'you must have some kind gentleman about you that will hear wot I have told you, and advise you wot to do?'

'I do,' she says. 'I have. Mr Brownlow.'

'Is he the kindly man Oliver spoke of, the elderly man who rescued him?'

'He is.' She pauses. 'But where will I find you again when it is necessary?' she asks.

'Will you promise that you will keep me secret strictly and come alone, or with this Mr Brownlow, the only other person that knows it, and that I shall not be watched or followed?'

'I promise you solemnly.'

'Then, every Sunday night, from eleven until the clock strikes twelve,' I tell her, 'I will walk on London Bridge—if I am alive.'

'Stay another moment,' Miss Maylie cries, putting her hand upon me arm. Close up I see how beautiful she really is. 'Think once again of your situation, and the opportunity you have of escaping it. Will you return to this gang of robbers and to this man, when a word can save you? What fascination is it that can take you back, and make you cling to wickedness and misery? Is there nothing left I can say to appeal against this?'

'When ladies as young and good and beautiful as you are,' I say steadily, 'give away your hearts, love carries you, bears you to heights and depths. When such as me, who have no certain roof but the coffin-lid, and no friend in sickness or death but the hospital nurse, set our rotten hearts on any man, and let him fill the place that parents, home and friends once filled, and that has been a blank through all our wretched lives, who can hope to cure us?'

And with that, I turn on me heel, open the door, close it softly again behind me, and fly down the stairs.

CHAPTER THIRTY-SIX

From here on, it is difficult for me to get away at any time. Perhaps Bill received a knock on the head during the break-in at Chertsey, for he ain't himself. He's on edge, like me. He's so on edge, I ain't seen his lobcock excited for days. He ain't got the appetite for you-know-wot, which is saying something. He don' have no work, either, and that adds to his condition. And he seems to watch me careful-like every hour of the day and night. Like he suspects I have done something, said something, or may *yet* do something.

We don' talk about it, but he knows I have feelings for the boy. And whether he is jealous of Oliver, or afraid I will do something rash, I do not know. And believe me, the boy is never far from me thoughts.

But Bill is a man after all, he is, and a mighty impatient and intolerant one at that, and on the third day arter I seen Miss Rose Maylie, when I been under his feet day and night, he has had enough.

'Get you gone, woman,' he says to me, when he finds me mid-morning a-sitting on the sofa where he likes to lay himself out.

'Ain't you got work to do? Why's it Fagey ain't sent you out?'—He means to visit a client—'Wot's happening there?'

Ah-ha, I think.

'Well, now you should mention it, I do have work,' I say, shifting over on the sofa. 'I have a number of them clients piled up—for it's been a while, Bill—and I ought to do something 'bout them, but I haven' wanted to leave you. You ain't been well, as you know.'

'Don' see why you carnt manage without me,' he says, lifting one booted foot and pushing me backside off the sofa. 'Tell you I don' rightly feel up to watching your arse while you work, and that's the truth. Run along and leave me be, there's a good little woman? And,' he says, sniffing, and glancing askance at me, 'if you don' go pretty smartly, I'll give you a reason to make you go.'

That there's an easy decision to make if ever I saw one. I don' need another belting, and I don' hesitate to take the opportunity to hasten out the door.

Perhaps I will go and do some work, after all? Perhaps it will take me mind off matters, is wot I'm thinking.

Outside, it's sunny and dry for once. And although the sun carnt exactly shine through the muck above me head, there's a bit of warmth in the air. It don' help with them smells, though. It makes them worse and I am almost inclined to hold me nose.

I stop by The Cripples first, out of habit, but also out of a longing for a certain man to save me from meself.

In truth, me instincts have been telling me I ain't likely to see Mr Rufus again. That he, Aunt Maud, and me association with them, are all behind me. I am confident she will have made allowances for Mr Rufus now, made plans. For she's been assured that he's an honourable and a good man, and it's my guess she were only a trifle concerned regarding that to start with. On the basis of this, it's also me opinion she may well give him his inheritance now. Then, he can truly look for a wife that befits his station. Which he has been unable to do up to this point. Yes.

This is all logical and reasonable, ain't it? But it doesn't account for the ache in me heart, or how close to tears I find meself most of the time.

Anyway, as a consequence, I am taken aback when Barney comes to the counter, says, 'Bere you bin?', as he seems to be making a habit of saying these days, and tilts his head towards a corner of the parlour.

Me instincts, I realise, have been wrong. Which is decidedly odd, but, then again, I ain't meself.

For sitting in a corner, his long-fingered hands clasped around a pint of ale, and staring fixedly at me, is Mr Rufus.

Mr Rufus, wearing a soft, flat cap and a corduroy jacket over a worn shirt. Mr Rufus dressed down, so he don' stand out like a lighthouse in The Cripples. Mr Rufus perhaps come to berate me—for, like I said, I ain't seen him in a while.

Oh, Lord, this is a bit risky, a bit too close to home! That is me first reaction.

A daring move on his part, I am thinking. And a dangerous one.

Me second is joy. I want to smile, I want to sing, I want to *tra-la-la* and leap around the room with the happiness of it.

But, weirdly, time stands still. Time teeters, for I lock eyes with Mr Rufus. I lock eyes with Mr Rufus and every clanging bell, every strident voice, every gossiping murmur fades away. The whole world winds to a whimper.

All you're conscious of, Nancy, is the man across the room, the man with the cinnamon curls and the deep-brown eyes that are locked on yours. The man who is licking his lips cos he carnt keep still.

You know he's not here to give you a talking-to.

You know.

You go rigid, perhaps. Maybe you bite your lower lip. Maybe you hear Barney say 'Bee's been baiting a bour', but you carnt be certain.

And then, Mr Rufus has left the table. Mr Rufus is alongside you, taking your arm, and steering you out of the bar and into the street. And you are *perambulating* along it, not saying a word, not looking at the man alongside you, not acknowledging him. It's like you have a predetermined *tryst*. The two of you. The two of you have some other place to be. Some other place it seems of the utmost urgency to reach. You are only conscious of the swing of your legs, of the shift of your skirt, of the pressure of his hand upon your arm, of the slight odour of the man beside you, the warmth of his body.

You carnt say how you get there, wot sights you pass, wot route you use, but you arrive at Number Fifteen, at the door of the tenement crib, and he unlocks it and propels you inside.

You come to a stop alongside the table in the room. You come to some sort of semblance of your senses. Perhaps it is the familiarity of your surroundings, the recollection of Mr Rufus sitting at the table reading the newspaper, and you making him a cup of tea, the remembrance of them foxes upon the hearth—

'Nancy,' he murmurs, behind you. 'Please,' he says.

You turn, and he lifts you under the arms and perches you upon the table and kicks the door closed with his boot.

He perches you upon the table and jerks you in towards him and kisses you, soft and sweet. And, no, he don' taste of oranges, not this time. He tastes of the countryside, he tastes of sunshine on wheat, he tastes of them bluebells under birches. He tastes of how you *imagine* these things. Then he kisses you long and hard, as his fingers fumble with your clothes, as his fingers undo you bit by bit, this button, that clip, this strap, and you are in a dream, a time of drifting and tasting and wanting and lusting and a-going on and a-going over, and over, and over. Stubble under your fingertips, silkiness of skin, dampness and wetness and hot, mingled breath, and then the nuzzle and the suck of it, the rocking and the wrenching, and the pause to make it last, the stop to savour it, the length to look at him, and for him to gaze at you, and the almost fainting with the agony of it all, and then, and then, then, then, the gasping for air, the gasping, and the ripple, the ripple of the wave and the wave coming, the wave coming, and coming, and the blissful agony of it all.

*

Later, when we are lying in the bed, I ask him to tell me something about Aunt Maud.

'I can try,' he says. 'But it depends on what your question is.' He pulls the covers back over us, for evening has fallen and it has grown chilly.

'Why … Why don' she have any maids—?'

'Oh, that. That's a story for another day, but I'll give you a shortened version. She, Aunt Maud …' He stops. 'No,' he says, 'let me start with Uncle Bernard, for he is, after all, the root of Aunt Maud's dislike of maids. They had maids when they lived at the Mayfair house, but no children, as you've gathered. Not that that makes any difference to what I am about to tell you, except to say that Aunt Maud has always been very kind to me. Uncle Bernard was devoted to her, *adored* her, but, alas, a certain chambermaid caught his eye and, as luck would have it, Aunt Maud caught them together in bed, and subsequently discharged every one of the maids, and the cook to boot. And she's never had another maid since. The only member of staff she didn't lay off was Foxley, on account of him having been in her employment since she was a child.'

'And wot about you, sir? You told me you are employed. Wot is it you do?'

He sighs. 'It is really nothing much. I can speak French and I do some translating for a lawyer. The work is quite boring, legal matters and so on, and also not particularly reliable. But it does bring in additional funds. Happy now?' he adds, gazing down at me.

'Happy,' I say.

'Good,' he says, and begins to kiss me. He starts at the base of me wrist and works his way up me arm, and makes me giggle.

*

He harps upon the marriage again—our marriage—at the darkened doorway, when I want to be leaving. Which completely confuses me. Because, why? Why does he need to marry me now? Surely Aunt Maud has seen sense and agreed to give him his inheritance at this point—rather than have him marry the likes of me? Perhaps I am wrong about her? Perhaps she wants to push him to see how far he will go to satisfy her? Is Aunt Maud playing games with us as we are playing games with her? And wot do I do? Do I tell Mr Rufus that she knows I ain't mute? Oh, Lord.

'I have a date in mind, and a church,' he says. 'And I would like you to meet me at the church to see if it's what you want—'

'I'm sure to like it, sir. I am,' I say.

He holds my hand and squeezes it. And I think: why's he bothering with me approving the church when the marriage ain't a-going to be genuine? Has he changed his mind? And how can I possibly marry him for real? Arghh. My head is so full I carnt hardly think straight.

'But I don' think marrying me is the answer. I … I …' I say but I carnt go on.

I don' know how to tell him about me background. I carnt tell him about Sikes and Fagin, and how they might very well do away with him, not to mention *throttle* me, if he marries me. I know too much. That's obvious.

'It is the answer,' he says. 'I must satisfy Aunt Maud. Sadly, she has made no indication of giving me my inheritance until I do. At least come and see the church with me. Will you do that?'

'Tell you wot, Mr Rufus, why don' you tell me which church it is and I'll have a look meself?'

'I want it to be right on the day, Nancy,' he says. He mentions a date ten days or so hence. It's a Monday, to me knowledge. Strange to choose a Monday, but that may be on account of the marriage not being genuine, of the priest having to be bribed, of papers having to be forged. 'And the church, the church is Saint Magnus the Martyr—'

'Oh, I know that one.'

'Do you now?' He raises one eyebrow and looks faintly amused.

I'm sure he's wondering how a girl such as I would know of the Saint Magnus church or any church, for that matter, and whether I'm telling the truth. There's a great deal he don' know about me and, most probably, never will. And that's the upper classes for you, not caring a fig for the likes of me. But that ain't wholly accurate, for he ain't wholly upper class, is he?

'You are going to turn up, aren't you?' he asks, interrupting me thoughts.

'I—er—er—I carnt promise, sir,' I say. 'Me life's not me own,' I say.

'What do you mean?' He frowns. 'Who's stopping you? Why don't you let me have a word—'

'No!' I blurt out. 'You must not, sir,' I say. 'You must not!' And I think of Bill and Fagin and wot they would do if Mr Rufus had *a word* with them. That, in spite of Mr Rufus's dark thoughts (which I have never told a soul about), he would not stand a chance, and I burst into tears with the worry of it.

'Nancy, Nancy,' he says, pulling me head to his chest and comforting me. 'There, there.'

'I'll do the best I can,' I murmur. Me mouth is somewhere near the vicinity of a naked rib and me voice is muffled. 'That I *can* promise, that I'll do the best I can.'

'Good girl,' he says. 'Remember that when we are married I will have my inheritance and none of this will matter.'

Perhaps not to you, I think. Perhaps *I* won't matter to you then, neither.

He puts me from him. He murmurs, 'I don't know why or how I thought you were like my mother for you're nothing like her at all, are you, Nancy?'

He takes one last lingering look at me, and I ain't accustomed to being looked at the way he gazes at me. With kind eyes. I ain't in the habit of being looked at … at … with what seems like *love*. Truly I ain't.

You will remember I said at the beginning I don' care if Fagey is a Chinaman, but in fact I do. I met a Chinaman once and he said something that stuck in me brain. He said something *touched* his heart. And that's wot it is, ain't it? This touches me heart. (Then it breaks it.)

Before I really fall apart, before I crumble, I pull away, ease out the doorway, and slip down the lane.

And I know you'll be wondering why I don' come out with it and ask him straight to his face, is this marriage no longer a sham, Mr Rufus? For you're talking like it's a-going to be genuine. You're looking at me like it's a-going to be real.

Well, I don' actually want to know. Strange, innit? See, if I know it's going to be genuine, it puts me in a right predicament. It tempts me to leave Bill, forget the consequences, and, worse still, abandon Oliver. If I discover it's fake, a pretence, I will be so disappointed in Mr Rufus, so utterly despondent, I don' know that I will be able to go on.

And go on I must. The boy is relying upon me to go on.

There's something else. It may not mean much to you. But to me it's so satisfying to know *I* can decide whether to ask him. Or not. Me. Nancy. No-one else.

*

I am crossing the muddy and mirey courtyard of The Cripples, thinking how much I would like a drink, how much a drink in the dismal and drear den of the front parlour would help me forget the many predicaments pressing in on me—like clamouring ghosts they are, coming and going, appearing and reappearing, befuddling me brain—but that I must get back to Bill, *I must*, when someone steps out from the shadows.

'Where you bin, Nancy?'

Another one asking me where I've been. Didn' I jus' say me life is not me own?

I pause. 'Shall we go in?' I ask, tilting me head towards the establishment.

'Best not,' Dodger says. 'Besides which,' he says, pulling one hand from a capacious pocket and holding a bottle out to the light, 'I got something.'

He raises his eyebrows, angles an elbow. I link arms with him and we backtrack and disappear around the corner. Into a dreary and dismal back lane. Where a stable of sorts is housed at the top end, and the landlord of The Cripples keeps a tired and rib-thin nag called Sally, and where a paling only needs a nudge to swing loose for the Dodger and me, both being rib-thin ourselves, to easily slip through.

Inside the dark stable it's warm and horsey-smelling. I *click-click* me tongue to settle the poor, old girl, but Sally knows it's us—she can smell us—and she don' need much to make her feel at ease.

We park ourselves down on the straw and I hear Dodger taking a swig from the bottle. Then he passes it to me, his hand bumping mine in the dark. The liquid is fiery and burns me throat and, for a second or two, I carnt get me breath, but then it travels down to me belly and gives me a lovely glow all over.

'Where you bin, Nancy?' Dodger says again, talking low-voiced, for you never know who might be bending an ear in the lane outside.

'Why? You asked me that already. Wot does it matter?' I pass the bottle back to him.

'It matters for I saw you wiv' a certain man. I saw you walking down the street together, bold as brass you were, like you were in another world. You should take care, Nancy.'

'I will,' I murmur, wiping the back of me hand across me mouth. 'I will. Right now, I ain't got a choice.'

'How's that?'

'You'll larf, you will,' I say.

'Try me,' he says, and pulls at the bottle again, then nudges me with it.

'I think I'm in love—'

He snorts with merriment, anointing me arm with a spattering of spirits.

'Oi,' I say.

'As I live and breathe!' he exclaims, and snorts a second time.

'Shh,' I say, thinking of wot Aunt Maud said about love, about how I would know when I were in love, how it would come to me …

'Wot you going to do?'

'Wot can I do? Bill will kill me.'

'And if Bill don', Fagey will.'

'Too right. Wot news do you have of the boy?' I ask, tilting the bottle to me mouth. 'Of Oliver?'

'Only that he's bin a-rescued and a-taken in by some leetle old ladies, in the countryside, and is engaged in a bit of nanty narking.'

Which, of course, I already know.

'So, nothing new, then?'

'No.' The Dodger sniffs. 'But I'd be careful, Nancy, if I were you. You know the old goat is scheming to get the boy back again. It's like his life depends on it. His ears are pricked, his eyes are out on poles. He's so wound up, he's talking to hi'self. More than usual-like.'

I nod. 'You won' tell anyone, will you, Dodge,' I say, feeling for his arm in the dark and laying me hand upon his sleeve, 'about wot I said?'

''Course not, Nance. Why would I?' He sniffs again. 'Where's that bottle up to?'

'Here.' I pass it over. 'I ought to get back,' I say.

'D'ye want me to come with you?'

'Thankee, but that'll only make Bill more suspicious, *and* he'll get in a right tizzy about you accompanying me home. He'll think you're encroaching on his turf and all.'

'S'pose,' the Dodger says.

'Dodger,' I say, casual-like. 'You know how you can read and all?'

'Mmm,' he says, swallowing.

'Well, wot do you know about libraries?'

'Them's those places in houses where people keep books, vast numbers of them, right? All in rows, alphabeticised.'

'*Alpha*—wot?'

'Alphabeticised. Like, from A to Z. They got to go in order, Nance.'

'I see,' I say.

I am quiet, thinking of Mr Rufus, of how he looked from the books to me and smiled gently. And I thought he were smiling at me cos I were doing the right thing by putting the books the right way up, and all the time, he knew! All the time, he knew.

He knows. He knows I carnt read. And it don' matter to him.

'Why?'

'Why, wot?'

'Why'd you want to know about them books?'

'No matter,' I say.

But then I take up even more of me courage in me hands. I'm on a roll, I am. 'Dodge, where'd you learn to read?' I ask.

He's quiet. Gone frozen. Like I asked something I ought not to have and he carnt find the words to begin. I know wot that's like.

'See, I … I were with someone, someone learned, before I came to the old goat. He … He taught me to read, before I run away, that is.'

I want to know why he ran away. I want to know where he went back to. But it ain't my place to ask anything further. I done enough enquiring for now.

I rise from the straw. 'This is me gone,' I tell him.

'Here,' Dodger says, 'lemme help you.'

He gets up, fumbles for the paling and swings it back, holding it ajar and letting in a smidgen of light. 'Look arter yourself,' he tells me.

Look arter yourself.

He's kind, he is. Who else would tell me to look arter meself?

He won' appear from out the paling same time as me. We don' do that. It's safer this way. He'll wait awhile.

And I can trust him. I know I can. I can trust him like he's me own brother.

CHAPTER THIRTY-SEVEN

I get back to the crib around eleven. I know because them church clocks have jus' chimed the hour. And before I even get in the door, sounds of disruption and chaos reach me, of things being thrown around and banged about and a great deal of clatter and of cursing, and it is with some trepidation that I push upon the door and enter.

'There she is! Where you bin? You—you—' Bill strides over to me looking thunderous, and behind his advancing figure I see the room has been turned upside down and topsy turvy.

'Bill—Bill—' I say, putting me palms up to keep him at bay. 'Remember, you sent me away? Remember, you told me to go to work?'

'I did?' He frowns. He grabs me wrist and staggers backwards and hauls me into the room, and I manage to sidestep the upside-down chamber pot that is fortunately empty and miraculously not broken.

'Wot's the matter?' I say. 'Don' be disputatious. Wot's a-troubling you?'

I try to speak calmly, although me heart is racing like a greyhound at the track and, with the amount of times me poor heart has been racing lately, it would not be surprising if it's taken kennelling and is a-boarding at the racetrack.

Is it Mr Rufus? Has Bill found out about him? Or is it Oliver? Has something happened to the boy, something terrible? Or—or—God forbid!—has Bill discovered I paid a visit to Miss Rose Maylie?

'Where—' he demands, halting in the middle of the room, his eyes sweeping the floor.

And I observe, by the light of the fire, the portmanteau, gaping and empty, to one side, and notice a glint of copper clutched in his other hand ... *the little copper jug* ... and it all comes back to me. I know wot he's on about.

'Where is that, that knick-a-knack, that curio, that gold baby charm call-it-wot-you-will-thingamajig you gave me! *Where*?'

He clutches me wrist tighter and yanks me over and begins to unbuckle his belt—

'Bill, Bill,' I say. 'Steady. Is—is t-that wot all this is about?' I get out, because me tongue has taken that moment to be seized by paralysis.

'Nah,' he says, 'not at all.' But he doesn't have the patience for sarcasm. 'Well, where is it, woman!' he yells, and now the buckle is undone and the belt is being slid from his breeches and he is breathing heavily through his nostrils and twisting the belt around one hand and a fog is drifting over, a fog is coming down over me vision, a fog—

'I hid it,' I cry out, near fainting and only not falling by stumbling against his chest.

'*You wot*? Stand up, woman!' he cries, and pushes me from him.

'I hid it,' I say again, swaying on me feet.

'I heard you the first time. And who, *who* may I arsk, gave you permission to hide it? And where's it at now? Where is it, girl!' He takes me wrist and shakes me like Bullseye does a rat.

'I've hidden it,' I say again, thinking fast, but nothing is coming to me.

'So you've said,' he says slowly. 'Now why would you do a thing like that?'

'Remember …' I get out, trying to invent something, to concoct a story, trying to *think* at all, 'Remember that you were sick, Bill? Poorly? Near delirious, you were. Remember? Well, I hid it for I were worried someone might take advantage of you—of you in—in your state, in your sickness. Someone might steal it from you.'

He frowns again. His grip around me wrist slackens. 'Wot? You stole it from me to protect me. I'm not understanding. *You*?' he thunders.

'Now,' he says, gripping me tightly again. 'I ain't forgiven you, jus' remember that. I ain't never given you permission, so I ain't forgiven you, and I want you to fetch that—that—knick-a-knack tomorrow sharpish, and jus' so there's no funny business, I'm a-coming with you, do you understand?'

I nod meekly.

I nod meekly, but me brain is whirling. Spinning on me shoulders. Me head has turned into a whirligig and is about to spin off into oblivion. How am I to get out of this?

*

'Course I don' sleep a wink, but the outcome of that is by the following morning I have half a plan in me head. Enough, at any rate, for me to creep out of the crib before it's hardly daybreak. Luckily, Bill has always been a man that needs a thorough jiggling to bring him back to the world, and I told you thieves don' do no deals before midday. I know I will pay the price for going without him, but there's naught I can do about it. I mean, jus' think on it—me, taking Bill along to Aunt Maud's? Ha! It's out of the question, innit?

Foxley answers the door to me knock. At first, he has big eyes. 'Miss Titania?' he asks half in shock. But I nod and he ushers me quickly inside, for naturally I am not in me finery and it wouldn' do to leave me standing on the doorstep, giving the neighbours something to gossip about.

'M'lady is not expecting you,' he says in the entrance hall. 'In fact, she is still abed.'

'Oh, dear,' I say, 'she's not poorly, is she?'

'No,' he says, shaking his head. 'She's not an early riser.'

Like Bill, I think, but for different reasons.

'There's something—' I begin. 'There's something I need to discuss with her if she can give me but half-an-hour?'

'Hmm,' he says. 'I will see what I can do. Come through to the kitchen in the meantime,' he says.

When we reach the kitchen, I see Foxley is in the midst of preparing Aunt Maud's breakfast. Eggs are waiting upon the table, and a number of rashers of bacon are sizzling in a pan, a covered plate sitting nearby upon a pot of simmering water keeping warm.

'Tell you wot,' I say to him. 'Why don' you let me take her breakfast up to her?'

Foxley shakes his head. 'Oh, I don't know that she would like that.'

'But I have something important to tell her about—about—'

'Mr Rufus?'

'You could say that.'

I ain't exactly lying, am I? It's more like one of them little white lies.

So I tell Foxley to put his feet up, which he seems altogether tickled by the idea of, and I finish the cooking, and take up the tray with the plate of eggs and bacon upon it, the toast on the side, and a pot of tea and a cup. And it all smells so very good it is a miracle it arrives in front of Aunt Maud without first being molested.

Aunt Maud is sitting up in bed, reading the newspaper with her lorgnette, when I knock and push upon her door.

'Come,' she says, deep-voiced.

A quick glance as I walk in shows me a sumptuously furnished room: fancy wallpaper, paintings, velveteen upholstery, brocaded bed covers, knick-knacks upon the dressing table. Not totally unexpected it is, knowing how ornate the drawing room is, how full of this and that.

Aunt Maud is engrossed for she don' glance me way—she thinks I am Foxley—but when I place the tray upon the bed, she almost drops the eyepiece.

'Nancy?' She looks at me; she seems unsure of me real name.

'The same.'

'What—what are you doing here, child? And why are you dressed as you are?' She eyes with some distaste me dress and shawl.

'I told you I weren' no lady, didn' I? And I am here for there is something I need to discuss with you—'

'A discussion? About what?' She sighs, closes the newspaper and lays it aside. A long grey plait hangs down the front of her blue velvet bedjacket and she tosses it over her shoulder. 'Please don't tell me you have altered your mind regarding the marriage arrangements?'

Pushing herself up in the bed, she taps the coverlet, and I pick up the tray again and place it in front of her. 'No,' I say. 'I haven'.'

'Well, then?' she says, looking at me, not the breakfast.

'Eat,' I tell her. 'Or it will get cold.'

She purses her lips as if affronted by me ordering her about, but nonetheless shakes out her serviette and picks up her knife and fork.

I perch on the edge of the bed. 'It's a long story,' I say, 'but I will try to be brief.'

She cuts into her egg, and it oozes out over the toast. 'Who made these eggs?' she demands, looking surprised.

'I did.'

'Hmph,' she says. She waves her knife in the air, indicating I should continue.

'There is a boy I know,' I say, 'whose life is in danger—'

She looks up at me in alarm and I break off. But I carnt keep stopping every time me words startle her, can I? So I go on. 'There is something I can do to save him, this boy,' I say, 'but it might well mean I endanger meself—and others who are the only family I have—in doing so. And I am torn in two. I do not know wot to do, which way to jump.'

'I thought you said it was a long story?' She speaks around a mouthful of food.

'Oh, that it is. Only … Only I didn' realise'—and here I feel sheepish—'I could achieve making it brief. I thought I were going to be long-winded, getting to the heart of it.'

'You surprised yourself, then?'

'That I did.'

'And what did you learn from that?'

Wot did I learn from that?

Oh, Lord. If I'd a-known this were going to be the Spanish Inquisition, I would not have come.

'Well?' she demands, looking at me.

'That …' I venture, 'that I don't know me own strengths?'

'Precisely. Lesson number one. Number two …' She pauses. 'I know you don't have children, that you are unwed, but let me tell you there is no greater love than that between a parent and a child. And while you are not the mother of this boy, I sense a deep attachment here, a deep bond between you and him—am I correct?'

I nod dumbly.

'So, therefore, you must do all you can to save this boy, even if it means endangering yourself and the lives of others, for'—she pauses again and looks meaningfully at me—'for if you do not, you will never forgive yourself. You will never live in peace again. You won't have a moment's respite. You will forever be haunted by a vision of this boy.'

A vision. That's precisely wot I called him!

'Need I go on?' she asks, putting her knife and fork together on the plate.

I shake me head. 'No,' I say. No, I say, for there is no need to go on. She has confirmed wot I have known all along.

I reach across and take the plate, but leave the tea with her on the tray. She has only eaten one egg, half the toast, and none of the bacon, but no matter. I will eat the remainder on the way downstairs. Lord knows, I need fortifying.

'Thankee,' I murmur.

'Is that all?' She picks up the paper and her lorgnette again.

'Yes,' I murmur.

'See you in church,' she says. She takes her eyes off the printed page to look directly at me, and I carnt help but feel it's a question, more than a statement. *See you in church?*

'Why, yes,' I say, airily, looking anywhere but at her. Oh, Lord. I believe she knows I have no intention of marrying her nephew.

To be honest, I am so overwhelmed by Aunt Maud's advice and this last interaction, I almost forget wot me prime objective was in coming here today. It is only when I reach the bottom of the stairs—after I've paused halfway down to scoff wot's left of her breakfast—that I remember.

Fortunately, I have come down the stairs slowly and quietly, for I been thinking, ain't I? I put the plate gently down on a stair and tiptoe off towards the drawing room.

It is all very easy. Too easy. Very often when things that ought to be difficult turn out to be easy, it is because you have omitted something—take me word for it—and all too often this omission comes back to bite you. But I carnt think of how to make this more difficult. Then again, perhaps it is all in me head? Perhaps it has already been difficult, and I am underestimating meself. I don' know me own strengths, like Aunt Maud said?

Back in the kitchen, Foxley's socked feet are raised upon the table, his head thrown back. He has dozed off in his chair and is snoring gently. I can see why. He is not young, and he is tasked with running the house and being at Aunt Maud's beck and call day and night. Very quietly, therefore, I go about cleaning up and restoring order. By the time the kitchen is gleaming, everything washed and put away, Foxley remains slumbering on, and I let meself out of the front door, and close it gently behind me.

*

Bill sleeps on, too, only he don' snore so gently.

If only the fairer sex had the same opportunity to idle about, do nothing, and snooze when it suited us!

I put the little *bambino* on the table, in clear sight, and then I hightail it. If he's a-going to explode since I went without him, then it's better that I ain't here.

I perambulate along the street, thinking. I don' have a fixed plan where I'm going. I'm simply roaming. And letting me mind wander.

Wot if I did marry Mr Rufus, I mean, *really* marry him, wot would I wear?

Oh, Nancy, Nancy, I hear you saying, stop dreaming. Wot does *that* matter when you have so much else, so many other *more pressing* concerns?

I'll tell you why it matters, sweetheart. I'll tell you why I'm allowing meself a few minutes to think on it.

It matters, for I never will have another opportunity to marry, will I? Another opportunity to dream of marrying.

I mean, think on it …

A girl like me? With a past like mine? And a future …

Wot future? I live from day to day, don' I? Sometimes even from moment to moment. Take the *bambino*. There are going to be consequences, ain't there, if Aunt Maud finds her curio gone a second time? But I'm not a-going to think about them. I will deal with them if and when I'm still here, won' I?

All this butting, all this iffing—*if* this, *if* the other—is making me right crazy, I think.

*

The church is quiet. Well, it is the middle of the day.

Strangely, with summer here and the weather heating up, you'd think it would be warm inside, but it ain't. It's cold. But the air is light and dry, not heavy and damp, and smells ever so slightly of floor polish, and when I pitch me head and look up, up, at the steepled roof, so very far away, the light seems clearer than usual.

Them candles at the altar are burning strongly with their flames straight up, not a flicker of a breeze disturbing them, and I think of the small effort required to blow a candle out, to douse the light. And I think of Oliver and how little it will take to snuff out his life … his light … and plunge me into darkness.

I find meself a pew near the back in a gloomy corner, and push meself into its nook. And I close me eyes, and put me hands together, and I pray.

Don' be fooled. I don' much do this. I don' know wot to say. I haven' a clue. Apart from *Oh, God, oh God*, and that's hardly to be considered a prayer, is it? But I am so betwixt and between right now, jus' the act of doing it has got to do me some good, surely?

Imagine wot I could wear to my wedding if I had the means … A lacy dress with a close-fitting embroidered bodice and long sleeves … Powdery blue to match me eyes? And a pair of soft leather pale blue boots that don' pinch, and lace gloves for me hands, a garland of flowers for me hair … Daisies, perhaps? I like daisies. They are simple. Humble. They have no airs and graces about them. And, yes, a nosegay of daisies to hold—

Nancy! Pull yourself together! This is downright trivial, innit?

CHAPTER THIRTY-EIGHT

The knowledge of the steps I have taken with Miss Rose Maylie works upon me mind. I remember that both Fagin and Sikes have confided their schemes to *me*, which have been hidden from all others, in full confidence that I am trustworthy and beyond the reach of suspicion. Other times, I reflect that Fagin (and Sikes) has led me deeper and deeper, down into an abyss of crime and misery from whence there is no escape. Still other times, I feel some relenting towards the old goat, lest wot I done be the undoing of him, that something should happen to him, something that can be laid fairly and squarely at me door.

Other times, all I think about is Mr Rufus and the temptation of this marriage, and how I wish he could magic me away from all of this. Make me disappear. But at wot cost?

Yet other times, I think of Oliver. And wot Aunt Maud said. I remember his hand trembling in mine. Recall the innocence of his face, the time he came to me and fainted asleep in me arms. That time was the nearest I ever felt to being a mother …

Day and night, I am plagued with uncertainties. I can no longer sleep, nor eat, nor behave in a normal fashion. I know I have grown thinner and am as pale as a candlestick, and that at times I find myself bursting into raucous laughter that is without merriment. Other times, I sit by the fire, silent and dejected, brooding.

If there is one thing that stirs me soul, it is that another waits for me, another desires me—even if it should not be! And there is another thing. It is that I am braver and stronger than I think.

Sunday night, and the bell strikes the hour. Eleven o'clock.

Fagin is here, talking to Bill, while I am crouched on a low seat before the fire. But they both pause to listen.

Sunday night, from eleven until the clock strikes twelve.

'An hour this side of midnight,' Bill says, raising the blind to peer out, and returning to his seat. 'Dark and heavy it is outside, too. A good night for business.'

'Ah,' Fagin says, 'what a pity, my dear, that there's none ready to be done.'

'You're right for once,' Bill says gruffly. 'And it's a pity, for I'm in the humour for work, too.'

Fagin sighs.

'We must make up for lost time when we've got things into a good train, that's all I know,' Bill tells him.

'That's the way to talk,' Fagin says, patting him on the shoulder. 'It does me good to hear you.'

'Does you good, does it?' Bill cries. 'Well, so be it.'

Fagin laughs. 'You're like yourself tonight, Bill, quite like yourself.'

'I don' feel like myself when you lay that withered, old claw on my shoulder, so take it away,' Bill says and shrugs it from his body.

'It makes you nervous, does it, Bill?' Fagin says. 'Reminds you of being nabbed, does it?'

'Reminds me of being nabbed by the devil,' Bill returns, 'not by a trap. There never was another man with such a face as yours, unless it was your father, and I suppose he is singeing his grizzled, red beard by this time, unless you came straight from the old 'un without any father at all betwixt you, which I shouldn't wonder at a bit.'

I rise from me place during this conversation—*Sunday night, from eleven until the clock strikes twelve*—because the Lord strike me dead, I can no longer sit by and do nothing! I find me shawl and draw it around me, and am at the point of tiptoeing across the room, when—

'Hallo,' Bill cries. 'Nance, where you going? Where's the gal going at this time of night?' he asks, turning to Fagin.

'Not far,' I murmur.

'Wot answer's that! Where are you going?'

'I say, not far.' I will not turn to look at Mr Sikes. I carnt.

'And I say, where?' Bill says in a loud voice. 'Do you hear me?' he adds.

'I don't know where,' I say. I have not thought of wot to say. Wot can I say?

'Then I do. Nowhere. You're going nowhere. Sit down.'

'I am not well,' I say. 'I need a breath of air.'

'Put your head out of the winder, then,' Sikes says, 'and take it there.'

'There's not enough air there,' I say, my heart yammering in me chest. 'I want it in the street.'

'Then you won't have it,' Sikes tells me.

He rises. He walks by me. He locks the door and takes out the key. Then, pulling at my shawl, he flings it from me. 'Now stop quietly where you are, will you?'

'It's not such a matter as a shawl would keep me,' I say.

Then, because I am almost out of me senses with despair—Sunday night, past eleven and counting now—I say, 'Do you know wot you are doing?'

'Know wot I'm—oh!' Sikes cries, turning to Fagin. 'She's out of her senses, you know, or she daren' talk to me in that way.'

'You'll drive me on to something desperate,' I murmur, and I place both hands upon me chest as if I can keep meself down, keep meself from some violent outburst. But it's no good, it's no—

'Let me go, will you!' I shriek, 'This minute, this instant—'

'No!' Sikes roars.

'Tell him to let me go, Fagin,' I cry, appealing to him. 'He had better. I won't stand for it! Do you hear me?' I stamp me boot upon the floor.

'Hear you?' Sikes repeats, turning to me. 'Aye, and if I hear you for half a minute longer, the dog shall have such a grip upon your throat as'll tear some of that screaming voice out. Wot has come over you? Wot is it?'

'Let me go,' I say with great solemnity.

Then I sit down on the floor before the door because me legs are quivering so bad they won' no longer hold me up. 'Bill, let me go. You don' know wot you're doing, you don' indeed. I only need one hour—'

'Cut my limbs off one by one,' he cries, seizing me by the arm and hauling me up, 'if I don't think you're gone stark raving mad. Get up!'

'Not till you let me go—not till—never—never!' I scream.

Sikes looks at me, and I tremble beneath that look, I do.

All of a sudden-like, he grabs me hands and drags me, struggling and wrestling as I do—into a chair where he holds me down by force. I am tempted to bite him, like a wild animal, to savage him, but I know wot the consequences will be. I will find meself halfway across the floor with a black eye. I will find meself halfway into the grave. And then wot use will I be to Miss Maylie, to Oliver?

And thus do I sit, imploring by turns, 'Please, Bill?' and struggling on occasion, until the hour passes and there is no point in going on, and I go limp in the chair. But not unconscious. I am still listening.

'Phew,' Sikes says to Fagin, leaving off pinning me down, 'wot a precious, strange girl that is.'

'You may say that,' Fagin says, nodding his head slowly. 'You may say that.'

'Wot did she take it into her head to go out tonight for, do you think? Come, you know her better than me. Wot does it mean?'

'Obstinacy. Women's obstinacy, I suppose, my dear.' Fagin shrugs.

'I thought I had tamed her, but she's as bad as ever.'

'Worse,' Fagin says. 'I never knew her like this, for such little cause.'

'Nor I,' Sikes says. 'I think she's got a touch of fever. She ain't well.'

Fagin nods. Bill goes on, 'When I was stretched on my back that time you were aloof, she was hanging about me all day and night. And we was very poor at the time and I think one way or another, it's worried and fretted her, and being shut up here so long has made her restless, eh?'

'That's it, my dear,' Fagin replies. 'Shh,' he says, then, for he sees me coming over.

I am so agitated, so tightly wound, I scarce know wot to do with me limbs, with meself. But I sit down, wipe my swollen eyes—swollen from bawling—and wrap me arms around meself and rock to and fro. Then I burst out laughing, for if I don' laugh, if I don' somehow expel my frustration, I think I might kill Bill. I will certainly have a go.

'Why, now she's on the other tack!' exclaims Bill. He looks over at Fagin with astonishment.

Fagin nods. After a moment, he leans over to Bill and, after glancing at me, whispers that he thinks I'm a-going to be all right now.

Wot would he know?

He puts on his hat and bids us goodnight and, at the door, asks for someone that would please light him down the stairs?

'Light him down,' Bill says, filling his pipe, 'go on. It's a pity he should break his neck himself and disappoint the sightseers. There, show him a light, Nance.'

And I get up and pick up the candle, for wot else can I do?

Fagin goes down the stairs, me following with the light. When we reach the bottom, he lays his finger upon his lips and draws me to one side.

'What is it, Nancy, dear?' he whispers.

Like I'm a-going to tell him.

'Wot do you mean?' I murmur.

'The reason of all this. If *he*'—he points with a skinny wrinkled forefinger up the stairs—'is so hard with you—he's a brute, Nancy, a brute-beast—why don't you …'

Fagin pauses. His eyes stare into mine. His mouth is all wrinkly like a cat's arse.

'Why don't I wot?'

'No matter just now,' he says, seeming to think better of wot he was going to suggest. 'We'll talk of this again. You have a friend in me, Nance, a staunch friend. I have the means at hand, quiet and close. If you want revenge on those that treat you like a dog—worse than his dog, for the man humours him sometimes—come to me. Come to me, I say. He is the mere hound of the day, but you know me of old, Nance, of old.'

'I know you well,' I say stiffly. I am not moved in the least by his impassioned speech, by his broken hints and meanings. I understand him only too well. If he means to do away with Bill, if Bill has become more trouble than he is worth, he will have to deal with me, first.

'Goodnight,' I say, wanting him gone now. For these troubling thoughts have set me mind on altogether another track. Wot if Fagin now tries to increase his influence with me? Wot if—just when I am involved with other so much more important things—he now lays a trap into which I walk?

He lays his hand on me arm, but I shrink back and go rigid. I am not in me right frame of mind. And I wonder if I will ever be again. 'Goodnight,' I repeat, in wot I hope is a steady voice, and this time I close the door, and go weakly back up the stairs to Bill.

CHAPTER THIRTY-NINE

You will remember how I said before that Bill don' let me out of his sight? Well, over the next few days, there follows a repercussion of this behaviour.

As before, Bill grows weary of me being under his boots, and his nose, and of being where he's a-wanting to be, and never alone. He grows impatient. And irritated. Is angry for little or no reason, like something about to go off, to explode—*boom*!—and that phrase *familiarity breeds contempt* were never truer than it is now.

I scarce know wot to do with meself. How to be? How to disappear? How to make meself insignificant and yet still exist.

How, I keep thinking, *how* am I to meet with Miss Maylie if this keeps up? For it's been almost a fortnight since I first saw her. And if I don' go a-walking on the bridge this Sunday night, she will give up. She will stop looking for me, waiting for me, and this will all be in vain!

Then, as suddenly as it started, Bill's watchfulness lets up. Not entirely, only a smidgin. As if Bill's been given instructions to let me get out on occasion. As if Bill's been told he *must* let me get out and about for the purposes of being followed. They don' trust me, anymore. I know this. For some reason, something's put the wind up them. And I carnt think who that might be. Not the Dodger. Dodger wouldn' do that to me.

Try as I might, however, I carnt ever find anyone following me … And then I start to wonder if it's all in me head? Is this awful and terrible burden I carry about the boy making me lose me grip on reality? Am I imagining things?

I said earlier, wot if Fagey lays a trap into which I walk? It means I dare not visit Mr Rufus. Much as I am crying out for him, longing for him, yearning for the taste and feel of him, I dare not be seen to be a-going to the ramshackle crib or to the posh Mayfair dwelling, for *if* they discover Mr Rufus, if they learn of his existence, I do not want to think wot will happen to him. I think about the forthcoming wedding, too, naturally. But, to be fair, there's so much else going on in me head regarding Miss Maylie, Oliver, Bill, Fagin, the man called Monks, and who's set me up, and who I can trust, and which way I should turn next, that there ain't a lot of space left for much else.

And then on the Friday, two nights afore Sunday, sitting in a corner in The Cripples before a pint of ale again, his long-fingered hands clasped in front of him, staring fixedly at me when I come in the door, is Mr Rufus.

If, before, I could not drag me eyes from him, this time I carnt look at him.

I *carnt.*

I carnt stop, neither.

There is too much at stake.

So I do the only thing I can. I turn and bolt. I run from the establishment and flee around the corner and up the muddy and mirey lane and stoop to lift the paling aside and throw meself into the stable and onto the straw and lie dead quiet, me heart yammering in me chest, while the rib-thin nag neighs softly in greeting.

And I think it is jus' as well. I think it is me only option for now.

I think if I were to be with Mr Rufus tonight I would tell all, confess to everything … And wot would that mean for me?

Wot would that mean for Oliver?

And jus' when I think it is safe to breathe out, to relax, to perhaps emerge and make me way home, the paling is shifted aside, letting in enough light to show me a body crawling in.

I go rigid. Me breath catches in me throat all over again and I dare not breathe.

The paling falls back. I am plunged into darkness once more. Only now there are two of us in here. And I have no idea who the other is. Even me nose is not telling me.

Is it Monks? Is it Monks been following me and come to *throttle* me?

Is it Fagey come to do wot he threatened to?

I hear fumbling, the sound of a match striking, and I push back with me heels on the ground until I am up against Sally's hide—

And suddenly there is light …

'Nancy?'

All the air is escaping from me lungs. I carnt speak.

The match goes out. Which is jus' as well in this place filled with straw and rotting wood.

And Mr Rufus reaches for me.

He reaches for me and holds me close, stroking me hair.

'Why did you run from me?'

'Oh, sir,' I manage to get out.

'You haven't changed your mind, have you, about the wedding?'

I don' answer.

'Nancy?'

'Sir … Sir, there are people who would kill me if they were to find out—'

'What people?'

'I carnt say.'

'You will be safe with me, I give you my word—'

'You don' understand, sir. Nobody is safe from them … *Nobody*.'

'We will run away, go abroad. Live in France. Would you like that, Nancy? I know I would.'

He settles himself better on the rough straw-covered ground, his back against a bundle of hay, and pulls me onto his lap and holds me like a child.

'Tell me about your mother,' I say, cuddling up to him and trying to distract him from the other topic. 'Was she very beautiful?'

He kisses the top of me head. 'She was,' he says.

'And she loved you a great deal?'

'She did.' He pauses, strokes me arm. 'But you don't want to hear about my mother. Not when … Did you know your mother, Nancy?'

'No, sir.'

'I thought as much.'

'Have you been poor and destitute like me, sir?'

'Yes. My father—who was Aunt Maud's brother—was a gambler. He lost everything, including our house, which is why Aunt Maud lent us her dwelling to live in, and moved to another. And, for a time, my mother and I were all right. Not exactly wealthy, but managing to keep afloat, to live in the style we were accustomed. But then the gambling began all over again until … finally … finally my father took his own life.' He pauses. 'Shortly after that, my mother died of a broken heart. She—she never recovered, not only from the disgrace of my father, but of losing the man she loved. For a long time, I pretended to Aunt Maud and to society that all was well whereas in fact I was penniless. Going to bed hungry most nights. That was when I moved out and went to live in the other house, which cost me next to nothing, and for which I did not require servants. And still I did not let on to Aunt Maud.'

'How did she find out?'

'She sent Foxley to find me. It took him a few days to track me down and, to cut a long story short, I was at death's door by the time he discovered me. I made him promise that he would never tell Aunt Maud and he has kept his promise. So you see, Nancy, I have been accustomed to living like you, even down to those who would kill me, since my father left a great deal of unhappy creditors when he died, and I am continually having to go around to them to reassure them that when I inherit I will reimburse at least some—I cannot pay all—of what my father owed them. This was the main reason why I was desperate to marry, Nancy. In addition, this was also my mother's wish, that the creditors be repaid—'

'So that explains why I saw you in The Horse & Groom?' I blurt out, without thinking it through.

'You were following me?'

'I was.' There's no point in holding that back.

'Why?'

'Aunt Maud asked me to—'

'Aunt Maud asked you to follow me?'

'She wanted to be reassured you were not up to mischief. I believe she wanted to be reassured that you weren' also gambling like your father.'

'And you reassured her? Without words?'

'I did.' A small white lie.

'Thank you, Nancy,' he murmurs.

'Could I … Could I make a suggestion, Mr Rufus?'

'You can always make one, Nancy. Whether I act on it or not is another thing.'

'Why don' you make a clean breast of it and tell Aunt Maud everything?'

'I've thought long and hard about that, Nancy, but I am afraid she will disinherit me.'

I think back to wot Aunt Maud said when we were talking about the boy, about a deep attachment, and about how I should do all I can to save him. I believe she was talking not only about me and Oliver, but also about herself and Mr Rufus.

'It's hardly likely, sir. You're all she has. She may act like she would disinherit you, but I don' for one moment believe she would.'

'What gives you that impression, Nancy?'

'Well, we have spent a considerable amount of time together, sir. And there's something else might convince you. When one of your senses is muted, you become more observant. You listen better. Your other senses become heightened.'

'Hmm,' Mr Rufus says, snuggling up to me. 'I believe you have a point.'

'Sir, how is it you know so much about doing a lady's hair and—?'

'Nancy, you must desist from calling me *sir*. Especially if we are to be married.' I carnt see him, but I think he's gazing down at me in severity. His tone is serious. I imagine his moustache might be bristling. And again I wonder wot he really means by *marriage*, but it does me no good to dwell on it. 'Now, say my name without the *sir* part.'

I sniff. 'Rufus,' I say.

'Good.' He kisses the top of me head again. 'Now what was it you were wanting to know?'

'How it is that you know so much about doing a lady's hair, sir.'

'Ah, that. When my mother took ill, I cared for her. I learnt to wash her hair and fashion it the way she was accustomed to wearing it. I dressed her every day, for the simple fact that we could not afford servants. And although this was a sad time, it was also the best time, for I became very close to her.'

He is quiet for a bit and I know he is thinking of his mother, of *Juliet*. It is a pretty name, is it not? I think it is like jewel, a little jewel. I wonder wot me mother's name were? I wish I had memories of her to dwell on, memories that would make me happy. Memories that would make me proud.

'Nancy,' he murmurs, 'I've told you a great deal about me, now it is your turn. Why didn't you know your mother?'

'Oh, sir, I carnt tell you that. It's better you don' know. The more you know, the more dangerous it is for you!'

'Then let us run away straight after we are married, as I have suggested.'

'I carnt do that, either, sir.' I pause. I gaze up at him in the dark, and it crosses me mind that jus' for a short while I have forgotten me troubles. Become content. But now it has all come back—Fagin, and Monks, and Sikes, and Miss Maylie. And Oliver. *Oliver.*

'There is one, a child, whose life depends on me. I must stay true to him, do what is necessary, before I can think of meself.'

He shakes his head. 'Why? Why must you do this!'

'I scarce know the answer to that meself. All I can say is that the child has a hold on me, that if I do not do this, I will never be able to live with meself.'

'You … You would give up your own happiness for this child?'

'Yes.'

'Oh, Nancy.'

He finds me mouth with his own then, and for a time I am in another world, a world where bluebells bloom under birches, where sun shines on wheat, and a stream gurgles through the woods. I don' know where these images come from. Maybe it would be like this in France?

And I start to think that maybe, jus' maybe, I will leave Bill. That perhaps I can find happiness with Mr Rufus. That maybe we *can* escape and get away and start a new life? Is it possible? Dare I dream of such a thing?

'Will you be at the church on Monday?' he asks, when we finally draw apart.

'I don' know, sir. But I will try me best, that I will.'

CHAPTER FORTY

The church clocks are chiming three quarters past eleven as I get meself onto London Bridge.

Two weeks since I last saw Miss Maylie! And I have been lucky—or have I been lucky because someone has planned it this way?—for Bill is out tonight and I been able to get away without a struggle, without almost losing me life. Fagin has sent Bill somewhere, on some errand, and he won' be back before daybreak. This much I know.

Me footsteps echo on the cobbles. It's a quiet and dark night, and cold. And the moon, that were only a sliver anyway, has long gone, slunk over the rooftops. I keep glancing over me shoulder, for although I'm alone and I've noticed no-one following me, I have this niggling doubt. A shadow hanging over me. A premonition, if you will. Real or imagined, I do not know.

I go across the bridge to the Surrey shore, scanning all the foot-passengers that I meet. But they are few and far between, and I come to an abrupt halt.

She is not here. Miss Maylie is not present. Nowhere in sight, at any rate. Then, again, perhaps I've not seen her. Perhaps … And I turn on me heel and cross to the other side of the bridge and return the way I've come.

At nearly the centre of the bridge, I stop again and stand in silence, looking out over the water. The water laps against the damp stonework like a thirsty dog. The mist hangs over the dank and dreary river, deepening the ruby red of the flickering fires that burn upon the small wooden boats moored off the banks. Smoke-stained storehouses loom like ghouls either side of the river and smoke drifts from chimneypots, a soft, black drizzle gone into mourning for the death of the sun. The tower of old Saint Saviour's church and the spire of Saint Magnus rise above the sleeping forest of masted ships, stretch into the murky night air, reaching for something I can only dream of.

I patter to and fro, and to and fro, thinking. Wot to do? Wot to do?

I will wait until twelve, that is wot I will do. And I have no sooner decided that than the bell of St Paul's tolls the midnight hour. *One, two, three, four …* The clang echoes in the fog like some death knell and a shiver runs up me spine. Oh, that I was not here! Oh, that I was safe in me own bed! But where would that leave us?

More important-like, where would that leave the boy?

Midnight gone now, and still no sign of Miss Maylie. And, again, I am in turmoil. *Wot to do?*

Then, appearing out of nowhere, two figures emerge on the bridge. One is a young lady, the other is a gentleman, holding her arm.

Wot a relief! I feel faint with it.

It seems I come upon them unexpectedly for they halt with exclamations of surprise. And, yes, timidity.

Then I understand why. For before I can say, *Miss Maylie?* a man in the garments of someone from the country brushes past me. I have not known he were behind me. He's way too close, considering a vast and empty passageway is on the other side of the bridge. I don' see his face. His hand is up against his hat. His hand is up against his hat, shielding his face, and I am spooked. All a-shiver.

'Not here,' I call hurriedly. 'Not here. Come away, down the steps yonder.'

The man takes that moment to turn. 'Wot you taking up the whole of the pavement for!' Real impertinent, he is. I don' like it one bit.

'Quick,' I say.

The steps to which I point are on the Surrey bank, on the same side as Saint Saviour's church, and form landing stairs coming up from the river. They consist of three flights, and I have reached the bottom of the second flight and can hear the tide lapping against the steps, when a voice comes from above.

'This is far enough,' the gentleman calls to me. 'I will not suffer this young lady'—he means Miss Maylie—'to go any further. Many people would have distrusted you too much to have come even so far, but you see I am willing to humour you.'

'To humour me? You're considerate, indeed, sir. To humour me!' I repeat. 'Well, it's no matter.'

'Why, for what purpose can you have brought us to this strange place? Why not speak to us above, where it is light, instead of bringing us to this dismal—'

'I told you before,' I interrupt. 'I am afraid to speak to you up there. I don't know why it is, but I have a fear and a dread hanging over me.'

'A fear of what?' the gentleman says, more gently. I return halfway up the first flight of stairs, and I see now in the half-light that he is elderly with grey hair. He must be Mr Brownlow. It seems likely from Oliver's description.

'I scarcely know. I wish I did. Horrible thoughts of death have been upon me all day. I swear I have seen the image of a *coffin* in everything I do, and they carried one close to me, in the streets, tonight—'

'There is nothing unusual in that,' the old gen'leman says. 'They have passed me often enough.'

'*Real* ones, that may be,' I say. 'This was not real—'

The old gen'leman makes a sound halfway between incredulity and irritation.

'Oh, please,' Miss Maylie says, 'please be calm. Speak to her kindly,' she says to him that I think is Mr Brownlow.

'You were not here last Sunday night,' he says to me, but he has taken her advice and his tone *is* kind.

'I couldn' come,' I say. 'I were kept by force.'

'By whom?'

'Him that I told the young lady of before.'

'You were not suspected of holding any communication with anybody on the subject which has brought us here tonight, I hope?' Mr Brownlow asks, anxious-like.

I shake me head. 'No. It's not easy for me to leave him unless he knows why. I couldn't have seen the lady when I did, but that I gave him a drink of laudanum before I came away.'

'Did he awake before you returned?' Mr Brownlow asks.

'No, and neither he nor any of them suspect me.' I cross me fingers behind me back when I say this, because I have me doubts about Fagin. Why has he taken the trouble to let me know explicit-like that Bill is away tonight?

'Good,' Mr Brownlow says. 'Now listen to me.'

'I am ready,' I say.

'This young lady,' he says—he means Miss Maylie, 'has communicated to me, and some other friends who can be safely trusted, what you told her a fortnight since. I confess'—he pauses and takes a breath—'that I had doubts whether you were to be relied upon, but now I believe you are.'

'That I am,' I say.

'I believe it,' he says. 'Now what we propose to do is to extort the secret regarding Oliver, whatever it may be, from this man Monks. But if—*if*—he cannot be secured or if secured, cannot be acted upon as we wish, you must deliver up the man called Fagin—'

'Fagin?' I cry, starting back.

'That man must be delivered up by you,' Mr Brownlow states, matter-of-factly, as if we are talking about procuring a jug of milk or delivering a side of ham.

'I carnt,' I say, shaking me head. 'I will not—I will never do that. Devil that he is, and worse than devil as he has been to me, I will never do that.'

'You will not?'

Mr Brownlow hikes his thumbs into his coat pockets. He seems prepared for this answer. Expecting it like.

'Never,' I say.

'Tell me why?'

'For one reason,' I tell him, 'that the lady knows and will stand by me, for I have her promise. And for this other reason, besides, that bad life as he has led, I have led a bad life, too. There are many of us. And I'll not turn upon them who might—any of them—have turned upon me, but didn', bad as they are.'

'Then,' Mr Brownlow says quickly, 'put Monks into my hands and leave him to me to deal with.'

'Wot if he turns against the others?'

'I promise you that in that case, if the truth is forced from him, there the matter will rest. There must be circumstances in Oliver's short history which it would be painful to drag before the public eye, and if the truth is elicited, they shall go scot-free.'

'And if it is not?'

'Then, this man Fagin shall not be brought to justice without your consent. And in such a case, I believe I could show you reasons which would persuade you to give it.'

'Do I get the lady's promise for that?' I say, for I can feel meself being swayed to Mr Brownlow's point of view.

'You do,' Miss Maylie says. 'My true and faithful pledge.'

'Monks would never learn how you knew wot you do?'

'Never,' Mr Brownlow says. 'The intelligence will be so brought to bear upon him, he will never even guess.'

'I have been a liar, and among liars, from a little child,' I tell them, 'but I will take your words.'

I proceed, low-voiced, to describe to Mr Brownlow and Miss Maylie the name and situation of The Three Cripples where Monks can be found, and Mr Brownlow brings out a notepad and makes some hasty notes. I tell them the nights and the hours at which Monks frequents the place, and the best position to watch for him.

'What does he look like?' Mr Brownlow asks, pencil lifted, waiting in the air.

'He is tall,' I say, 'and strongly made, but not stout. And he has a lurking walk, and as he walks he constantly looks over his shoulder, first one side, then t'other. And don't forget that his eyes are sunk in his head so much deeper than any other man's, you might tell him by that alone. His face is dark, like his hair and eyes, and although he carnt be more than eight and twenty, his features are drawn and haggard … And, and his lips are scarred with teeth marks, for he has desperate fits, and sometimes even bites his hands and covers them with wounds. Why do you start so?' I ask, for Mr Brownlow seems to shiver.

'It is nothing,' he says. 'Go on, please.'

'In all truthfulness,' I say, 'I have only seen him twice, and both times he was covered up by a large cloak, but I have learned all this from others. Particular-like, upon his throat, so high that you can see a part of it below his neckerchief when he turns his head, there is—'

'A broad red mark, like a burn or scald,' cries Mr Brownlow.

I utter a cry of surprise. 'How's this? You know him, then!'

For a moment, I go rigid with fear. I am, at any rate, so frozen that I feel the breeze whispering across the river.

'I think I do,' Mr Brownlow murmurs. 'We shall see. Many people are singularly like each other though, so it may not be the same.'

He pauses.

And I, too, am quiet, for I have naught left to say. Except … Except …

'How is it you know each other?' I ask. 'Can you tell me that?'

'Ahh,' Rose says.

'Of course,' Mr Brownlow says. He looks at Rose.

'Mrs Maylie and I were in London for a few days,' Rose says, 'en route to the coast with Oliver, when Oliver came to me to say that he had seen the gentleman who was so good to him: Mr Brownlow, of whom we had so often talked about. Oliver saw him getting out of a coach and going into a house. I took the boy directly there, without a moment's loss, and you can imagine the outcome when I brought Oliver into the room. Such a happy occasion,' Rose says, wiping at the tears that have sprung to her eyes.

'Now,' Mr Brownlow says, quietly. 'You have been of invaluable assistance and I wish you to be the better for it. Is there something I can do for you?'

I shake me head.

'You will not persist in that,' Mr Brownlow says with a voice of kindness. 'Think now. Tell me.'

'Nothing, sir,' I say. 'You can do nothing to help me. I am past all hope.'

'I do not say it is in our power to offer you peace of heart and mind,' Mr Brownlow says, 'but we can offer you a quiet asylum, either in England or, if you fear to remain here, in some foreign country. And this is not only within the compass of our ability, but our most anxious wish. Before the dawn of morning, before this river wakes to the first glimpse of daylight, you shall be placed entirely beyond the reach of your former associates, and leave an absence of all traces behind you, as if you were to disappear from the earth this moment. Come,' Mr Brownlow says, looking at me encouragingly, 'I would not have you go back to exchange one word with your old companions, or take one last look at any old haunt, or breathe the very air that is pestilence and death to you. Quit them all, while there is time and opportunity!'

'Oh, please,' Miss Maylie says. 'She will be persuaded now. She is hesitating, I am sure.'

They are both staring at me, waiting, anticipating …

'I fear not, my dear,' the old gen'leman says to her. How it is he seems to know me own mind in so short a time, I do not know.

'No, sir,' I say. 'You are right, I am not persuaded. I am chained to me old life. I loathe and hate it, but I carnt leave it. I have gone too far to turn back now. And the fear comes upon me again,' I say, looking hastily around, for I swear them shadows are moving. 'I must get on. I must get home.'

'*Home*?' repeats Miss Maylie. As if the likes of me could have such a thing!

'Home, lady. To such a home as I have raised with the work of me whole life. Let us part. I shall be watched or seen. Go, go. All I ask now is that you leave me and let me go me own way alone.'

'It is useless,' the old gen'leman says with a sigh. 'We compromise her safety perhaps by staying here. We may have detained her longer than she expected already.'

'Yes. Yes.' I agree. 'You have.' And another shiver goes down me spine.

'What can be the end of this poor creature's life?' Miss Maylie blurts out. She is speaking out of turn, such is her distress.

And I ask you, wot about me own distress?

'Look before you, lady,' I say. 'Look at that dark water. How many times do you read of such as me who spring into the tide, and leave no living thing to care for or bewail them. It may be years from now, or it may be only a few months, but I shall come to that at last.'

'Do not speak thus,' returns Miss Maylie, practically sobbing.

'Do not concern yourself, miss,' I say. 'It will never reach your ears. Now, I really must go!'

Mr Brownlow turns away, but Miss Maylie cries, 'This purse, take it for my sake. That you may have some means in an hour of trouble and need.'

'You don' understand,' I say. 'I have not done this for money! I have done this for the boy, for the child. For Oliver. For children are innocent and should be treated as such. Let me at least have that.'

They are quiet, then. They regard me. I believe they are taken aback, surprised that someone like me is capable of such a thought. But surely this has crossed their minds? Surely they don't believe that if one is poor and needy, one must also be dim-witted? Or without principles?

'Give me something that you have worn, if you must,' I say gently to Miss Maylie. 'I should like to have something small—

'No, no, not a ring'—for she is removing her gloves—'perhaps a handkerchief? There, a handkerchief will do.'

Miss Maylie quickly retrieves one and reaches out to press a square of white lace into me hand.

I do not linger any longer. I pass them by and head up to the bridge.

'Bless you,' I say, looking over me shoulder at them. 'Goodnight.'

'Goodnight,' they respond.

Is there any good to be found in the night? Is there any good to be found in a place without light?

I have been absent too long. Much too long. And I take the stairs as fast as me legs can carry me and get as far as the stone pillar upon the bridge. Me pins won' hold me up no longer and I sink to me knees in the shadows.

A hackney coach goes by, but all I hear is them horses' hooves hitting the stones. Me vision is blurred. The fog has come down. All is darkness.

After some time, I come to. I rise and get to me shaky feet, feeling more in charge of me senses. The clock is striking one as I melt away into the darkness, but it seems to me to be the single loneliest sound I have ever heard.

CHAPTER FORTY-ONE

I am awoken by a horrific noise. And, befuddled with sleep, I half raise meself and gaze about in the semi-dark. The day has padded into the room, I see. Faint and grey, it sits behind them curtains like a curious cat, waiting to see wot will happen next.

Someone is trying to get in and the door is not having a bar of it. The door is resisting attempts to open it—on me behalf. It has, it appears, a mind of its own.

'Bill,' I cry, as the ruckus becomes too much and I start from the bed—

But the door is thrown violently open, juddering upon its hinges.

Sikes.

His shirt is hanging out, his brow sweaty, his hair wild. He looks half-crazed. Maniacal.

Me heart begins to panic, to thrust against the ribs imprisoning it. It fears wot's coming.

'Hallo, Bill, sweetheart,' I say, gently, quietly.

'Get up!' Sikes orders, and he draws the candle that burns upon the table from its candlestick holder, and hurls it into the grate.

I push aside the bedcovers to rise, to open the curtains, but he thrusts his hand before me.

'Where do you think you're going?'

'Bill,' I say, 'why d'you look like that at me?' For he stares at me in an unpleasant way, like he has a stench under his nose.

His nostrils are dilated. He breathes hard. It is like he is possessed.

'Nancy!' Sudden-like, he grasps me by the throat, drags me off the bed.

Stumbling, I manage to regain me balance, to stay upright.

But he claps his heavy hand across me mouth and, 'Bill,' I gasp, struggling, me voice muffled by his hand as he yanks on me hair. 'I-I won' scream—or cry—not once.'

He says nothing. If anything he pulls harder. Me hair feels as if it's about to come out by its roots. All I can think is that this is about last night. This is about me meeting Miss Maylie and Mr Brownlow. Or is about Mr Rufus? And how does Bill know?

'Speak to me,' I get out as he releases me mouth. 'Tell me wot I have done!'

'You know, you she-devil!' he cries. 'You was watched tonight. Every word you said was heard.'

'Then, spare my life, for the love of Heaven, as I spared yours.'

I turn in his clutches, much as it pains me scalp, and cling to his arms.

'You cannot have the heart to kill me,' I say. 'Think of all I have given up only this one night for you!'

He bites on his lower lip so hard I wonder he don' draw blood.

'Bill,' I cry, fighting to lay me head upon his chest, 'the gen'leman and that dear lady told me tonight of a home in some foreign country, where I could end me days in solitude and peace.

Let me see them again! Let us both leave this dreadful place and lead better lives and forget how we have lived. It is never too late to repent. But we must have time—a little time.'

With his free hand, he pulls his pistol from his back pocket.

He's still clutching me by the hair, tearing at it, and I teeter and stumble at his feet and he swings the pistol around one-handed. Swings it, raises the butt, brings it down.

Brings it down upon me face.

I stagger away. Fall from him. Fall to me knees. The pain is horrific. The blood, wet, sticky and red, runs down me cheeks and alongside me nose.

On the floor, on me knees, I fumble in me pocket for the handkerchief, the white handkerchief, and I hold it up in me folded hands as high towards Heaven as I can. I mumble something. It may be the Lord's Prayer that desperation makes me recall. *Our Father, who art in Heaven …*

For a moment, just a moment, when nothing further happens, I think I am safe. I think it is over. But it is always when I think it is over that it is jus' beginning. And somehow I remember the words and I go on praying ...

Forgive those who trespass against us as we trespass against them …

Then something club-like and heavy strikes me head and I sprawl sideways. I am undone.

For ever and ever. Amen.

CHAPTER FORTY-TWO

I lie in the centre of the room surrounded by me blood, blinded by it coursing over me eyes, and feel meself rising from the floor. Rising from the floor and floating into the air.

It is the strangest thing because I *knows* I'm still lying there. I can *see* me own body, quiet and still, and not moving.

And yet, here I am, wafting weightless up towards the ceiling. And just when I think I'm a-going to bump me head on the rafters, just when I can see the sharp splinters of the rough beams, I stop and hover. *Hover*, I tell you.

Wot is this?

A cold shiver runs down me back, only I carnt feel it. It's not even a sensation. I carnt feel nothing. It's the body on the floor it's happening to.

I realise wot's going on. Wot I'm doing up here, looking down on meself. Wot I am. Wot I have become.

I'm a spirit that ain't departed.

And who knows how long I drift up here while I lie down there below, while he lies half-propped against the wall, while

Bullseye lies down in a corner with his head upon his paws, while the world continues to turn? Because time seems to have no meaning. It could be half the night. It could be half a year. It could be half a century.

It is the sun that bursts into the room with radiance and clarity. That bright ball that brings back not light alone, but new life, and hope, and freshness to mankind. I tell you, anyone would think the sun were glad to see the end of me …

But it is the sun that gets things moving.

It lights up the room where I lie. In all that brilliance, it shows me Bill Sikes clambering to his feet. Bill Sikes looking at me body with horror. Bill Sikes flinging a rug over me as if he cannot stand the sight, and then just as quickly yanking it off again. Why, I don' know. Maybe it is me eyes he doesn' like, for they are open. He won' come near me to close them. And so I lie staring up at the ceiling.

The man moves around me like a puppet, jerking and shaking in fright. He tries to strike a light, clumsily dropping the match the first time and cursing and trying to pick it up between two fingers, but trembling so hard he cannot. Finally, he gets a second one alight, and kindles the fire and thrusts the club into it. And my hair, which is caught upon the end of it, blazes and shrinks into cinders and, caught by a draught, whirls up the chimney. That frightens him, that and the smell, for he steps back. He remembers, then, he's still clutching the club and holds it in the fire until it breaks in two, then pushes it deep into the embers to burn away.

All the while, Bullseye sits motionless in the corner, gazing on.

Sikes fills a bowl with water from the jug in the corner and washes himself, but there are stains and splashes upon his clothing that will not come out, and he takes the scissors to them and cuts them loose, so his jacket is mottled with holes, and throws the bloody tatters upon the fire.

He calls to the dog, but Bullseye won' move. Sikes stumbles over to him and drags him backwards by the collar—never taking his eyes off wot lies in the middle of the room—to the door.

Then they leave the room. Sikes shuts the door softly behind him and locks it. I hear them going down the stairs. I bob down to the window and gaze out. Bullseye pauses at a lamp post to lift his leg. Sikes stops to look up to the window. He doesn't seem to see me, even though I put up me hand. I put up me hand and me fingers go clean through the glass and I draw them back in and gaze at them in consternation. Then I push them out through the glass again, further this time.

Sikes whistles to Bullseye. I follow them from above, the sun sparkling off the dew on the clustered and chimneyed roofs, as they wend their way down the lane through the fog.

There is fog everywhere. Fog up the river, where it flows among the meadows; fog down the river, where it rolls among the shipping masts. Fog hovering in the rigging of the great ships. Fog lying out on the yards, drooping on the pens of Smithfield, dropping from the ears of beasts. Fog, as if we were in a balloon and hanging in the clotted clouds.

The man and the dog go through Islington, walk up the hill at Highgate on which stands Dick Whittington's stone and the cat upon it. Bullseye makes a wide berth of that, then they turn down to Highgate Hill. They strike off to the right again, taking the footpath across the fields and skirting Caen Wood, and coming out on Hampstead Heath. Their route seems unsteady of purpose, and Sikes keeps looking over his shoulder with a haunted look in his eyes. As if he can see me. As if he knows I am following.

He reaches the fields at North End and lays himself down under a hedge and tries to sleep, but it don' last long before he is up and away again, heading back to town, then back again, then drinking from a ditch, then laying down, then getting up, then wandering again for miles. It's like he carnt make up his mind which way to turn.

Finally, an abandoned shed, tumbledown and half-hidden by three tall poplar trees in a field, offers shelter. He enters, Bullseye following.

It is dark inside, and the wind moans through the trees. A rusted plough share stands forgotten and forlorn in one corner, some farming tools in another. Sikes looks about, then lays himself down on some matted straw, the dog close by. The dog, I notice, is not inclined to hang about Sikes's side. The dog, I reckon, has been taking notes.

But Sikes is no sooner down than he starts up and rushes pell-mell back out, calling to Bullseye and shielding his eyes from the sight of me.

When he and the dog finally lay themselves down under yet another hedge, Sikes trembles and cold sweat seeps from every pore. I leave them be. I have things to do with me time and, to be truthful, I ain't got any idea how much time I do have. Who's to say I might any minute now disappear all of a sudden-like?

CHAPTER FORTY-THREE

I ain't forgotten wot day it is today. As if I could.

When I reach the church they are all already gathered inside. They are gathered inside and glancing at their fob watches. They are gathered inside and the light from them vaulted ceilings is drifting down upon their heads like hallowed fairy dust. They are gathered inside and Mr Rufus puts his hands in his pockets, shifts from one foot to t'other, and gazes worriedly up the aisle. Foxley is the best man and is talking low-voiced to the priest, who looks concerned.

The only guest not anxious about me absence is Aunt Maud. Aunt Maud is in a wheelchair positioned at the side of a pew. She wears a bright, aqua-blue dress that I ain't seen before and is watching Mr Rufus, her chin propped upon her hand, her rings catching the light. She seems to be in a pensive mood. I believe Aunt Maud has the same sixth sense I do—and I think instinct already told her I ain't going to turn up. I think instinct told her a while ago I were never going to. I believe she has been playing a little game with me while I've been playing a little game with her.

She suspected I had no intention of marrying Mr Rufus. See, she's a canny old bird. She knows wot I am. She's seen wot I am, and wot I discussed with her about Oliver would've only cemented this opinion. This little ceremony here is a test she has laid out for Mr Rufus. She wants to see how far he will go to please her. It is also why there are no invited guests.

In the long run, I believe it don' matter. I believe she has made up her mind wot she is going to do about him and the house. She has a gruff exterior, but a soft inside, and I believe she will do the right thing.

There are no wedding flowers in the church. Where the wedding flowers should be, there is a big copper bowl of oranges. Ha!

Aunt Maud beckons to Mr Rufus, who comes over.

I carnt hear wot they're saying, but Mr Rufus, in his wedding finery, goes down on his haunches to talk to her. He is wearing a tawny-red patterned waistcoat the same colour as his hair and stuck into his cravat is—if I am not mistaken—a small brooch of a fox.

Mr Rufus smiles. He looks kindly at his aunt. Together they gaze at the oranges. I believe he is explaining the reason for the fruit, for I hear him mention me other name, Titania, and Foxley, who is listening in, smiles and looks touched. Dear old gent that he is. Mind you, he's probably smiling for he knows me given name. I wonder if one day Aunt Maud and Foxley will let on to Mr Rufus that they knew the real me? I do hope not.

Mr Rufus returns to stand down the front alongside Foxley. Foxley pulls out his fob watch and glances at it yet again. He shambles back up to the enormous front door, opens it and peers out.

And returns to Mr Rufus's side. They confer. The priest joins in.

After some minutes, Foxley goes to Aunt Maud and turns her wheelchair around and they go back up the aisle, Aunt Maud steepling her fingers together. I believe she is thinking.

The priest begins to talk to Mr Rufus. Perhaps the priest is telling Mr Rufus it is a good thing I have not turned up.

It *is* a good thing I have not turned up. It is a good thing. *A good thing.* If I say it enough times, perhaps I can believe it?

Mr Rufus and I were not meant for one another. It might well have been all bluebells blooming, sun shining on wheat, and the scent of oranges, but it was unlikely to last. Not unless I changed and became someone I am not.

It is better he has a broken heart now than later. Later, when he would despise me for me lack of education, for the way I speak, for wot I am—was.

I know he will find someone once he has his inheritance. Someone who is more suited to his circumstances, someone refined. Someone, I hope, who will love him as much as I do. As I did.

Who need never know that once upon a time he were poor, that once upon a time he took a girl like me into his bed, and into his life. That once upon a time he showed me a love that I did not know nor yet can ever forget.

Oh, Lord, I am getting sentimental!

The priest has disappeared. Mr Rufus is still standing at the front of the church, only now he has turned his back on the others disappearing out of the big door, and is gazing forwards, one hand on a church pew.

Roo-fus. His name on a level, but for a small peak of excitement that's not obvious, that he tries his best to hide, his name stays the same. Smooth and even. Steady and reliable. Like the man.

Mr Rufus is gazing forwards and, even as I watch, a tear slides down his cheek. He puts the back of his hand to his nose and sniffs. Then, stepping forwards, he bends and picks an orange from the bowl. Just the one. He puts it gently into his pocket. Then he turns and walks up the aisle and out of the church door. He don' look back.

And it strikes me that perhaps I have misjudged him. Perhaps he truly does want to marry me. Loves me. At the start it was but a scheme, perhaps? But as he grew to know me, and me to know him, he found he loved me after all, as I loved him. I mean, the bowl of oranges and the brooch of a little fox, they surely must mean something?

One day, I think to meself, he might be in his library. The library as belonged to Aunt Maud's deceased husband, Mr Bernard. The library that will soon, I predict, if me instincts are correct, belong to Mr Rufus. One day, he might be in this library, and he might recall the books need rearranging—putting back in *alphabetised* order—for that were the thing I omitted to do, the clue that woulda given away me lack of literacy skills, and about which Mr Rufus never remarked, for he is too kind. Anyways, he will be pulling all these volumes out and reordering them, and he will see something glittering, something shining, at the back of a certain book with a large *N* in the upper third of its spine, and he will reach for it and come away with an amethyst and pearl necklace clutched in his fingers like a fistful of stars, and he will remember me. I hope he will remember me. And think fondly of me. That is me wish, at any rate.

The church now is empty. The church is deserted and I hover down to where the hallowed light drifts upon the pulpit and upon the altar. And upon the place where Mr Rufus and I might have stood together, and gazed into each other's eyes and exchanged vows, which would have meant the world to me. I hover down and wait in the light that is like fairy dust. I look up and am momentarily blinded.

I am momentarily blinded, waiting in the light. Or is it that I wait in the light and am blinded momentarily? Or, am I waiting, momentarily blinded by the light?

So many ways to say something.

So many ways to live a life.

So many ways to bestow warmth, kindness and love.

And although I wait and although I am blinded, no longer momentarily, I am still here.

Still here.

CHAPTER FORTY-FOUR

Strange that I presumed I would disappear. Pffft! Like that. That the church would be the time and place, only it weren' to be. Obviously.

For here I am. Drawn across the city to the noise, to the clamour, to the hue and cry.

Near to that part of the Thames on which the church at Rotherhithe squats, where the buildings on the banks are dirtiest and the vessels on the river blackest with the dust of colliers and the smoke of close-built low-roofed houses. Here is the filthiest, the strangest, the most extraordinary of places known as Folly Ditch.

To reach this place, you must go through a maze of close, narrow and muddy streets, thronged by the roughest and poorest of water-side people. Like me, they are. Tottering house-fronts lean over the muddy pavement, the rooms small and filthy and the air tainted.

And here, in one of these tumbledown shacks, a man has emerged by a door on the roof. He has planted a board firmly against the door, and is creeping over the tiles and looking over the parapet, and that man is Bill Sikes.

Following him, but unseen by the man, is a dog—Bullseye. Something tells me Bullseye ran away when his master, knowing the dog at his heels would assist to identify him, tried to drown him in a pond and failed. Bullseye, not knowing which way to turn, has been skulking behind his master ever since. Poor thing. But dogs are like that, aren' they? Loyal and true. Never wholly deserting their masters.

A crowd has gathered below, which is the noise I've been drawn to, for alongside the house the tide is out and the ditch is a bed of murky mud. On the opposite side of the ditch, a mob has entered the dwellings and thrown up the sashes and there are faces pressed to every window, all shouting, and some raising their fists to cry, 'They have him now! They have him!'

'I promise fifty pounds,' cries an old gentl'man, who I recognise as Mr Brownlow, 'fifty pounds to the man who takes him alive.' And a roar from the crowd goes up.

The man shrinks down against the rooftop, bullied into submission by the fierceness of the crowd and wot seems to be the impossibility of escape, then springs sudden-like to his feet.

For the exit by which he crawled out upon the rooftop has been breached, and he is roused into new strength and energy. He sets his foot against a stack of chimneys, fastens one end of a rope brought out with him tightly and firmly around the stack, and with the other end makes a strong noose with his hands and teeth in almost seconds. Now he can let himself down by the cord to the ground and he takes out his knife ready to cut the rope and drop the remaining distance into the mud.

And he brings the loop over his head prior to slippin' it beneath his armpits. And Mr Brownlow warns those about him the man is about to lower himself. And, at that instant, the man looks behind him on the roof, throws his arms above his head and utters a yell of terror.

For I have wandered over and perched upon the roofline.

'The eyes again!' he screeches and looks directly at me as if he would sear my soul with his gaze.

He staggers as if struck by lightning. Loses his balance. Tumbles over the parapet. At his neck is the noose, and it runs up swift as an arrow with his weight and tight as a bowstring. At his neck is the noose, and he falls for five-and-thirty feet. A sudden jerk, a convulsion of the limbs, and he hangs there, the open knife clenched in one hand. And no matter how I look at it, there's still a part of me that's sorry.

Bullseye has been standing, cowering, behind me. Now he runs backwards and forwards along the parapet, howling. I call to him—he ain't never done anything to me—but he is a lost cause, and collecting his hairy and dirty self on the edge, his less than white front paws padding against the gutter, he springs forwards. He jumps for his master's shoulders, but misses. And, his body, turning over as he goes, falls to the stones below.

I do not look to see wot happens. I carnt. I have seen too much already.

CHAPTER FORTY-FIVE

Time, I have to say, seems to have a mind of its own while I am in this state of flux. That when I am not bearing witness to something of note, I am neither here nor there.

At this point, however, I were here bearing witness and I went along for a ride, so to speak. Yes, a ride. Well, a carriage were involved and a trip to the country, so I am not stretching the truth. See, I found meself in a travelling coach together with Oliver. Yes, Oliver! It does me heart good to know he's safe and well. Also, in the coach are Miss Rose Maylie, and the elderly Mrs Maylie, the lady who owns the Chertsey house where the failed break-in took place, and a lady with a familiar face. I believe she is the one who stuck her head out of the window of Mr Brownlow's house on the day I were watching and a dog was making a ruckus. Mrs Bedwin, her name is. There is also an elderly man, the same one I saw with a limp going into the house, and I hear him being called Mr Losberne.

I am up near the roof, keeping out of harm's way. Travelling behind us in a post-chaise is Mr Brownlow, accompanied by another man whose name I know, but whose name I do not like saying. It is around three o'clock, judging by the position of the sun and shadows, and those in the carriage have not spoken to one another since I been on board. They each seem to be in a state of preoccupation, and I wonder wot they are thinking, and where exactly we are bound for? For we seem to be travelling, not in the direction of Chertsey, but somewhere else. And we come now upon a village, and here Oliver becomes animated.

'See there! There!' he cries, eagerly clasping Miss Maylie's hand and pointing out of the carriage window with the other. 'That's the stile I came over. There are the hedges I crept behind for fear anyone should overtake me and force me back,' he says, and I believe he is describing to Miss Maylie leaving the sad and sorry places of his childhood, and his trip into London. And I recall the first time I saw him in the streets with Dodger, and me instinct telling me we were inextricably linked. Well, I weren' wrong, were I?

'Yonder is the path across the fields leading to the old house where I stayed when I was a little child,' he says. 'Oh, Dick, Dick, my dear old friend, if only I could see you now!'

'You will see him soon,' Miss Maylie replies. 'You shall tell him how happy you are, and how rich you are grown, and that in all your happiness, you have none so great as the coming back to make him happy, too.'

'Yes,' Oliver says, 'and we'll—we'll take him away from here, and have him clothed and taught, and send him to some quiet country place where he may grow strong and … and … Shall we?'

Miss Maylie nods, for the boy is smiling through such happy tears, it is clear she cannot speak. And I wonder whether they will indeed rescue this other poor child called Dick from his plight, and how many other poor children they can rescue before they admit the number who are despairing and in need of assistance, the vast quantities of children who are beyond hope, is beyond them?

'You will be kind and good to him, for you are to everyone,' Oliver says, turning to Miss Maylie and patting her hand. 'It will make you cry, I know, to hear what he will tell you, but never mind, it will all be over, and you will smile again. I know that, too—to think how changed he will be. You did the same with me. Dick said God bless you to me when I ran away. And I will say God bless you now to him, and show him how I love him.'

The carriage makes its way through narrow streets and, like Oliver, I peer out the window. He seems to see a number of houses and places he remembers, for he cries, 'There's the undertakers'—Sowerberry's, I think he told me it were called, the place where Oliver slept among the coffins—'and there's … and there's …'

We drive straight to the door of the town's hotel and everyone alights and goes in. I follow and hover in a cosy sitting room, which is very grand, near Miss Maylie and Oliver, who have sat down and speak in whispers, as if they are afraid to hear the sound of their own voices.

Mr Brownlow does not join them, but remains in a separate room, while Mr Losberne and another gentlemen I do not know hurry in and out with anxious faces. Once, Mrs Maylie is called to that room and, after being absent for nearly an hour, returns with eyes swollen with weeping. This makes Miss Maylie and Oliver all the more uncomfortable, for she will not say why she has been crying.

At length, I am almost beside myself with impatience. But not boredom, never boredom, for I once told you I could sit and look at the child for a good, long while. At length, Mr Losberne and the unknown gentleman return to the sitting room, followed by Mr Brownlow and Monks.

Yes, Monks is the man who accompanied Mr Brownlow in the other carriage. *Monks.*

Monks, not at all happy about being here, folds his arms across his chest. His eyes are black sockets, his mouth a slit in his face, the broad red mark vivid upon his neck.

'This,' Mr Brownlow says to Oliver, indicating Monks, 'is your brother.'

The boy starts from his seat. Monks casts a look of hate upon the astonished Oliver, and sits down near the door, hunched forwards, his arms upon his thighs. And Mr Brownlow, who has papers in his hand, walks to the little table near where Miss Maylie and Oliver are seated.

'This is a painful task,' he says, 'but these declarations, which have been signed in London before many gentlemen, must be in substance repeated here. I would have spared you the degradation,' he says to Monks, 'but we must hear them from your own lips before we part, and you know why.'

'Go on,' Monks says, looking at the floor. 'Quick! I have done enough. Don't keep me here.'

'This child,' Mr Brownlow says, drawing Oliver to him and laying his hand upon his head, 'is your half-brother, the illegitimate son of your father, my dear friend Edwin Leeford, by poor, young Agnes Fleming, who died in giving birth to him.'

'Yes,' Monks confirms, scowling at the trembling boy. 'This is their bastard child.'

'The term you use,' Mr Brownlow says sternly, 'is a reproach to those who have long since passed. It reflects true disgrace on no-one living, except you who use it. Let that pass. He was born in this town?'

'Yes. In the workhouse of this town,' Monks replies sullen-like. 'You have the story there.' He points impatiently to the papers.

'I must have it here, too,' Mr Brownlow says, gazing round at the listeners. He wants them to bear witness, he does.

'Listen, then,' Monks says, 'and I will tell you, if you must have it from my lips.' His voice softens, like he has given up fighting against wot must inevitably happen. 'Oliver's father, who was also my father, long separated from my mother, was taken ill at Rome and died. Among the papers left on his desk were two, dated on the night his illness first came on, one directed to Mr Brownlow, which enclosed a letter to Agnes Fleming, who was the boy's mother. The other paper was a will.'

'Tell us about the letter,' Mr Brownlow says.

'The letter was a confession. My father had told Agnes there was a mystery to be explained one day that prevented his marrying her, which was that he remained married to my mother, and Agnes had gone on trusting him until she trusted too far, and lost what none could ever give her back. She was with child, with this *boy*'—he indicates Oliver. 'My father told her in the letter all he had meant to do to hide her shame, if he'd lived, and begged her if he died not to curse his memory, for all the guilt was his.'

'And the will?' Mr Brownlow asks. 'Tell us about the will.'

Monks is silent. And unmoving. It seems he will not talk of the will.

'The will is in the same spirit as the letter,' Mr Brownlow says. 'Edward Leeford talked of miseries which this man's mother'—he indicates Monks—'had brought upon him, and how she trained Monks to hate the man who was his father, but that he left Monks and his mother each an annuity. The remainder of his property, he divided into two equal portions, one for Agnes Fleming, Oliver's mother, and the other for Oliver. However, the boy was only to come into the inheritance on the stipulation that he should never stain his name with any public act of dishonour, meanness, cowardice or wrong. This was done by Edward Leeford to mark his confidence in Oliver's mother, Agnes, and to state his conviction that the child would share her gentle heart and noble nature. If he was disappointed in this expectation, then the money was to go to Monks, for then, and not till then, when both children were equal, would he recognise Monks's prior claim upon his purse, for he had none upon his heart. Monks had from an infant repulsed him with coldness and aversion—'

'My mother,' Monks interrupts, 'burnt this will, and the letter never reached its destination.'

'And years after this,' Mr Brownlow says, 'Monks's mother came to me. Monks had left her when he was but eighteen, but not before he, her own son, mark you, robbed her of her jewels and money and fled to London, where for two years he associated with the lowest of outcasts. His mother told me she was sinking under a painful and incurable disease, and wished to recover him before she died. Inquiries were set afoot, strict searches made, unavailing for a long time, but ultimately successful, and Monks returned with her to France.'

'And there my mother died,' Monks says, 'after a lingering illness, and on her deathbed she bequeathed these secrets to me. She did not believe the boy's mother had died. She had the impression that a male child had been born, and was alive, and I swore to her that if ever the boy crossed my path, I would hunt him down to vent my hatred and drag him, if I could, to the very foot of the gallows. And my mother was right, for *he*'—Monks breaks off to glare at Oliver—'came in my way at last and, if not for babbling drabs'—he means Fagin, Sikes and me—'I would have finished him as I began. I would, I would!'

I won' go on with them details. You get the drift. In a nutshell Oliver is going to be all right. Of course he is. *The changeling survives.*

He will be adopted by Mr Brownlow and will come into money. He will be adopted and have his head filled with Mr Brownlow's stores of knowledge, and will rest easy in the knowledge that the gen'leman has his best interests at heart. Most importantly, Oliver will be adopted and will be *loved.* Loved by the gen'leman, by Mrs Maylie and Miss Maylie, and by all them staff at Mr Brownlow's.

Ol-uh-ver. Oliver *is three rungs of a small painted wooden staircase, the paint perhaps being a bit chipped and mouldy in places, but it's three steps up. Starting low and rising. Starting small but having prospects, going places. Becoming someone.*

I told you Monks was altogether evil, didn' I? Apparently he has been given an ultimatum. He is to pay back Oliver's rightful inheritance, and to leave the country. There is talk in this very sitting room he is going to America.

But there is another surprise ...

Oliver's mother had a young sister. And I won' go into the ins and outs of their long story, you'll jus' have to trust me.

Now who do you imagine that young sister might be?

Why, none other than Miss Rose Maylie!

Strange, how things turn out. See, Rose is actually Rose Fleming, and was but a girl when her much older sister, Agnes, found herself with child, with Oliver. And after her father died, and Agnes was gone who knew where, she was adopted by Mrs Maylie, and became Rose Maylie. Wot a coincidence! And didn' I rightly warn you against coincidences, saying the world is full of them?

A great deal of other shenanigans against Oliver took place, too. Double-dealings. Similar to those me and Mr Rufus and Aunt Maud partook of, only much worse. Ours were tame, by comparison. And if your head is spinning, I carnt say I blame you.

A great many tears are shed at this aforesaid meeting, and I do not linger once I have the gist of matters. It is a hard thing to weep when I carnt actually produce tears.

And, talking of tears, I have not been able to bring meself to mention that the Dodger has been nabbed for stealing a silver snuff box in the interim. Oh, woe! It breaks me heart, it does. I imagine he made a great show of impudence in the courthouse, most likely declaring his attorney were a-breakfasting with the Vice President of the House of Commons, and generally behaving like a poncy gen'leman, swaggering to and fro with his hands in his pockets, and that the old goat probably declared the lad were doing full justice to his bringing-up, establishing for himself a glorious reputation. I fancy Dodger was right pleased by all that. Right full of himself for all the attention. He is not to be hanged, there is that small mercy, but is to be transported to Australia—for life. Oh, woe! I say again. Dodger was kind to me in a world where there were very little kindness. Dodger was me friend.

But, on the other hand, reflecting now, it may be this is good thing: a clean start for Dodger. Another world. A new life.

Me consolation—yes, there is something! Me consolation out of all of this is that I overheard Mr Brownlow say that the murder of Nancy, that is of *me*, brought down Fagin's entire gang, and if it weren't for me death, he doubted whether he would have found Monks.

So ain't that nice? I done some good, after all.

CHAPTER FORTY-SIX

You could say that me work here is done, but for some strange reason I appear to be loitering. I think it is because there is one last thing I must bear witness to.

By the time I reach Newgate, night has fallen, and the trial at the old Bailey is well and truly over and the verdict given. *Guilty.*

Cells for the condemned are in the oldest part of the prison, and the doors are four inches thick, the walls mildewed, dense and damp. In each cell is a small window, high up and doubly grated, giving me enough light to see the man cowering in the dark upon his stone bed.

The man's head has been bandaged with a cloth. It must have been hurt by missiles from the crowd on the day of his capture. His matted, red hair hangs around his dirty face, his beard is torn and twisted into knots, and his eyes sunk into his head like holes in a mask. Fagin mutters to himself. 'Good boy, Charley, well done! Well done. Now where's that girl, where's Nancy? Where's she got to? There's something I must tell her.'

Outside, in the yard, is the noise of hammering and the throwing down of boards. They are erecting a scaffold.

'Oliver!' Fagin has just said, 'take that boy away to bed,' when the jailer appears at the gate.

'Fagin?'

'That's me,' Fagin says. 'An old man, my lord, a very old man.'

'Here,' the turnkey says, coming in and laying his hand upon Fagin's breast to keep him down. 'Here's somebody wants to see you, to ask you some questions, I suppose. Fagin? Fagin, are you the man?'

Fagin looks up. 'I shan't be a man long,' he tells the turnkey. 'Strike them all dead!' he says, and his face contorts with rage and terror. 'What right have they to butcher me?'

'Steady,' the turnkey says.

He turns towards the door, towards the stranger who has been quietly waiting there.

'Now,' he says to Mr Brownlow. 'Now, tell him what you want, quick, if you please, for he grows worse as time gets on.'

Mr Brownlow steps into wot light comes through the barred window. 'You have some papers,' he says to Fagin, looking intently at him, 'which were placed into your hands for better security by a man called Monks.'

'It's all a lie together,' Fagin says sing-song, 'I haven't—not a one.'

'For the love of God,' Mr Brownlow says solemnly, 'do not say that now upon the very verge of death, but tell me where they are. You know that Sikes is dead, that Monks has confessed, that there is no hope of any further gain. Where are these papers?'

Fagin says nothing. He looks at the ceiling, and then at the floor, and then towards the high window.

'Let me try,' a small voice murmurs. 'I am not afraid.'

Relinquishing Mr Brownlow's hand, stepping out from behind him, a child moves into the light.

'Oliver!' Fagin cries with glee.

'Here,' he says, drawing the child towards him, 'here. Let me whisper to you. The papers,' he murmurs, 'are in a canvas bag, in a hole a little way up the chimney in the top front room. Now, I want to talk to you alone, my dear. I must talk to you. There's something you must tell Nancy.'

'Let me say a prayer?' Oliver entreats. 'Do let me say a prayer, say only one upon your knees with me, and then you can talk till morning.'

Fagin rises. He pushes the boy before him towards the door.

'Outside, outside,' he says. 'Tell them I've gone to sleep,' he mutters to Mr Brownlow. 'They'll believe you. Tell Bill never mind the girl. Tell Nancy! Tell Nancy—'

At which point the poor child bursts into tears. 'Oh, Nancy!' he cries. 'Oh, Nancy.'

At which point my heart breaks.

'What should I tell Nancy?' the child asks.

'Tell Nancy—' Fagin begins, then breaks off and looks at Oliver in alarm. 'Where's the Artful?' he says. 'Where's the Dodger?'

Oliver lifts his little shoulders. He don' know. Why would he know?

'Tell Nancy that the Dodger—' Fagin begins again, but the cell door opens and distracts him, and various attendants return and lay hands upon him. 'That's enough, sir.' Gently, they untangle Oliver from his grasp. Push the old man back towards his stone bed.

But Fagin writhes and struggles with the power of desperation, shedding flakes of dry skin. He shrieks and kicks, and hisses like a snake, startling a mouse that skitters across the damp stones.

In consternation, Mr Brownlow lays his hand upon the boy's shoulder and gently leads him out of the cell. They go out and disappear into the darkness, Oliver's little frame shaking with distress.

They disappear into the darkness, but they go out into the light.

Into the light. Into a future bright with prospects.

The back of the boy with a face like an angel is the last I see of him. The last. And I did so want to hold his golden head to me breast once more.

Little by little, Fagin's shrieks turn to sobs, bit by bit his sobs become moans and his moans whimpers, and then there is nothing but gulping. Nothing at all but gulping and hiccoughing. And the attendants leave us and go out of the cell again.

And I say, although I carnt of course speak, 'Wot of the Dodger? Wot of Nancy and the Dodger? Wot do you mean to tell the girl?'

Fagin looks up and stares wild-eyed at me as if he has heard me, as if he can see me clear as day. 'That he's her brother,' he says. 'Nancy's brother.'

Wot?

The Dodger, me own brother?

'Oh, yes,' he mutters. 'I fed her lies, didn't I? I concocted a tale about finding her in the street—I *suggested* I may have—and she believed me and took it on as her own. And the Artful? And their mother? What a piece of puppetry she turned out to be, selling her own children like that, one after t'other, although the Artful came to us later, didn't he? Well, never mind that now, my dear—Oliver! Take that boy to bed.' He sits down heavily, puts his head in his hands, and rocks himself gently to and fro.

I stand to one side. Too stunned to speak. If I had tears, they'd be a-running down me face.

I have family. I have a brother! *A brother!*

And that brother is the Dodger. Jack Dawkins.

All this time and I never knew. All this time and me brother was by me side most days. All this time …

And yet. And yet when I look back on it, it's almost like I *knew* he were my brother, innit? I surely treated him like a brother.

Thought of him as a brother. Only … Only I never put it into so many words.

Oh, if only I could see him one more time. Hold him warmly to me one more time. The Dodger. Me own brother.

God forgive this wretched man, indeed, for keeping this from me!

*

I sit with Fagin through the night, keeping him company, sometimes with my hand upon his, not that he feels it, for he is quiet now.

Day is dawning when I emerge. And it seems to me I come out of Fagin's cell, not of me own free will, but through some otherworldly force.

Outside, I find a great multitude assembled in the yard of Newgate. And the barred windows are filled with prisoners staring mindlessly out, or smoking and playing cards to pass the time. The people are restless, pushing, quarrelling and joking. 'Fagin! Fagin! Fagin!' someone cries out, and the crowd takes up the chant and carries it until it dies away to a whisper.

In the centre, in the middle of all this life and activity, is a dark cluster of objects standing quite still. A black stage, a crossbeam, a rope, all the apparatus of a hanging. Of death.

The scene before me fills me with dread. I don' linger. Surely there's no further reason for me to remain?

And filled with expectation, I lift up me eyes to the murk above. Lift up me eyes through the muck and the smoke and the soot, and into the vast and open sky.

Starting off low and ending up high. Finishing bright and cheerful-like. In the clouds.

That's me. Nancy.

ACKNOWLEDGEMENTS

Thank you, Nicola Robinson, for suggesting Nancy when I turned to you after *Estella* and said, what now? Thank you, Jo Mackay at HQ, for your continuous support, and for such a lovely evocative title. Thank you, Suzanne O'Sullivan, Laurie Ormond, Sherryl Clark, and all the lovely staff at HarperCollins Australia who worked and continue to work so tirelessly on *The Scent of Oranges*. It has been a pleasure and a delight to work with you all. Thank you to Darren Holt for such a stunning and eye-catching cover.

Sharyn Pearce, to whom this book is dedicated, has been a kind and wonderful reader and editor, and I am very grateful. Thank you, Rosemary Rust, my English cousin, for your meticulous research, and my readers, Linda Brucesmith and Toni Lucke, and my dear friend, Merryl Powell. Thank you, Jodie How, for your precious friendship and all things writing. Thanks to my writing mates, especially Laura Elvery, Les Zig, and Rebecca Jessen—knowing you are in the background and never too busy to dispense words of wisdom is of great comfort. I'm grateful to my agent and friend, Sally Bird, as always. I'm also indebted to the Queensland Writers Centre for continued support. Thank you to my family and, most of all, to Tim.

I cannot close without mentioning Nancy herself. Some books are more special to their authors than others. (Is this like admitting you have a favourite child? Oh, horrors, I don't know.) All I can say is that Nancy became very dear to me during the writing of this book. She was smarter, braver and kinder than I ever could've imagined, and she brought me to tears several times. I admit that delving into her life has made me a better person, more empathetic towards those who suffer poverty and who deal with violence and exploitation on a daily basis. And I hope her story goes some way towards acknowledging girls and women like her everywhere, both in the past and present.

I was privileged to travel to London while I was writing this book, to stand upon the chequered floor of St Paul's, to walk down the steps leading to the Thames, and visit some of the places that Nancy might have frequented. All experiences that made Nancy more real to me, that brought me closer to her, that made the writing of *The Scent of Oranges* easier and such a pleasure. And I say thank you, Charles Dickens, for creating Nancy, and for writing *Oliver Twist*, for without that book I never would have written this one.

RECOMMENDED READING

Oliver Twist by Charles Dickens

Fingersmith by Sarah Waters

talk about it

Let's talk about books.

Join the conversation:

@harlequinaustralia

@hqanz

@harlequinaus

harpercollins.com.au/hq

If you love reading and want to know about our authors and titles, then let's talk about it.